Greenthorne

Alec S. Ireson

MAKER BOOKS

Copyright © 2025 by Alec S. Ireson

All rights reserved.

No portion of this book may be reproduced in any form without written permission from the publisher or author, except as permitted by U.K. copyright law.

First edition

Cover design and author portrait: Nishat Artz

ISBN: 978-1-0682743-0-5

No generative AI tools were used in the production of this work

Contents

Dedication	V
Epigraph	VI
1. Preamble	1
2. Little Peep	13
3. Odd Fellows	32
4. Cranford Electric	52
5. Athletic Pictorial	72
6. Enfants Terribles	97
7. Utter Rhubarb	122
8. Backstreet Dandy	145
9. Heartsore Lady	166
10. Butler's Brouhaha	190
11. Nether Moor	213
12. Indoor Sports	230

13. Tungsten Flame	256
14. Busman's Picnic	278
15. Sincerest Condolences	295
Acknowledgements	300
About the author	301
Also by Alec S. Ireson	302

For Russell and Agnes

Bethink one face you knew before. No one wears that face you knew. Death has made it its nevermore.

– Henry Pearson White

Preamble

Oliver, unable to afford anything more flavoursome than bread, pitied himself as he trudged towards Jennings the Baker. Without question, a loaf would be his most sensible purchase; although unappetising, it would fill his belly, at least, and keep suppertime's hunger at bay. Along the way, he tried not to look at the tangles of liquorice laces and slew of gobstoppers in the General Stores' windows.

An ice cream sundae, courtesy of Mrs Spence, became far too tempting the instant that he glanced towards her tearoom, however; although he liked to pretend otherwise, he had never really allowed rationality to interfere with his whims. Accordingly, he aborted his mission to Jennings immediately and headed straight for her establishment instead. He preferred to live in the moment, after all; he had long ago predicted that he would grow up to become a hedonist. This affirmation had mostly been made in defiance towards his late mother's insistence that he square his shoulders, buck his ideas up, and learn to approach life sensibly.

As one of her few regulars, Oliver appreciated the discount that Mrs Spence offered him while feeling unperturbed that he had only a single penny left to pocket once he had paid her. He had learned some time ago that it was best not to fret over such impulsiveness in the shorter term because the regret, hunger, and suffering that came later always passed eventually; it passed once he had weight in his pocket again. That will only be forty-eight hours away – it will all be fine come Thursday, he reminded himself as he trousered the coin. Although unpalatable, he had a stockpile of suet massed in his larder as a last resort, should that forty-eight hours become too gruelling for him; Greenthorne's darkened streets had plenty of dustbins to rummage in too.

His first spoonful served as a confirmation that he had made the correct purchase; delightful varicoloured dollops of fruity ice cream sprinkled with sugar, topped with cherries, wedged with wafers, and zinging with terrific taste proved to be just the ticket! The sundae's shades of magic mint, carnation pink, and sunshine yellow made it as much a feast for the eyes as it was for the belly. This sundae, devoured in this setting, was a common indulgence of his; forever finding himself at loose ends, it was another way to idle away his days – he had long been out of work.

Oliver liked to champion poor Mrs Spence's teashop anyway; it felt like a charitable act because she was a woman for whom he had tremendous sympathy. He liked to think that in his own small way, he was contributing towards the modest profits that she could only have earned from her little business; moreover, it had always felt like an excellent way to prepare for the usual daily excursion on which he would soon set off.

Unexceptionally, her tearoom was quite empty that lunchtime. Inside it was a little cooler, at least, while outside, as so often of late, the heat's intensity was beyond description; the summer, like the spring before it, was unseasonably hot and humid – for the north of the country, in any case.

Behind him, she wiped down her counter tops in silence. Rose Spence was a widow whose grief seemingly had no end – such had been the strength of her bond with her late husband. She functioned nonetheless although she looked as if she perpetually walked a tightrope; all too often, the moistness of her eyes made one worry that she might lose her balance at any moment and plummet into despair. Today, her eyes appeared very moist indeed, so it was not at all surprising that she had been rather short with Oliver when he had ordered his midday snack from her, despite the lengths that he had gone to in thanking her, so as to not seem unappreciative. She was always polite, however, always managing the teensiest of smiles, but she was still too choked by melancholy, even after all these years, to make even the smallest of small talk.

A glance at her wedding ring provoked an unexpected shudder – the ghosts of her past were not as literal as his own, after all. He managed to resist a nervous glance over his shoulder in case his own were lingering, as they so often were. This was a queer matter; it was often disturbing, and it was occasionally sad. He distracted himself from brooding upon it all with another spoonful.

The sundae aside, violets wilting in dusty vases were the only splashes of colour about Oliver; otherwise, the place looked cheerless in almost every respect. While glancing idly about at the tearoom walls, which were entirely unadorned except for peeling and browning wallpaper, he remembered the film posters that Mrs Spence had, way back, furnished the place with; he would seldom forget that she had been the Greenthorne Palace organist. This had been a role that she had relished until Mr Spence had perished upon the battlefield, grief and melancholy had taken her over, and the frivolities of the films that were screened there had become far too jarring for her to play along to. She had quit her job at the town's little picture house then, quite understandably. The pretty frocks that she had apparelled herself in were confined to her wardrobe, and she had worn mourning attire ever since, dressing drably.

A wistfulness abruptly overtook him then because he had a few precious memories of that generally long-forgotten place. He then found himself harkening back to the impressions that he had left of being taken to the Greenthorne Palace, once or maybe twice to the children's matinee – or the 'nippers' stampede', as it had been called back then; cartoons, hushed voices, and sweets sucked in the darkness – although dimly remembered, these impressions remained quite enchanting.

Later on in his life – quite recently, in fact – Oliver had frequented another picture house that had not been closed down, and the cinema had had an even greater impact upon him then. He had packed the flicks in eventually, however, for not dissimilar reasons to Mrs Spence, funnily enough; owing to this, he liked to imagine that had they not been so reserved, and had their lives worked out differently, there was a great deal that he and she could have talked about, exchanging movie trivia and their impressions of screen idols in particular. He often wished that they could while he would sit with his back to her in silence; neither of them had much company otherwise, after all. Since she had an acquaintance with his late mother's friend, Olive Solby, Mrs Spence must have known a little of his own backstory; as such, he liked to imagine that they could have understood one another's difficulties and could have consoled each other to some degree. But near silence prevailed once again while on the wireless, its volume dialled down extremely low, a soft voice murmured '*And smile alike, my loveliest dear, while I wipe away each tear…*' These wistful lyrics from *Heartsore Lady*, accompanied by such a gentle melody, did nothing but thicken the sense of poignancy that saturated the stagnant air.

Draw closer my heartsore lady
Cuddle up and don't feel blue
All your woes will diminish greatly
When you see, dear, that I'm all smiles for you

When glancing outside in preparation to head off, the streets appeared to be ablaze, as if the sunshine was hotter than Spooner & Sons' foundry; this blaze of light danced through the spinning fan above to mesmerising effect. While not feeling as daunted by the blistering heat as perhaps he should have, he readied himself for the long hike ahead. He savoured his last spoonful and listened to the song's last chorus.

Every cloud must have a silver lining
Just wait until the sun bursts through
And smile alike, my loveliest dear
While I wipe away each tear
Or else I shall be heartsore too

Looking as shabby as ever, dear old Clive Turner, a veteran who had lost one eye and one arm upon the battlefield, squatted on the curb adjacent while playing the mouth organ in the hope that passers-by might sling their spare change into his upturned cap. But only stray dogs passed, sadly; with the heat so overpowering, those that could remain indoors had done so wisely. Wisely, as Oliver quickly discovered because once he had bid Mrs Spence farewell, waved to Mr Turner, struck up a smoke, and set off, he had only managed to stagger less than a mile before the heat had begun to thwart him. He found himself longing for cloud cover then – real cloud cover, not the fumy drifts of smoke trapped in the baking air above; he yearned for the lost skies of his youth then, pining for their cover during autumn and winter in particular – especially when scattered with clouds emblazoned with a sunset's pinkness. As a child living in Thorny Grove, he would sit in Ashurst's conservatory and gaze up in rapture at those skies while listening to the warbirds practising evasive manoeuvres at the nearby aerodrome; when thinking back, such moments still seemed his life's most blissful.

Back in the present, when smacking his lips together, he realised that to have brought tap water would have been sensible; his smoke seemed to have wicked the last beads of moisture from his tongue, and a dryness seemed to wend its way down into his parched innards. Regrettably, his hip flask remained in his bedroom's shady confines; he had not thought of it because he was all out of gin. Furthermore, the sundae sitting on an empty stomach found him feeling increasingly nauseous. Sadly, then, he could only return home.

'Tricky today, this lark,' Mr Turner said imploringly as Oliver obligingly threw his last coin into his cap; after frittering away any chance of a rudimentary supper with that oh-so sickening dessert, it seemed no great sacrifice to reward Mr Turner's efforts with the last of his shrapnel. Oliver's pockets were entirely empty then, and although he had felt quite proud of himself when he had paid the Electric Power Company utility bill on the Thursday prior, he found himself wishing that he had not bothered. He had become close to being cut off again, but being without electricity was not too problematic in the summer months with the benefit of candles; it was only during wintertime that it drove him nearly mad.

The remains of the day were, and could only have been, a matter of endurance once Oliver had returned home because, even for such a solitary creature, he never felt particularly at ease in his own company; the more he animated himself, which mainly meant taking himself on long walks, the less this solitude felt apparent. But today the heat, a looming headache, and his upset tummy had checkmated him entirely, so he had only his homebound boredom and the usual depressing silence to deal with – neither of which he found easy to bear. Cigarettes aside, he had no other distractions at his disposal – nothing else to thinly paper over his loneliness, just like Mrs Spence had done with that peeling wallpaper once she had torn her cinema posters down.

Glancing wistfully up at the old telephone, he again wished that there was a line to the spirit world where he could reach his dearly missed nana. He had allowed the line to be cut off long ago, however; the operator had never been particularly chatty, and the only other person in his telephone book was Uncle Sheldon, who would invariably bark something along the lines of –

'What's that Oliver... something sensible to say for once? What? Bad line... speak up! Christ! Do you seek something? Look, sure it can wait till next Thursday, whatever it is!' before hanging up on him, and before Oliver ever managed to get a single word in edgeways.

An analgesic took only the edge off of Oliver's achy head while seconds felt more like minutes and minutes seemed more like hours, despite the frenetic ticking of the mantel clock – a sound which increasingly grated on him.

With his sketchbook's blankness seeming like too much of a mirror, he found that he could not even pick up a pencil – such was his leadenness. Cigarettes felt much lighter, however, and as he lit up again, his compulsion to toss the match to the floor took him quite by surprise.

Oliver's abode was in a state of complete disarray, as usual. Along with his and his late mother's jumble, old tea chests, chock-full with goodness knows what, and countless piles of faded old newspapers made for lethally-combustible kindling, potentially; it did indeed feel quite desirable to toss the match and dispense with it all – and perhaps it felt just as desirable to dispatch himself along with it all too.

While looking contemptuously at it all, it no longer seemed excusable with a little humour; when he was not entirely in the depths of despair, he liked to joke that these messy piles, scattered the length and breadth of his abode, were his, with the French pronunciation, *'arrangements'*. It was a handy way for him to reframe and excuse the chaos in which he lived – to pretend that this shambles was actually a meticulously arranged still life, ready to render on paper or canvas. That aside, with another hour having slowly passed, Oliver had toyed with his pyromantic fantasies enough to imagine that he had grown wilful. He struck another match and peered as dispassionately as he could into the heart of its scarlet flame, yet he still could not quite muster the nerve to do it – there were less agonising and histrionic ways to die, surely?

Predictably, hunger had become his tormentor by then, and, needless to say, he wished he had bought that bread from Jennings after all. Upon scampering to the larder with half a mind to swill down a cup of suet, he found that he could not imagine actually ingesting any when faced with the clotted goop that he had prepared; he tossed it into the sink instead, along with all the other cups' worth that had met the same fate, all of which sprouted mouldy blooms in a staggering array of greens and greys. He only ever bought suet because it seemed like a sensible staple, even though he had not even the slightest clue how to cook it or cook with it. His mother had made it a common ingredient in their diet, yet he still could not recall what on earth she had done with the stuff; he would just let it pile up in his larder while waiting for the day that the penny would drop. It was only ever in utter desperation that he would whisk some up with only a dash of tap water for the least offensive consistency, and force it down himself while fighting to suppress the reflexive protests of his tightening oesophagus and heaving diaphragm. Fortunately, however, as the world outside darkened a little, his indigestion had eased enough for him to be able to drown himself in the half full bottle of gin that he had remaining. This reaffirmed itself as a superb tactic that he had discovered some time ago: gin on an empty stomach transported him to a realm where his body lost its command over him. Later, once the gin had worn off a little, he found that his hunger had waned because his body had given up upon its insistence on being fed and demanded sleep instead. The sun had graciously set by then – a blessed sign that the ordeal of the day had passed.

Tomorrow will be different, Oliver assured himself as he staggered giddily towards his bedroom, casting a habitual, tentative glance at his mother's old bedroom door as he passed it by.

Although weary, he felt fidgety – much to his frustration. Despite the absorption that they usually afforded him when sleep eluded him, a well-thumbed pile of books stacked upon his nightstand failed to entice – he had ended up feeling too sick and tired with everything. Even the smattering of cinnamon toffees that he found hiding in his bedsheets failed to cheer him; he just piled them upon his nightstand.

His bedroom looked quite colourless with such little moonlight; it merely looked silvery, much like a cinema screen, which set him thinking about the cinema in general, and the Greenthorne Palace and Blandishford Picture House in particular, once again. Glancing around at the most recent additions to his bedroom's adornment, a room that otherwise amounted to a museum of his childhood, Oliver surveyed the promotional images that he had torn from the Blandishford Picture House's programme notes on *Follow the Band*; it had had Randolph Stewart at the helm – a blond Adonis that Oliver had decided was more or less his double.

Oh, how the movies had wooed him at first, and musicals especially! For a while after discovering the nearby town of Blandishford's own dream palace, the cinema had given him a weekly excursion to look forward to, until the novelty had worn off finally – at least that is what he liked to think had happened. In truth, as his liking had led to obsession, as it so often did with him, the cinema had become yet another Pandora's box. It had unleashed a chaos of opposing desires that he had been ill-equipped to govern; quite sensibly, then, he had packed it in eventually and had torn down his cuttings of film icons, but had kindly allowed Randolph Stewart to remain. *Follow the Band* had been the last film that he had seen, and a good one to go out on in retrospect.

Despite this eventual difficulty with it all, the cinema had indeed been a revelation at first. He had had nothing but admiration for the Hollywood heroes that he had tried to emulate, and he had adored the heroines even more so because Greenthorne had never afforded him the chance to fawn over such ravishing creatures in real life! Also, the films had, suddenly and amazingly, come with actual sound, so poor Mrs Spence, once the Greenthorne Palace organist, would have lost her job eventually anyway. The cinema had, for a time at least, seemed the perfect antidote to the miseries of his hard-worn life – to the point where the dreams that the Blandishford Picture House had stirred in him had felt essential for his spiritual survival; he had nearly always left its auditorium walking on air once he had sharpened his tastes in films. With the exception of George Berrycloth, who was a pretty good giggle, he had found that he simply could not bear gritty working-class films – the cinema was supposed to be about escapism, after all! The newsy shorts that they had screened before the main feature, featuring local soccer teams and the like, had had their appeal, however; he had willingly lent his hands to the applause for those.

American films had turned out to be quite a different story, thank heavens, because they had transported the spectator to exotic, far-off places, otherwise unimaginable. Even though they had spoken English, and they had had American accents in Roman Italy and even in Arabia, which had seemed as daft as daft could possibly be, Oliver had still felt that he had learned much about the world's history, its legends, and its myths.

Patricia Lombard, who, with her blonde hair and well-favoured features, was virtually his mother's twin, had required the widest berth, of course, but all too soon, as they had become increasingly more bold and more luminous, almost all other starlets had embraced roles that had framed them as conniving femmes fatales – also bringing his mother too much to mind. It had seemed as if women had finally had enough, had clawed their way out of their domestic traps, and had revolted against men ferociously and by any means necessary; often, this had required that they carry a gun on their person! For the first time ever, they had had all the power – until they had become spectacularly unstuck, of course, which they always had done by the time that the credits rolled; while they had been all the more magnificent for their sudden supremacy, no matter how transient, he had had to admit that it had unnerved him greatly.

Edith Granger, on the other hand, had been quite a different character. She could never have been conniving or cruel; she was not capable. Oh, Edith! Such warmth, poise, and such a terrific dancer! Although the films were monochrome, he had almost been able to see the redness of her hair, like waves of finely spun copper, layered upon the silver screen.

Unfortunately, however, it had not been long before Oliver had found that he could not enjoy the sense of escape from life's hardships that stars like Edith Granger had gifted to the common man without subverting their generosity. His desire for the gods and goddesses of the silver screen had provoked an excitability that had greatly detracted from his ability to follow the films' narratives, and from his overall enjoyment of them; thus, it had become an impossible task to sit back, relax, and find his way back into the story unfolding before him once he had been particularly struck by an ingénue's shapeliness, or by a suave topliner's smouldering gaze, to name only two of many such stimuli. This had quickly become a hefty frustration while one day the penny had dropped that it had, in fact, been a common difficulty. When glancing towards the back of the auditorium, he had discovered that other spectators had been aflame themselves; couples, similarly overcome by the films' provocations, obviously, had canoodled shamelessly in the centre-back row. That row had, as he had quickly discovered, been chock-a-block on the otherwise quieter afternoon matinees.

While feeling mightily indignant that he would never have a lady friend to accompany him back there – women were a complete and utter mystery to him – Oliver had felt compelled to seat himself in the centre-back row anyway; at least there he had been able to observe the spectacle unfolding on the seats beside him as well as the one unfolding upon the auditorium's screen.

Once, having seated himself thus, and right next to one such couple, he had been amazed when the young lady sitting in his neighbour's lap had reached over, grabbed his hand, and pressed it to her bosom; even more astonishingly, her gentleman friend had not seemed to mind this too much – well, it had been hard to gauge in such dim light.

It had soon dawned on Oliver that all this must have been a deliberate part of the picture house's design because the centre-back row nestled in a shadowy eave under the projectionist's booth and was entirely discreet; the staff's attitude had seemed to confirm his theory because they had clearly been aware of its goings-on, but they had never once taken exception to them. Even the mobile ice cream lady, when flashing her torch, had not batted an eyelid; he had purchased mint imperials, golden humbugs, rhubarb and custards, lollies, and a strawberry cornet from her while seated next to this couple who had so charitably gotten him in on their act. He had thought this was rather civilised of her too. In summation, it had all seemed a frightfully modern attitude, and he had quietly thanked her and the Blandishford Picture House's architect, management, and staff for having adopted this forward-thinking approach.

It had been upon this particular occasion that the feel of pert bosom, the taste of strawberry ice cream washing over his tongue, and the spectacle of the breathtaking architecture had all combined as a magical, dizzying assault on his senses that, for Oliver, meant the Blandishford Picture House had earned its right to be called a dream palace too; accordingly, the place had become an even more compelling weekly excursion.

Before long, his visits to the Blandishford Picture House had become incentivised more by the draw of the centre-back row's activities than that of the films themselves; this was not least because, as the months had flown past and he had grown increasingly dissatisfied with his own lot, the films had made for a harsh contrast with how beggared his own life had become, despite the escapism that they had once afforded him. By that point, the overly privileged and overly beautiful giants posturing upon the silver screen had filled him not only with lust, but also with jealousy, and even hatred; their wealth and status had also begun to grate on him, as had the fact that they had had nothing better to busy their pretty little faces with than performing the Dance of the Seven Veils, or committing the diabolical murders of their husbands or love rivals while dressed in sharp suits, cloaked in furs, or dripping with pearls. Since he had never been lucky enough to have been afforded such wealth, nor had opportunities for such whimsy in his own life, the expense and effort of traveling to Blandishford and back just to have his face rubbed in it all had no longer seemed worthwhile; additionally, he had in theory been able to get the only bonus he was left with upon the heath without all that journeying, with no admission fee to pay, and he could take his own sweeties with him.

'Granny' Rogers, as she was affectionately called by all that dearly loved her, informally sold sherbet lemons, cinnamon toffees, liquorice twists, and all manner of other confections, along with cigarettes, from her cottage's front room window – only several strides away from the heath's border. She had once told him that she did this to supplement her pension. Thanks to all such convenience, he had at last been able to avoid so much detriment to his mood and dispense with those maddening films.

Back in the present moment and while turning over in his bed, Oliver realised that in remembering all of this, his mind had been wandering into that impressionistic stream of consciousness that precedes sleep, thankfully. Tomorrow... will... be... different, he once again assured himself as he drifted off.

Little Peep

Barley sugars, mint fondants, pear drops, coconut kisses, sugared almonds, vanilla fudge, mint imperials, lemon sherbets, buttered brazils, liquorice, and toffees of any kind all seemed to be the perfect accompaniment to heath excursions; today, however, Oliver had only a handful of his cinnamon toffees left, which were stale and hard at that.

Using a birch tree's shadow as his retreat from the sun, he found that the heat was inescapable there, too, and just as merciless; the sweat continued to soak his clothing and pool beneath his Derby tweed, but as part of his armour, he never took off his cap as a rule. He remained unwavering on the matter while supposing that the toffee he had just unwrapped might serve as a slight distraction from all such discomfort. On popping the sweet into his mouth, however, he was delighted to find that the heat of his pocket had rendered them far more palatable than expected; they were deliciously gooey, in fact, and he felt richly rewarded for having remembered them.

'Mmm... yummy... just capital,' he murmured while things felt a little less cheerless for him – momentarily, at least.

Oliver had discovered this spot some fifteen months prior on a cool, damp spring day while wandering across the north's heathlands on one of his aimless jaunts. A derelict tennis pavilion appearing on the ridge had intrigued him; once closer, he had realised that he was standing on what, way back, were trim tennis courts. Nowadays, they were overgrown with weeds and moss. He had supposed that this must have been the lawn tennis and golf club that his uncle had spoken of – the one Sheldon had frequented as a far younger man; Oliver had also supposed that it was yet another amenity forsaken during the economic downturn when many of Greenthorne's wealthier residents – the company executives, bankers, industrialists, and such – had upped sticks and headed south to less depressed areas. But after thinking back on all this and then finding his mind back in the present moment, converging on the hijinks at hand, Oliver remembered that he had not hiked all the way out there to simply rehash this spot's history for himself.

Seemingly, hours had passed already, and without happening upon what he had always sought when going there, the heathlands had failed Oliver miserably thus far. To pass the time better, he attempted to sketch a view of the place instead – one that he might watercolour once he had returned home. Having been there so many times already, he found that inspiration eluded him, however. It was too great a challenge to make it all out with sufficient clarity anyway, owing to the sunlight's intensity.

When inspired, he much preferred to sketch and paint indoors from memory, while outdoors he often felt thrown by the infinite blankness of an empty page without really knowing why – especially when it reflected the sunlight's glare back at him so blindingly, just as today. He had half a mind to put his sketchbook away then because, despite his genuine love of art, in this setting it served more as a prop than anything; while posing as a landscape artist, it lent him a convincing cover with which he could scrutinise the grasslands, thicket, and underbrush very carefully. It prevented any chance of reproach from passing ramblers who might otherwise have guessed what he was really doing, and he felt free to peep to his heart's content; it was no great secret, then, that all manner of extremely indiscreet behaviour took place there.

To Oliver, his initial naivety to it all seemed amusing in retrospect; it had been quite a shocker at first, though. Although it had lain abandoned and tumbledown for a good few years, the heath and the old sports club had turned out to be quite lively still. Nowadays, however, they were frequented mainly by townsmen who enjoyed an entirely different kind of sport. He had quickly gathered that the fellows who scrambled inelegantly through the bushes were there for a single pursuit: theirs was a game that, after the thrill of the chase, ended in the same activity for which the town's darkened alleyways became the venue at night.

Perhaps even more shockingly, lewd liaisons could sometimes be spotted between men and women. In these rarer instances, it appeared that only a rather exotic breed of female leant herself willingly to such exertion in this particular habitat, however. It was notable that these ladies never came alone – they came with their fellas under the pretence of picnicking, but, of course, certain other activities took place on their spread-out tablecloths. These were outlandish and somewhat notorious creatures like Gertrude Woolgar. For them, the Oddfellows snug bar was a no go due to the chily reception that they received from the 'normal' townswomen.

Downing pints at the billiard hall instead while playing footsie under the table with anyone that would play along, the likes of Gertrude had a witch's cackle, wore no drawers by most accounts, and yet they felt naked unless they caked themselves in rouge and eyeshadow. They would also cuss and spit scrims of saliva on the pavement without thinking twice. These women were not 'putting out' for recompense either – they merely put out for fun! Finding that pretty mind-boggling, to say the least, Oliver deemed Gertrude and her kind quite extraordinary while rolling his eyes at anyone who dared to characterise them as anything remotely subhuman. Today, however, while reflecting upon all this exotica, there was no sign whatsoever of 'Dirty Gertie', 'Hefty Hattie', or any others from their tribe, sadly for him.

All in all, what took place there was provocative without often being titillating exactly; he found it shocking, funny, occasionally unsavoury, and very rarely boring, depending upon his mood, but beyond all that the appeal refused to properly explain itself. He knew that everyone did it, mostly in the confines of their bedrooms, but on the heath he was being given a chance to see something utterly mysterious, and he had little else to do, after all.

'Not a bloody dickybird,' Oliver muttered as he pressed his sweaty palms over his face, making a shield of sorts from the brilliance of the afternoon sun; orange sunlight still seared painfully through his eyelids–while the world sounded uncannily quiet. Quiet, except for the choruses of crickets and the murmur of stale air shifting about the lifeless remains of hawthorn and bracken. Then, gulping down the toffee's sweet kernel, he peered about again; as hard as it was to adjust to the sun's brightness, he could still discern that nothing had changed, and his heart sank for the sake of the heath's utter desertion. Lighting up and smoking his penultimate cigarette, he continued to wearily wait things out as wisps of silver and cerulean wafted about him.

A shrill whistle sounded in the distance, marking the change of shift at Watkin & Rees Engineering & Manufacturing; it was a sound which always brought a jolt, bringing their tyranny to mind when he had been one of their employees. Once he caught his breath, however, it became a sound that conversely comforted him. It reminded him that their reign over him had been short-lived, at least, and that he was free of all their nonsense nowadays. Glancing up, he saw another dense plume of smoke seep from its chimney which, like a water colourist's brush, painted the fumy air above the town a deeper hue of beige; funnelling from that stack, and also from the chimneys of Spooner & Sons and Sharpe & Beard, these ugly drifts of smoke had loomed over Greenthorne for years. The particles of soot they had dispersed had slowly tarred the length and breadth of its already dreary rows until each square mile looked quite grey; even the townsfolk did too – their faces had a similarly ashen hue.

Watkin's dreadful exhaust had diffused the sunlight, at least, but once Oliver could see more clearly, looking back at the heathlands with Greenthorne in the distance, it all appeared just as dreary. It more resembled an infertile dust bowl than England's green and pleasant land; the entire landscape had become a dreadfully dreary-looking wash of burnt orange on a canvas that was already primed with brown ochre – the drab and muted shades of a parching and seemingly endless summer. Vast swathes of purple and yellow flowering heather and gorse, that he had always so adored during their flowering seasons, had become little more than browning skeletal bushes while the regions of tiny, many-coloured meadow flowers between them had all dried out.

Resisting all this was the stippling of vivid green that remained, marking out Thorny Grove where his Uncle Sheldon lived, and where Oliver had once lived with his family in more prosperous and hopeful times. Featuring a finer sprinkling of violet, mauve, and cornflower blue, this splash of colour indicated the blooms of well-watered chrysanthemum, geranium, and rhododendron bushes; the hosepipes of Greenthorne's more affluent enclave had run continuously all summer long, keeping such blooms and its lawns and bushes resplendent while everything around it had wilted and then withered away.

While spotting and following a motor car heading west and away from the grove, he wondered if it was his uncle's Bentley, although it was too far away to be sure. He felt peeved nonetheless because he had already convinced himself that, in all likelihood, it was Uncle Sheldon on his way to some high society function, or perhaps to pricey grandstand seats at the races. How lovely would it be to have been invited to tag along, after all, which he never had been. Oliver could not tear his eyes from the vehicle, and he followed it until they incidentally met a building in the far distance that had once been Cranford Electric – his late mother's last place of work. Thoughts of that place and, by association, thoughts of her always seemed best avoided, so catching sight of Cranford's ruins stirred cold draughts straightaway in closeted corners of his mind; they blew open doors that he often struggled to keep shut. Slamming shut and bolting those closet doors immediately, he then turned back to his sketchbook.

Squinting down at the few faint pencil marks that he had scribbled within the last hour, Oliver still felt uninspired; no, for him this was going absolutely nowhere, and having failed to find artistic inspiration as well as the spectacle that he always sought, this exercise had become nothing more than tiresome time-killing for what had felt like an eternity already. He began to regret going there in the first place; the other idlers, artists, and ravishers had not bothered, likely knowing that it was not sensible in this heat. But, desperate for a way to occupy his afternoon and getting up to his usual antics, he had foolishly been undeterred by it again.

While acknowledging his nitwittedness, he looked about glumly. All remained eerily still and disconcertingly silent, except for the occasional gust of stale air rattling the stalk tops; even the starlings and sparrows were too overheated to twitter, to hazard a guess. Then, whirling about each other in an amorous frenzy above the skeleton of a blackberry bush, two cabbage whites echoed what he had failed to find.

Peering back in the direction of the tennis pavilion's ruins, there was still not a dickybird, but he found himself musing on his uncle's patronage there many moons before; although Uncle Sheldon was drawn to more physically demanding games such as polo and cricket, he had been born to gentility, in a way, and thus meant for more leisurely forms of sportsmanship. But has Sheldon even played golf? Oliver wondered because it was quite hard to imagine, but he had definitely played croquet, and Oliver had seen golf clubs and balls about his uncle's residence, Ferndale House.

Giving up on his landscape because his mind kept wandering off to such speculations about the subject, he attempted a self-portrait instead; with five minutes having passed, however, he gave up on that, too, since he quickly found that he could do himself no justice. Indoors or out, portraits had never been his forte, and the face that he had just outlined had missed the mark by a mile, by his reckoning; he felt that it looked far less handsome than it should. With its inadvertently downturned mouth, it also looked quite miserable – just as miserable as he had begun to feel out there alone in that hinterland.

While looking back at Greenthorne, the details of which danced in the season's perpetual heat haze, he wondered whether to chalk it all up, put away his sketchbook after all, and make his way home for refreshment. A pint at the Oddfellows would be better still, although sadly his pockets were still quite empty. Reaching again for a smoke, he then remembered that it was his last, which he took as a sign that he should just spare it and pack up after all. Just on the verge of doing so, however, he felt peculiar tingles along his spine and noticed movement asudden in his vision's periphery.

Hoping for a moment that his fortunes had changed, Oliver quickly gathered that they had not, unfortunately. It was not the cabbage whites either, which had tumbled away across the grasslands and towards the dales. No, it was only a faint shimmer, but it was not the ambient heat haze either since it was not that gentle. Feeling instantly unnerved, he looked closer and tried to attune his eyes to the sun's glare being deflected back at him. But nothing could be seen above the brambles and briars then, although this was not reassuring in the least.

'Oh no, not today... Please!'

He closed his eyes forcefully shut and tried to shove his apprehension aside because it was hardly the first time that he had witnessed this phenomenon or fretted over its implications. While noticing the blood pulsing and hissing in his ears and feeling that he must distract himself, he imagined a cool pint of ale standing on a bar top in a tavern's sanctuary – a thought that, at any juncture, easily dispelled all others.

Shrugging it all off as best as he could, he wended back towards Greenthorne across the sun-drenched heath, feeling dwarfed by unsightly, towering electric pylons that had only recently appeared on the landscape. They had seemed improbable and unsettling upon their sudden arrival, and they still suggested an otherworldly invasion by sinister forces. The electric hum overhead still seemed just as menacing as the sun glittering off their ugly metallic branches. Little appreciating the utility of this peculiar technology, Oliver always feared that he would be electrocuted as he followed their march of steel.

***

The next Dales Express train was already on the horizon, but Oliver had not come to mark down the locomotive's engine number. In the long run, trainspotting had proved to be just as tiresome as when his late mother, Marion, had once suggested that he busy himself with stamp collecting instead of idling. Unsurprisingly, then, he had already burned his little numbers book and briefly warmed his hands during a frostbitten winter two years prior.

Clattering along the Chalk Hill to Blandishford branch line, the locomotive passed through the old, disused station where Oliver loitered, leaving the vicinity as quickly as it had come, and leaving dense drifts of steam behind it. They engulfed the crossway that reached over the station's tracks. He then stepped quietly into this silvery exhaust and into its thrilling anonymity. He had to grip the handrail for support as he found his way up the steps and through the dense eddies of steam. Once inside the crossway's core, all was quiet except for the locomotive's distant clatter.

While creeping along this overpass, Oliver's breath quickened upon observation of a dim, shifting silhouette in the dense steam ahead, so he slowed to a shuffle and then a tiptoe; how unsuspecting the courting couple were to his approach, despite him reaching such nearness to them, reaffirmed his extraordinary stealthiness. While he watched them clutch each other tightly, he strained fruitlessly to make out their whisperings.

Supposing the fellow was a factory floor worker of some sort since his silhouette sported the requisite felt cap, Oliver was surprised that he was not pawing at his lady friend, as was often the manner of such ogres; this was an observation that he had arrived at through many months of this mischief. In this particular case, however, there was actually a perfectly respectable restraint about the pecks that they gave one another.

Once he had inched even closer to them and saw the chap more clearly, he knew him immediately: he was Dennis Bannister, a steel worker from Watkin & Rees. Dennis had always been a popular fellow, and he was a finely rendered one at that, with striking blue eyes, the colour of chicory petals. In fact, Oliver had barely been able to take his own eyes off Dennis when they had been co-workers. They had never found occasion to speak, however; regrettably, just like everyone else at Watkin & Rees, Dennis had seemed to regard him with the utmost suspicion, but Oliver could hardly have helped that! Envy followed as Oliver felt rather cross with Dennis' lady friend for snagging one of Greenthorne's finest sons; who on earth is this temptress? he wondered because she was still something of a mystery, with her back turned to him all the while.

Suppressing a cough and remaining perfectly still while he waited for the lovers to slowly shuffle around, Oliver had to withhold a gasp of astonishment once she had unwittingly revealed herself to him. She was quite the picture herself: poised perfectly upon her swanlike neck, her face was quite round and yet her features were delicate and sparrow like. All this, and the way her silvery-grey eyes sparkled, put him in mind of a cinema starlet. She was more than Dennis' match in her comeliness, and she was turned out very nicely, too, with her blue glass dingle-dangle earrings and her green felt fedora. Oliver then forgave her unhesitatingly for her ensnarement of his former colleague and heartthrob; clearly, this exquisite young lady hardly deserved his cattiness. Instead, he aimed his resentment squarely at Dennis while wishing that it was he that gazed into her wondrous eyes and not his former colleague. Furthermore, and much to his surprise, he found himself wanting to kiss the moist berries of her lips himself.

What is Dennis' secret? he had to wonder because they were comparably good looking, Dennis and he, yet women barely noticed Oliver at all. It had always seemed to be an anomaly – perhaps the greatest of all life's mysteries – that even though men of a certain persuasion seemed to like Oliver a great deal, women – all women – seemed inexplicably immune to whatever charms he might have possessed in their regard; the heartbreaking perplexity of this had forced him to bury his desire for the fairer sex so deeply that it was most surprising to be so struck by her in this moment.

With Dennis still nuzzling her neck, Delilah, as Oliver decided to call her, stared dreamily into space as if communing with her own personal god; or is her mind simply on other things? he wondered. He had overheard that most women – civilised ones, at least – preferred kitchens to bedrooms, and that, by many accounts, housewifery meant everything to them; it seemed likely, then, that her mind was indeed elsewhere. Whatever she was dreaming, it was all too apparent that Dennis and Delilah were on two different wavelengths entirely, despite the physical closeness they shared; it was a curious phenomenon and yet a commonality to nearly all courting couples that he had studied so closely.

Although she was lost in thought, and perhaps dreaming of domesticity after all, he began to worry that Delilah might notice him because she was staring blankly in his direction then, and the veil of steam was finally thinning out; with his nerves about to get the better of him, he considered a hasty retreat until a sudden deafening choo-choo signalled that the next Dales Express was about to whoosh past below. It had Dennis and Delilah leaping from their skins while clutching each other tighter as it clattered underneath them; suppressing a chuckle, Oliver took great delight in their fright.

Blown into the crossway by the north-easterly breeze, fresh eddies of swirling, silvery-blue steam cloaked the three of them once more; Oliver decided to stay put then. Delilah was clearly at the height of her powers, and, feeling that he had congratulated this seductress for long enough, what consumed Oliver in the next moment was how she in turn had been wooed by Dennis. Once again, Oliver quickly found himself resenting him for this; resentment and desire made for quite an inflammatory blend, however, particularly when inspired in equal measure, and he also imagined that he could lose himself in Dennis' firm embrace more than ever. Unsure which of the two sweethearts he wanted and which he would rather be, Oliver found that envy and irritation had suddenly taken him over, and then they had to open their silly mouths and make it worse –

'What time'll you be home, Dennis?'

'Not sure, pet, Watkin wants us all on overtime tonight.'

'Ah suppose you'll be wantin' a spot of late supper when you get in?' she asked while handing over a weighty-looking lunch bag.

Dennis grinned.

'What we 'avin'?'

'Suet pudding an' cabbage, if you please,' Delilah answered, seeming inexplicably pleased with herself.

Oliver almost guffawed because the banality of their utterances seemed so unseemly; unfortunately, however, while trying to swallow this reaction, a splutter forced its way out of him anyway. He was so stunned that he hardly registered that he had revealed himself, the steam was thinning out anyway, and that they were both staring at him then with looks of angry astonishment.

'Creep!' yapped Delilah.

'Sod off, slutchy-eyed twat!' seethed Dennis.

Oliver obligingly made an abrupt about-turn and took leave of them both, clambering back through the flurries of thinning steam. An eyes-into-the-back-of-you sensation prickled between his shoulder blades, and it seemingly intensified the further that he withdrew, until he found himself shivering with the troubling sensation of finger tips crawling up and then down the knots of his spine; this bothered him far more than what had just transpired with Dennis and Delilah – a not unfamiliar peculiarity that made him quicken his step. Then, having rushed down the steps and nearing the crossway's exit, he felt a hand firmly grip his shoulder and he could only let out a yelp.

He had quite forgotten the strength of the sun's rays, and he found the ambient heat to be just as overwhelming as he emerged breathlessly from the lingering swathes of steam. Panting with the effort, he crossed the old station's slip road and scurried down the grassy verge and on through patchy woodland, back towards the heath's border. While pausing to catch his breath where the woodland opened into an expanse of dried-out grassland, he realised that the sunlight was even more bedazzling there. While forcing his eyes shut, he noticed how queerly his body still tingled. There had been nobody else in the crossway, and on such grounds he had no doubt whatsoever whose icy-cold hand had clawed at him in there.

Oliver already wished to drown his sorrows; if the funds for such remedial measures had blessed his pocket, then his feet would not have stopped until he reached the nearest public house because the shame of his desires, and of idling his time away on such wretched pursuits, had swiftly become a bitter taste in his mouth that he could hardly bear. It was a taste that he wanted to wash away with a jar of pale ale as soon as humanly possible.

His mother had often branded him a 'little peep', and he suddenly felt a rather sorry one at that. Upon discovering the old station's crossway, which served as this lovers' lane of sorts, many months back, he had been quite charmed by its romanticism – it was somewhat more civilised than the heath, at least. He had wanted to be a Romeo just like Dennis Bannister, naturally, but had soon settled on the role of voyeur, albeit with great reluctance. He had come to realise that, much like the heath or the Blandishford Picture House's centre-back row, he would never be lucky enough to have a lady friend to accompany him there, while a gentleman friend, although considerably less unlikely, would be equally out of the question – far too controversial. Despite the poor visibility within the crossway that had served him so well, when he was occasionally caught out, its users were having none of it; it had not taken long at all for his resentment towards this forbiddance to lead him from rhapsody to all this.

Oliver had walked away with a kick in the shin and a flea in his ear several times already, but his curiosity had continued to outstretch his principles, which, despite his mother's best efforts to save him, were loosely defined, to say the very least. He had soon become stealthier while becoming emboldened enough to risk his chances of being caught. Thereafter, he had treated the crossway like a curiosity shop, craving its spectacle more and more often.

Regarding all this and the morning's pursuits in general, 'Sorry Mother' was all he could mutter while staggering back to the signal box. As he collapsed into its shadow, awash with guilt as much as with sweat, he swore that he could almost hear her cries and curses.

The vague, hazy figure that Oliver had glimpsed earlier on the heath was something that he had seen more and more often in the last twelvemonth, with that shimmer slowly taking on apparitional form. He had no doubt that it was his mother – Marion's spectre lurking in the tall dead grass and watching with her eyebrow cocked in disdain.

In retrospect, it was not surprising that she had returned because she had so often reminded him that she would do just that –

'You needn't think, Oliver, that you'll be off the hook when I'm gone. I'll return to check on you... and on your thoughts... each and every last one of them! So, you needn't fret about that!'

Plucking another 'gasper', as his dear departed nana used to call Marion's cigarettes, from his pocket, and forgetting that it would be today's last gasp, he lit it with trembling fingers. With nervous puffs, he drained it of its nicotine yield while its tendrils of grey smoke crept and coiled around him. He kept his eyes downcast all the while, afraid to look up and witness her ghostly figure lurking in the scrub again.

Casting his mind back across the last five years, it seemed surprisingly nostalgic how utterly alone Oliver had felt in his solitude, despite how unhappy he had been. He had already been fatherless and grandmotherless by the time Marion had passed away, and the echo of his footsteps had seemed to ricochet unnervingly around him everywhere he went – an awful sound which had assured him of his loneliness with each new step. He certainly had not found the freedom that he had longed for. Thereon, with his mother and his nana gone, birthdays came and went with no salutations. Despite such hard knocks, however, he had never, not for one moment, wished that his mother would come back to him. Once she had, he had increasingly taken umbrage – he would prefer to be horribly alone than horribly un-alone any day. Soon enough, he had found himself hankering after that solitude and the freedom that it had afforded him to do exactly as he liked; upon hearing those echoing footsteps again, they seemed more like a pleasant rhythm that should have percussed his daily stroll to freedom.

It had become just as frustrating as it had been alarming. Soon after she had begun to creep back into his world, he had felt so antagonised by her that he had snatched the photo of them both that he carried from his wallet and then scratched out her face with his thumbnail. He had become convinced that this was the thing that still tethered her to him across realms. But despite this evasive manoeuvre, he still sensed and saw Marion with increasing frequency; at first, it was merely a feeling, but then, more worrisomely, he had occasionally begun to glimpse her from the corner of his eye at home. Soon after, he had also begun to sight her lurking in the darkening alleys that flanked Middle Row as the sun had crept down. She had even started popping up at Ferndale House lately, and he knew that Uncle Sheldon, if he had also been able to see her, would not have been too thrilled either.

'And now, to cap it all, she's made her debut in the ruddy crossway,' Oliver muttered to himself as he remembered with a shudder how firmly her hand had clenched his shoulder in there.

With the sun painfully searing through his eyelids once again, he tried to free his mind of his mother; he quickly found, however, that he could not do so any more than he could refrain from fretting over what she had so often caught him up to. She was right, then: not only was he a 'little peep', but he was also a 'good-for-nothing', a 'dirty little grub', a 'never-do-well', and all the other utterances with which she had characterised him; once again, he found that he could hardly pretend otherwise. Feeling utterly ashamed of it all, he became filled with much dread and sorrow.

Washing through his veins, this dread and sorrow froze Oliver's glands like ice water while the blood hissed and thumped louder in his ears; as his mind raced with these emotions, gathering charge, Oliver feared the onset of yet another migraine.

While he smoked with his eyes tightly shut, that electrical-sounding drone in his ears seemed too exasperating to be borne. The sweat, pooling uncomfortably in every fold of his trembling body, felt just as excruciating. Once he dared to open his eyes finally, glancing down at the nicotine stains that seemingly tattooed the fingers of his right hand while he snuffed his cigarette out, he made up his mind to head back to Greenthorne once he had mustered the nerve to get up – to get away from the heath and from her.

Trudging back towards town with his eyes kept safely downcast, Oliver stopped after ten minutes or so to rub scratches from nettles, thistles, and gorse on his calves and knees; the itching seemed to serve as a slight distraction from that eyes-into-the-back-of-you feeling that still prickled between his shoulder blades. While that whining sound in his ears was fading, he was thankful that his pulse had resumed its normal rate, and he was glad that his vision had cleared; his mind felt far less achy and agitated in general. Feeling relieved to have some clarity again and seizing upon this straightaway, he looked around and was satisfied that she was not following him. The coast seemed to be clear again, for the time being, at least.

It struck him then that Marion had managed to become just as insufferable in death as she had become in life. Only a year ago he had been blessedly free of her, and there had been no repercussions to face before she had crept back into his life. Once again, his resentment rivalled the unease to which she had habituated him.

'Enough is enough, though, surely?' he muttered to himself. When she had been alive, his mother's belligerence had kept him similarly heedful of her, to the brink of nervous exhaustion; she had still found plentiful occasion to have his guts for garters, however, no matter how hard he had strived to behave himself.

The only logical course of action Oliver could determine when thinking back on all this was to carry on regardless; whether his mother was right or wrong in her views, he knew, deep down, that he simply could not help himself. There could be no pleasing her, and moments of remorse such as this were always half-hearted and never lasted long; they lasted not much longer than her appearances, in fact, which, although getting more and more frequent, were always fleeting.

'So be it!' he muttered with his former nonchalance overtaking him; he swore once again that he would not change his ways, despite Marion's continued attempts to police him. A devil-may-care smile crept over his lips. While wishing that he had a toffee left with which to jubilate his renewed spirits, he found himself checking every fold of his pockets for the sugary morsel that he hoped he had overlooked; striking gold, he immediately stripped it of its wrapper with steadying fingers and administered its gooeyness to his tongue. It was still very early, and the day was not to be spoilt just yet – of this he was determined. Returning his thoughts to Dennis Bannister and Delilah instead, he sniggered to himself, and the queer matter of his mother's return was quickly shelved, he chuckled heartily because the look on both their faces seemed priceless in retrospect, and he had to remind himself that it was not as if he had harmed them in any way. Having already shrugged off pretending that his behaviour was a form of anthropological fieldwork, Oliver knew it had become nothing more than shameless tomfoolery; duly, he could hardly fault their reaction.

That aside, a pint seemed called for since Oliver had a slight anxiousness lingering that he needed to suppress. More importantly, though, he needed that pint to celebrate his growing immunity to his mother's visitations, and, of course, with which to toast his increasing command over his own life. He then remembered with a jolt, however, that his allowance was gone; he had none of those tarnished copper discs left, which, despite their deceptively small size, always had so much power over him. By consequence, he found himself entertaining thoughts of sneaking down the Oddfellows' side steps and breaking into its beer cellar; it certainly would not be the first time such daring action had been warranted.

While resting on a stile at the heath's border, he was pleased to find that his mind was already finding its way elsewhere; already, a precious memory of Jonesy, his former pet feline who was much loved, presented itself. Emotional elastic tied between them had often tugged Oliver's little friend as far as this stile while in pursuit of his master. On reaching the perimeter of his own world, however, Jonesy had always become too anxious to follow any further; he would always stop and howl as Oliver continued into the distance. Nothing had been more gladdening upon Oliver's return than seeing Jonesy still waiting there, seeming relieved and overjoyed that he had not been abandoned after all; his whiskers, and indeed his whole body, had always quivered visibly with this elation, but the sweetness of such memories had a melancholy carryover nowadays. Jonesy's passing had left Oliver utterly alone. Oliver had not cried at his mother's or even his nana's funeral; instead, he had battled with remorse for having dared to think that he might be better off without Marion, while he had simply felt numb at his nana's funeral, despite how much he had adored her. To this very day, however, he readily sobbed his heart out at the slightest thought of Jonesy; still flooding his throat with wayward tears, this sorrow had almost drowned him after discovering that his little sidekick had passed in his sleep, curled motionless at the end of the bed. For a long while afterwards, catching sight of auburn flecks of cat hair, still stuck to the settee cushions, had unleashed a grief that had felt crushing in his innards. Nowadays, however, he embraced this grief, and he greeted it like an old friend that he never wanted to lose touch with; it had become a deep melancholy in which he would willingly submerse himself while pushing all feeling for everything else away.

Sobbing quietly as he squeezed through a side alley and turned to walk the length of Meadow Lane, which was horribly littered, he then passed derelict-looking workshops and tin shacks that nowadays served as the shoddiest of housing for residents who had little choice but to grow their own veg in nearby plots. Mirroring his own internal landscape perfectly, Greenthorne had become increasingly desolate-looking in recent years; despite this parallel, the affinity that he had once felt for the town had dwindled in such times, however. While plodding past their dusty, desiccated allotments, clustered in the barbed shadow of the gasworks, he tried to ignore those square yards of despair where townsfolk struggled to grow potatoes to supplement their meagre diets, and 'petty capitalists' kept pigs to procure and sell their manure.

On reaching the corner finally, Oliver wiped away those tears and steeled himself to face the crowds on Greenthorne's main thoroughfare, Middle Row.

Painting its east side with a yellowing wash while blocking out its west side with an indigo tinged darkening matte, the sunlight seemed even more garish there than where he had just been; against this blinding light, and against the swarms of gnats, midges, and horseflies that flew about him, Oliver kept his eyes downcast as he headed through the milling crowd.

While panhandling as usual, Mr Turner offered his upturned cap to everyone that passed him by. He had been well decorated, and his tarnished war medals still swung from his grubby, sweat-soaked blazer. What has this valorisation done for him, though? Oliver wondered; not a great deal, by the looks of things! Seeming to have been forgotten, just as his brave contributions to the war effort had been, Clive seemed to be similarly adrift from the world and its history as Greenthorne itself had become.

'Fag for the corporal, Oliver?' Mr Turner asked.
'All out I'm afraid, Mr Turner. I was going to ask the same of you, actually.'
'Pity.'

He looked so old, perhaps beyond his years? Oliver often wondered; one could not really tell. Noticing that Mr Turner was once again selling those decorative little crosses which he crafted from cigar boxes, and with which passers-by took little interest, Oliver found that his eye was still caught by Clive's handiwork, and he wished that he could purchase one.

Soon after, while passing by the billiard hall, Oliver could barely suppress a grimace once more; the place was beyond terrifying, and it was an absolute no go thanks to its rough clientele. Patrons like Dirty Gertie and Hefty Hattie aside, most that drank there were embittered former miners who, having lost their jobs due to the depression, would have no doubt fancied him as an ideal punch bag with which to take out their frustration; this seemed to be confirmed by the thousand-yard stares that he always received from the hard nuts spilling out of its doorway. He had had the foresight for once to avoid an undesirable outcome without having to learn the hard way, however; he had never dared to venture in. Then he had found his own sanctuary anyway: the Oddfellows. This other drinking establishment was far less dangerous, and it was a place where he could, at the very least, be tolerated – something that he was more than thankful for.

Feeling that he had lost his nerve to break into the Oddfellow's warm and fragrantly yeasty cellar, Oliver decided that he would try his luck by batting his pretty eyelashes at the pub's barmaid-in-chief instead. Doris was the closest thing that he had in the world to a friend, after all; it sometimes worked, and, in all earnestness, he would have hated to have hoodwinked her again by sneaking in downstairs.

Although it had long ago lost its core industries to overseas competitors and new forms of power, their shadow still loomed large in Greenthorne – the shadow of coal mining especially. Despite the local pit closures and the years passing since, a woman's place among all that had not changed a great deal, much to his annoyance; following this convention, the Oddfellows' snug bar had been reserved exclusively for ladies, as had the saloon for gents. He could not possibly enter the snug, then, as much as he might prefer to; the townswomen may have treated him as if he were invisible – that perpetual mystery that never ceased to baffle him – but when he thought of the reception that routinely awaited him in the saloon bar, he would have preferred invisibility to always standing out so starkly.

Odd Fellows

As the saloon door swung shut behind him, Oliver heard Doris yell down to Hard-Faced Auggy that the pale ale barrel needed changing, but he simply could not wait for the incurable slowcoach to make his preferred tipple available again.

'Nice drop this,' Doris said of the pale ale's substitution.

'Thank you so much, Doris... Really... I can't thank you enough,' Oliver whispered.

'You're lucky Bossman's at t' brewery... Ah couldn't if 'e were 'ere,' she replied, just as hushed. 'Watches me like hawk, that fella, even after all these years.'

Doris was absolutely his angel, and her kindly light brown eyes – those warm pools of molten toffee – were quite beautiful, but they always caught him a little off guard; they served as yet another reminder that he had completely given up on womankind, having no insight whatsoever into their puzzling natures. But the woman smiling at him from across the bar was one of the few folks in the world who had any good words for him, which was all that really mattered, and, in fact, it meant the world. It was not as if the conversation flowed easily after initial pleasantries, however; with nothing much else to say, he quickly assured her that he would sling the cost across her palm at the very next opportunity, and tentatively made his way across the room.

While discussing local soccer matches and the horse racing results from Amthorpe in a spirited manner, Roy Wilks, Grahame Lowndes, and Bert Greasley sat pouring over copies of the *Greenthorne Gazette*, the *Blandishford Comet*, and the *Daily Herald*. Unfortunately, the mean-spirited sun's rays, slicing through the saloon bar windows, betrayed Oliver as he tried to sneak past them; while tiptoeing to his usual seat in the corner, they cast his shadow across them, and the room fell silent as the men looked up from their papers. He was no stranger to their scrutiny, nor was he unfamiliar with the clammy bodily sensations that accompanied it. He could only hope they would soon forget him; they always did eventually.

He had some inkling of why he bothered Roy, at least, since he had knocked elbows with him in the darkened alleys that odd fellows tended to roam; he hid his secret life well, however, he had to admit of Roy. It was quite a big secret too – much like the heath, the carnality of the alleys was absolutely shocking! Only recently, in fact, he had seen Roy's darkened silhouette kneel before another man's like a loyal subject before a king. But Bert and Grahame seemed to find his presence just as troublesome as Roy did, and that was far more perplexing; they lived on the straight and narrow, after all, and could not have known about such activities, surely? Nonetheless, their penetrant stare felt much like how the darts being flung at the dart board might feel if they were being flung at Oliver! Why, then? he found himself asking, just as so many times before, and while feeling somewhat exasperated.

'Starin' owt 'em winders, 'e looks like a phummock peepin' out an ivy bush,' Oliver heard Grahame mutter while the lingering tension in his tummy worsened; he had no idea what he meant, but he had no doubt that it was yet another put-down, and that he was the 'phummock' in question. It felt especially exasperating because he had gone there to calm and compose himself after what had just transpired, the atmosphere was otherwise pleasant, and there was even soccer on the radio –

'... They're off again... They're changing over... Pearle's taking it... He's kicking to the left...'

A cooling draught wafted from out the back and across Doris' bar, and then it circled pleasingly around the room; he had her nailed as a secret wizardess for conjuring it. It felt extraordinary, actually, but although it felt cooler than anything that he had felt for aeons, he still felt hot and bothered thanks to Roy and company.

'... Wales defending the south end now... Harding throwing it in... A fairly long one... England have it... Down on the ground... England have heeled... Out to Laughton...'

People-watching through the saloon bar windows was usually pleasing for Oliver, although the view across Middle Row to the draper's opposite was limited. Market stall holders' banter from further up the street was ordinarily music to his ears, too, and it formed lively images in his mind's eye; owing to its relative liveliness on this late afternoon, Middle Row's bluster should have been as easy to visualise as the clash between England and Wales –

'Carrots, sweeds, an' turnips for sale... Come get thy veg, ladies n' gents... Fresh from t' field!'

'... Now to Laired... Corbet... Out to Gibbs... Gibbs is going down the line... Keeping his pecker up... Up to twenty-five now... Well done sir...'

As he tried to sup without slurping, Oliver remained so tense, however, that all this sounded like more of an irksome, cacophonous jumble of noise; fearing another bad head, and another afternoon and evening lying prostrate in agony at home again, he knew that, difficult as it was, somehow he must relax and refrain from trying to second-guess the reasoning behind Bert and Grahame's wariness.

'Nesh little gnat!' he then heard Bert whisper to Roy, who tittered, unsurprisingly. Oliver knew he had the air of lost wealth – Clive Turner had kindly pointed this out to him; as such, he supposed that the problem might be that he simply puzzled them. He had never found a job that suited him, and he supposed that he might therefore be classed as 'idle poor' also, but his weekly allowance from Uncle Sheldon meant that he could afford beer most days of the week if he made tough sacrifices; the latter point made their indignance seem quite unwarranted if his assumptions were correct. But was this actually what annoyed them? He supposed that it was a plausible explanation, having heard that, even after a hard day's toil filling mould castings in Spooner & Sons' foundry, Bert and Grahame had to tire themselves with all kinds of legitimate and illegitimate measures to simply make ends meet. Meanwhile, Roy secretly fraternised with the gentlemen of the shade, and his fiancée, Pearle, kept looking at her wristwatch, no doubt.

According to Grahame, however, who had just flicked open the *Blandishford Comet's* sport pages and skimmed the headlines, Jock McAlloran had beaten Moe Taylor to the northern region flyweight title at the Blandishford Corn Exchange – excitement enough to forget Oliver for the time being. Feeling greatly relieved to hear that they had at last returned to sport, and from the gee-gees to boxing, Oliver felt lighter asudden. Breathing a deep yet hushed sigh of relief, he greedily glugged his bitter down while peering through the stencilling on the window's frosted glass. He watched a chap walk his lurcher past the drapers while their window was being redressed by Mrs Woolgather and her plump, sullen daughter, Sybill, whose sulky, mindless glare through steely eyes he had always found oddly arresting. Seeing Roy on his arrival had briefly revived his remorse – that he had ever known the heath and those alleyways himself, even if only from a spectator's viewpoint – but already that remorse was becoming a far less troublesome itch with every sup; with his pint washing through his veins, he quickly felt calmer. Odd glances and untoward commentary aside, the Oddfellows, of all Greenthorne's public houses, intimidated him the least; the likes of Bert and Grahame were coarse, but they were hardly hooligans. They understood that even if you did not like someone, lamping them was usually not the way to go; Doris would have none of it when they did occasionally resort to fisticuffs anyway, growling 'Not on t' premises!'

Middle Row's least precarious watering hole also had a sporting orientation that Oliver greatly appreciated: the walls were adorned with pictures of racing greyhounds, whippets, and horses. One could play cards there, or dominoes, if one had an opponent, and the spirit of friendly competition permeated the smoky air. Just like today, there was usually soccer or horse and dog racing on the wireless too – another plus and something else for him to focus on while he drank alone. Over some time, while doing just this, he had gradually grown accustomed to being the unaccompanied odd fellow in the corner who was begrudgingly allowed to settle in; Roy's, Grahame's, and Bert's distrusts were crosses that he had learned to bear, so long as he could sit with his back to them and observe life on Middle Row while forgetting Marion's atrocities from the afterlife and his woebegone life in general.

Already, Oliver felt less troubled by his mother's earlier appearance because, although lonesome, the Oddfellows felt much like a sanctuary of sorts from all malign energies. The saloon bar was a cavity of bismuth yellow – the colour of his late nana's tea caddy – which, with the sun's rays pouring in through the saloon bar windows, shimmered a golden colour and lent the place an air of consecration; furthermore, the place was usually busy enough to give the spirits scant elbowroom.

While feeling appreciative again of Doris' charity, he found the bitter's tartness, seeping beautifully through his parched interior, soothed yet invigorated him greatly. While feeling equally invigorated by the prospect of having his allowance paid out again after tomorrow's visit to Uncle Sheldon, Oliver remembered how unexpectedly tiresome these visits were becoming of late, but for this essential monetary reimbursement they were inescapable.

He found himself craving another cigarette then; it always felt nightmarish when he ran out – smoking helped to occupy his hands as well as steady his nerves. Without a fag to clutch onto, those hands of his became impossible to ignore; they became cumbersome appendages that trembled, taking on their own life. Finding himself unable to resist fixating on their rough and sinuously knotted appearance, which seemed so incongruent with the rest of him, he felt repulsed. Layer upon layer, he also hated it when he found himself fretting over them; bringing a deep sense of alarm connected to worries that ran deeper than the cosmetic, this agitation caused his fingers to tremble even more.

Having only had a few grains of oatmeal left to peck at on rising, and a half-eaten Eccles cake that he had spied lying in Jennings' entranceway, which he had scoffed for elevenses, Oliver felt increasingly lightheaded while his tummy rumbled in complaint;

he felt famished, actually. Remembering the all but empty larder at home and knowing that he had no remaining purchasing power left, it then struck him that supper was entirely off the cards again. Anxiously, he took out his wallet and checked for any extra coins that may have secreted themselves in its folds; while searching, the photograph of his mother and he that he had defaced, yet still felt compelled to carry, slipped out onto the table.

Propped on the living room's mantel at home were others from this set that had all suffered from the same ill-treatment over time, with his mother's face becoming a ghostly, scratched out blur in all of them; having only made them more unnerving, he still could not bring himself to dispose of them either, despite what he had done to them. In the case of the photographs of Marion and a far younger Oliver together, of which this was one, he had left his own face intact, of course, which unfortunately made them even more jarring; those had become the most troublesome of the set. These photographs had once been happily associated with his last truly joyful memory of life, when they had also lived in Thorny Grove, just around the corner from Uncle Sheldon, who he presumed must have photographed them with his Coronet camera. The occasion had been a family picnic which had been held in the common land just beyond the low wall of Ashurst's rear garden. They had been relatively prosperous then, and accordingly his mother had still behaved reasonably. It was also a time when she and his uncle had seemed to have some rapport. It was when Sheldon had been relatively young and handsome. It had also been when his dear nana, God rest her, had still been alive. Gigi, as they had all called his nana, had always lingered out of frame in his imagination, hovering just beyond the photographs' periphery, just as she had in reality; she had been so convinced that a piece of her soul would be stripped from her with the shutter's closure that she had always stepped aside. But how Gigi had beamed that day, despite her cataract, while carrying out a tray of refreshment! While picturing as best as he could how the coral glow of her gown had matched the tint of the cordial glasses, he always found it quite the pity that he had no record of this – especially now that she had passed away.

Sadly, upon growing older and more visually perceptive, Oliver had eventually come to notice that something was a little off with these particular photographs, and he had realised that the floral meadow backdrop was, in fact, a painted studio backdrop. Once he had realised that this set had not captured the occasion that he so dearly treasured in his memory – one that was dimming in his mind with every passing year – resentment had followed; resentment had soon turned to loathing, however, owing to Marion's piercing gaze in the photographs. Once seeming somewhat queenly, that gaze had conveyed her dependability even if it had never been the warmest of looks, but later on in her short life and beyond, that gaze had become unsettling, oppressive, and increasingly difficult to bear. Her eyes, seeming to follow him around from any photograph that she had wound up in, had become unbearable to behold; this was the reason that he had scratched them out, and soon afterwards her entire face. He had straightaway felt guilty for doing so, however, each and every time.

While attempting to snatch the photograph up and return it to his wallet's darkness in an involuntary reflex borne of the regret and anxiety it had come to stand for, those unruly, trembling hands of his had lost all their dexterity; he knocked his bitter over with a loud clatter instead. The remainder seeped over the tabletop in a syrupy puddle. The suds ran off the edge, and, since he was in short trousers, dripped uncomfortably down his calves and into his socks and brogues; with deep agitation also seeping through him, he wished that the saloon bar floorboards would splinter open and swallow him whole. The gents behind graciously jeered and clapped, and while flying over with her rag, Doris squawked –

'Ah give you a free pint and you wash t' floor with it... What a caper!'

'Sorry Doris,' Oliver replied sheepishly.

'Never mind, poppet.'

Winking again at him, she then turned to his audience, flicked her rag at them, and they quickly piped down when she snapped –

'Put a sock in it or sod off, you lot!'

Then, plucking the sodden photograph from out of the puddle, she asked –

'What's this? What a shame, you've ruined your photo!'

Flipping it over and studying the faded logo that he had never been able to make meaning of – 'V.S.' inkstamped on the back – she quickly exclaimed –

'Vale Studios!'

Feeling horrified that Doris was clutching the wretched item, and as much as he felt compelled to snatch it from her, get it out of sight and out of mind again, and then deflect by changing the subject, he did not; instead, he found himself asking with some urgency –

'You know it? Where is it, Doris?'

'Ah thought it might be 'im. 'E took our Ruby's photos. Lovely photos they were too. 'E's down in the Old Stores, behind Ash Brothers... if ah remember rightly... but that were a while ago... Wonder if 'e's still there?'

'He?'

'Albion Roper's 'is name. Ah remember 'cause ah went to school with the feller... Nice feller, in fact.'

Handing it back to him, she asked –

'Who's this anyway? It's you, isn't it? Aww, cute. An' who's this?' she then asked of his defaced mother.

'No one, Doris,' he said on rising. 'Must... ehm... dash, though... I'll see you soon.'

***

Although he had assured himself that he would just have a brief look and then pass on quickly, Oliver found himself staring up at a sign, which was so old and weathered that the words 'Vale Studios & Photographic Services' were barely legible, for quite some time; a smaller sign asked that inquirers ring for attendance, and independently of his better judgement, his index finger had immediately followed the instruction upon his arrival. As much as he would have liked to have left, it would have been rude not to wait in case Mr Roper was home, regrettably. While waiting in the shadow of the Old

Stores, it felt weird upon reflection: it was as if a silent wind had wafted him there, or as if an invisible hand, pressed firmly between his shoulder blades, had ushered him the entire route. Having arrived, however, the place felt completely unfamiliar, and he suspected that it was probably better left that way; with the short shrift that he gave the past in general, and his mother's memory in particular, he had no idea what he was doing there or hoped to accomplish. This was a thought which found him glancing nervously around, for fear that she had followed him to find out what on earth he was up to. While keeping his head down as he had left the Oddfellows, he had made sure not to glance into the side alleys, where the shadows of the approaching evening would have already been thickening; Mill Lane was still reasonably well-lit, however. Glancing tentatively around, he felt optimistic that he was alone for once. That perpetual, shimmering heat haze had died down a little, owing to a slight drop in temperature; Marion's discarnate figure was not discernibly lurking behind him anywhere.

Feeling greatly relieved that nobody had answered and about to make his getaway, he then heard an upstairs window slide open, and, looking up, he saw the silhouette of a man against the undulant, ashen sky. The gentleman rubbed his eyes as he yawned sleepily and then called down –

''Ow do?'

'Mr Roper?'

'Aye, that's me.'

'M-may I have a word?'

'Aye, lad. Ah'll be down shortly... Was just takin' a nap, sorry.'

Oliver pushed the door open and stepped in with some apprehension. Once inside, Vale Studios felt stuffy and airless. The lathe, among other machinery, revealed tell-tale signs of its former utility as a manufacturing works of some kind, and the old workshop was quite a mess: gloomy, dusty, and forlorn looking. It was hard to imagine that the outfit was still in business at all. With the lights flickering on finally, Mr Roper poked his head in behind, saying 'Ten more minutes, lad... Sorry,' before disappearing again. Upon swerving around, and without getting a particularly good look at him before he shot out again, unkempt hair of the darkest shade imaginable was all Oliver could ascertain of Mr Roper.

While waiting, and while trying to breathe through his mouth to bypass his nasal cavity, he found the studio's odour deeply unpleasant: the stench of industry that always brought Cranford Electric, and therefore his mother, to mind. Around old machinery, rusty bulkhead lights, and brittle, yellowing wall notices, a gallery of townsfolk was on display.

Then, browsing hurriedly through a display album of Vale Studio's sitters, featuring ill-fated infantrymen, drab debutantes, and glib graduates – all spotlighted in the emerald glow of the lily lamp that Mr Roper had placed just so – he swallowed hard. It felt ghoulish to console himself with the knowledge that many of these proud-looking soldiers were long dead, and that he was not, therefore, the only fatherless orphan of war; it was a thought that comforted him nonetheless until he carelessly knocked the ornamental crinoline lady, who had stood next to the album, to the ground. While cursing those trembling fingers of his yet again, he saw that he had smashed her into smithereens; after the initial jolt, ensuing heart palpitations, and worry of upsetting Mr Roper, the jagged green shards of pottery scattered about his feet found him feeling just as fractured.

When turning then and noticing the canvas backdrop heaped carelessly in the corner of the room, Oliver felt his heart palpitate! While immediately recognising the once lushly rendered meadow, with its fine splattering of versicoloured meadow flowers, it first struck him how pitifully it had faded and browned, perfectly mirroring just how dreary-looking the lands around Greenthorne had become that long, hot summer. It also confirmed what he had guessed already: the sorry sight of that meadow's artifice proved that the family photographs that he had once cherished, and then came to despise enough to vandalise, had not captured the special memory that he recalled so fondly – the one with which they had been associated for so many years. It was without question, then, that that glorious occasion had not been captured on photographic paper and only remained hazily documented in his mind after all. He had already asked Uncle Sheldon if he had taken any such snaps with that Coronet camera of his, but Sheldon had merely shrugged while saying that if he had, he likely would have thrown them out amid a spring clean or during the renovations – unthinking goon, if he had.

''Ow do lad, what brings thee?'

Swerving around to find that Mr Roper had quietly snuck in behind him, Oliver saw that he was indeed dark – sable dark. With the way that his host rubbed his eyes while smiling, Oliver could only think of a badger waking from a long hibernation when coaxed from his den by spring's calling. It seemed surprising that he did not remember Mr Roper either once he had dropped his hands and revealed himself to be a leanly built fellow with a pleasing, if a little careworn, face because he was distinctive looking. Yes, the photographer was only a decade or so his senior, to hazard a guess, but his facial lines, although charming, seemed at odds with the youthful lustre of his glimmering eyes. Oliver felt curiously drawn to this stranger. Revealing thin, sinuously carved forearms, Mr Roper wore a shirt with rolled-up sleeves beneath a Fair Isle woollen vest that did not quite meet the baggy, threadbare slacks draped over his narrow hips – all just as endearing. Oliver then became mindful that he had almost forgotten what it was like to be so genuinely struck by first impressions; it felt odd – novel even – but knowing that he was not on the heath or in the crossway, and how rude it was therefore to stare, he realised that he must speak up –

'Thank you for seeing me, Mr Roper. I–'

''Old on.'

Although Oliver deemed it quite unnecessary, Mr Roper saw fit to switch on the photographic lamps while saying 'There, that's better,' and the room became even brighter than midday sunlight; a faint electrical whine also filled the air. Feeling their surprising warmth on his skin, Oliver quickly understood, when thinking back on the family picnic, how easily the rays from these photographic lamps could have been confused with the warm sun of his childhood; it also helped explain how, if the distillate of his previous visit with Marion was bottled, cobwebbed, and closeted somewhere in his mind's recesses, those occasions had become so muddled in his mind.

Having to screw up his eyes to be able to see at all then, with the light so bright, he ascertained that Mr Roper's eyes were just as dark as his hair, keener and sharper than he had previously noted, and that the photographer returned his gaze quite intently too. Having only just been slickly backcombed, Mr Roper's blue-black hair was rebelliously shaking itself loose already, owing to the early evening's humidity. While nimbly rolling a cigarette with long and delicate yet thickly knuckled fingers, Mr Roper smiled so very pleasantly and then said –

'Dunno if ah can take thy portrait today, the place is a flamin' bombsite, as tha can well see... But don't thee fret, there's nowt in 'ere will bite thee.'

He then finished the flawlessly assembled roll-your-own, lit up, and added while soft ringlets of smoke wafted about him –

'So... tha'd like an appointment, lad? That it?'

'Oh no, Mr Roper, you see... we've actually met before and–'

'Oh, we 'ave? Well, ah am surprised to 'ear that, ah must say, as ah don't remember thee at all, lad... which is odd... ah've a memory for faces.'

It certainly is odd, Oliver thought. He was in total agreement because he usually did, too, but then –

'Well, it was rather a long time ago, Mr Roper. You see, I wondered if... Well, I've mislaid a set of family portraits which were taken by your good self... and I wondered if it were at all possible to get them replaced... They were genuinely treasured.'

Feeling surprised to hear all this spill out, Oliver realised that on his way there, a barely acknowledged plan of atonement had been subconsciously devised; with the regrets and worries of the day still weighing upon him somewhat, he had decided, then, that he would mend his ways, and meanwhile he would replace the photos that he had so heartlessly defaced in apology to his mother's spirit.

'Oh... well... how long ago?'

'Well, it was over a decade ago, Mr Roper. Eleven or twelve years, perhaps.'

Although it was beyond doubt that Mr Roper wanted to help him, the change in his expression indicated straight off that his chances were slim; his face fell immediately.

'Oh dear... ah'm sorry to say... ah think it quite unlikely, lad. Ah do 'old on to negatives, but that were quite a while back... Let me 'ave a look, just to be sure. What's thy name?'

While feeling both disappointment and relief, and conceding that it had indeed been folly to come after all, Oliver answered anyway –

'Oliver Gidley, and my mother's name was Marion... Marion Gidley.'

'Right... well 'old on... ah'll be back in just a tick... Ah'm Albion by the way,' he called back once out of sight.

With his host rummaging in his storeroom, Oliver, knowing that he sometimes went overboard when minding his 'p's and 'q's in the company of strangers that he felt compelled to impress, worried that he was sounding a little too lofty – grandiloquent even; perhaps he sounded a complete twit to Mr Roper, then, who was clearly the salt of the earth. Deciding to tone it down a little because, for some reason, he still found himself caring far more than usual what this gentleman – a total stranger – thought of him, he then noticed how sodden his shoes and socks still felt from the bitter that he had spilt over himself, and he worried how much he might reek as such. Remembering with another jolt a far more pressing concern – his act of inadvertent vandalism – all this became eclipsed for Oliver; while wondering what on earth Mr Roper would make of his faux pas, if he had not noticed already, Oliver sheepishly ventured –

'Mr Roper, I can't apologise enough. I should have told you as soo–'

'The crinoline lady? Ah noticed. That's alright lad, we'll live, even if she won't,' Mr Roper called back with a chuckle.

Feeling relieved to be forgiven for his ham-fistedness, and then realising that he had an opportunity to step out of his spotlight and find a shadow's refuge – somewhere that he could address Mr Roper with more confidence – he quickly gathered there was none available. The lamps were so dazzling that they brilliantly lit every corner of Vale Studios without leniency; accordingly, he felt increasingly tense and sweaty, but the aroma of Mr Roper's rolling tobacco lingered behind him and was surprisingly soothing in a way. It was sweeter smelling than any kind that Oliver had tried; seeming to be somewhat of an antidote to all such anxiety, it tickled his fancy for another puff himself. When wondering if he could be brazen enough to ask Mr Roper to furnish him with one of his roll-your-owns, he immediately thought better of it when heeding his own tobacco-stained fingers; just shameful! he thought while tucking them behind him, out of sight.

Clutching an envelope, Mr Roper flew back into the room with a look of apprehension on his face. Oliver wondered if the photographer had encountered a ghost back there, before his host turned to him and loudly exclaimed –

'Oof, but ah remember these clearly now... and thee, and thy poor, dear mother!'

'I'm sorry?'

'Oh, she did give me a fright... 'ow she jus' lay there... twitchin' on t' floor... It were awful. All warmth were washed from 'er face... Small wonder tha were so upset, lad. Remember?'

Quite stunned, Oliver could only nod at first, having no idea what to say. Then he could only offer –

'Not so very well to be frank... What happened, Mr Roper? She passed out, then, I gather?'

'Aye, she did at that. Couldn't stop thee bawlin'... 'Er nose trickled with blood, like a leaky tap, an' wouldn't stop. Well... we called Doc' Fairbrother and they 'ad to get her to the infirmary. Ah stayed with 'er while my assistant, Violet – ah 'ad an assistant in those days, see – she took thee to thy nana's on t' train to Blandishford... Remember that?'

'Well... yes.'

Yes, although he did not remember the studio, Oliver certainly remembered ending up at Gigi's. While taking an unexpected detour to Blandishford and then juddering along a rutted byway to another place called wretchedness, his life had changed dramatically owing to the very moment that Mr Roper was unveiling! The room blurred at the edges as he connected the photographer's account with his stay with Gigi above the grocers, and he remembered how, upon his mother's return from the infirmary, even though the doctors were at a loss to find any cause for her collapse except for malnourishment and exhaustion, the light had gone from her eyes; her conviction that the hospital doctors were incompetent quacks, and that something which they had missed entirely was terribly wrong with her health had persisted, however. Although she had never exactly been the warmest of mothers prior to this, Marion had always been reasonably tempered towards her only child, at least, having already claimed her stake to the good life before he had been born. But because she had abruptly become convinced that her good life was in jeopardy, there had newly been a subdued quality and a coolness about her that had saddened and unnerved him as a child, while she had also become uncharacteristically curt with him on occasion. He also remembered how she had begun to frown when Gigi, with the second sight, had tried to reassure Marion that his father's spirit was still around them; Gigi would cry out, 'I can see 'im... 'e's right there... an' 'e's smilin'!' while pointing to a dusty mirror that reflected nothing of note; Marion would only smirk at her disbelievingly by then, however.

Bringing his mind back to the present moment and to Mr Roper's preface to all such difficulties, Oliver remained vexed that he could not remember any of it – especially since this preface was a pivotal moment in all their histories.

With sickly sensations churning in his entrails, he seemed to be sweating even more profusely too; it seemed quite understandable how his mother had wilted beneath these hot lights! Feeling dizzy and exhausted, as if reliving her pain, he then had no doubt that he should not have gone there to tinker with the past, and wanting to leave immediately, he mumbled –

'Yes... well, I'm sorry... Sorry to have troubled you, Mr Roper. I... didn't come here to upset you... so I'll just be–'

'Oh no, that's alright lad... tha's not upset me. It were just a shock for a moment... Brought it all back. Tha's lucky thy mother only wanted the first half a dozen of these posted, although she paid for the whole set, of course. S'pose it were understandable, seein' as what 'appened. But there's a few gooduns left.'

'A-are you sure you wouldn't mind?'

'Mind? Ah'd be delighted, in fact... Well, ah'll be delighted to 'elp thyself out is what I mean... They were lovely photos, an' it were a good sittin'... at least it were before all that.'

Feeling too much like a moth on a pin, Oliver felt far too tight-chested and anxious to properly process it all. Meanwhile, the incendiary glare of the photographic lamps became overpowering; he had to blink repeatedly, but their sunlike yellow coronas left afterimages that lingered, seemingly burnt into his retinas, and they cluttered his vision, which had already become quite unfocused. Unable to bear the pungent smells either – the burning off of layers of dust by the scorching lamps, the queer aroma of hot fuse wire, and the vile metallic and chemical smells of industry that still bedevilled the place – he almost retched while imagining that Cranford Electric would still smell much the same.

'She recovered, thy mother? 'Ow is she? Ah often wondered... but then... when I received 'er cheque, ah assumed all came right for 'er.'

'Well... she... er... I'm a-afraid s-she d-di... she's passed on,' Oliver said, feeling that he was about to pass out at any moment.

Mr Roper's face fell instantly, and with his eyes glimmering with genuine concern, he exclaimed, 'Good Lord, ah'm sooo sorry to 'ear that!'

They were perhaps becoming a little too penetrating, however, those remarkable eyes of his, while Mr Roper then asked –

'Thy father? He still about?'

In obligation to Mr Roper's sincerity, Oliver felt that he could only answer truthfully, as much as he wished to avoid this question too –

'Well... he passed away too... before her, in fact... The war... you know... shot down in air-to-air combat.'

Straightaway, Oliver realised that he had stumbled quite carelessly into rather dangerous territory. The doors to his mental closets were being tugged open with a loud creak by a rather nosy parker indeed, albeit a well-meaning one. He had to break from Mr Roper's heightened gaze then, and he glanced back at the studio momentarily; despite the lamp's visual echoes cluttering his vision, he had no doubt that he saw a somewhat indistinct figure hover and then collapse onto the floorboards with a sickening thud – felt more than heard – before paling into nothingness. His heart raced faster as the finer hairs on his neck and arms bristled and stiffened; in tandem, the blood sang even louder in his ears, sounding more like an electrical hiss. To cap it all then, Mr Roper did the darnedest thing: he stepped closer and took Oliver's sweaty, trembling hand in his own, holding it quite tenderly and patting it gently.

'Ah'm sorry, lad... Life 'asn't been fair to thee at all, 'as it? My condolences for thy losses.'

With the greatest of regard for Mr Roper's good intentions, however sweetly expressed, Oliver still felt that he could not suffer this interrogation from the owner of the twinkling eyes any longer – eyes which under any other circumstance he would have happily gotten lost in; reclaiming his hand awkwardly then, he looked elsewhere. Not liking folks talking about his father's sacrifice as if it were a tragedy either, he felt that he should speak up –

'Well, I suppose that he got the glory he sought in the end... Well, that's what my mother said anyway.'

''E were a pilot?'

'A pilot officer, yes.'

'Oh aye? Which squadron were that?'

'I... uhm... I've no idea!' Oliver exclaimed with some surprise and disappointment at his lapse of memory; he did not want to misplace what little detail he had archived in the mental dossier of his father, after all.

'Was 'e stationed out at Nether Moor?'

'Y-yes... out at the aerodrome.'

'Aye, ah knew by thine accent thee weren't from these parts. Where's thy family from?'

'Er... well, my mother came only from Blandishford, as a matter of fact, but my father was from down south.'

'Oh, she were local... Well, she really didn't sound like a northerner... an' nor does tha, for that matter!'

Oh dear, oh dear, Oliver thought after hoping that he would succinctly satisfy and conclude Mr Roper's line of questioning with his response. Every question that he answered led only to being probed even further, while it struck him rather coldly that Marion was probably hearing all this too – the careless raking up of her past; she would not be best pleased either! It then dawned on him that the crackling electrostatic interference that he could hear was her signature tune – on grounds that she spent half her life in Cranford Electric's spook house of unearthly-sounding hmmzonks, hmmdinks, and hmmzaps. Yes, she is here, he thought; I have just seen her, haven't I? The smell of her brought even more certainty: burning fuse wire and the noxious chemical smells that she had always reeked of by her shift's end. Once again, he could see her apparitional shimmers and swirls forming in the periphery of his vision; snapping his eyes shut then, Oliver pretended to wipe them.

'No... Well, she attended private school in the south somewhere... Sorry... something in my eye. Where was it now? Highborne, possibly.'

'Well it clearly paid off. She were a fine woman. Spoke an' carried 'erself very well, from what ah can remember... an' she were a pleasure to photograph.'

Struck asudden by the distance between appearances and the truth of things, Oliver instantly let his mother's visitation slip again while poking around his own migrainous mind, rummaging in those mental closets himself. A fine woman indeed? Yes, people had often thought so... but he had known the person behind the facade. Her iron will, for instance, and the temper so easily lost if her desire to have her life and the world just so met with any obstruction. He also remembered the derision with which his mother had so often spoken of her parents, and how, in all her snobbery, she had hated being the daughter of a lowly grocer – from Blandishford, of all places. Gigi had usually brushed over her daughter's acidity, but in a rare moment of transparency, she had once revealed how Marion had worn his grandad down with all her demands; Gigi had whispered that despite securing a loan from Uncle Sheldon to pay for her first two terms, his mother had still needed money for the charm schooling upon which she had insisted. Uncle Sheldon was not really an uncle, but merely a cousin of Marion's – Oliver could not imagine how on earth she had forced his hand to write that cheque! His grandad had gotten into debt, despite working all the hours God sent, to pay the remaining balance; Gigi had even implied that it was part of what had sent him to an early grave. That charm schooling had clearly been too monstrous an extravagance for someone from such humble origins! Next, Oliver recalled Sheldon's tattletales of how his mother had never forgiven his grandad for not quite managing to pay the school's fees thereon, but she had quickly married Oliver's father instead, and in doing so, she had also married into the affluence that she had sought all along. Once satisfied with her new social standing, she had mellowed substantially by most accounts, and she had swished airily through life, as they all had, until the war had widowed her, and fate had put her right back in her place, reshaping her over time into a different creature altogether. In summary, she had succumbed beneath an onslaught of untoward events. Finally, she had come to resemble one of the cracked and chipped chalkware figurines that were damaged in the move to lowlier quarters once she had no longer been able to afford the rent in Thorny Grove. But no, he could not mention all that to Mr Roper, who clearly thought he had his mother pegged. One should not speak ill of the dead anyway, of course!

'Sorry, Mother,' he muttered for the second time that day. He had gotten quite carried away, it seemed, and while closeting these skeletons, he made up his mind to leave post-haste, even if it meant stooping to rudeness. Anyway, feeling nauseous and with a thumping headache already, Oliver could hardly see straight at all, and he knew that he must put himself to bed.

'Goodness, Mr R-Roper... I didn't realise how late it is. I really m-mustn't keep you any longer, and I really must dash.'

'That's quite all right... an' please call me Albion,' replied the charming draggletail with the smiling eyes.

'A-and how should I p-pay for the remaining photographs?' Oliver croaked as he paced towards the door, desperate for the comfort of night's darkness.

'Tha can 'ave t' photos lad, no worries... No use 'em rottin' out back if tha can 'ave t' benefit,' Mr Roper said while pressing them into Oliver's shirt pocket with a pat.

'An' no payment needed... there were nowt outstanding anyroad. But perhaps tha might do me a favour an' come back Thursday week. Ah'd like thee to sit for me, that's only if tha wouldn't mind, of course... Practise me portraiture, see?'

'Well... if you think that'd be helpful, then I'd be only too happ–'

'Fine, that's settled, then.'

It was not fine at all, of course. Although he hated to disappoint, Oliver felt that he would have had little alternative than to do precisely that, could he have mustered the nerve and impoliteness to say 'no'; every cell in his body screamed 'no' resoundingly. No part of him wished to return to this portal to his prickly past.

Having left Mr Roper standing on the front steps of the Old Stores, still grinning at him, Oliver was already fretting over other matters: was it just the echo of his own footsteps or the tapping of Marion's work boots that he could hear upon the cobbles behind him? While feeling afraid to look around and witness his mother's unlikely embodiment and, since it was dark, that eerie luminous light that suffused her ghostly figure, he staggered onwards with his gaze fixed firmly ahead. Once he had passed Ash Brothers and managed to reach the intersection of Gas Lane and Mill Lane without tripping over or retching on the cobbles, he heard Mr Roper call after him –

'Mind 'ow tha goes now... an' see thee next Thursday... Tha's grown into a reight fine young feller, tha' knows Tha can't 'alf see the resemblance. Thy mother'd be proud, ah reckon!'

Cranford Electric

Shards of broken glass glittered in the evening's garish light while the sun, unrelenting in its violence, crept slowly towards the chimney tops.

'Thunderation! Dadgummit! Gnashbarbs!'

Oliver had nothing to take the edge off his achy head except a caustic-tasting analgesic. That pint of bitter, half of which had seeped into Doris' rag anyway, had not been nearly enough either – especially with all that had transpired since then. Instead of smashing empty gin bottles, he considered seizing a knife from the kitchen rack and slicing through his skin, but he managed to resist this familiar compulsion; he had collected quite enough scars that route.

While glancing at the defaced mantel photos, which were awaiting their replacement with the contents of the envelope that was tossed on the living room table, he decided that those replacements would never see the light of day after all, and he stuffed them into a drawer's darkness. It was easier anyhow to look at the mantel, where his father's photo took centre stage, while his mother remained faceless. When meeting his gaze with his own, his father still looked as dashing and heroic as a pilot officer should, in his tightly collared and buttonless tunic, his side cap, and his shiny swagger cane; the portrait had not been hand-tinted, but Oliver could still see the spun copper for hair that Marion had described, the grey-blue of his eyes, and the beige biscuit crumbs of his freckles. But suddenly the surrounding defaced photographs of her, and of mother and son together, could not be ignored; they bothered him even more now that they marked the precise moment that all things had changed for the worse.

While rummaging frantically through the living room chests with half a mind to scour the streets for discarded, smelly butts if he had no joy, he finally found a pack of filterless cigarettes that had been stashed in a rare moment of prudence and then altogether forgotten. With enormous relief, he removed the picture card inside, lit a cigarette, and smoked until his airways felt satisfactorily singed; this calmed him tremendously. He examined the picture card of a monoplane. Having almost completed this 'Pioneers of Aviation' set, he already looked forward to carefully pinning each of the thirty or so cigarette cards around the photographs of mono, bi, and triplanes; windsocks; and aerodrome hangars that already adorned the wall opposite his bed – his shrine to his father.

The evening's stillness seemed somewhat ominous. Only the mantel clock and moths colliding with the windowpane could be heard, and thus the evening's quietude seemed equally haunting, so Oliver flicked on the wireless: his Cranford Radiophonic E37. Although he was not keen on electrically powered machines in general, he made exception for wirelesses because he simply adored what they brought to the world. Soccer! The clash was narrated by a distinctively clipped and relentlessly chipper commentator; the whole thing should have been music to the ears. But as so often of late, the damned device coughed and spluttered; he was once again unable to find a reasonable reception with which to enjoy the match.

'Barker now... pop... He's off past Andrews... Up to the... crackle twenty-five... pop... crackle... He's made a mark inside his own... pop... twenty-five... crackle... splat... hsszap... Saved himself from... hsszap... an awkward situation there...'

Since it had been getting progressively worse all summer, he could only hazard a guess that it was due to the unusual atmospherics. He switched it off with a grimace because those clicks, pops, and crackles felt like they might perforate his ear drums. Scouring the table's clutter then, he looked for the dampened tea cloth that he had thrown over his latest painting to prevent that singular shaft of sunlight, which pierced the drawn curtains and penetrated the gloom of his living room, from blanching it with its withering rays.

Oliver found and threw it off, revealing the painting that he had begun of Uncle Sheldon. Its initial function had been to ridicule that fattening face with which Oliver had become increasingly displeased. He instantly noted that he had caught the precise shade of Sheldon's deathly pallor perfectly – utterly bloodless, in fact – and he had perfectly captured those scarlet bruises, patterned with dark purple threads, that his pretend uncle tried to pass off as cheeks. His eyes, that were once so eerily arresting, were suitably sunken, like currants sinking into cake dough. Although all the pieces seemed to be there, somehow or other the sum that they added up to was not faithful enough, however. Sheldon's face, once so well-balanced aesthetically, had rapidly become a quarrel of form in recent years, but this was not the portrait's great failing either because he had captured that perfectly too. It felt doubtful that he could distract himself from all lingering agitation by finishing it because, although he had reasonably captured his pseudo uncle's likeness, he had failed, more crucially, to capture his essence, which was deeply disheartening. Even if it had felt worth persevering with, he did not have any sauce in his system to steady his hands and tremulous fingers – it always did the trick.

His one true love was art, so it was painful to have failed in this instance, although when he did triumph, he felt indebted to his old secondary school's darling of an art teacher, Mrs Dennis-Hunt. St Mark's had failed him miserably otherwise; omitting dear Mrs Dennis-Hunt, their staff had been unable to recognise his potential, let alone foster it if they had. Slim chance he had had of reasonable exam results, then, thanks to the sheer blandness of its hopelessly middlebrow teachers; Mrs Dennis-Hunt had indeed been that rare exception, though, and art became a subject that had had his full attention. Owing to her inspirational teaching, he had discovered that he greatly enjoyed sketching, drawing, and watercolours, and that he loved oils in particular, which was fortunate since it provided him with an activity with which to while away his empty evenings nowadays. The skills that he possessed did not suffer at all from his usual state of inebriation either – they were actually improved by it. Along with smoking, artistic endeavour also gave him another way to occupy his restless hands, which Mrs Dennis-Hunt had described as 'delicately wrought and beautiful'. Their deep lines and knots, according to her, were signs of an acutely artistic temperament – this he had been rather incredulous of until he had noticed that her hands were similarly ugly.

There were aspects of art that Oliver excelled at and those that he did not; Mrs Dennis-Hunt had remained convinced, however, that he would conquer all aspects if he stuck at it enough. He had always excelled at still life and painstakingly precise landscape pictorialism, photographically remembered from wanderings outdoors. He also adored colour and combinations of colour: 'colourifics', in her words. He had collected countless pockets' worth of boiled sweets – the rewards she handed out – for excelling at the rendering of light sources' highlights and shadows; it had not been long before he had begun to reward himself by purchasing his own with his lunch money. With Mrs Dennis-Hunt's encouragement, it became an obsession of his to name the exact shades of things, so that he would know how to blend them in retrospect; if he could not find the corresponding shade, then he would name and concoct his own. Ash grey and shivering blue had been required in this instance, to accurately depict Sheldon's peculiar-looking pallor, and raw red, of course, for those unfading bruises that were once rose petal cheeks.

Regrettably, however, despite Mrs Dennis-Hunt's efforts to see him make strides, his great failing, his blot on the landscape, was the human figures that he placed there. He had always struggled to portray them in any naturalistic way, with only quite a stylised technique at his disposal; he had learned this technique by copying from the illustrations on sewing patterns and the clothing advertisements that he had torn from Marion's magazines. This inconsistency was becoming a severe source of frustration because he had grown bored finally with rendering deserted panoramas and still life arrangements that had interested him, after painting corners of the horse hospital and parts of Greenthorne and Ferndale House for which he had a photographic memory.

That said, even when Oliver did occasionally pull off a more naturalistic rendering, something still felt amiss, just as it did in this instance; again, he was reminded that portraits had hardly been his forte. As such, he had lost all interest in finishing this piece because it had failed – no, he had failed once again – to capture the essence of the subject, and he felt dashed. Uncle Sheldon's avarice had not been a problem either; somehow, that was hinted at, too, but some hint of the popinjay, the Byronic scoundrel – a role that Sheldon had once so perfectly inhabited – he had not captured at all. Oliver liked to think that this was still Sheldon's essence, even if this kernel had become buried beneath so much blubber in recent years; it still vaguely suggested itself if one looked very carefully. Since all great portraits must capture the subject's essence, and Oliver would accept nothing short of greatness, this failure was relegated to the drawer's darkness along with Mr Roper's photographs. As he slammed it shut, these musings on portraiture found him querying once again what Mr Roper's intentions may have been when he took his hand and asked to photograph him. The invitation seemed as enigmatic as the bearer in retrospect, but revisiting that place, and his encounter with Vale Studio's enigma of a leaseholder, had only distressed him by having been interrogated on a past that was too painful to recall; as follows, he was visited again, and unfavourably, by the image of the crinoline lady made into a mosaic of jagged barbs by his carelessness. Perhaps she is in the dustbin now, he wondered, forlornly awaiting a reassembly that was beyond the realm of possibility.

Feeling shattered himself, tiredness had crept up on him while he continued to search for distraction, and hunger stirred again. There was nothing to be had from the scraps of stale food that were scattered about the table, however, nor was there any refreshment to be had from the mouldy tea leaves swimming in his mother's treasured pewter teapot; it all seemed to be nothing more than dreadful clutter, so he lit another filterless, shrouding himself in grey-blue haze while irritably shaking off his shirt and slapping his chest vigorously. This tactic left behind only a dull pain which served as a rather wanting distraction from his lingering angst.

'Too bloody warm,' Oliver muttered; his abode trapped the heat all summer long like a greenhouse. Presently, he despaired of this ramshackle apartment, which was carved into the attic of what had once been called Partington Stables and then had become Greenthorne's horse hospital, more than he had ever done. It smelt simply atrocious, although he knew that only he could be blamed for the ingrained aromas of rotting food and cigarette smoke; the stench of the winter's wet rot, baked in by the summer's heat, was equally assaulting. And there often seemed to be yet another pong that found him searching endlessly among the flat's clutter for the rodent that he was sure had died somewhere, without realising that its source was the acrid-smelling sweat of his rarely washed body.

As he so often complained to himself, the way Marion had decorated the place certainly had not helped; she had painted it the same cadmium green that had looked so impressive in Ashurst, the town house they had rented in Thorny Grove. Here, however, it served only to make the room seem dark and forbidding, even in the yellowish glare of her moth-eaten lamps all switched on together, or with the curtains opened during spring and autumn. Regrettably, it had also been the colour of her prying eyes. Even the hallway had been daubed an unnerving hue: mantis green, sloshed patchily over vile old Victorian damask. It always felt much like an insect's mouth about to swallow him whole when he dashed through it to his bedroom.

Despite his great love of 'colourifics', green had become his least favourite colour of the spectrum since it had become completely emblematic of her; she had even worn green – green and grey mainly. It was a colour that had come to speak of her envy, her pride, her snobbery, and then over time it had become the colour of embitterment, despair, rage, disease, decay, and finally death; owing to all this, even green fields and such had come to look somewhat strange and unnatural. Thank heavens ten year old Oliver had fixed upon fairytale faun brown for his own chamber, but had settled for nut brown instead when Marion had implored him to be practical.

The contents of these ghastly green rooms – green like the sourest of grapes – had not changed much in the last half a decade either; he was quite aware of the irony that, while trying to keep his and his mother's past securely closeted away in the dark corners of his mind, he still lived in a fastidiously curated museum of their life together. No, he had not touched or moved any of her things – he did not dare to – which all still lay exactly where she had left them; her embroidery and gardening magazines, copies of *The Lady About Town* periodical, and unreturned library books remained in a pile on the settee while her bobbins and her sewing machine still sat on the shelves.

In life, Marion had been a modern woman who had always gotten rid of the outdated 'junk' that cluttered any house that she took over. That junk resided in the disused stables downstairs and smelt of manure and saddle soap, but the geometric lines of her modern knickknacks – the metallic barbs and sharp edges of her picture frames and her mirrors – looked harsh and out of place upstairs; in that setting, they were merely more junk. Despite all her efforts, it remained dingy; they had fallen more than a station or two and nothing that she had tried could have disguised it. Her attempts felt contrived and vain to this very day.

Then, as so often before, while bemoaning all of this and while foraging for any other forgotten gin bottles, Oliver tripped over another of his *arrangements:* his old stroller, which sat rusting in the corner of the room, piled high with ancient, yellowing copies of the *Greenthorne Gazette* and empty beer bottles. While the green could not be overlooked, otherwise he had, in the years since her passing, learned an essential focal trickery, wherein he could look past all other remnants of his mother with a selective visual focus, so that they became fuzzy and indistinct. In practise, this forced near-sightedness, along with his frequent insobriety, found him feeling rather giddy as he crashed about the place; forever butting elbows against cabinet doors, stubbing toes on old tea crates, tripping and grazing knees on rough floorboards, and scraping shins on chair rungs, he would scream out his favourite hyphenated expletives.

'Arrrhhh! Crappity-gummit-gummit-gummit!' he cried once again as the pain juddered through him, and he despaired even more of his untidiness.

'But all artistic geniuses live in chaos, surely!' he reassured himself as he slammed the final drawer of old, empty bottles shut with great irritation – not even a dribble of extra dry left in any of them, much to his sorrow; the accursed heat had evaporated all the little beads leftover that he would normally harvest. It would not be the first time that he had gone to bed sober as well as hungry either, not by a long chalk, but it was not something for which he had much endurance.

Sometimes it seemed as if he should follow Grahame Lowndes and Bert Greasley's tenacious example, who he had heard went poaching rabbits by night, or who thwacked pigeons with their catapults in order to put meat on their loved ones' tables; Oliver had never really felt himself capable of such acts, however, not least because it seemed desperately sad to kill animals, so he was not even able to supplement himself with this free source of food. This was a conundrum that often found him chewing on mouldy crusts instead, and it was not the mould per se, but rather its unnerving shade of green that bothered him; penicillin was mould, after all, and that was very good for you. But all of this, sadly, brought Jonesy to mind because Oliver had often been similarly inept at catering for his dietary requirements – to the point that poor old Jonesy had gotten quite skinny himself at times; although he had howled unhappily at this, his nature had been so agreeable that he had always forgiven his master's shoddiness the instant that food was dished out again.

'Oh, Jonesy,' Oliver whispered sorrowfully into the living room's emptiness.

His exhaustion could no longer be ignored, and there seemed to be little else to do but to carry himself off to bed then, risking the terribly green hallway and creeping silently past Marion's bedroom door to get to his own bedroom safely, and taking his prized cigarette cards with him.

Arriving safely at the hall's far end without incident and ducking into the tiny bathroom opposite his bedroom door, he splashed his face with water. A lingering glance in the bathroom mirror cheered him no end – his young body, which his mother had mocked for its thinness among many other attributes, had changed a great deal in recent years. Being a late developer, he had watched with relief as a little muscle had grown and had finally separated skin from bone – muscle that remained despite his increasingly lacking diet; he was slender nowadays, but he was raw-boned no longer. And he had only just recently come to appreciate just how refined his facial features had become. His father's chiselled looks mingled sublimely with his mother's sharp lineaments. Oliver's high, rosy cheeks; olive green eyes; thick brows; and straw-blond hair – bleached so very bright by the heath's sun – had all become as pleasing to him as they had to those luckless fellows that had so vainly tried to ensnare him on the heath or in the alleyways. He would never forget that heady day when it had dawned on him that adolescence's huckery and ungainliness had been replaced with a steadier gait and good looks; it had been so heady, in fact, that he had actually wept! They were not tears of self-congratulation either – he had simply become overwhelmed by nature's benevolence – at last he had a redeeming aspect!

Over time, as Oliver's self-satisfaction with his appearance had grown, he had found himself increasingly too distracted by his reflection upon entering the bathroom to properly bathe, but he had decided that to remain unwashed did not spoil his bloom, which on the heath and in the alleyways and other such places, had already become legendary. Thanks also to summers spent on the heath, his skin had become so delightfully dusky that one hardly noticed the grime anyway. He had also decided that his blackened fingernails served only to accessorise him with more character. Only the exceedingly beautiful can get away with not bathing – this had been his decree.

Feeling relieved to sprawl out on his bed, despite the mattress' exposed springs perforating his skin a little, Oliver found that the day's worriment and exasperation had finally become the vaguest itch that he hoped would be entirely gone by morning. Even thoughts of Marion, and the remorseful mindset that accompanied such thoughts – exacerbated by her earlier appearance and as much by his ill-considered visit to Vale Studios – had begun to lessen. He always imagined that her spirit, which crept around him so much of the day, had retired to her own bedroom by that late hour anyway – just as she would have when she had been alive.

Despite this, all the childish things that Oliver had clung onto remained his allied forces – his tattered cloth bears, model aeroplanes, tin soldiers, and his dear dangling parachutist were still his guardians and his protectors from her. He had collected more recent keepsakes, of course: Randolph Stewart; newspaper cuttings regarding the victories of soccer teams that he had come to support; his cigarette card collection of footballers, boxers, and jockeys, which he knew served much the same dubious purpose as Uncle Sheldon's gallery at Ferndale House; and photographs of landships and warbirds that fought on and above the battlefield, alongside their heroic pilots – images that he had torn from his treasured *The Great War, a Pictured History* periodicals.

The night was too dark, with the moon in the wrong phase to provide sufficient illumination to see any of this clearly, but he still dared not use the work lamp which Marion had pilfered from Cranford Electric. She had done so to furnish him with the bedside illumination required to read his adventure capers. He still hated that thing, with its engine green flaking paint and machine-like appearance. To make matters even worse, the mains connection must have shaken itself somewhat loose because it flickered and strobed when switched on of late. It also emitted the not-so-sweet fragrance of burning dust and warming fuse wire, so he, more often than not, left it off nowadays, preferring moonlight instead. He had never dreamt of trying to fix it as he little understood, nor liked, electricity; to him, it still seemed an uncanny, preternatural energy – the stuff of nightmares.

While scanning the collage of cards, cuttings, and photographs pinned to the earthy-coloured walls, Oliver's eyes came to rest on a cutting of a shamelessly naked lady. She had been pinned there for several years already, and he had unwittingly made her into an artwork via his signature blend of desire and shame, and by his attempts therein to ogle her naked bosoms, then to protect her modesty by painting on a robe, and then allowing it to slowly flake off again, several times over. She had been affectionately named 'Big Sis', and the name had stuck despite how inappropriate it had become at times. He was too tired at this present moment to remember the emotional and hormonal strife that Big Sis had caused him over the years, however, and he merely admired her 'pippins', now that her robe had flaked away again for the most part. Those twin flesh buttons, glued perfectly in place on such modestly sized yet pleasingly pert-looking bosoms, filled him with wonder. They still seemed somewhat alien and sexless, however, perhaps because women and he had seemingly given up on each other; he could not imagine how they might feel – the picture house incident being too far back to remember with any clarity – and this he blamed for struggling in recent times to find the eroticism in them that he felt he ought.

Sex had always been a confusing concept anyway since his only frame of reference to actual congress was when he had had shambolic fumblings – only once or twice and instantly regretted – with the sort of odd fellow that Roy Wilks secretly mingled with. In doing so, Oliver had quickly learned that the alleyways and such did not lend themselves any better than the crossway did to his romantic yearnings; for some reason, what he would have preferred out of all the possibilities that they might have afforded him was merely to peer into a pretty pair of peepers, have sweet somethings whispered in his ear, and feel a body close to his while in rapture – much like Dennis Bannister and Delilah had been doing earlier that day. Unfortunately, however, it had all been much more about frenzied groping and the demand from his opponents for looseness of the lowest order; it had bordered on the repugnant, in fact, and had bitterly confirmed that shame and even disgust were the shadows of desire – despite the temporary boost to his ego and his attempts to convince himself that he was beyond shame in the first place. So, he had remained elusive thereafter, settling once again on the role of voyeur. Happily, the odd fellows never tired of chasing him, though, nor dared brand him a tease; his elusiveness appeared only to add to his mystique, while such attention provided him with an adrenaline rush that found him feeling better, temporarily at least, than he had since he was a seven-year-old presented with a new train set.

All that aside, the moon had kindly crept up a little, allowing Oliver to make out a bottle of extra dry gin that he had quite forgotten, glittering in the depths of his toy box; its contents were not nearly enough to guarantee undisturbed sleep, but he glugged it down anyway.

The hands of his Cranford Tempograph alarm clock marked one o'clock in the morning, yet that meant nothing whatsoever. It was another beastly item that he would have tossed out of the window if he felt that he could get away with it; 'Quality products at popular prices', give me a break, he had so often thought because the clockworks had quickly lost their accuracy, and the time that it showed haphazardly lagged. Only somewhere between seven and eleven hours to go, to hazard a guess, between himself and remuneration; tomorrow would be Thursday – payday thanks to Uncle Sheldon! What a relief, he thought as he began to drift off; his hunger, which he had been trying to ignore all day, would at last be satiated. Once again, his only hope was that his sleep would be dreamless.

***

A constant trickle of water from leaky cisterns sent echoes pinging off the walls; it was a washroom of sorts, and Oliver had the queerest feeling that he had been there before. Thinking back, there was only a darkness where one normally remembers the sequence of events that trickle to the present moment; he was at a loss to explain his presence there.

Its mildewed walls were daubed engine green, which suggested pounding pistons, whirling spindles, and scorched engine oil. Illuminated from above by two machine-like lamps, two wash basins of black faux marble sat below two grimy, circular mirrors which had already lost much of their silvering; he appeared quite wearied in their patchy reflection. With no window in the washroom, he had no idea if it was day or night.

'Where on earth am I?'

Oliver supposed that if he thought hard enough, the answers would all be there and it all would make sense. As he pondered, odours of soap, turpentine, and methylated spirits wafted about him on a cold draught and were companioned by an even greater sense of familiarity. The answers still did not reveal themselves, however. His next tactic, then, was to screw up his eyes and simply wish it all away, but once he had opened them again, nothing had changed. Feeling quite lost, he stepped out of the washroom to ascertain his whereabouts.

He immediately recognised the wide, darkened hallway outside; this place was, as confirmed by company advertisements hanging proudly on display, the Cranford Electric Appliance Company. It was an outfit that manufactured modern household appliances such as alarm clocks, wireless radios, and even newfangled televisions. With no idea what cause he had had to visit this firm, Oliver's familiarity with it felt entirely illogical.

The large circular window at the hallway's far end framed a waxen-looking moon in a cloudless night. Moonlit Greenthorne looked otherworldly, although the outline of the tannery opposite was reassuringly familiar: Sharpe & Beard. Beyond it, the grimy frontage of Spooner & Sons Manufacturing also loomed. It seemed peculiar that their chimneys belched their exhaust into the night sky because most factories were not operational in the night-time. Huddled far beneath these monoliths, tin-roofed workshops housed smaller outfits such as Burbage's Chemicals, Pie & Co. Manufacturers of Physical and Electrical Instruments, Drake's Haulage & Warehousing, and Crowther Overall Manufacturing.

Below the window's wide aperture was the desk where Harriet Blake, the company clerk, had once sat with piles of invoices towering over her, but there was no sign of friendly, efficient Hattie. Instead, her desk was littered with electrical parts: turning coils, switch headers, coil holders, condensers, panels, valves, and power amplifiers. They all seemed like creepy parts of some diabolical automaton, awaiting assembly by a mad scientist straight out of one of his future-fantasy story anthologies.

Oliver's familiarity with the place seemed to crystallise more and more with each passing second. He remembered others then: Alec Solby, the factory foreman, came to mind, and so did his wife, Olive. But how on earth do I know these folks and their names? he had to wonder. The place seemed deserted, at any rate.

Hoping for more specificity, he remembered that there had been a large wall clock near the coat rack at the hallway's other end; he found that it was still there, and its luridly luminous hands and figures marked a quarter past two. This luminescence seemed to have a special significance for him that he also could not explain – all very baffling indeed.

While pacing back down the hallway, Oliver could no longer ignore how cold the tiles felt underfoot. When looking down, he realised that his feet were bare and somewhat grubby. He was wearing only his nightclothes: a sort of all-in-one that he favoured in the summer months.

The overhead lighting began to flicker, which, along with the blackening brickwork and the fetid aroma of the place, summed Cranford Electric up to somewhat of a spook house. While peering through porthole windows in the doors that flanked this hallway, he saw workshops with row after row of empty booths upon which sat vials of unearthly-looking luminous paint and brush holders; each holder was stuffed with umpteen finely pointed brushes. Swiftly, he recalled how these tools assisted Cranford's dial painters in the monotonous task of painting the hands and figures of their Tempograph alarm clocks with this lurid green colourant; faint luminescent dust swirled in the air above while spectral-looking fingerprints of shimmering green also matted near every surface of those booths.

The doorway to painting booths five, six, seven, and eight felt especially familiar, and he felt quite drawn to it; it seemed as if he must have passed through this entryway many times before. On account of this, Oliver had a growing suspicion that his familiarity with this firm was via someone that had worked at one of those booths – someone of tremendous significance. But this certain someone he could not place at all, despite knowing Hattie, Alec, and Olive. While pondering this anomaly, his eyes fixed on the signage above that doorway, and he felt curiously drawn to the figure eight; it somehow seemed to be an eternal loop of wearying toil.

Feeling compelled to enter and investigate further, he pushed through the groaning wooden doors and stepped into the gloomy interior of the workshop with some hesitancy.

Inside, it felt airless; breathing was quite the effort. An old wireless, resting on some metal shelves at the back of the room, rasped away on a dead frequency. Peering around, he noticed that the brickwork was pinned with a smattering of yellowed, brittle-looking, and densely worded notices, which spoke of discipline in the main: the importance of proper procedure, punctuality, and courtesy.

Inside as out, it was gloomy – ill-lit in the dullest cast of light imaginable. This scant illumination seemingly leaked in drips from above since the overhead lighting continued to flicker and flash intermittently; electrical cabling must be loose as usual, Oliver guessed because the place reeked of singeing, overloaded fuse wire. He then remembered that the place had always been so poorly maintained; the main fuse blew so often, and somehow he also knew that the pile of rusted and cracked gas lanterns, which served as a precaution for those all too frequent power cuts, had never helped a great deal.

Without warning then, the echoing splutter of Cranford Electric's tannoy system fanfared around him –

'Booths four, seven, eight, and eleven… afternoon break will be forfeited until output meets vending quota!'

Oliver was suitably startled and bewildered until, steadying himself and catching his breath again, he stepped closer to booth eight and surveyed that quota of alarm clocks awaiting the grind of having their figures and hands painted. Oh… yes… of course… the dial painters had all been women, hadn't they? he thought; so, whoever this person was that had drawn him there – this enigma – they were female, and Cranford's dial painter number eight!

Bottles of turpentine, methylated spirits, and denatured alcohol dressed the stage of the dial painters' thankless task, and while clumsily toppling a few of them over, he could not resist running his hands under the magnifying lens – the one that facilitated the dial painters' precision – but before he could become too absorbed in his dislike of them, the tannoy erupted again –

'Elsie Smith and Lou Bormann, stay behind until further notice!'

Although it was not entirely unfamiliar to Oliver, this second noisesome outburst was equally startling as he looked anxiously around. Who on earth is operating the tannoy? he wondered since the deep, rasping voice of the higher-up was not familiar in the least.

'Lissie Draper and Rose Houghton, please clean your magnifying aids and remember to point your brushes!'

While all this rumbled about his ears, another cool gust of air seemed to emanate from nowhere specific. The luminescent whorls of dust hovering above seemed to form tendrils then, much to his disbelief, reaching for him like long, clawing fingers.

'Oof, cripes... What the heck?'

After making a sharp exit from the painting booths, and while the door swung shut behind him with a creak, he noticed a downward staircase opposite; the stairwell led down into darkness, and it seemed ominous, giving him the seemingly arbitrary impression that it led to a lightless, labyrinthine substructure full of jeopardy.

The stairs were obviously a no go, but Oliver then remembered that there had been an exit at the hallway's far end, which led down another short flight of steps to an outside lean-to. While he glanced quickly in that direction, about to turn on his heels and make a dash for it, ominous rumbling sounds bounced up the stairwell's iron rungs, rapidly becoming louder; their acuteness seemingly equalled that of the thickening air pressure because his ears quickly had that dreadful feeling of being overstuffed – as if their drums might burst at any moment. Meanwhile, a noxious pungency of methylated spirits, boric acid, denatured alcohol, turpentine, and swarf stung his nostrils.

Fast becoming overwhelmed by this acute sensory overload, and while remembering the workshop's sinister spectacle only moments prior, he felt his heart race as, paradoxically, his blood seemed to run colder and colder in his veins.

'Who's that?' he muttered with a shudder; clearly, someone was following him from that very workshop, with their slow, stealthy approach betrayed by the clickety-clack of their work boots on the tiled floor.

Oliver attempted to bolt then, but while zigzagging around in frightful confusion, he crashed full impact into an unseen wall because his vision had already become entirely unfocused. Buckling up in pain and collapsing with a thud, he somehow found the willpower to pick himself up immediately, but then he realised that blood streamed from his nose, which he feared might be broken.

Upon hearing the workshop doors groan open behind him, he froze with his feet seemingly glued to the floor. His ears, increasingly suffused with blood, began to purple as the webbing of nerves in their dark whorls began to create their own stuttering electrical hiss – or was that raspy syncopation coming from outside of him? He was not sure. It quickly overwhelmed him with its din and discordance.

The air's increasing static charge tugged at the downy tufts on Oliver's neck and forearms while he began to suspect that she – his mother, of course – who else could it be? – must be stood right behind him by then, with that all too familiar prickling sensation between his shoulder blades growing in its tactility. He dared not glance around as the galvanic current emanating from her electrified fingers crawled up and down his backbones. The draught then felt freezing while the blood running from his nose became a torrent. He could not contain his distress any longer and emitted a blood-curdling scream that served only to frighten himself even more. As he became increasingly agitated, his vision began to glitch and jitter, overlain with what looked like electrical static in its patterning. Meanwhile, what echoed up from beneath him bounced sonically around what seemed to have become a maze of walls that had crowded tightly around him. But then utter silence except for the hiss...

'I know I was wrong,' Marion murmured from behind him in a surprisingly hushed, meek manner that was deeply uncharacteristic of her; despite her tone's inconsonance, he felt just as unsure of her as he had done in life, however, and had no idea how to reply. Her voice sounded most peculiar too – tinny, as if filtered through a badly tuned wireless.

'I shouldn't... splutter... zap... crackle... have said it,' she whispered, sounding just as off-pitch and just as meek.

Despite the mildness of her approach, however, Oliver's horror and stress only seemed to intensify exponentially as eddies of soft, pale luminescence swirled about him, clouding his vision's periphery. It was that peculiar phosphorescence again: the soft green shimmer of zinc doped with silver and copper, apparently.

'S-said what?' he finally stammered.

'Immaculate thoughts, Oliver... zap... Scrawny little sprat... crackle... Daddy's going to be away much longer than we thought... hmmmmzink... clunk... pop... I've seen the way other mothers look at me... I shall have to have difficult words with... pop... Little peep... Dead, just dead... hummmzink... Dear oh dear... Hmmmmmzonk... Whatever shall we do about you... crackle... Do you do it on purpose somehow? Pop, pop, pop... Then you'll be a happy little... crackle... snap... hissssssssssssss...'

***

Being unaccustomed to waking so early, birdsong was something that Oliver had not heard for quite some time. He wiped the rheum from his eyes and checked whether his nose was bleeding. While feeling relieved to find that it was not, and that the nosebleed had only featured in the nightmare that his alarm clock had gallantly delivered him from, he then remembered that it had also rescued him from his mother's bewildering advances.

The room to which he had awoken appeared to be drably painted with a gloomy purple-grey and bluish-silver palette. Amid the gloom, that familiar feeling that he often awoke with, one that could best be characterised as 'God-awful', still possessed him while dimly rendered impressions of Marion and Cranford Electric remained as unsettling imprints upon his mind's eye; he hoped that the dream would soon be forgotten entirely while feeling sorry that he had not drunk anywhere near enough to sleep deep, dreamless sleep. He knew that he had only himself to blame for the night terror, however, for going to Mr Roper's studio and dredging up the dreadful days of yore; what on earth had he been thinking, then?

Oliver plucked a filterless from the pack left on his bedstand, lit it, and lay there for a while, blowing garlands of smoke upwards, where they caught the first dappling rays of morning sunshine while drifting around the tinplate airplanes strung from the ceiling; it was the only civilised way to start the day, after all, especially if one had an unemptied bottle of gin to hand – which sadly he did not.

As his mind wandered, he found that he could not help but muse on Mr Roper again – his affability and his endearingly shopworn appearance especially. He then came to mind as a charmingly bedraggled-looking chimney sweep, with his soot black hair and his lustrous eyes widened as if he had just seen Father Christmas' sleigh sail over the rooftops. He was one of those locals who still spoke with 'thee's and 'thou's too – a trait that Oliver had always found rather endearing. The way that he had taken his hand while asking to take his picture, however, felt puzzling with hindsight; could the latter have been a thinly veiled excuse merely to have the pleasure of his company again? he had to wonder. Mr Roper had the air of a 'confirmed bachelor', just like Uncle Sheldon, after all; whatever the truth of it, it only seemed civil to show up as promised. But with second thought, Mr Roper aside, it had been quite traumatic returning to that place; furthermore, as much as the fellow had intrigued him, his artistry had not at all – not by any stretch. Do I really want to feature in that drab display album anyway? he had to ask himself because the work itself showed little of the passion that Mr Roper's eyes so obviously brimmed with; it was clearly a matter for further deliberation.

All that remained of his nightmare by then was the barest muddle of its disordered parts, glimmering in the dark recesses of his mind; he had only a vague impression left of having been frightened, of chasing around some ill-lit maze – no longer sure where – and of being cornered by some antagonist that he had already forgotten.

Snatching up another filterless, Oliver lit up while trying to draw himself away from these lingering abstractions by looking at old Jonesy's favourite spot near his feet; preferring to immerse himself in bitter-sweet memories of his old comrade, he allowed a few tears to prickle up in the corners of his eyes. It did the trick, as always; although it was saddening, those tears washed away the last traces of the more troublesome mood that he had awoken in, and prepared him for the day ahead.

With his cigarette put out, and while straightening the kinks in his spine as best as he could, he peered through his bedroom window's smearing of bird droppings and soot. The sun was already above Greenthorne's chimneys. Knowing that before long the heat would be throttling, he sighed wearily. Since the blistering summer days had become too long, his general strategy had been to lie in for as long as possible and shorten them considerably – with exception for early crossway and heath excursions if he woke feeling particularly spritely.

Why am I up so early, then? Oliver quizzed himself. He did not remember setting the alarm, while there was rarely any reason to do so due to its wild inaccuracy. Remembering that he had been particularly shambolic the previous evening, he presumed that he had been worried about sleeping through the entire day, as he sometimes did; that generally led to mass disorientation that took weeks to recover from, and it was best avoided, naturally, yet that still did not quite explain it all.

What to do with the day, then? he wondered just before it dawned on him that it was Thursday – his allowance day, which was perhaps the reason that he had feared oversleeping. He dressed hurriedly and with a bellyful of butterflies because because a melancholy emotional residue remained. It commingled rather uncomfortably with the tension that thoughts of Uncle Sheldon stirred.

Athletic Pictorial

Uncle Sheldon asked if he could take a peek at his nephew's moral compass, so Oliver dutifully plucked it from his jacket pocket and handed it over.

'Hmm... quite lovely isn't it... Gosh, solid silver casing! Wherever did you get it?'

'It was a gift from Mother, on my eleventh birthday, if I remember rightly.'

'Wonderful craftsmanship... Marion always had terrific taste, I'll give her that. Know where she got it?'

Oliver shrugged and then replied –

'Fensters, I suppose. She bought everyone's gifts there, at Easter, on birthdays, and at Christmases... Even the Christmas hampers.'

'Ah, never did like those hampers.'

'You didn't like the cognac butter puddings?'

Uncle Sheldon shook his head.

'Not struck at all.'

'What about the brut reserve?'

Uncle Sheldon shooed the question away with his hand.

'Only liked the piccalilli, otherwise just a lot of pricey gubbins in my view, yet I'm sure this was worth every penny she paid,' he enthused while holding Oliver's moral compass to his ear and tapping its rim to gauge the silver's thickness, 'and the filigree flourishes on its rim are quite charming!'

'Aren't they just.'

'Points you in the right direction, does it?'

'If you like,' Oliver answered, but the way his eyes glittered betrayed him entirely.

'What do you suppose it's worth now?' Uncle Sheldon then asked.

'Absolutely nothing.'

'Good answer!'

Rising ceremoniously from his armchair, Uncle Sheldon tossed the instrument onto the Persian rug between their feet, and then, with his cigar clenched between his teeth, he stamped on it with all his might, but except for a small fracture in its glass, his nephew's moral compass remained defiantly intact.

'Fiendishly solid construction,' he wheezed, rapidly losing puff while hopping up and down on it with both feet. Oliver had to agree –

'Sturdy little item, isn't it?'

'Oliver, could you fetch me a mallet from the tool caddy in the cupboard under the stairs… The biggest bugger you can find.'

'As you wish, Uncle.'

A smile crept over Oliver's lips, and he dashed to retrieve the mallet, then skipped gaily back, handing it over.

Thwack!

Uncle Sheldon knelt and walloped his nephew's little moral compass with all the might that he could muster, smashing it into pieces with a surprising savagery. The cogs, springs, smithereens of steel, slivers of silver, and shards of glass glittered in the morning's sunlight while Oliver tittered hysterically.

'There, that's better!'

***

ALEC S. IRESON

After nodding off for a few moments, Oliver awoke from his snooze on the chaise longue, and upon consulting the wall clock, he felt quite cross that Uncle Sheldon was thirty-three minutes late for their appointment already; how many times had Sheldon reprimanded him for his own poor time keeping, after all! But Sheldon's tardiness aside, Oliver was, in truth, quite happy to be alone in the more than pleasant confines of Ferndale House – alone except for Ferndale's maid, Maxine, of course.

He switched on the wireless, an outmoded, yet still very impressive, thickly varnished walnut wood monolith with all manner of sexy switches and dials: Sheldon's once top-of-the-range Cranford Aurora two-valve K63. Oliver really did love radios, despite the dark energy that powered them. It was a Plakativ Apparat rip-off, but a fine-looking contraption all the same.

Dance, Dolly, Dance chimed over the airwaves, so he snapped his fingers and could not help shuffling his feet; he had only just begun flinging his arms about when he heard Maxine scamper close by, so he quickly packed it in for fear that he would make quite the spectacle of himself.

A pair of timeworn pugilist's gloves hung from the dado rail, and Oliver could still smell the adrenaline of the fight within that heady, aromatic blend of sweat and old leather; it always brought agreeable images to his mind. The bookcase below them was crammed with rows of books on subjects as scintillating as corporate law, trade regulations, industrial practises, electronic manufacturing guidelines, and hazards in the workplace, along with the ledgers and business contracts for the Bradshaws, the van Hildas, the Cranfords, the Chivvers, and the Spooners; Sheldon had been their legal and financial advisor and confidante, after all. Once again, Oliver picked up one ornament from the ostentation of pewter peacocks that were placed upon the bookcase's top shelf, and he tugged at the tiny metal pry bar discreetly hidden beneath it that he had happened upon months ago. Once again, the bottom shelf, which was loaded with a row of encyclopaedias, slid out and tipped forward without the books falling out – they were glued together and in place. Behind was a secret rearward shelf with a very different set of volumes altogether. Upon discovering this secret, it had not been the van Hilda's tax evasions nor other such scandals that had caught his attention; nor had it been the stolen blueprints for a revolutionary Bavarian-made vacuum triode, marked 'For God's sake keep this under lock and key, and at the slightest sign of trouble, bury it as deeply as the rest – Edwin'; nor had it been a briefing on the practical applications and dangers of radioisotopes, entitled 'Lessons hard learnt'; nor had it been the radio receiver and transmitter trade secrets to which Cranford had no right either.

He picked one of the more unexpected discoveries out: a well-thumbed publication entitled *Athletic Pictorial*. This one, like all the others, served up the repurposed flesh of unsuspecting young men, who were merely enjoying their bodies in healthy and natural ways, as pure erotica; naturally, then, there was always a pair of swimming trunks, a pair of shorts, a pair of cropped pants, or some such nonsense protecting their modesty, despite the generous amounts of flesh on display. They had already lost their novelty for Oliver, but it was still hilarious that they unveiled Sheldon as such a harry hoofter! He tittered to himself as he put *Athletic Pictorial* back, slid the bottom shelf back, and returned the peacock to his flock.

He took out his lighter and lit up another cigarette, and its wisps of blue-grey smoke gently coiled and knotted into the air around him. After plonking himself back on the chaise, he put his feet up. Oh, how he enjoyed visiting Ferndale House, with a reception room for every day of the week, and imagining it was his! All this was the life he was born into and meant for, after all! The plush velvet upholstery against his bare legs felt exquisite as he stared dreamily up at the chandelier. Although Ferndale was generally impressive, everything looked a little worn upon closer inspection, but this only added to its charm – as did the clutter of Sheldon's sport miscellanea. It seemed peculiar, however, with Sheldon favouring the gentle curve and simple geometry favoured within recent trends in interior design, that everything did indeed appear a teensy bit shabby upon closer inspection. Did he buy it all as second-hand booty from the house clearance sales of other social climbers that had lost their footing? Oliver wondered; perhaps Sheldon was feeling the pinch, too, and could no longer afford the calibre of living to which he aspired. Judging by the shroud of dust on everything, and by the bronzes rapidly growing verdigris, Maxine's hours had been cut too. But if anything, all this made Ferndale House all the more endearing. Ferndale's signature aroma: a blend of wood polish, salts of lemon, pipe tobacco, and Sheldon's pomade was charming in unison with the former.

Oliver had grown to adore this room in particular. It was not a traditional drawing room, but more of a curious combo of salon and sports clubhouse, and it was all the more tasteless for it. The china blue and salmon pink cloth carnations looked wonderfully wretched against the peppermint and black cherry of the walls and wainscoting respectively. It was a sort of colourific violence: an assault on the eyes that, for most, would have been more than a step too far, but Oliver did not find it objectionable at all.

A handsomely framed gallery of sportsmen from all disciplines and eras densely cluttered the walls: turn of the century pugilists, jockeys, golfers, cricketers, Soviet gymnasts, and acrobats that hailed from the Baltic region. He had already studied each and every photograph keenly, learning the names that belonged to these winsome faces and impressive physiques. He also knew that, having no genuine interest in sport whatsoever, Sheldon's interest in these athletes was just as questionable as his own. Oliver smiled all the same as he noticed new additions to this gallery; for his attention an Olympic fencer, pentathlon champion, triple jumper, and Greco-Roman wrestler jostled, or perhaps jousted, with their peers upon the mint-coloured walls.

He plucked an orange from the fruit bowl, feeling thankful that Sheldon was one of the few whose fruit was not ceramic; after nimbly removing its peel, he delved into its delightful citrus flesh. Occasionally he understood the importance that people placed on food, especially when as hungry as this. He helped himself to another, then another.

Noticing that another portrait of Svetlana Popov had appeared, he then snickered to himself upon remembering how, after seeing Swan Lake and returning from London one evening, Sheldon had tipsily knelt before the assembled Bolshoi ballerinas upon his wall and had doffed his boater hat to them. He had been unable to get up again, then he had collapsed rather awkwardly on the floor; Oliver had laughed so hard at the drunken sycophant that he had shaken loose a rather long and rasping toot, which had only added to the slapstick vulgarity of the scenario.

Letting out a belly laugh as he mentally replayed this moment again for his own amusement, Oliver then heard a watery splash from outside, which pulled him up from the chaise; a spray of water poured down from the heavens. He stepped closer to the window to locate its source, and there was Maxine up on the balcony, hosing down the flower beds. While Greenthorne had wilted and shrivelled all summer long, Thorny Grove's fine houses still stood in grounds full of lush green shrubs sporting blooms of cream, purple, and pink; it was easy to imagine that those shrubs had sent out armies of overly long roots in all directions, robbing the town of all remaining moisture. But no, it was merely that the maids and gardeners, the Maxines and Mr Doubledays of this world, had spent their summers pointing hoses at their flower beds or flinging pails of water among their grounds.

Then from this vantage point, glancing up between the balcony posts, Oliver caught flashes of her bare knees, calves, and ankles, which, combined with the scent of the garden's wet sprays, was utterly intoxicating; by stark contrast, this drawing room, this shrine to the male physique, suddenly seemed a charmless and rather absurd exhibition, and he also felt faintly sick at the thought of its exhibitor's imminent arrival. In fact, he suddenly found himself wondering if perhaps he had become rather blasé about men in general: indifferent to their rough-hewn bulk, and even repelled by the smell of ale and factories if you were harebrained enough to get too close to them. Maxine meanwhile smelt of flower gardens, and her legs, which were usually hidden beneath ugly brown stockings, were revealed to be so soft-looking and curvaceous, tantalising him with an as yet unexplored alternative to men.

Suddenly, the apparent ease with which men could be wooed, if one so fancied, seemed pitiful, and their plentiful supply in the town's alleys, the heath, and other such places abruptly felt like overkill. Meanwhile, it seemed noteworthy that when chancing upon a desirable filly, he had never once been smothered in petticoats and other more exotic undergarments in the nearest vacant lot; it was fascinating, actually, that women rarely went beyond the limits of what was considered normal while men did much, much more often.

As Oliver puzzled these mysteries, from the corner of his eye he registered movement as a breeze kicked up the heavy sash curtains, bringing with it more of that wonderful aroma of wet earth, moistened flora, and freshly clipped topiary. This unexpected motion startled him momentarily, and he imagined for a moment that some intruder must have secreted themselves in the room's corner; once again, he found himself suspecting that someone was there, just beyond edge of his vision, but he dared not turn his head for fear of being proved right. Pale luminescent vapours began to swirl in his vision's periphery then, around the club chair close to that bookcase – about to take on apparitional form, no doubt. Oh dear... she's here... waiting to catch me out... again! he thought worriedly.

'No... not now, Mother... Just a little peace for once... please!'

'Immaculate thoughts, Oliver,' was her stern whisper.

'Yes, but of course Mother,' he answered while trying to suppress his indignance.

Oliver snapped his eyes shut then, hoping that Marion would soon retreat, but he found himself wondering once again whether those electrical-sounding whines, pops, and splutters were emanating from the wireless, from her, or from inside his own head – he could never tell. He focused on what he could smell instead, getting wafts of ginger wine above that rum-smelling aroma of burning fuse wire that always accompanied her; with his mouth watering, he decided that he would help himself to a slug from the decanter once he had found the nerve to get up.

Upon hearing the crisp crumpling sound of Sheldon's Bentley pulling up on Ferndale's gravel drive finally, his fake uncle's arrival sent his mother packing, presumably because she had always quietly despised Sheldon and in the long run had barely been able to stand being in the same room with him. Her presence paled away accordingly while a different tension rose in Oliver because, as much as he needed his allowance, he found himself wishing that his faux uncle was stranded with a puncture in the next village after all, so that he might enjoy the finery and stillness of Ferndale a little while longer, and play master of the house with Maxine.

Sheldon was making his approach, however – Oliver could already smell the commingled stench of sweat and pipe tobacco that always introduced him – so he realised that he better attune his mind to the task ahead; that aroma had already made his stomach turn, just as it had increasingly of late, yet despite even this, he still felt somewhat drawn to the unarticulated tension between them.

Today, however, after the revelation of Maxine's bare legs, he felt less drawn the moment that Sheldon billowed into the room. Sheldon looked to be as fat as butter, and he had an unexpectedly nonchalant air himself, barely looking at Oliver at all while he threw off his jacket, huffing and puffing. Although only moments prior, Oliver had been wishing that flat tyre on him, his alleged uncle's unpunctuality suddenly felt like enormous disrespect. Still, only twenty minutes stretched between this moment and getting his allowance paid out, which was all that really mattered.

The room had seemed comparatively cool while he had waited, but Sheldon seemed to be a radiator of sorts, bringing all the heat of Greenthorne with him while muttering something about a 'ruddy racket', and retuning his Cranford Aurora until he found Patrick O'Mally crooning about Cupid's tears – a singer that Oliver had seen on cinema newsreels and with whom he had never been particularly struck.

What irked Oliver even more in the next moment was seeing how much heavier Sheldon appeared to be since last Thursday's meeting – increasingly engorged with the indulgences of his intemperate lifestyle. His mock uncle had once looked devilishly handsome; the sharp, striking lineaments of his face had seemed to perfectly mirror the aesthetic favoured by trendsetting artists at the time. Now he looked quite different, however; still, this spoiling, Sheldon's rapid and unexpected physical decline, had not seemed to be too much of a concern for Oliver, at least not at first, but he wondered if perhaps he was beginning to feel differently. For starters, he felt unimpressed with Sheldon's ruddy cheeks, once rose petals, now more reminiscent of overly ripe plums – the same deep maroon that Sheldon had assigned to the wainscoting. Additionally, perspiration might be unavoidable at this Fahrenheit, but are those rivers that run from Sheldon's nose and brow absolutely necessary? he also had to wonder. Yet another baggy, shapeless suit hung off him, too, when he had previously looked so sharp – as much beyond excuse, in Oliver's opinion.

Sheldon stuffed and lit his pipe, then he checked the timepiece strung to his pocket while Oliver struck up another cigarette himself. After a stilted silence, punctuated only by their puffs and while the air filled with Sheldon's thick, strong-smelling exhaust, Sheldon asked finally –

'Hmm... Well now, Oliver... I hope I find you well?'

'Yes, Uncle Bainbridge, quite well... thanks for asking.'

'Oliver, I still find it rather peculiar that despite my requests, you still do not address me by my first name. "Uncle Sheldon", if you please.'

Sheldon had encouraged Oliver to call him 'Uncle' ever since he had been a boy. Oliver later realised that it was wholly inappropriate; nowadays, however, this was something that he took inappropriate pleasure in. Since Sheldon was merely a cousin of Marion's, Oliver could never quite decide if that meant they were related in any meaningful way; the blood they shared was minimal, after all. But either way, contrary as ever, he refused Sheldon the familiarity of addressing him by his Christian name, and to maintain a certain playfulness, he simply called him 'Uncle' or 'Uncle Bainbridge'.

'It is meant sincerely and as a mark of respect, dear Uncle. One should mind how one addresses one's elders and one's betters, after all. You know my mother taught me so.'

Oliver had to present himself as well as he could under the circumstances, but he could not resist toying with his enunciation in Sheldon's company, and he excessively stressed the cut-glass vowel sounds that he had learned from his mother; this he did out of insolence because he enjoyed overplaying his verbally dexterous hand to see if his 'uncle', who was undoubtedly silver-tongued in utero, would notice what he was up to. Otherwise, in Sheldon's company especially, he liked to splatter his internal monologue with crude insults such as 'bastard tuss' and 'sodding fool'.

Sheldon cocked his eyebrow, shrugged, and collapsed into his chair.

'If you say so, Oliver... and so... how has your week been?' he asked in a decidedly disinterested tone, which made answering feel just as much of an effort –

'Rather dull and much like any other, I'm afraid,' Oliver replied mechanically.

'Yes, well... things are what you make of them, as I've so often pointed out... What say you, Maxine?'

'Indeed they are... Listen to your learned uncle, Master Gidley,' Maxine called back despondently from the hall. 'He's no fool.'

He bloody well is, and he's a fat-arsed effing golumpus at that, Oliver thought.

'I've lost count of how many times I've tried to draw your attention to this,' Sheldon added with an inattentive, downcast gaze as he drew on his pipe, 'but do what you will, then.'

The deep brown scent of his tobacco thickened, as did the air between them, but as much as its noxious aroma had begun to repulse him, Oliver's fingers were already fidgety, and he found himself reaching for yet another smoke himself.

'Oliver, you know my other nephew, Tristan Bainbridge Junior, is as much the success as his father is – the apple of his eye, in fact. Furthermore, he is always so immaculately groomed. You should take a leaf from his book. He'll be visiting soon enough, then you can see what you should be aspiring to.'

What on earth? Oliver thought; Tristan has a son? I have a rival? Oh dear, oh dear! In light of this, Sheldon looked too bored – thoroughly disinterested, in fact. Oliver found himself fretting over whether he was being too much of a smart aleck then, and was surprised to find that, despite his sudden nonchalance, a deeper part of him still required his phoney uncle's attention; Sheldon had become quite an eyesore, but he had wealth, status, and power, after all, with each of those having strong merit. Oliver felt that he could kick himself then, for not following through with the plan he always leaves Ferndale with but forgets entirely in the interim: to return armed with a long list of fictions about his week, meticulously crafted to maintain Sheldon's interest. Since they did not meet at any other time and they lived at opposite ends of town, Sheldon would surely never suspect that such stimulating anecdotes were utter lies, but now he would have to invent something on the spot, which he was never very good at. And the difficulty with Sheldon was that nothing much held his interest unless it was money or sport oriented, with exceptions for African explorers of the late nineteenth century, the British Raj, the ballet, the male nude as depicted within classical art, the history of the Austro-Hungarian Empire, or psychoanalytic dream analysis – the last item being only a vague dabbling, in order to not seem too out of his depth with his brain doctor friend, Dickie Shoosmith.

'Oh... dear Uncle... I clean forgot... There's been a rather exciting development that might be of some interest to you.'

'Oh, yes?'

'Yes... regarding... well... dare I say it, a possible new vocation... Well... a route to be explored anyway...' Oliver said as his mind raced to cast his narrative spell and flesh out the details of the boastful fib that he was about to stun Sheldon with.

'Goodness, what on earth might that be?'

'Well... you remember the Chivvers?'

Sheldon merely winced.

'Well... I rather fortuitously bumped into Avril last Tuesday... I'd been out taking the air and our paths crossed.'

'Run the other way, did you?'

'No, she was nice as anything, actually. It turns out, Uncle, that she has become an equestrian show jumper of some renown. Furthermore, she even let me ride her warmblood. It was the most marvellous afternoon.'

'Did she now?'

It seemed a pretty quick-witted and clever fabrication because this accomplishment was precisely what the tiresome little twit had hoped of her future when they were children; she had never stopped wittering on about it, in fact. What also shielded the lie was that Sheldon took no interest whatsoever in women's sporting events, thankfully; he would swallow the rhubarb whole, no doubt.

'Yes... she said I was a natural... Never once above the bit, kept good contact, and had an excellent seat. All the earmarks of a potentially accomplished rider, to quote her verbatim.'

Sheldon obviously knew what he was alluding to –

'How extraordinary... the races, here we come, eh! Horse racing, Oliver... the sport of kings!'

'Well... I wouldn't get too carried away just y–'

'That's funny, though, Oliver, because I bumped into Margaret Chivvers only just recently. As always, the old boot was exceptionally charmless. I enquired of Avril's modus vivendi, naturally. One must at least try to appear interested. Old Chivvers said the dreadful little twit has saddled up with the Mayor of Snobbshill, and reading between the lines, she whiles away her days frock shopping nowadays, along with throwing extravagant soirees, heartily draining his bank account, and by the sounds of it, little else.'

Oliver did not know what to say except –

'Well... you must have misheard Mrs Chivvers, Uncle... Avril did let me ride him... and she did say as such... I swear it.'

'Quite so, then,' Sheldon replied wearily while gripping his pipe with both hands so forcibly that it looked as if it might snap. He was obviously disbelieving of this twaddle; 'Let's leave that!' his look said plainly. A painful silence followed while Oliver's lip trembled. He actually heard Maxine tut too; the nerve of her! he thought of Sheldon's sexy-legged flunky and apple-polisher because servants were supposed to know their place.

'Keeping off the sauce?' Sheldon asked while drinking freely from his sherry glass.

Well, that's a welcome change of tack, but rather rich coming from you, Oliver thought because he knew Sheldon's cheeks had not become ruddy of their own accord.

'As I've told you, Uncle, a tipple helps me sleep soundly and without disturbance I still suffer from frightful nightmares.'

'Really?'

'It does the trick.'

'And this is preferable to you?'

'It is.'

'Hmm... your mother drank, didn't she?'

The wireless crackled. Oliver would not answer this. He did not like Sheldon talking about his mother; there was a specific tone of derision that he reserved for speaking about Marion, and, in fact, reserved for speaking about women in general, come to think of it. That aside, Oliver still felt that only he had the right to mention or even contemplate his mother's shortcomings – not that he often dared; if anyone else had the nerve to do so, he immediately leapt to her defence or fell into a sulky silence. After yesterday's ill-conceived foray into Vale Studios, and all that that had dredged up, more ruminations about Marion and picking over the tragic particulars of her undoing was the last thing he needed! Moreover, Oliver was all too aware that Sheldon's concern for his welfare, using Marion's drinking as a cautionary tale, was no more genuine than his interest in sport; it was all a thinly veiled excuse to have a handsome boy indebted to him and within his control.

'I think you should heed her fate with regard to drinking.'

Even greater indignation welled within Oliver while that electrical crackling audibly resurged and sounded in tandem with his quickening pulse.

'I'd prefer not to talk about that. You are too uncaring some days.'

'Oh, a thousand pardons, then, but I daresay I'm pessimistic about your own outcome.'

Oliver shrugged and looked away.

'You still look rather grubby too. Perhaps we should strip you off and have Maxine turn the hose on you – what!'

Oof! Oliver could only cringe while fretting that Sheldon's tedium had driven him to entertaining himself with such crassness, making a pig's ear of what Oliver felt had been a silver purse – the delicate ambiguities that they had once exchanged. Irrespectively, however, this observation provoked an incredibly awkward and humbling memory of about twelvemonth before. This was the day that Sheldon, tipped off as next of kin by a busybody clerk from the Labour Exchange, who had presumed Oliver dead for being a repeated no-show, had forced open his front door. He had found Oliver in rather a sorry state to say the least: dirty, malnourished, and coiled in the living room corner, wearing only his underpants. Oliver had had no food or electricity, had run out of foodstuffs, even suet, and, more crucially, had run out of alcohol; he simply had not coped. This collapse had followed a month of despair and disorientation following his dismissal from his post as a sweeper-upper at Watkin & Rees' manufacturing plant for unpunctuality and absenteeism; after the initial sense of release from Watkin & Rees' tyranny, his gay feeling of being 'let go' had not lasted more than a few days.

The labour exchange had not been of much help either because that clerk, who had tried to be friendly at first, had only whispered to Oliver that most jobs in Greenthorne were obtained through 'contacts': friends of friends, essentially. He had only been able to point out to this clerk that since he had none of the former, he obviously had none of the latter either. He had then refused a pittance's worth of work at Drake's Haulage, feeling that it was somewhat beneath him, and in the ensuing argument, while beating the horse until it was dead, he had taken exception to the clerk's insistence that he attend one of the exchange's initiatives for the hopelessly workshy instead; Oliver had vehemently protested that, in his view, such initiatives were akin to concentration camps. Learning that he had had no other choice, he had begrudgingly attended, had not been struck with it all, and had popped back a few days later to share his testimonial with the clerk: 'Naff'. Unsurprisingly, then, Oliver had had to forfeit his dole for such an insolent attitude, and he had consequently lost all grip on life once his last pennies were spent; in doing so, he had perhaps become the most shining example of what the state meant when it described the unemployed as 'ill at ease'.

Thus, Sheldon had found him in complete meltdown, and after chuckling at the sight of his late nana's horse brasses, had drunk in the sight of Oliver's near-nakedness also while alluding to the likelihood of incarceration in St Mary's sanatorium unless stringent remedial measures were quickly taken; Sheldon had cleverly bargained for weekly visits to discuss Oliver's welfare in exchange for an allowance that fell vaguely between meagre and modest in its sum. Sheldon was good at this sort of tidying up – of somehow turning disgraceful behaviour and even scandal to his advantage, ultimately to serve his nefarious endgames; that was his half-baked profession as a company lawyer, specialising in malfeasance, after all, when he had headed that crooked little outfit, Bainbridge & Company, and before he had taken loafingly early retirement. Oliver had to remind himself that two were playing this game, however, and that he had his own nefarious endgames to work towards.

'I simply had no time to bathe today, Uncle. I am rather busy, you know.'

'Cleanliness is a form of personal order and is the best place to start. We don't want you slipping back into the disarray of last summer, do we?'

'Why must you always talk about the past, Uncle? Isn't it the future that we should be looking to? Is the past really so important?' Oliver yapped back at Sheldon while knitting his brow.

'That's for you to ponder in the interim, Oliver, and I must be getting on now, I'm afraid.'

Sheldon pulled himself up from his chair with considerable difficulty and panting with the effort. He looked like a hot hound trapped in a boiling Bentley with the windows wound tightly shut on a blistering summer's day – and still not so much as even giving him a momentary glance.

'So, next Thursday is struck from my diary entirely. Off to Whitebaston for the cricket, and then another drive to dinner at Hanley on Linett with my old and rather dear friend, Doctor Dickie Shoosmith. And that reminds me, I have a book for you, Oliver, as recommended specifically by dear old Dickie.'

Sheldon snatched up a book from his side table and brushed the pipe tobacco scattered upon it onto the floorboards for Maxine's benefit.

'And do read it, Oliver. It'll do you some good... and if you don't, I'll get Maxine to give you a good thrashing – what!'

Sheldon guffawed and cracked a grin finally –

'Come Friday instead, I will attend to you then. Maxine will see to your allowance. She has it tucked away somewhere.'

***

Well, that was all pretty queer, Oliver thought as he wended back through Thorny Grove; is Sheldon questioning his commitment to this arrangement? He surely wouldn't cut off my allowance, would he? I'd actually been hoping for a raise and a substantial one at that.

It also felt troubling – mortifying, in fact– to think of his former collapse being retold in detail to a complete stranger – Sheldon's couch doctor chum, Shoosmith. Remembering the book in his hand, he flipped it over and read its title: *Psychoanalysis for the Feeble Minded* by Geraldina Carter. Is it a joke? he wondered; what rubbish because I'm much better now, am I not? He had always made sure that he gave Sheldon his best possible impression, so he failed to understand the need, nor see the funny side if it was meant as a pun. He slipped the book – utter rhubarb – back into his satchel and out of mind.

Suddenly his remuneration dawned on him, and he dispensed with all thought of that prankster.

'Bravo!' Oliver cheered while punching the air in exaltation; his spirits soared whilst taking lungfuls of the grove's clean air. What struck him in that moment was how loudly that air rang out with the twitter of house martins and the cooing of wood pigeons, and how it all sounded alive and rather gay, whereas the extreme heat in less salubrious parts of Greenthorne seemed to have driven them all away. The gentle bubble of hosepipes and the hiss of sprinklers sounded equally pleasant, while the latter wet his nose and ears with dewy mists of water vapour that were thrown in the air before drifting back to the lawns that flanked Hill Drive.

It was all quite lovely. A bonfire, charring redundant oak pews on the corner by the old chapel, released a smoky, woody aroma that smelled remarkable commingling with the sweet fragrance of honeysuckle. He was always particularly struck by the glow of mauve elderflowers too – the pretty garden variety that flanked hedgerows of waxy privet and ivy-clad trellised arches, which lead to greenhouses crammed with palms and baby sunflowers, to babbling fountains, to fragrant herb gardens, and to trees laden with berries. He would scrump the lush fruits of those secret gardens if he could get away with it, he told himself while hunger pangs stirred in his belly; he would gorge himself on the succulent flesh of their fat gooseberries while butterflies adorned his hair – if they had not employed gardeners that would rat him out to the owners, of course.

As much as Oliver admired and admittedly envied those owners, their wives felt like more of a sore point because this was once his world, too, and he dared to believe that it still was; the puzzled looks that they gave him on passing assured him that he was mistaken, though, and he hated them for it. He could not help but envy their spoilt little brats, however – the kiddies gently dozing off beneath the parasols that saved their delicate skins from the withering sun while being watched closely by hired nannies. Whatever they did, they were endlessly entertained and cared for. It seemed that little could go wrong for them, despite the fact that it had for him. Along the lines of such thoughts, he found himself stewing over that 'insufferable little tuss' that he had just lied about so incompetently: Avril Chivvers. She had worn pink ribbons tangled in her flyaway hair, for heaven's sake, and she had kept French saddle ponies that she had never let him ride, not even once. Having just learned that she had become a moneyed lady of leisure made him feel quite peevish – just as peevish, in fact, as she had so often been with him. What on earth had our mothers meant, saying that they should 'knock our bloody heads together', and that we were 'as bad as each other'? he carped to himself; they were always so mistaken!

Walking past the towering van Hilda's Regency residence and the large Tudor-bethan dwelling of the Grosvenor's property opposite, he soon passed what had been the Cranford's Georgian town house before they had vanished into air. The Bradshaw's modern and stylish number opposite that, with its sleek curves reminding him of a yacht or ship, brought their plucky little dog, Slate, to mind, who would always greet him at the property gates.

Whatever happened to Slate? Oliver wondered, but then he guessed the answer immediately with a sigh: that was thirteen or fourteen years ago, at least. And there, at the far end of a cul-de-sac, was the more modest yet still quite lovely townhouse called Ashurst; it had been his childhood home which they had rented until it became beyond their means, and they had mournfully had to leave. Finding himself barely able to look at it again, the memories that it stirred were too bittersweet to bear, and so he quickly moved on; the happy, trumpeting spirit that the Grove always inspired had already dispersed into the hot air above before he had even left the vicinity, and he found himself sinking leadenly into the hot, oily tarmac beneath him. Sparking up another filterless then, he huffed it down glumly.

On passing the grove's last outpost, the upmarket Jolly Gamesman on Salt Street, he let out another sigh. It had seemed more his sort of place than the likes of the Oddfellows at first, but with his increasingly dishevelled appearance, which somehow he could do little about, his licence to drink there had been revoked some time ago; with that in mind, the reality of the life that he was lumbered with nowadays presented itself as he turned the final corner into Greenthorne proper.

There was quite a clamour on Middle Row that lunchtime; it was extremely busy and positively throbbed with that workaday yet lively mix of dereliction and thrifty enterprise that Oliver found so overpowering. Even in such stifling heat, sweaty townsfolk, who tenaciously pressed on with their challenging lives, ran market stalls selling earthy-smelling crates of homegrown carrots, cabbages, and such in front of boarded-up shop fronts; their aggressive sales pitch boxed his ears as he passed them by. It then struck him just how many more stores had closed their doors permanently in the last month; at least half of Middle Row's stores lay empty, in fact.

His mood levelled once he had become engaged in the pleasurable activity of spending. Alfred Goldfinch, the grocer's son, said 'Alright mate!' as Oliver entered his father's store, but having never been particularly awash with social attention, and with his ears poorly attuned to it, Oliver was also too consumed with his shopping spree to notice that lunchtime.

Determined to allocate his allowance sensibly this time around, he bought lettuce and apples because Marion had always insisted that fruit and vegetables were essential to good health. Jennings the Bakers was his next port of call, for bread to stock his larder with for a day or two. Oliver then stopped at the Greenthorne General Stores for barley sugars, frosted mints, pear drops, and packets of filterless, now that he fancied a change from his usual smokes. He called in on Badcock's Pharmacy lastly, to replenish his stock of analgesics and purchase spirits with which to clean his sable brushes.

Upon today's approach, Mr Turner appeared to be unusually down in the mouth.

'Top of the morning, Mr Turner. How are you this fine day?'

'Fucked and ah've had no fun.'

'Sorry to hear that.'

'Where you soddin' off to, then?'

'The pub.'

'Have a drink for me, then, eh moneybags.'

'Alright, I will.'

'Ta-ra, then, Oliver. Enjoy that quail pipe up your backside.'

'I certainly shall, Mr Turner.'

'Oh, ehm... 'old on,' he called out as Oliver moved on. 'Any chance of a coin or two? My stomach swears my throat's been cut.'

With plenty of brass in his pocket for once, and feeling sorry for the old grouch, Oliver was more than happy to oblige.

'Ta. You can shove off now.'

The Oddfellows was usually Oliver's next port of call after his visits to Sheldon, where he liked to celebrate receiving his allowance in great style – alone in the corner seat getting soused. But alas, it proved to be too busy for him this afternoon, with his usual seat having been pinched by Roy, of all people, who was scoffing the contents of his lunch bag. It may have been for the best, however; Oliver sensed, as he peered into the saloon bar, that there was an air of aggression about the place – likely due to the stifling heat, which had become a little much for everybody. The townsmen were clearly spoiling for a fight, and Doris had her work cut out for her.

It was therefore impossible to pass a decrepit and ownerless-looking lockup on Primrose Passage, the dark secrets of which had become common knowledge to all except local police constables, without slinking into its discreet side door; for years, Murray Pierce had brewed and sold cheap, unlabelled bottles of black market grog from there. Once again, Oliver emerged from its illicit darkness somewhat weighed down; the price could never be argued with, after all. He had purchased so many bottles, in fact, that he struggled to carry them home while scouring dustbins for freshly tossed newspapers with which to wipe his behind – more expert frugality.

Oliver whiled away his early evening shrouded in a smoky haze, smoking one cigarette after another and scribbling idly on his sketchbook. Although it still did the trick – he was quickly sloshed – Murray's latest brew was a little vinegarish; upon noticing that there was even silt in the bottle, Oliver decided that he would treat himself to a clear bottle of extra dry gin the following morning, the very moment that the General Stores reopened its doors.

After a passable salad of lettuce, slivers of apple, and homemade croutons, followed with pear drops for dessert, he turned to his art and tried to capture Maxine's legs on paper; he had seen women's legs before, of course, but hers had been so standout! He quickly realised, however, that he struggled to remember this remarkable sight at all. All he could picture of her was her horse-like teeth and her overly strong jaw – features that he knew would prevent her from ever being called pretty, yet for him they merely added to her allure, due to their sublime incongruence with her daintiness otherwise.

Instead, then, Oliver sketched and then painted a portrait of Sheldon, just as young and handsome as he had once been, and the way Oliver had preferred him during that early period in his childhood when things were relatively cordial between the family, and they had visited him often. While working quickly but carefully, he remembered that this was when Sheldon had first asked him to start calling him 'Uncle' while thrusting Athletics Guild periodicals and boxing programmes into his 'nephew's' eager little hands. While affectionately calling him 'champ', Uncle Sheldon had had grand designs upon Oliver's future, and he had been expectant that his new nephew would grow up to be a sportsman one day; they had discussed this exhilarant fancy so often, but the only practical tuition in sportsmanship that Oliver had ever received from his new uncle was a few games of croquet that had been played on Ferndale's lawns, when he and his mother had dropped in on distant summer afternoons. Naturally, their visits had been received with a cordiality that had turned out to be insincere; much later, with Marion's health faltering after she had been laid off, and when she had requested financial assistance, Sheldon had recoiled, dropping her – well, dropping them both, actually – like the hottest of bricks. He had even been so very wicked as to cite her illness as –

'Self-delusion if one were being kind, but if one were being realistic, much more likely to be deceitful trickery with the intent of eliciting attention and, in all likelihood, to extort money – more money.'

Oliver's grandparents on his father's side had recently done the same thing, more or less; they had never warmed to the 'greedy' grocer's daughter either. Still, before his truly spineless disposition became apparent, it had been fun for Oliver to have his fair-weather uncle's undivided attention. Before things had turned sour, the parties to which Marion and he had been invited had been a blast, too, because in those days, Sheldon had indulged in endless pageantry and banqueting. Sheldon had even had a live-in housekeeper and cook back then: Mrs Fairfax, who had previously been in a countess' employ. She had talked animatedly of the rest of her culinary repertoire while she had stuffed pheasant, deep roasted quail, and simmered onion soup *gratinée*. And silly old Sherbert Saunders, Oliver thought when thinking back on his former party playmate in particular; what the blazes had Lady Saunders been thinking when naming him Sherbert?

Ferndale had never looked so alive, not before or since; electric lights had been strung between the grounds' shrubs, and the other guests had mingled beneath their varicoloured blooms. Inside, Sherbert and he, both age seven or thereabouts, had sneakily acquired their first taste of alcoholic beverage, and they had both agreed that gin and Dubonnet made for a good introduction. Spectacular spreads, whipped up by Mrs Fairfax, had been laid out too – smorgasbords of oysters, dry caviar, and even octopus. For little Olly, however, the napkins had been the greatest attraction: manufactured in deep empire blue satin and with an exquisite gold-fringed and pinked trim, they had harmonised the buffet's visual presentation charmingly.

Thinking back to those better days, Oliver found himself thinking wistfully of the indoor sports room at the end of Ferndale's side passage – the one that he had been denied access to since he was a child. It had once been absolutely his paradise; he had often pretended to play table tennis there with an invisible ball because there had never been any opponent available that had the slightest ability to bat a real one back. He had also enjoyed being surrounded by Sheldon's trophy collection, and he had enjoyed a strong sense of sporting achievement, just as Sheldon had, by close proximity to this dazzling array of golden cups, which he could only imagine that his imitation uncle had acquired from the house clearance sales of recently deceased and financially ruined sportsmen. Then, once the decorators had been and gone, Oliver had discovered that the newly laid linoleum was an invigorating shade of gin fizz grey-yellow, but the walls had been daubed a rather sorry colour that had become a sore point between them ever since; it had possibly been the reason that he had been denied entry to that hallowed hall thereafter because Sheldon never could take criticism. Despite his protests on the matter, Sheldon had, by Oliver's estimation, blundered terribly; the walls were not racing green but bilious green – of that Oliver was certain.

Presently, other shades came to mind and were being carefully applied to younger Sheldon's portrait; colours such as wintry off-white for his purported uncle's skin were blended with the palest tinge of dark orchid greyish-violet because there had been something somewhat deathly looking about 'Uncy Sheldon' in those days, which would have been utterly revolting had he not been so very handsome. Yes, it had all worked: the pinkness of his cheeks had made no argument with his waxen pallor otherwise, and had only augmented his rather unnerving and unique allure. Moreover, how wonderfully he had attired himself in his dapper days! Bow ties, regatta blazers, three-piece suits, tuxedos, white slacks, pleated fronts, leather britches, and plus fours in the great outdoors had all become him, with grave exception for that silly boater hat, of course. The cigars that he had smoked in those days had suited him far better too.

Having finished his portrait, Oliver assessed its merits and its imperfections thoroughly, and he felt rather pleased overall; he congratulated himself for successfully capturing the Uncle Sheldon that he so desperately wanted back. Where has this handsome, if somewhat spooky looking, uncle of yesteryear gone? he wondered while finding that he missed the scowling mouth; dark glittering eyes; high, flinty cheekbones; rosebuds lips; and rose petal cheeks, which he had found so arresting as a child, rather terribly.

He was all too aware that his attempts at rendering human figures were rarely up to snuff – they were often too stylised, mimicking the fashionably geometric and elseways streamlined aesthetic as applied to the human form that he had copied from popular artists' work sourced from the printed press; in this case, however, the likeness was one of his best. This was not so much because his technique had improved overnight, but it was more due to the fact that Sheldon, in his younger years, looked as if he had been drawn by one of these artists too; naturally, then, it was quite easy to get the likeness.

Yes, this was the Uncle Sheldon that had unnerved and thrilled him once with an eerie and savage beauty – unfortunately all but a distant memory nowadays. Finding himself seriously doubting whether he could bother anymore with his inferior replacement, Ferndale's roly-poly imposter that bored him so, Oliver had to remind himself that it was not the fuller figure per se that he found objectionable – far from it, in fact. Derek Munyard was rather rotund, after all, but Oliver found him to be as cute as a button, and Alfred Goldfinch, the Grocer's son, was a very big boy indeed, but Oliver had often found himself gazing into the blue irises of his oh-so pretty eyes while grinning like a madman. Sour-faced Sybill Woolgather, the draper's daughter, was also a fascinating and alluring enigma, whose thunderous face and thighs he would more than make allowances for. Unfortunately, however, Sheldon's portliness suggested ill-health, verging on the impression of full-bodied gout, if such a thing were possible. Either way, it was perhaps, as exemplified by his coarseness earlier that day, the decline of his once sharp and sly wit that had become the greatest tragedy.

Nowadays, Sheldon had become such an embarrassment, in fact, that during a toe-curling attempt to re-enact one of Oliver's childhood rituals last August, merely tapping the ball with the croquet bat had had the fairy elephant panting and breaking out into a sweat while swiping a tall glass of lemonade that Maxine had produced promptly upon his urgent calls for refreshment; what a sorry state for someone only in their early forties! His older brother, Tristan Bainbridge Senior, was still as dashing as Sheldon had been, and he still took London by storm, apparently; with a heightened and ambiguous sexuality, he scandalised London's beau monde with great aplomb, and he always got away with it, of course, because good looks and charm trumped moral rectitude without exception, in his circles, at least.

A better approach to life, Oliver then savvied, was to cut loose of his odious faux uncle and forge his own destiny. The only way of doing so, he supposed, was to secure gainful employment and pay his own way through life; he would have no reason to keep up these tiresome charades with Sheldon then, which were clearly going nowhere anyway. In the next moment, this sudden vow of self-sufficiency felt more like a dreamer's feeble conviction, however – deep down he knew that he was nowhere near capable, as confirmed by the unease that he felt in his tightening diaphragm. He then found himself fearing losing his allowance more than ever, owing to its grave consequences. And what about Tristan Bainbridge Junior? His imminent arrival was hardly going to help matters any.

Feeling weighed down by this sense of helplessness, and also by the worry of it all, he rose leadenly. The mantel clock marked that it was already morning, so he trudged down the hallway, but he crept as silently as possible past the door to his mother's bedroom, so as not to wake her spirit. Putting himself straight to bed then, he still felt half-cut, but that was the point of getting so glazed in the first place – how he preferred long-lasting, deep, and dreamless sleep, and the lengths he would go to to get it!

Enfants Terribles

Despite last night's unease, Oliver had slept soundly and had awoken feeling surprisingly light and refreshed. The day that stretched before him seemed likely to be as uneventful as his sleep had been, which was quite alright by him – he was in an unusually neutral mood. But then, while feeling dismayed to find that his supplies of bread and lettuce had dwindled far quicker than he had expected, he became gripped by a familiar worry that if he bought more food, he would soon run out of funds for the staples upon which his daily survival depended: pints of bitter – his new favourite, boiled sweets, bottles of extra dry gin, and cigarettes or packets of filterless if he so fancied. Accordingly, he felt disinclined to buy more foodstuffs while realising the need for unsparing attention to his balance books and extreme frugality, with only half his allowance remaining already, if that.

After a breakfast of lettuce sandwiches – the most satisfactory one he had had for days and one which helped considerably with his hangover – he had a sudden hankering for something altogether different, which took him quite by surprise. Could I really do that? he wondered of the shenanigans that had just occurred to him; to hell with it! Why not? Bloody Nora, I'm a brave bugger! Accordingly, he thought that he had better give himself a wipe down with a damp flannel. Quickly throwing on a shirt then, he stepped into his shorts, yanked his socks up, donned his Derby tweed, and with sudden abandon he grabbed a considerable chunk of change from his bedstand. He then filled his hip flask with Murray's liquor, snatched up his smokes, jumped into his brogues, and headed out into warming Greenthorne, forgetting his sweeties in the rush.

All but empty of folk, Middle Row baked silently beneath the smokiness of the yellowed sky. With all the filth that sullied Greenthorne's skies generally, Oliver often felt that he had forgotten what blue sky looked like, and white clouds, for that matter; he found himself lamenting this once again while the tar underfoot melted and stuck to his soles.

While passing the Woolgather's and Goldfinch's empty stores, he neared his favourite watering hole and felt his allowance scorching holes in his pockets. He had missed his customary splurge the previous afternoon, after all, but although he felt quite parched and the Oddfellows looked invitingly cool and peaceful, he had even greater urges calling; thus, on passing the place by, he merely tapped on the windowpane and waved to Doris, who was wiping down the bar tops. Above him, perched on a ladder's top rung whilst washing soot from the pub's upstairs windows, Grahame Lowndes cast him yet another off-coloured leer; Oliver quickened his pace then, muttering 'Push off, tuss,' and 'Don't look at me, dullard,' under his breath.

While doggedly refusing to disband, despite the pit's closure, and still rehearsing in the old fire station only a few streets away, Nether Moor Colliery's Brass Band struck up a rather plodding dirge, which seemed hell-bent on wrecking his mood; it sounded too much like the blue notes in his life's melody, so he hummed *Ten Green Bottles* to keep his spirits buoyant.

Ten green bottles standing on the wall,
Ten green bottles standing on the wall,
And if one green bottle should accidently fall,
There'll be nine green bottles standing on the wall...

Cheerfully, little Wally Shanks came to mind then – a childhood chum from Thorny Grove, who had taught him the melody and lyrics of this little ditty. He had been quite a gas, little Wally – his plentiful dripping excrement had, on a daily basis, been an offering to his mother, the intention behind which was to drive her to distraction with its unorthodox presentation. Oliver had always found the little rascal's party piece quite amusing, however, even if no one else had.

Up ahead, dear old Mr Turner, appearing to be in a far better mood, had claimed his usual pitch opposite Mrs Spence's tearoom, and he was slumped on the pavement, smoking a roll-your-own.

'Good morning, Mr Turner.'

'Fancy readin' a book, Oliver?' Mr Turner asked enthusiastically while gesturing to a small selection of grimy paperbacks scattered on the pavement beside him.

'Gosh, yes... I'd be only too happy to purchase one.'

'Ta, lad. You'll be my first customer.'

In truth, Oliver felt torn; the last title that he had bought from Mr Turner, *A Dictionary of the Vulgar Tongue*, had proved to be invaluable, but he did not have much of an appetite for proper reading nowadays, and with quite a distance to trek, he felt weighed down by his satchel's contents already. On consideration, however, he still felt that he had to indulge Mr Turner; he liked the old chap and admired his ceaseless entrepreneurship. Beggardom had become an art for him.

'What titles do you have?'

Mr Turner reached over and picked each up in turn, squinting to read their front covers aloud –

'Well, let's see now, shall we? What we got 'ere... ehm... *Call of the West Book of Tours, Lawn Tennis for Beginners, Maps of the Outer Hebrides, Socialism Defined, Thirty-Three Uses for Suet*, and *The Picturegoer's Who's Who and Encyclopaedia*.'

'May I just ask, Mr Turner, purely out of curiosity... where did you get them this time?'

'Nicked 'em from the t' library,' Mr Turner replied with a hearty chuckle. 'Couldn't lie to ya now, could ah?'

Oliver could not suppress a snigger.

'How on earth did you get away with it? Old Chivvers has one eye permanently peeled. Sleeps with it open, I'm sure,' Oliver said of Greenthorne Library's infamous manageress and Avril Chivvers' mother.

Mr Turner belly laughed.

'Oh aye, ah'm sure she does. Well, the trick with 'er is... she got an Achilles heel, that woman. Loses 'er rag a little too quick.'

'How on earth did that serve your enterprise?'

'You 'ave to create a distraction, ya see.'

'And how did you create this distraction?' Oliver asked between snickers.

'Well, my mate, old Snaggs, ya see... 'e's got this speciality: belches on command and up to a maximum duration of twenty-five seconds. Fancy that, eh?'

Oliver cackled out loud.

'Really?'

'Oh aye... Well, you can imagine old Chivvers' reaction. It were like a red rag to a bull when ah signalled fer 'im to open 'is bone box and let rip. A real ear-splitter it was too. Never seen a woman so enraged... Near as lost 'er mind, she did. Meanwhile, ah shoved all these in my carryall.'

'That was quite an act of bravery on the side of your friend. She'd have barred him for life, surely?'

'Oh aye, ah've not seen an explosion like that since the Battle of the Somme, nor sensed such potential bloodshed. His feet barely touched the floor as she got rid. But poor old Snaggs, 'e got the cancer, ya see... Won't last till the winter... an' why on earth would you want to go to the library when the heatin's off anyway? No loss fer 'im.'

'Well, I'm sorry to hear about Snaggs.'

'Aye, that's life, though, aint it? Life and death go hand in hand, don't they? Any road... any catch your fancy? Sit yerself down an' 'ave a browse if you like.'

'Well, you both deserve medals for your bravery, I should say. Not that you haven't been well decora– Sorry... I didn't mean to demean–'

'Oh, don't be so daft, son. Ah'm not that easily offended.'

Oliver crouched, picked up *The Picturegoer's Who's Who and Encyclopaedia*, and sat flicking through its pages.

Hmm... I'm really not sure, he thought. It was likely to be a dangerous acquisition since already the book's film listings, script synopses, and star profiles had all begun to seduce him a little while he also remembered all the tumult that the cinema had caused him in the long run. But upon remembering that the Blandishford Picture House was where he had acquired his first and only handful of intimate female anatomy, his voyage of discovery beckoned him even more compellingly. He supposed that come winter he could burn the book and warm his hands if it really did grate on him, and feeling anxious to hurry things up and get back to business, he asked –

'How much for this one, then?'

'Oh, a penny'll do. It'd be cheeky to ask ya for more now that ah've told ya where ah got 'em.'

'Here... I award you two... for astonishing acts of bravery.'

'That's kind of ya, lad.'

'But would you mind holding on to it for me, Mr Turner? I've got quite a walk ahead if me, and it's quite a heavy volume to carry.'

'Oh aye, where you off to, then?'

'The pub.'

'Again, eh? Bit early for the Oddfellows, ain't it?'

'Trying somewhere new.'

Turning then and catching sight of Mrs Spence's teashop, Oliver found that her sensational ice cream sundaes called to him as loudly as Doris' wares had on passing her establishment, but even greater hankerings still called louder; even the extra dry would have to wait.

'Thanks, Mr Turner. I do hope you shift them all.'

'Ah 'ope so n' all. Ah need the gravy 'cause rent man'll come seekin' soon enough.'

A few hundred meters on, while passing a modestly sized row of terraced houses, the front gardens of which had once expressed the pride of their owners, he despaired, as he so often did, that those gardens were blossomless nowadays and overgrown with weeds, or paved over for the convenience of not having to bother with them at all. Nowadays, too, only a few of them had followed their exemplary monarch's shining example of replacing geraniums and such with cabbages and potatoes, but just ahead was Olive Solby's front plot, which was always the exception to all this desperation and neglect. And there was Olive herself, looking rather old these days and tending to her trim little garden, as always, with her enormous and ancient tortoise, Archie, still going just as strong as she was. It took shelter in the shadow of her gladioli stands; their velvety petals still entranced butterflies and bees as much as they did Oliver.

His heart sank again upon seeing Olive. She had either forgotten him entirely, or she simply no longer recognised him as the boy that she had once warmly welcomed into her thriving, colourific garden to play with his old *amie*: her daughter, Abigail, who had been about the same age. They had had a special name for those picnics that they had held in that garden, but he could not for the life of him remember what that name was anymore; irrespective of that, they had been fine dining indeed, those picnics, wherein Abigail and he had munched on pickled onions, cubed cheese skewered with cocktail sticks, and lemon curd sandwiches. Meanwhile, propped on the gateposts or sitting at the kitchen table, Olive and Marion had discussed the price of household commodities and such, or they had engaged in shoptalk because their careers had mostly moved in tandem through the various factories that employed womenfolk; they had both been machinists at Crowther Overall Manufacturing for several years, and then they had been tanners at Sharpe & Beard before winding up at rotten old Cranford Electric. Despite her increasingly festering bitterness through all of that, Marion had always had nothing but warmth for Olive – she had always been surprisingly convivial toward those that she truly liked.

Thinking back on all this, he wondered what on earth had become of sweet, amiable Abby after he had harmed their rapport so spectacularly; wherever she had disappeared to, he hoped that she had not forgotten him entirely either, although he did hope that she had forgotten his pathetic advances towards her. That aside, with all this poignancy flooding through him, that brightly coloured mirage of better days appeared quite lucid, but then it folded away into nothingness as he briefly met Olive's blank stare and then moved quickly on.

When passing the primary school that Abby had once attended, Oliver neared the corner where he would turn into the old tramway, but he found himself dragging his heels as he peered ahead, squinting at the point where the town's main artery became dustier and less distinct while becoming increasingly flanked by haulage warehouses, textile factories, the leatherworks, the sealed colliery, and the abandoned cotton mills. Even from this distance, he could see that the wooden lean-to on the side of Cranford Electric still stood, even after all these years of weather and neglect. This was the closest distance that he would allow himself to be to it nowadays – never any closer; as much as he would have liked to pretend that that factory had never existed, he never could suppress the involuntary reflex of glancing at it. In doing so, he always feared that he would see Marion's phantasmal figure waiting for him with bared teeth upon its shadowed steps. Despite such fears, he also permitted a few memories to resurface; they were hard to curb considering how many times he had waited for her to finish her shift while sheltering under that lean-to.

While thinking fondly of Alec Solby, Olive's late husband and the works foreman, who would sometimes sit and chat with him while he waited out the gap between the end of school and Marion packing up for the night, Oliver smiled. Once double shift had eventually become mandatory for her, he was finally furnished with a key with which to let himself into the horse hospital, much to his preference. But before that, sitting and conversing with Mr Solby in Cranford's lean-to had been very entertaining, wherein he could only marvel at the sheer size of Alec's hands and how much they resembled the hide of his pet tortoise. Alec was perhaps his only pleasant memory of that place, however, because he had visions of his mother emerging from its darkness already, tired, grey, and clawing her hair away from her face with that increasingly withering look for him; upon remembering this, he realised that he better forget it all and move on.

With half a mind to turn back, purchase some liquorice, and go to the crossway or heath instead, he found himself feeling torn suddenly because his plans seemed a little far-fetched by the light of day, but the yearning that he had awoken with still called to him, like a siren's song, and he remained fixed on a very different destination. His mind seemed to be made up because the sense of mischief that still brimmed inside of him after seeing Maxine's bare legs the day before could not be suppressed; he realised that the voyage of discovery which that spectacle had inspired could not be given up on.

Oliver began to tremble with the anticipation of what potentially lay ahead; the fine hairs on his arms and neck bristled and stiffened with trepidation, and he felt breathless, too, while the shrill whistle of a Dales Express train sounded in the distance, which he interpreted as a signal that he had made the right decision to press on with his plans. Looking eastwards down the old tramway at Iron Bridge, Oliver saw the locomotive and its carriages clatter over the rusted viaduct at its far end, leaving dense plumes of pale, vaporous exhaust behind it; they, thanks to the breeze rebounding off Tamworth's frontage, were buffeted down to street level and lingered there, cloaking the secrets within the viaduct's shadow. This was, in fact, where he was heading – a place where he had heard that the mysteries of women, who were similarly shrouded in ambiguity, might be solved.

***

While eavesdropping in the Oddfellows and learning a great deal about Greenthorne's neighbourhoods and their history before the rapid economic downturn, Oliver had overheard many stories about this particular area. Once a centre of industry and productivity, Greenthorne East, nicknamed 'Iron Bridge', had even had its own little hub of commerce, with several stores, a bowling alley, and even a picture house among other establishments; these firms had gone out of business once the downturn had hit and the tramway became surplus to requirements and was no longer maintained. What had followed had made for colourful stories, to say the very least: stories of loose women, violence, and racketeering. When picturing Greenthorne's black spot, he could only imagine a Sodom shaped by the grievance and disenchantment borne of the depression's human cost, yet a locale which conversely compensated Greenthorne's townsmen for all their losses with its lawless enticements; he had also heard that this district had a reputation that still lingered even after the focal point of that ill repute, a once rather lively establishment, the Queens Head Public House and Hostelry, opposite the Greenthorne Palace, had also been closed down by the town council.

But while feeling quite disappointed now that he had arrived, Oliver could only guess that Iron Bridge's dubious reputation lingered in the stale air because the townswomen still insisted that it was off limits when their men were off the leash. The only sounds that he could hear, apart from the odd gust of wind and distant cricket song, was mental chatter regarding the lore of the sirens of the Queens Head, which perhaps was only a legend after all because amid such desertion, he could not imagine any creature living there – real or mythical.

Workshops that skirted the old tramway's entirety, that had once been so productive, appeared to be utterly derelict; their fences of corrugated iron were rusted to almost nothing. The tramway, all the way along, was still scattered with the remnants of their manufacturing: all manner of rusting and mouldering industrial offscourings. Warm gusts of wind blew all that litter about as a tattered Greenthorne Fayre poster flapped around Oliver's ankles, and then swirled away along with the nostalgia it had aroused: the taste of honeycombed toffee and candyfloss, the challenge of the coconut shy, and the ding and dong of tin can alley.

Further along, a torn and twisted barrage balloon trailed listlessly across the forecourt of yet another empty lot – its fabric now rotted to a pulp; the sad sight of this ancient-looking wartime relic triggered another recollection of times past, when he could only have been an infant, and when his mother had pushed him virtually the length of the tramway in search of gainful employment.

The barrage balloon had been airborne then because the ministry kept them afloat for many years after wartime; perhaps they were left hovering as an emblem of victory – a reminder that Britannia had quashed numerous foes already and would remain eternally unconquerable. Oliver could suddenly envisage how in those days, there had been a light about Marion – an almost regal seeming glow that came from inside, much like one would imagine of Britannia herself; perhaps this was the reason that this memory was not instantly dispatched back into his subconscious the moment it had surfaced. She in no way resembled the figure so transformed by embitterment and illness that she had become later in her life, so he allowed this memory to linger, too, albeit fleetingly.

There had been a dark period prior, naturally, but by this point in time, Marion's luminosity spoke of how determined she had become not to let her widowhood define her, which was most surprising with hindsight because later on she had developed quite a taste for victimhood. Prior to all this, work had been avoided at all costs and her annual garden fêtes, in support of the Red Cross or the Royal British Legion, which took place in the quintessential English country garden that she had been working so hard on, were merely a form of atonement for otherwise being an utter vulgarian – if one paid heed to Uncle Sheldon drivelling on while calling the kettle black. It was quite surprising that when having little choice but to work since his father had passed away, this change of circumstance had not seemed to faze her at first – such was her defiance – but she had yet to realise just how dearly it would come to cost her. The harsh realities of how wearying labour would be in a time of such rapid economic decline were unimaginable; her naivety as to what really lay ahead – all manner of gruntwork, essentially – veneered this memory with even more poignancy as he suddenly envisaged the balloon's shadow falling across her hopeful face –

'Look Oliver!' she had cried as it had twisted in the breeze and his stroller had trembled on the cobbles. 'That balloon protected us all once, just like your father did.'

Perhaps the only solace of Marion's widowhood had been that her husband had been a hero; it was something that she had never stopped talking about, in fact – perhaps boasting about if one were thinking unkindly. Either way, he had certainly earned the glory that he had sought, and he had surely earned his place in Valhalla – no one had argued against that; he had done his bit, just as that balloon had done its bit, so it had symbolised the bittersweetness of both her loss and her pride.

While thinking of other widows such as Rose Spence, ever alone in her teashop, and poor old Auggy, who nowadays had every right to be hard-faced, faded and tattered posters that read 'God speed the machine and the woman who works it!' and 'For every fighter a woman worker!' spoke to Oliver of bruised hearts once limbs and lives had been lost in that infernal war.

While reflecting upon all this adversity, he stopped minding his step and tripped over the tramway's rusted tracks; while steadying himself, he abruptly had that familiar feeling of being followed, but when turning around and looking back the length of where he had come, there was no one to be seen. Resuming his quest then, he trudged along the old tramway with optimism and determination, just as his mother had done.

With his crosshairs usually aimed at Uncle Sheldon's living standards with great accuracy, Oliver, despite his initial dismay with the place, found himself becoming surprisingly drawn to it. Wouldn't it be grand to up sticks and move to this neck of the woods, he speculated; its dereliction felt unexpectedly appealing. It might also facilitate the life that he so often hankered after: one spiced with absinthe, opium, and hashish. He would be away from prying eyes, after all; moreover, he was no stranger to isolation. As if signalling its approval, another Dales Express choo-chooed across the viaduct while a motorbike beezumped past him, quickly dissolving into the drifts of steam that lingered ahead; he had just time to discern that it was a military motorbike – its rider was likely to be another aeronaut from Nether Moor's aerodrome.

With his urge to press on feeling hindered by unease again, he began to wonder if he was about to make a total idiot of himself. Stopping then and anxiously smoking the first of a new pack of filterless while taking generous slugs from his flask, he noticed that among the rubbish that littered the tramway, a child's toy pram had been smashed into it and had remained there on its side ever since. A doll lay motionless in the road nearby; clearly, the accident had been fatal.

Finally, after some time wondering whether to turn back or persevere, he carried on because his inquisitive and unprincipled nature had won the toss once more.

With the viaduct finally looming, Oliver heard jazzy music that crackled and spluttered; someone was running a wireless up ahead, in the viaduct's dark shadow where the Queens Head Public House and Hostelry should be, with the Greenthorne Palace opposite. The wireless had a poor tone and was tinny sounding, but the music was nevertheless gladsome. Perhaps the sirens are real and not myth after all, he dared wonder since he had met one of them once, but he had found her so implausible upon reflection that he had decided he must have dreamt her up; after all, she had seemed more like a character from a fantasy film, or the heroine of some luridly penned novella, or some such fiction, than any real-life person that he had ever met. The possibility that she had been real after all was a prospect which both excited him and made his anxiety rise; the downy tufts of hair on his forearms and neck bristled again while he became filled with huge anticipation.

He cast his mind back to conversations that he had overheard between Roy, Grahame, and Bert in the Oddfellows. Apparently, there were three women that still offered a business of sorts from the remains of the Queens Head, and their names were Ava, Kitty Kat, and the last one went unnamed – she had been a bit too tall and gangly for anyone's taste. Yes, all three would, to Oliver's astonishment on hearing this for the first time, fornicate with you at a price; upon learning this, he could only imagine the ruined shell of what once was the Queen's Head with the sweating bodies of filthy harpies cavorting on the hostelry's dirty mattresses. Soon afterwards, however, to the shock of all the pub's patrons and the town in general, Grahame Lowndes had brought one of these women into the Oddfellows on his arm; this was Kitty Kat, or 'Kitty' for short. As soon as Oliver had clapped eyes on this rare creature, he had realised just how mistaken he had been because she had been more finely apparelled than any woman he had ever seen, and she had also looked more pristine than even his mother's best impression, but yet she had acted as much the court jester as a Shakespearian fool. She was by no means the 'crazy, cockney tart' that the townswomen had so ignorantly called her that night; she was, in fact, a lovely Londoner who had learned her craft, while also crafting her persona, in bohemian Soho.

He had found Kitty visually arresting because she had worn the heaviest of make-up, as if to project herself to the furthest row of a theatre; the high arches of her blackened brows, ruby-lipped cupid's bow, beauty mark, and expanse of petrol blue eye shadow were all painted upon an alabaster mask framed by a platinum mass of curls. He could not imagine what she might have looked like beneath all that, nor particularly cared. Her style was very carefully considered; 'Weimar Republic hostessen,' was how she had explained it. Those words, 'Weimar Republic hostessen,' spoken rather proudly in that cockney accent of hers, was a marvellously clashing juxtaposition. He had also eavesdropped keenly on all her froth and bluster when speaking of the 'Shim Sham', the 'Caravan', and the 'Afghan'; with no clue if these were people, dances, or positions for fornication, he had approved of it all anyway. Hers had certainly been the most compelling of all the utterances he had ever overheard in the Oddfellows.

Although Oliver had guessed that Kitty's company took up most of Grahame's wages, he could tell by the look on his face that, for him, she was worth every penny paid. In the saloon, of all places, she had seemed entirely incongruous; she had worn natty little high-heeled shoes, black culottes, and a pinstriped gentleman's waistcoat. Her pearl necklaces had obviously been fake, but the blue rose pinned to her fedora had looked genuine and not at all made of cloth; it had been head-scratching, actually, because Oliver felt sure that blue roses did not exist in nature. It was this anomaly that had convinced him that she had merely featured in a dream, or had been a figment of his vivid imagination, until on one drunken, haphazard afternoon, he had glimpsed her on Middle Row; even then, once he had sobered up, he had not been entirely sure.

For all this, he decided that she – well, all three of these women – could be nothing short of enchanting sirens – not the screen sirens that the Greenthorne Palace, opposite the Queens Head, had been intended to showcase, but they were sirens nonetheless! But as much as Oliver had found her quite devastating and had admired her in general, Kitty was far too intimidating. Fortunately, however, he had heard that there was another young lady available, whose name was Ava – a local lass, by all accounts, who apparently looked like one of those department store mannequins. He still supposed that he had his sights set on this one of the two, although he had never even clapped eyes on her. The third one that he had heard about was obviously a no go – the terribly tall one, although he was sure that she was a lovely lady, all the same. That was one of his late grandad's famous pearls of wisdom apparently –

'They're all marvellous, it's just that some are less marvellous than others.'

What a thoughtful and generous approach to womankind, Oliver had thought on hearing such savvy.

While remembering all this, Oliver crossed the tramway to the opposite side, so that he might approach the Queens Head unnoticed because he still felt at rather a loss as to how he might approach this affair.

Astonishingly, there were two women stood just outside the place, and he watched them silently from only a short distance while crouching low enough to be somewhat obscured. With the sun directly behind the Queens Head, it was hard to make it, and them, out at all, but he could just about discern that so far the two women – merely silhouettes – had yet to notice him. His heart thumped in his chest, and he felt awfully sweaty, which did not help bolster his confidence at all; he knew that women were different to men and that, for them, such things mattered. Since in the excitable rush of the morning, he had not tended to his personal hygiene nearly enough, he suddenly felt at even more of a disadvantage.

Creeping across the sun, a swirling drift of cloud softened its glare considerably and the sight of the Greenthorne Palace shocked him with more clarity; he forgot everything for a moment.

'Good grief!' Oliver gasped. Although it was fashioned with the streamlined curves and geometric contours with which most dream palaces had been built, the picture house's brickwork was of the dullest grey imaginable; furthermore, it was disappointingly small. Its signage was quite weather-beaten and was falling off its supports. The windows were mostly cracked, as was the frosted plate glass in the old foyer's revolving doors – the endless circling of which had been dizzying and utterly mesmerising when he and Abigail had been taken to the 'nippers' stampede'. Although he still could not for the life of him remember what films they had seen there, it had anchored itself in his heart as a place of tremendous significance. Not long after those outings with Abigail, he had been dismayed to learn of its closing due to rapidly dwindling attendance, with folk giving up on the flicks altogether, or preferring to ride the Dales Express to champion Blandishford's far glitzier picture house. But then, having awoken from his reverie, he remembered that this excursion had hardly been conceived as a trip down memory lane.

Looking back, there, out front of The Queens Head opposite, was the bawdy harlequin herself, Kitty Kat, sporting black stockings that reached just above the knee, revealing thighs that were as porcelain white as they were gymnastic. She sat on an old tea chest, blowing discordant notes from a trombone with an air of great amusement. Her face still wore that mask of alabaster and petrol blue, with ruby lips and toffee apple cheeks that were clownish without being in the least bit silly; she somehow married sophistication with lampoonery. She wore that improbable blue rose pinned to her fedora again, and she still appeared to be just as terrifying as she was improbable overall.

Standing ten or so paces away, the brunette stood beneath her pollen yellow parasol, garlanded by merigold yellow off-the-shoulder ruffles that were pinned with a salmon pink rose, she must surely be Ava, he thought. She smiled back at her friend so sweetly.

Although Oliver could not quite make out her responses to Kitty's chit-chat, she spoke with a northern dialect, which he could not locate in its precise geographical origin, but was surprisingly soft and treacly in its enunciation. She appeared to be perfectly charming, of course, but perhaps a little too charming for what Oliver had in mind; she looked like the sort of lady who was only capable of thinking immaculate thoughts, and for whom you could only have the deepest of respect while holding hands with her on gay picnics and canal boat excursions along sun-dappled water ways. But, then, word about her was quite to the contrary, of course.

With each young lady standing either side of the Queens Head's entrance, his eye felt drawn to graffiti on its frontage, just above that entrance, where somebody had scribed the word 'Sisters', with the outline of a love heart etched around it in white paint; this he found utterly charming, and it seemed to be spot on, too, because the closeness and camaraderie that they shared was heart-warmingly apparent. In view of all this – such a visually arresting tableau – and perhaps for the first time ever, he regretted that he had not brought his sketchbook out with him with genuine intention, nor had Uncle Sheldon's Coronet to hand because he felt that he would far prefer to be a photographer than a little peep – if there was much difference between the two.

But oh dear! he thought because it was no longer a case of being undecided as to which one of the two he favoured; Ava, although she appeared to be somewhat softer than her sister in every regard, was also quite intimidating. It had become depressingly clear that he was out of his depth entirely; what had he been thinking? He would be returning home with his head in his hands. But just as he was about to do so with tremendous botheration, and with as much self-loathing, he heard the pub's front door creak open.

The young lady that emerged was quite extraordinary, and Oliver felt immediately enraptured by her while the other ladies rapidly paled into their surroundings. The colourifics of her outfit were eye-catching, the vermillion, claret, fuchsia, and deep greens, but her face – oh, her face – that pale, freckled round framed by an elegantly scissored blonde bob! Even from this distance, he could see that her piercing eyes were a rather intense powder blue. She had been looking straight at him from the moment she had stepped out onto the street; he could only suppose that she had spied his dashing self from the vantage point of an upstairs window and had rushed down to win him.

With Ava and Kitty following her gaze, all three were looking at him then – the point at which he very nearly turned and fled, but the sweetest of smiles broke out on the sirens' lips and he felt, quite simply, aflame. They then exchanged looks – a wordless exchange where each negotiated with the others over who would next have weight in her pocket; clearly, he would have had little say in the matter even if he could have found his voice. It quickly became apparent, however, that this goddess had won the bout anyway. It seemed likely that the other two would have understood that he was hers from the moment she had emerged anyway; there was a crackling of energy in the air between them that no one could have missed.

This prize-winner, who had won Oliver's rapture as well as his custom, was no more tarty-looking than her sisters; she was merely magnificent, transcending any such unkind description. Her glow – an incandescence that came from within – was ethereal somehow, although he quickly decided that 'celestial' was a more fitting description of her otherworldliness. He watched as she plucked a hand mirror from her pocket and checked herself in it; warm pools of light refracted pleasingly across her face.

All worries over how to proceed were quickly forgotten because there was a kindliness about her gaze, and a steadiness in her approach that kept him quite spellbound while somehow reassuring him that she would guide him through the entire transaction with ease; with his eyes fastened on her in awe, he merely awaited her command then – the bedazzled subject of an empress-queen.

Once she loomed closer, Oliver realised how tall she was, and he could see those intense powder blue eyes quite clearly, her faint freckles, and her sheeny blonde hair – the colour of straw, much like his own. She wore a vermillion-coloured felt bowler and an old wine-coloured graduation gown, which was cleverly repurposed for its flowing lines that billowed around her curves and was pinned with a rose fashioned from *citron vert* cloth. She also sported bottle green nylons while, perhaps most striking of all, her eyelids were painted seafoam green! While a little tattered and threadbare, her enterprising outfit, which looked to have been cobbled together from thrift store bargains and cast-offs, was somehow just magnificent; they were queenly robes all the same!

'H-hallo,' she said softly.

He could not quite catch her accent but knew instantly that she was a Johnny Foreigner; he quickly realised that this transaction could not be as wordless as it so easily could be with the townsmen in the alleys. Christ, how on earth can I sustain a conversation with this creature? he thought, feeling out of his depth already while also feeling, especially with her height, like an ant in the shadow of a giantess.

'Are you... okay?'

'S-sorry, I-I'm Oliver. What's your–'

'Simone,' she replied with a smile; her accent was, in fact, French.

Her scent was heavenly, too, and Oliver wondered if he should congratulate her on it; notes of lavender, rose, orange blossom, rosemary, and geranium wafted about them both. *Très bon* indeed! This aromatic fragrance was oddly familiar, however, and while lost in momentary déjà vu, he could almost hear those notes wafting about him; he could not account for the tune's familiarity, though.

'S-s-sorry... what was your name again?'

With his nerves as they were, he had forgotten already.

'Simone... Joséphine... Marianne aussi... W-whoever you want me to be.'

'Okay, I shall call you Simone, then, if that's alright?' he replied, having no idea what she had meant with all those names. 'Or would you prefer another?'

Simone merely laughed.

'I'm Oliver, by the way.'

She nodded.

'Would you... l-like to come i-inside... Oui?'

Ava and Kitty had taken leave of them and tactfully made their way inside already. Oliver looked up at the Queens Head, which, although ugly and dilapidated, was hardly the pigpen that he had imagined, but it still felt too foreboding.

'Oh, I-I c-couldn't.'

'Non? Then... y-you will like me to come to y-your... ehm... maison?'

'Ehm... is that agreeable?' he asked anxiously.

'Oui... but of c-course.'

And so they set off quietly, side by side. While walking between the tracks, by the time they had reached sight of the barrage balloon trailing in the distance, he felt pretty deflated himself, preferring to call the whole thing off if he could have. I really am quite the wretched article, he griped to himself. He was unable to think of anything of worth to say, nor was he able to even meet Simone's eye. Finally, after fifteen minutes or so of walking in complete silence, with his nervous glances met only by an agreeable nod of reassurance, he felt that he had to come up with something not too idiotic to say, or all would be lost –

'You are French?'

'Oui, mon chéri. Parlez-vous français?'

'Non... afraid not.'

Oliver dared to think for a moment that he might try to impress her with the moderate amount of French that he had learned from his mother's books – say 'enchanté' or some such thing, but he feared that he would sound far too stilted if he did. What on earth is she doing here, in wretched Greenthorne anyway? he had to wonder. It seemed so incongruous while all he had wanted was some uncomplicated slap and tickle with a subhuman, if he were being truly honest with himself. Yet here he was trying to converse with a woman who was clearly brighter than a penny, and who, despite being impoverished, had the nerve to be dauntingly courtly and refined seeming, just like his darned mother had done. Oliver despaired; why is my life always so complicated? he thought peevishly, then he found himself feeling that perhaps she should explain herself –

'Why Greenthorne, I mean of all places?' he snapped.

'I m-married an Englishman. A usine... non... a f-factory man... He brings me here.'

'A factory worker?' he asked with his voice shooting up in incredulity; it seemed so unlikely, and he just could not imagine anyone, let alone a factory worker, snagging her, much less bringing her to ghastly old Greenthorne.

'Non... a boss.'

'Oh... well, why aren't you with him?'

She shrugged airily, 'I k-know not where he... be.'

'I'm sorry.'

'Nothing to be sorry a-about,' was her genuinely nonchalant reply; again, though, Oliver could only nod and otherwise find no response. His sudden sympathy for her had nipped his former angst in the bud, at least. After a long, untimely pause, Simone finally offered him a little more detail –

'He was... mal... non... a bad man... Treated me bad, just as one of his workers. Got rich working employees to the bone. Cutting... how you say? Cutting corners... then runs away with all the... ehm... money... yes?'

'I'm sorry to hear that.'

'Nothing to be sorry about,' she said with decision.

Feeling abruptly perturbed by the possibility that this young lady was lowering herself out of financial desperation, Oliver wondered if he might be accused of aiding and abetting her crimes against herself if they carried on with this business; it might take him far beyond the threshold of how much depravity he was comfortable with – which he supposed was saying something. He then realised that he had thoughtlessly assumed, after seeing Kitty in the Oddfellows, that this game was always a jolly old caper; now, however, he found himself feeling rather concerned for himself and for all three of the sirens too. But then, thinking of the confidence that all three were armed with and Simone's peacefulness in particular, he wondered if he was getting too carried away with his worries. Why, oh why can I not just relax and enjoy life, like Grahame and Bert? he then had to wonder, yet he still had to ask –

'Are you new to this game, then?'

He regretted opening his big mouth instantly; she did not appear to be offended if she had understood, though. He had heard euphemisms such as 'game', 'brass', 'knee-trembler', 'spreadeagled', and 'shady-lady' while eavesdropping in the Oddfellows, and they rolled off the tips of Bert and Grahame's tongues with regularity and ease. With second thought, then, it seemed a safe assumption that the sirens were used to hearing such commonplace descriptions of themselves and of the services they offered – the parlance of the backstreet industries.

'G-game? Sorry?'

'Are you new to this... ehm... business?'

'Non... ehm... no.'

Her stilted reply allayed his fears, at least.

'I see... well...'

He could not think what to say except –

'I'm sorry it's so far.'

This all feels too surreal, Oliver thought because he knew that he was certainly under her spell, but what kind of spell was it? It did not seem like the sexy sort of enchantment that a comely wench would conjure, and it felt like something of a much higher order; Simone seemed to be a little too angelical for what he had in mind. It was not what he had hoped for, which he had come to realise might be at the expense of her virtue anyway; he could not even imagine her naked, and, in fact, it was beginning to feel wrong to even dare to.

Perhaps I should just take her for a drink instead, then? he wondered; to talk over her problems... but then... perhaps that isn't the done thing in this 'game' and risks more offence to her? But he then realised that, either way, even if she did have worries to discuss, he had not exactly put her at ease enough to open up to him; it was another regrettable quandary for which he had no answers nor means of inquiry, which only added to his growing sense of wretchedness.

Oliver desperately searched for a way to calm himself, but as the extent to which he was out of his depth dawned on him, he felt his heart sinking; this folly already seemed to be the harshest of reminders that women were quite beyond his understanding, and as they passed that discarded pram and the child's doll lying in the tramway, he felt chilled by the heartlessness of the little madam that had tired of playing mother and had left her child to perish.

'A-are you okay?' Simone asked, clutching his shoulder.

Oliver had not imagined the extent to which his agitation was showing.

'I'm sorry.'

'Relax... I am s-shy too, en tous cas... I enjoy walking. Exercise, non? I'll sing you a chanson... a... ahem... a song to re-relax you... écoutez-moi... listen, okay?'

But Oliver could only wonder that she did not enjoy walking with him at all and was merely being polite; the French were revealed to be far more civilised than he had been led to believe.

The ditty that she came out with was a gentle-sounding siren's song that soothed him greatly while she took his hand, which surprised him a little, and swung it in hers as they continued down the tracks. She threw him a coy smile then, and he, without too much difficulty, managed to return the gesture, surprisingly. Out of nowhere, Simone radiated an eroticism that caught him quite by surprise; feeling far more at ease then, thanks to the accord and flirtatiousness that they had suddenly stumbled upon, he felt reassured that nothing could jeopardise the risqué delights that they had to look forward to. An unexpected confidence swelled inside him, a sense of fun even; he smiled again because, for him, they had both become akin to the most darling of children, on their gay way to a picnic in a magical forest. Or perhaps, more aptly, they had become akin to enfants terribles – his recall of French was improving now that he had relaxed – ready to raise merry hell in Gay Paree while fireworks of red, white, and blue bloomed above them. Since she was smiling, too, his gay mood seemed to be taking her over; he would not have been at all surprised if they had both begun skipping then. But just as he was about to clutch her hand tighter in preparation for such frivolity, he, without warning, felt a tingling sensation between his shoulder blades; it was that familiar eyes-staring-into-the-back-of-you feeling that he knew all too well from the crossway, the alleys, the heath, and other such places. He thus found himself looking over his shoulder, for fear that his mother was following him once again.

The wide expanse of the derelict, littered tramway seemed to be empty, although the ambient heat haze kept all its details quivering infinitely, which only made it harder, as it had done all summer, for Oliver to ascertain whether Marion's hazy figure was lurking somewhere behind them. Feeling too unsure, his heart sank; the whimsy Simone had whipped up, bordering on the hysterical and rivalling the morning's enthusiasm, was fading fast. All he could then hope of Simone was that this sorceress had other spells up her claret-coloured sleeves.

Sensing his downwardly spiralling mood, Simone gripped his hand even tighter, hummed louder, and quickened their pace. It felt as if he were being frogmarched by the loveliest sergeant major in all the known universe; while somewhat endearing, it felt infinitely, infinitely awkward.

I simply must get a grip, Oliver thought. If Marion was following them, then he would simply have to outright ignore her. Aptly enough, like mother like son, his pig-headedness won the moment – focusing on the task at hand, a sense of determination rose in him as he pulled himself together. He would see this venture through, whatever the result; naturally, however, he would aim for no other outcome than to rouse Simone's passions. The fat lady has yet to sing, he reminded himself while also remembering how handsome he was – surely half the battle already. Furthermore, he had heard Bert and Grahame describe the act itself with such clarity: 'In-out, in-out, like a fiddler's elbow', apparently. Not too difficult, surely! he told himself.

Forcing a smile for her, he began to search for lively topics of conversation; he thought it best to just keep quiet until he had armed himself with a long list. It seemed a pity, however, that she had given up humming her little ditty in the interim and looked rather disheartened herself. He supposed that it was his turn, in that case, to provide the musical accompaniment that had made things feel so convivial between them only moments prior; he found himself humming the only tune he could think of again, and without the greatest of tunefulness, admittedly. He still felt enormous gratitude to little Wally Shanks, however, who had taught him the ditty.

Ah, little Wally... what a gem! Oliver thought as he hummed Wally's song; he had to smirk, too, when remembering how his childhood chum had been so insistent upon his mother's tears that he had crapped himself with unfailing regularity, and she had had to keep a hanky tucked in her sleeve at all times. He certainly had not been afraid of women and had always known how to assert himself with them! Oliver then felt assured that wherever grown-up Wally Shanks was in the world, he would definitely be in more command of his life than he himself was of his own.

Simone laughed at his song, at least, which surely was a new beginning! Her newly improved spirits did not last long, though, because the ditty quickly appeared to lose its novelty for her. He then became convinced that she had not only tired of it, but had tired of him in general; with his new mandate of determination, he could only view this as another challenge, however, to be heaped on a pile with all the others towering over him.

While casting her yet another nervous glance, he quickly felt daunted by the intellect that she so clearly brimmed with, so he mentally tore up that list of stimulating conversation points that he had been working on – he did not have anything written on it yet anyway – and he threw it to the dogs that he felt snapping at his heels. The problem was that, with the greatest of respect to Kitty Kat, Simone was not the sort of cheerfully dim floozy that one might expect of Bert and Grahame.

Then to his great relief, Oliver heard her humming again, but her tune had a different sort of tone; it seemed likely that its purpose was to sooth her, rather than to cheer him, as she walked beside him, looking bored beyond belief and keeping her gaze downcast. Well, at least she has some activity with which to console herself and while away the long journey ahead, he thought; he had only this to console himself with by then because she had clearly had enough of him altogether.

Back at the old schoolhouse finally, and while turning the corner onto Middle Row, Oliver remembered the manner in which he lived and the shambles that awaited them; he had not thought that it would matter that much because he had all too conveniently assumed Kitty to be a rare exception, and the grubby harlot whom he had expected to snare that morning would not have cared.

'It really isn't that far now, I promise you.'

By the time they reached the horse hospital finally, the silence that lingered between them became even more intolerable, and the echo of their footsteps on the cobbles sounded suitably grating.

Utter Rhubarb

Oliver appointed himself as his least favourite person in the world as he rushed down the hall to tidy his bedroom; while doing so, he tried to reassure himself that the Queens Head had been no palace either because oh, the shame that had indeed washed over him the moment that they had passed the horse hospital's threshold!

He found himself wishing that he had a motor car again because the hike home had felt excruciating; for the greater duration, each new step had seemed to bring them no closer to their destination. He could only imagine that time must have intentionally slowed itself down for that very purpose, and to create a fertile breeding ground for his anxieties to flourish. He still wished that he had accosted Uncle Sheldon and secured him in Ferndale House's damp cellar, stolen the Bentley, and whisked his new fair lady off there; its charm might have compensated her for his utter uselessness thus far, he thought while looking around at his abode with horrified amazement, as if seeing it for the first time.

Heaving open the bedroom window, Oliver allowed new air to circulate for the first time that summer while wiping the sweat from his brow. Models and toys that were not strung from the ceiling or nailed to the walls and rafters were thrown into a tea chest, along with the others that he clung onto, and kicked into the corner of the room; regrettably, he had no time to deal with the remaining ones. While wondering for a moment if he should snatch down Big Sis, he guessed that it was unlikely that Simone would object to her; still, except for Big Sis, it was a boy's room and not that of a man, which felt mortifying.

'Too bloody late now,' he grumbled because it could only be a matter of just getting on with things; in fact, he simply could not wait for the whole ill-considered affair to be over and done with, so that he could get on with the shame and remorse that would naturally follow, once he had found the energy for it all – and to suffer his mother's displeasure, of course – for her to fracture another finger, perhaps.

It seemed unforgivable to have left Simone unattended in his outrageously ramshackle living room after dashing in panic to freshen and tidy the setting of their pending transaction. Then he felt even more of a louse upon realising that he had forgotten to even offer her a seat; he felt that he should have switched on the wireless, at least, which may have helped with the strained atmosphere. But without offering refreshment or explanation, he had just left her. However, he then made an educated guess that, with her nervous glances at the fermented tea with its scrim of mould, the spoilt food rotting on his living room table, and the swarming blue bottles that lay their eggs there, all of which had greeted their arrival with fetid aromas, Simone probably would not have felt particularly inclined even if she had felt peckish. That aside, she had been a vision of straw yellow, wine red, and deep fuchsia against the cadmium green of that living room – cutting an arresting figure that he presently felt more inclined to paint than undress.

While tiptoeing back down the hall, his nerves threatened to render him rigid.

'Qui est ce bel homme? Non... W-who's this handsome man?' he heard her call out just as he reached the living room door's aperture, but much to his shock and dismay, it was not Simone that he found upon turning into the living room, but his mother standing before the mantel while the lymph froze in his glands! Stood motionless, Marion peered down at his father's portrait, clutching its tortoiseshell frame rigidly, with her eyes wet and her shoulders slumped.

'It looks like Daddy'll be gone far longer than we thought,' she said weakly. How ponderously tall she is, Oliver thought of her loftiness while feeling equally struck by her fragility because she was usually quite formidable looking with her height, her striking looks, the luminosity of her platinum blonde hair, and her piercing green eyes especially. But the sum that these characteristics usually added up to fell short because, with the terrible news she had just received, she looked brittle and weakened – utterly defeated, in fact, like a wounded bird without use of its wing.

'Dead... Gone... I just can't believe it,' she whimpered. But then something undetermined flashed across his vision and quickly paled, so that once he had blinked and clarity had returned, he found that it was Simone standing there again – same hair, same height, but otherwise quite different, examining the portrait that she had plucked from the mantel.

While awaiting the answer to her inquiry, he saw her expression shift as it dawned on her that the question may have been too intrusive. Realising that he must appear visibly shaken, he felt too frozen to offer her any reassurance while she returned his father to his spot on the mantel, brushed her faux pas quickly aside, and then pressed on with her usual tenacity; turning then and fixing on him, Simone stepped a little closer while unbuttoning the bodice of her dress and allowing it to slip just a little, revealing her smooth, freckled shoulders.

'Don't look so worried, mon chéri.'

While coughing loudly because a lump had formed in his throat, Oliver wondered if he might pass out as she floated towards him. Through the diminishing interference that still crackled in his ear canals and fogged his vision, he had a vague sense that Simone was already leading him along the hall towards his bedroom's open door, but on passing the door to Marion's bedroom, that electrical hiss resurged while waves of electricity washed over his skin, tugging at the fine hairs on his arms and neck, causing them to stiffen and bristle – tugging them, and him, towards her door.

***

Oliver watched Simone smoking from the corner of his eye. She, at least, seemed unperturbed by the awkwardness of the transaction that was blessedly over and done with, and she also did not seem as drained as he felt by it, and by the considerable legwork required to get to it in the first place. He, at least, felt thankful to her that her only complaint had been that it had been too hot for her indoors because no breeze whatsoever came through that newly unlatched window on such a murderously muggy evening; this conundrum had found him scampering around in his underwear, like a frenzied handmaiden searching for a solution to her plight, just before 'getting down to business', as he had heard they call it in the trade. He had thankfully found and fetched the electric fan that he knew was buried in the living room somewhere; its whirring blades still fanned the stagnant evening air and whipped her cigarette smoke into a fierce frenzy.

With hindsight, he realised that Simone could not have been any more considerate, and she had been awfully sweet; she had managed to fill the wastelands following the fiasco of their so-called coition with her second surprisingly authentic-seeming performance of the day. It had been a monologue, her second performance, littered with many long pauses – excruciatingly long if he were being brutally honest, yet it was a thought she did not deserve – while searching for the correct English verbs, adjectives, nouns, and such to adequately convey just how much she admired his toys; that she quite understood; that she really did get it; that she did – really; that she had her own collection of porcelain *poupées* held in storage in some far-flung attic somewhere; that she intended to have them sent the very moment that she could put down roots; that he should never, under any circumstances, get rid of any of his; that he should always have them on display *parce que* everyone should, according to her design for life, collect and play with dolls and toys; that if they did, everyone would be far happier for it; and that the world would generally be a better place for it; rah, rah, rah... All utter rhubarb, obviously, but spoken with good intention: to make him feel less ashamed of himself. He still had to award her points for trying because it seemed mean-spirited not to do so; however, dare he admit it, he felt equally relieved that this performance was over too.

Having piped down and busied her mouth with smoking and humming her little tune instead, he enjoyed listening to Simone's lullaby while admiring her striking profile. Her eyes were Tiffany blue then; he knew that, in truth, the long-standing game of naming colour shades with expressive appellations was a form of poetic play, more than anything; there was only so much truth in what the eye perceives at any given moment, after all. Lighting created variance; when it came to people, however, this variance seemed greater for some folks more than for others. It then dawned on him that this might be because emotions lend their own colouring; accordingly, her eye shadow then appeared to be lime green. She was rather zesty, after all. The *café au lait* freckles on her *décolletage* looked wonderful against the shimmery chocolate brown satin of the bodice that she had already slipped back into so gracefully; all in all, then, if he had had his way with Marion and painted his own walls fairytale faun brown after all, the sight of her reclining on his bed would have been utterly exceptional. Although the room was already darkening, the evening's sunlight, tempered by the thick scrim of pigeon droppings on his windowpane, dappled them both and the room about them with warm drifts of orangey light; yes, the visual feast of form and colour before him would have been pitch and picture perfect – not that it was far off in that moment!

While feeling quite ridiculous for becoming so emotionally overwrought during the eternity that it had taken to walk home together, Oliver realised that he had shot himself to pieces with worries that, as it turned out, had no basis. The growing animosity towards him that he had suspected of Simone in her silence had turned out to be a misreading. It had merely been a challenge for her, their long hike in what had felt like sub-Saharan temperatures – something that he now realised he should have been upfront about. He had feared, though, that the distance that they would have to trek would have put her off the moment that he had realised the Queens Head was a no go; as soon as they had crossed his threshold, however, and she had splashed her face with water, she had been as sweet as strawberry *bonbons*.

How could her husband have left this kind, beautiful, and intelligent *femme*? he had to wonder; had he been in his right mind? Oh, yes... he remembered then... something about him being a complete cad and then scarpering. Pity for her, he thought; but, then, perhaps not... She had an air of freedom and liberation about her that could be palpably felt.

'So why did you choose this... life?' he ventured timidly while feeling that his choice of words was as dismal and dangerous as ever.

'I could n-not... be, how you say it... be... exploitée... by the... bourgeoisie,' she explained. 'In the... er... usine... non, f-factory... I became... very sad. I felt more ehm... e-exploited in my body as un travailleur.'

'I see.'

'When a woman is abandoned in a foreign land... with no work available... no work that's r-reasonable... what can she do?'

Oliver turned to her, asking –

'Who abandoned you?'

Simone leaned in and whispered –

'I told you... some... étincelle brillante... so... ehm... vaniteux that he thinks he may have o-others... ehm... to be bought, sold, screwed or... w-worked to d-death.'

'I'm sorry,' he said, while wanting to pat her cheek, although he felt that he better not. 'How could someone do that to you?'

'No loss... if one know him un... s-shown... as an enfoiré.'

'He sounds like quite the rascal. Did he get away with it all, then?'

'They not call him bright spark for nothing, mon chéri.'

He nodded. She seemed so wise, so deep in her thoughts – big thoughts – as if she could see the world and its problems in aerial view while exhaling those voluminous clouds of cigarette smoke that funnelled and swirled endlessly above them; he then found himself scanning those bluish-grey garlands for any symbolic clues – a secret communiqué that she might imbue him with on the subject of how he might have been a proficient lover. But the smoke only formed ugly phantom faces that glowered at him – ridiculing him for his woeful cocksmanship, as well as for the scrawniness of his body, which she could so easily have crushed. Luckily, however, Simone had been very coolheaded about his utter uselessness; she still appeared to be so unperturbed, in fact, that it was another reason he had just about managed to remain at her side and not run tearing down the hall with the intention of head-butting the living room wall.

After glancing up at Big Sis, however, he found himself realising that the truth of the matter, if he were being unusually honest with himself, was that he knew this was the first and the last time he would ever have a *femme*, let alone such a beauty, in bed with him; what fellow in his right mind would leave her side, he had to ask himself while knowing full well that most chaps would not, even if the blankets were on fire. She looked like a movie star; it made no sense that she was stuck in ghastly old Greenthorne when Hollywood casting directors would have snapped her up the very second that they had clapped eyes on her, without realising that they had missed out on a golden opportunity because the casting couch would hardly have been a deterrent to her. She was demonstrably good at acting too; she was so good, in fact, that their latest starlet would have been out on her ear the moment that she had dipped her finely polished toe in the Pacific Ocean – of all this he had no doubt whatsoever.

While admiring her still from the corner of his eye, Simone looked pleasantly adrift in her seas of wisdom as she hummed her melody, and he noted that it appeared to be much like meditative chanting while she returned those wispy wreathes of smoke to the air. Again, she looked utterly divine, straight out of *Aladdin and his Magical Lamp* or *Baghdad Mystery* now that she sported a jade-coloured satiny turban that she had slipped on to keep the smoke from her hair. Oliver then realised that he had managed to concoct a situation that would have him beating his breast for the rest of his life – to have bedded a creature that was to die for and to have made such a pig's ear of ravishing her.

He thought of her breasts then: those curious appendages rising and falling before him only minutes prior. They had felt somewhat strange – not unpleasant in the least but peculiar all the same. He thought of his own body next; despite his usual self-satisfaction with his appearance, his confidence had waned upon undressing. He had felt too exposed asudden, with his legs appearing much like spindleshanks again while also feeling too spindly of arm, with elbows so sharp that he had feared he might do her injury. Her sex remained a mystery still; somehow, he had not even seen that mysterious opening that, without the precautions that he hoped she had taken, was where all life begins. He was not even sure if his member had managed to find its way inside her either, while he also began to fret over whether it had even become sufficiently enlarged enough to do so in the first place. It was not that he found her unappealing because she was quite the revelation when naked. But it was as if his spirit had retreated to the far corner of the room, and had watched with terrified amazement his lank body mechanically going through the motions of what he had assumed screwing should be. All the while, he had felt completely detached and unable to feel anything; it had felt quite bizarre, and it had all been rather awful to be frank. What he then found himself wondering was: if he had asked Simone to furnish him with a 'tuppence', a 'knee-trembler', or had requested to be 'spreadeagled', whatever those things meant, would things have gone any better for him?

Meanwhile, what barely lingered in Oliver's mind, since he had unwittingly become fairly adept at despatching the memory of Marion's visitations back into his subconscious each time that they occurred, was that while his disembodied spirit had sat watching his body do Simone an enormous disservice, he had also been assaulted by sporadic flashes of his mother's visitation by the mantel, accompanied by rasps of white noise. He had become painfully aware that he was displeasing both women simultaneously.

It had seemed likely – obvious, in fact – that they were crocodile tears that Marion had shed. He had sensed his mother's game alright: it had all been a pathetic, jealous act to make him feel sorry for her and to compete with Simone for his affections. At that juncture, it had seemed the lesser of two difficulties to ignore Marion's theatrics rather than get rid of Simone; it would hardly have been fair to do so anyway because

Simone was doing such a gallant job of pretending to jockey him to the imaginary finish line.

Yes, Simone's virtuosity seemed boundless to Oliver when thinking back. Sensing his unease, she had drawn on all her tact and professionalism to enact the first act's performance: one that played out the idea that all was going well and was quite satisfactory for them both. Despite his disembodiment and Marion's interference, his body had just about managed to play along. Then, just as now, he had felt entirely in her debt because he had understood her selfless motives; she had obviously realised that it would have been even harder on him to have called time and stopped altogether – to live with a sense of even greater failure. Finally, she had performed the moment of completion convincingly and had somehow managed to convey the sense that there had been a mutual explosion of sorts, ending it with a sigh of mock satisfaction. Then she had gently rolled off of him while the frosted mints, which had found their way into the blankets the night before, had scattered about them.

'I'm sorry.'

'Nothing to be s-sorry about, mon chéri... It was nice... Grande plaisir for me... Très bon!'

'It's just that... you reminded me of someone...'

She appeared to be genuinely interested.

'... someone I was trying to forget.'

'Ah... mais... but a b-broken heart will... how you say... fix?'

'Oh, it's nothing like that!'

'Well... there is time, if you... p-prefer to talk, peut-être? To help you... for-forget?' she said after consulting her wristwatch, but for Oliver, straight off, the idea of forgetting provoked a rather guilty feeling.

'I don't want to forget! Well, I only wanted to for a moment or two, really... I'll still pay you.'

'Oui, b-but of course,' Simone said as she clutched his shoulder to manoeuvre her way out of bed. Oliver stared hard at the floor because it felt strangely inappropriate to watch her dress. This little peep could not quite help himself, however; out of the corner of his eye, he watched how she managed to dress quite gracefully, keeping her smouldering cigarette poised between her lips the entire time. I like the style of you, he thought.

'You're very pretty,' he said, feeling that he had better offer her some reassurance of her attractiveness, in case he had worn away at her confidence, then he immediately felt ridiculous for doing so. They both knew that the problem was not hers, but his; she hardly needed reminding that she had nothing to worry about. Simone's lack of response confirmed that she was indeed quite sure of herself, and that the whole thing had blown over her like sand over a dune, just as his efforts had – he had felt like sand blowing over a dune too.

'Cinq... ehm... five pounds... oui? As we said.'

Oliver handed over most of his remaining allowance in cumbersome amounts of clunky change, and without resenting her the money one bit; he found himself feeling a little uneasy at how little was left, however. Perhaps I should just say 'To hell with it!' and give her the lot, then? he wondered; as compensation for my inadequacy and the terribly long journey home ahead of her. Or would that make things even more awkward between us both? he also queried while hating the world more than ever for its densely complex social mores.

'I-I let myself out, Oliver... It was nice to meet you.'

He found himself merely nodding while realising that the proper etiquette would have been to get up and kiss her hand, doff his chapeau to her, or some such thing; he remained under the bed covers instead, preferring to lazily berate himself for his bad manners. Unperturbed as ever, Simone came closer and cheerfully ruffled his hair, putting him in mind of a spritely grandmother doting on her freckle-faced grandson.

'Doux et beau!' she cried with a smile and a wink, then she turned and paraded out of the room, leaving a wispy trail of blueish smoke wafting behind her. Oliver listened to Simone pass the threshold and clatter down the stairwell outside, then he sighed deeply – partly with relief, partly with sadness, and wholly with despair.

'Adieu,' she called up from the cobbled yard, with her voice echoing peculiarly around it; he still felt too stunned by his own discourtesy to call out a reply, however. He knew that he had absolutely no excuse for not being a gentleman and showing her out, but despite her best efforts to pretend otherwise, in arguing his case he would say that it had all been too disastrous and humiliating to have any grace left with which to perform the usual social niceties. She had left her lipstick and hand mirror on his bedside cabinet, and he had not even called after her; he had just let her go without it while not knowing whether to pine, sigh, or cry.

While smacking himself forcibly in the chops, Oliver noticed that a rather ripe body smell hung in the air, which seemed even more regrettable – an odour that he suspected he was more to blame for than she was. Striking up yet another gasper, he then crammed his mouth with barley sugars; they helped take the ghastly taste of his fags away, at least.

Once he had heard her footsteps on the cobbles fade to nothingness, he pulled on his underpants and stomped back into the living room, ready to tend to his regret and self-hatred. The cigarette that he had lit made him feel light-headed and queasy, so he stubbed it out immediately. Night had finally enwrapped Greenthorne, so he switched on all the dreary, cigarette smoke-stained lamps that were once so golden, and he shooed away the moths eating them. He unscrewed a bottle of Murray's finest and gulped it down, nearly choking as he did so.

Abruptly, Oliver was reminded why he had, for the most part, forced women out of his mind; his forays into their territory had always been utterly disastrous! Thinking then of his dear old Abby, he again felt the resulting heartache that had followed once the romantic love that he had professed for her at the tender age of eleven had propelled her into the arms of another boy, Johno Webster. How he wished that he had had the gumption and strength to have smashed that boy's sodding head in! This blockheaded twit that she had favoured had been a hardy, sporty lad, but he was hardly the brightest spark and was nowhere near as well-mannered as Oliver. Oliver had realised that Marion had been correct all along, though: he was not at all what women wanted. His mother had been hugely relieved, having never approved of this sudden infatuation with Abby anyway. But how he wished he had kept his unreciprocated feelings to himself because he had thoroughly demolished their bond by declaring them; they had lost touch with each other from that point on, leaving him with only his mother.

'Mother!' he gasped, followed by a full-bodied jolt of delayed trauma. How could he have forgotten her visitation by the mantel? All thoughts of Abby and Simone were instantly blot out as Marion leapt back into his mind; right away, he could hardly pretend that her lament had been anything other than painfully authentic.

She had looked so corporeal too; wearing her favourite green gingham frock with her shoulders slumped and her eyes so wet, she had been such a pitiful sight! The past suddenly shocked Oliver – how could I have forgotten the weight of its sadness, he demanded of himself while feeling at rather a loss as to how he could not have retained some sense of the heartbreak that was perhaps the primary ingredient in her broth of bitterness.

Additionally, it had seemed somewhat unprecedented to him because, as solid as she had appeared, Marion had seemed utterly devoid of spirit, and it had always been the other way around – even more so since she had passed away. It was how utterly bereft that she had looked which had shocked him and not the visitation itself because he was so used to still having her around much of the time; her face had been empty of the derision that he had spent his adolescence marinated in, and it did not at all inspire the usual shame and self-hatred that engulfed him when she did appear. This baffled him somewhat, and it also seemed unprecedented, considering all that was about to transpire at the end of the hall.

While the evening wore on and the world outside melted into hues of pink and orange, the living room had become a muddied-looking quagmire with this change of light. Greenthorne sounded even more muted than usual – virtual silence, in fact, except for the echo of the ticking mantel clock. Meanwhile, Oliver could still not stop glancing at the mantel where his mother's body had strangely supplanted Simone's only an hour or so before.

His father's portrait normally took centre stage on that mantelpiece, but now that Simone had meddled with the arrangement, another photograph, usually tucked behind it, had become visible. This prodded a recollection of when, in a rare moment of apparent generosity towards its staff, Cranford Electric's management had come up with the bright idea to hold a beauty pageant: a competition among the female workforces. This, of course, was later revealed to be a sly promotional initiative timed to coincide with a prototype portrait camera that they were bringing to market; it had been the machination of some higher-up, perhaps even Edwin Cranford, the top brass himself.

The cheerfully impoverished-looking women in the photographic record had assembled cast-offs and hand-me-downs, most of which may well have belonged to their mothers originally, to assemble threadbare outfits that looked a little contrived and dowdy to be frank; they were lovable all the same, though. 'The Dishwater Dollies of Greenthorne', Oliver called them but meant it affectionately. Olive Solby, with her hair all done up in a twist, had won the title for that first and only year – the folly was never repeated; she was duly crowned 'Miss Cranford Electric'. Looking at Olive, it seemed surprising how old she had looked on passing the day before because the beauty that stood before him in the photograph was only seven or perhaps eight years younger. Alec Solby, the works foreman, stood stage right and looked on in wonder at his wife, who was draped in her satin sash while clutching her prize: her very own Cranford Tempograph alarm clock, with which she looked dutifully thrilled. In the photograph's periphery was his mother, of course, a rather grumpy and unenthused-looking runner-up. Marion had still been quite beautiful then, even though the drudgery of working at Cranford Electric and her resulting debility had already begun to sully that beauty a little. For Oliver, Olive's win had always exemplified that beauty is not entirely skin deep, however, and that it stems from character as much as appearance. Had she not felt so wearied, he knew that his mother would have looked even more ungracious for having not won outright and claimed the title for herself; while the other women laughed and smiled at each other, Marion looked straight through the lens with a gaze that was broody and intense.

'Goddamn your eyes!' he barked because it was hard to maintain this newfound sympathy for her while she eyeballed him in such a manner. When casting his own eyes away from her, he realised that he could no longer overlook things that he was previously able to ignore. The living room was entirely rendered in painfully sharp detail, and he could no longer tune out his mother's belongings in particular: her faux mother-of-pearl vanity set – green of course; her hairbrush, still matted with mounds of her ever loosening and greying hair; rose-tinted glass jars of face cream with which she had tried to smooth away her lines; and that other pile of empty liquor bottles that was piled in the corner of the room – Marion had also become one of Murray Pierce's best customers towards her end. He was no longer sure which of those empty bottles had been his or hers. Empty cartons of her slimline cigarettes also littered the floorboards, as did the poetry, fiction, and French language books that she had never returned to the library; for someone so busy policing his own conduct while acting as if she was perfectly attuned to the workings of an orderly and civil society, she could act with surprising illegality sometimes! Travel guides to Borseau and Paris, that she had also effectively stolen from Greenthorne's library, were also scattered about, but she had never managed to visit either place, sadly; these were some of the books of 'hers' that he had read himself, and with the same wistfulness. Her shawl had become little more than a heap of tangled woollen fibres on the floor – the one he had dutifully placed over her before tottering off to bed to read adventure, spy, and war stories, then drifting off and dreaming of flying on his late father's wings.

Marion's walking stick still leant against the cabinet, and it still seemed to point to the first aid tin left open upon its top. This sorry sight sparked an awful recollection of one of her frequent nosebleeds.

'Go back outside Oliver... I'm fine. It'll stop in a minute.'

But she had not seemed fine at all; her eyes had been quite wide and jittery, in fact, while she had tried to brush it all aside, and it had never stopped, not really. Although Sheldon had sent her for a private consultation in the hope that it would quash her hypochondriasis and relieve any burden put upon him by result, and even though Doctor Dryden had insisted that her nosebleeds and such were little to fret over, they, along with her aches, her migraines, her heart flutters, and her bleeding nose and gums, had served only to pillar her belief that something had still been terribly wrong with her – and that all doctors were utterly incompetent. All this worry had peaked around the time Cranford had shut up shop, and she had been laid off along with all the other dial painters; from that point on, Oliver had lost count of how many times he had been sent to purchase liquor from Murray Pierce on her behalf, how many cigarettes she had smoked, and how many times she had found cause to scold him for reasons that made little sense to him. Her rage had exponentially intensified, and as numerous new and admittedly rather vague symptoms had appeared, her frame had appeared to crumble along with her coherence.

Before long, all of his mother's essentials had been kept within clawing distance of the settee, where she had eventually taken permanent residence; throned there on its leathery folds and crowned with wisps of cigarette smoke, she had grown greyer and more brittle looking by the day while she had cursed, drank, and smoked innumerable cigarettes, or 'coffin nails' as Nurse Cruikshank, the district nurse, had later called them. Her hair, that had once appeared platinum, flaxen, or like straw in a summer meadow, depending upon the light, had been quite grey by then too; she had also looked a little yellow due to her alcoholism. The mound of settee cushions still bore the imprints of her increasingly crumpled body; 'bent like a broken hairpin,' Cruikshank had said. Meanwhile, the bond between Oliver and Marion had become similarly askew.

He could suddenly picture, and with painful clarity, the final act – the time when Marion had become so resigned to her fate that she had practically lived on that settee, sleeping there also. It seemed unsurprising in retrospect, given her frail, ghoulish figure, so gaunt in its knotted appearance, that she would soon die there too. He felt that he dare not look at the settee then, for fear that she might appear there also, staring at him in shock as she replayed her final few minutes for him – those distressing moments wherein her heart had finally failed, and her eyes had rolled back in their sockets while the searing pain had shot down her left arm. With his gaze downcast, fearing that he would become unglued if she was preparing to re-enact that terrible spectacle for him, he lit another coffin nail and clouds of grey smoke fogged the air about him; his chest tightened because the room was increasingly perfused with a strong-smelling miasma. Silence once again, except for the mantel clock's ticking and that faint flutter of hornets and hawk moths against the tattered shades while he inhaled his smoke's savourless vapour.

'So, that's how things were at the very end... How could I have forgotten?' Oliver mumbled contritely to himself while remembering that perhaps the most troubling aspect of it all was that the same virtual silence had permeated what turned out to be their last days, hours, and minutes together. It then came to mind that by that point in time, he had had no idea what to say to her, or even think of her, since he had no longer had any idea what his bottle-brandishing, perpetually drunk mother had thought of him once she had lost the will to live, let alone speak. The heart attack had been about to pounce and despatch them both from all her misery – almost an act of mercy, dare he even think it – and he would never know, or be able to hazard the slightest guess, whether, in her final moments, Marion's feelings towards him had softened at all. The last time she had had anything to say, she had been a wailing banshee full of pure spite. One senseless row had followed another; by then he had spent too many years drowning in her disapproval, to the point that he had become convinced that her sentiments towards him had become unbending.

Did I really drive her to madness with my bad behaviour? Oliver occasionally asked of himself and found himself asking again. It hardly seemed likely, although he sometimes became susceptible enough to the argument to wonder if it were possible that he had, and then to despise himself for it. More often, however, he cursed himself for having believed her, for having allowed her to trick him into remorse – as if he had somehow been to blame for her fate! What a nonsense! Other times, if she had truly been diseased after all, then he found himself hating the mysterious malady that had perplexed the doctors, and he hated her just as much for having succumbed to it in the first place. What on earth had happened to that grit... her wilfulness? he often wondered when thinking along such lines. Mainly, however, he had come to resent his mother deeply for having become so embittered by everything, and particularly for her drinking, perhaps unfairly because he had since fallen in love with the bottle as much as she had. Thinking of her time in the infirmary, was it any wonder that she had had such an awful clinical presentation when she had drunk so much? he found himself asking. Yes, on some level he dared to suspect that Sheldon was right: the hypochondriac had simply drunk as well as willed herself to death while blaming some imaginary illness for her demise so that she did not have to take any responsibility for giving up on life, on herself, and on him. She had simply thrown her hands in the air and then around his neck, metaphorically speaking; so, all this animosity had stewed wordlessly between them as her body had weakened, her heart had finally shuddered to a stop, and her already dimmed light had finally gone dark.

As if all that was not enough, while seemingly glued to his seat and lost in these quibbling thoughts, he then became haplessly assaulted by starkly lucid flashbacks of the start of her unravelling also; they were homespun and densely woven – a racing kaleidoscope of impressions in his mind's eye. A toy tin plane stalls in mid-air, dives, and then plummets to the floorboards while its pilot, poor young Oliver, unwitting to its unfortunate symbolism, yelps as her fist meets his ear. Toytown on Children's Hour with a drunken Marion snoring so loudly that he could barely hear a bloody word. Sloshed pea soup accompanied by screams of reproach and knuckles rapped – all cringeworthy vignettes from the two-man show that they had played out together to an increasingly empty feeling theatre.

All this raced through his mind while all too familiar chemical and metallic smells drifted about him. The air's static charge tugged once again at the downy tufts of hair on his neck and forearms as he began to suspect that his mother was hovering behind him then, with that familiar prickling between his shoulders growing in its tactility. He dared not look around as her bony, electrified fingers crawled over his goosebumps, and static danced behind his eyelids; anxiety and Murray's gut-rot churned sickeningly in his innards, too, while his head pounded, and he expected another migraine's onset. The light became unbearable as his eyeballs throbbed. About to vomit, he hurtled with his eyes closed, crashing into the door frame before feeling his way along the hallway, lurching out of the front door, and then staggering down the side steps; he did not quite make it to the outside lavatory before retching hard as he vomited upon the cobbles of the horse hospital's shadowed courtyard.

Staggering back up the outside steps while wiping a scrim of vomit from his lips, Oliver noted that he felt lighter already. The purging had brought instant, blessed relief, and not only of his inflamed stomach's contents, but also from his mother's botheration – as he stood in the living room doorway and tentatively peered in, it seemed to be empty. If Marion had been there moments ago, as he had suspected, then she was most definitely gone for now.

After polishing off the last stale crusts from his cottage loaf, to stuff his entrails and mop up the last of the acidic stew that his mother had just cooked up for him, he tried to lose himself in sketching and painting while scoffing his remaining barley sugars. It hardly seemed sensible to drink any more of Murray's vile liquor – turpentine would be more palatable – and he wished that he had purchased the extra dry gin after all. Uncle Sheldon in his salad days was banished to the bottom drawer, along with the passion that he once stirred, and along with all the other forsaken subjects.

The enchantment of Simone's perfume still lingered; its various floral nosegays taunted Oliver by whispering sweet nothings that spoke of what pleasures might have transpired had he been the Romeo that he so desperately wished he could have been. He then decided that he would at least try to capture her on paper – ravishing her the only way he knew how. The vividly colourific impression that she had made while standing amid the living room's greens had been glorious. The sun-dappled sight of her propped upon his bed was too scrumptious to forget, too, but he needed to forget it all; he could only hope that if he got it all out of his head and onto paper then he could comfortably forget Simone altogether.

He chose to depict her standing in the living room while fully attired, of course, respecting her dignity; it felt bothersome, however, that although he had seen almost every square inch of her, it felt as if the only one of them that had lost their dignity was him, and why was that? That aside, was he trying to reframe the embarrassment that had taken place in his bedroom by imagining that instead she had only come to his atelier by appointment to pose for his latest masterwork? A part of him wondered if this were so. It had been the first time he had had anyone in his bed apart from Jonesy and it had felt rather crowded in hindsight. Whatever the truth of the matter, he pressed on, smoking one coffin nail after another as he worked, and peering at her through the silver clouds of smoke while sucking hard on his sweeties, then crunching them until he had made painful cuts in his gums with their jagged shards.

Her willowy frame was easy to sketch, just like a fashion illustration featuring in one of those magazines of Marion's from which Oliver had drawn so much inspiration. The colours, meanwhile, were a wonderful selection to work with: modifications of crimson and purple madder, such as claret, mulberry, deep fuchsia, various other pinks, various other purples, and greens for the rest – bottle green and *citron vert*, of course. Starling purplish-black matched the charming wee feather threaded into her hat's band. For her eyes, however, he had no idea which shade to settle on since they had been different with every passing second; finally, he fixed on cerulean blue.

Rendering her attire, and her gown in particular, had been an unexpected jollity, but her face proved to be a different story, and he quickly realised that he would fail to capture Simone; it already seemed to be his mother staring back at him. Addedly, despite how spellbound he had been, he realised that, strangely, he could not picture Simone with any real clarity already. Furthermore, he wished that he had not chosen to render it in watercolour because the paint ran and blurred in the perspiration that dripped from his brow, giving her figure a phantasmal quality and bringing Marion even more to mind. He flipped her face down then and sat in wretched silence with his eyes drifting nervously to the mantel once again.

'Oh, Gigi,' Oliver whispered when catching sight of the collage of picture postcards pinned nearby that she had sent over the years. He was all too aware that for the greater part, his attempts at coping with his nana's loss were to imagine that she was still caravanning somewhere; a smile crept across his lips when remembering that he had once accompanied her and his grandad on one such holiday, during one grey and blustery April when they had ventured very far south into seemingly unchartered lands – which had felt rather exotic! They had wound up in Allworth Cove, where he had triumphantly claimed a sliver of fossilised wood from its craggy shore. It had been such a terrific trip, wherein on cosy, rainy nights when the caravan's windowpanes had become delightfully misted, the tin camping kettle's whistle had announced that hot cocoa would soon be sipped while Gigi had read to him from one of his absolute favourite fantasy stories. And there it still was, atop a pile of his mother's stolen library books by the settee. He picked up *Geronimo Bill* and flicked through it. Having read it for the umpteenth time only the week before, it felt too early to revisit Bill and chums, despite the comfort and nostalgia that the book always afforded him, and as much as he cherished their camaraderie.

Needing something else to occupy his mind, he stooped to switch on the television – a rather bulky chunk of ornamental wood with only a tiny circular screen, upon which one could just about discern its programming if one stretched one's imagination in the cumbersome task of decoding its murky images – his Cranford Chromax E37. For young Olly, those images had seemed risible; they were monochrome, after all, while the world was a riot of colour. Films got away with this, of course, because they were crystal clear photographically and often beautifully shot. Meanwhile, the television had spooked him more than anything, seeming to be a dingy, clouded portal to an alternative universe where things had lost their form, disturbingly; it was not at all the marvel that he had imagined after hearing all Marion's unrestrained enthusiasm regarding this new technology during her early days at Cranford Electric.

'Goodness... the sound is terrible, as always,' Oliver grumbled to himself, remembering then, as he twisted its dial, that the programming was so scant that you were lucky if you found anything to view at all on most evenings.

Some crude images did appear, however, along the theme of goodness knows what; he could not follow the narrator because, just like the wireless, that ominous-sounding electrical clicking, humming, and crackling played havoc with it all. Even worse, somewhere in the background, behind all that interference, music, and the rich, deep voice of the commentator, there also seemed to be another voice of a higher pitch repeating a word that sounded oddly like his name. He switched it off at once!

The virtual silence felt insufferable again; the distant clatter of a goods train travelling along the branch line was a blessed relief, but it swiftly dimmed again, leaving only that ceaseless paper-soft colliding sound of the moths against the window pain and that relentless ticking of the mantel clock. He strained his ears and discerned faint chatter and laughter in nearby streets as well as the traffic up on Moorside and Brewery Lane.

The barley sugars had also been scoffed, every last one, and the remaining pear drops? He had no idea where he had misplaced those.

Within an entire sweep of the cabinet clock's second hand, Oliver had not moved an inch except to glance between his upturned palms and the mantel. Circling his palm continually with his opposing thumb, he found that it still surprised him that they had not become hirsute, just as Marion had assured him that they would. That aside, in this mood he would probably have sucked his thumb, as he often had as a child, if his blackened fingernails were not so unappetising. The sensation was soothing, at least – that circling motion of skin on skin, just as his mother had done with the bud of his ear lobe when he was just a wee one – long before he had become the fly in her ointment, of course.

When looking up finally, now that he had removed *Geronimo Bill* from the top of the pile by the settee, his gaze fell upon Marion's favourite poetry collection, the works of D.S. Eades to date, and these lines flit through his mind –

Hyacinths for my beloved,
Arms laden, your face aglow,
Heed the light, the silence,
And come unto me.

Although Oliver felt that he had never really understood this poem, he had loved those particular lines and the vision of the enchantress that they conjured, whoever she was. The image lingered as dizziness and exhaustion took him over asudden; he was still half-cut despite his emptied innards. With his head bobbing and swaying, his eyes fluttered shut, and then he fell instantaneously into slumber, slumping forward and hitting his head on the table, causing its jumble to clatter.

***

Oliver asked Marion if he could ride the carousel of woe; it was his absolute favourite of all Greenthorne Fayre's attractions. He had already been down the helter-skelter of shame, and he had ridden the Ferris wheel of regret several times; she had all but emptied her purse on the little bugger, but she would allow him one more ride, even if he should have outgrown it all by then. In fact, if he had not asked then she most definitely would have insisted.

He climbed excitedly aboard, and soon the carousel of woe gaily flung him around and around while she smiled and waved from the sidelines, holding his toffee apples and his candy floss.

Just as she had expected, Marion could see that the 'little peep' was already staring at the derrière of the young lady seated on the steed in front of him.

'Can't you make it go any faster?' she asked the fairground attendant.

As if under her spell, the attendant dutifully sped the ride up, flinging Oliver around and around with increasing velocity, until he and all the other little brats were screaming and making rather a mess of themselves.

'Faster!' Marion ordered.

While clinging on for dear life, Oliver sobbed bitterly as the bag's worth of honeycombed toffee, which he had just scoffed and then vomited, adorned his favourite sports jacket; he also became painfully aware that another young lady, who was flailing about beside him, looked likely to furnish him with the nougat that she had polished off earlier.

'There, that'll teach him.'

Backstreet Dandy

On waking from his slumber and while wiping the drool from his chin, Oliver peered about. A dim sunlight filled the room, and he presumed that it must be very near dawn, yet the mantel clock insisted it was twelve. The television set hissed away in the living room corner on an unused frequency. It was odd, he was convinced that he had switched it off already. Its faint luminescence, flickering upon its narrow screen, did nothing but accentuate the peculiar atmosphere. As he rose to switch it off again, with those crackles, clicks, and pops fraying his nerves already, a loud rat-a-tat-tat on his front door was so alarming that he almost leapt from his skin! While looking sharply around, he noticed that in the deep green shadows of the hallway, a singular shaft of sunlight sliced through the high stained-glass window with the flourishes painted upon it, dyeing that light magenta; rising tentatively and creeping along the hallway to answer the front door, he became crowned by this hue as he passed the door to his mother's bedroom – an unnerving aperture at the best of times – and he dug his filthy fingernails into the patterned relief of the wallpaper, gripping the wall for support.

With his elongated shadow and its perse corona falling upon it, much to his disbelief and his horror, that door unlatched itself and began to swing open with a deafening electrostatic crackle. Condensing from the air's wetness, swirling eddies of luminescent sift appeared, the coiling tendrils of which clawed at him like fingers through the gap where the door swung ajar. While he tried to slam that door shut in alarm, somebody – his mother, of course – was tugging at its handle from the inside. An upsurge of electricity coursed through his body again while the pungent aroma of hot fuse wire invaded his sinuses.

With all this uproar underscored by that urgent knocking on his front door, Oliver could have screamed! But, upon managing to slam Marion's door shut finally by placing his foot against the door's frame for leverage, all unnatural energy was finally contained with a clatter. Knowing that there must still be a key scattered somewhere in the clutter of the living room that would secure his safety from her, he despaired of his disorderliness; he would be safe if only he could lock this bloody door! But the unexpected visitor was still knocking at the front one, and with greater urgency, it seemed.

With great irritation, since his nerves already felt shredded raw, upon throwing the damn thing open, he barked breathlessly –

'Yes, can I help you?'

Instantly regretting his discourtesy, he found Simone perched on the top step, staring back at him with that marvellous moon face of hers, those *café-au-lait* freckles, and those ever-changing eyes – periwinkle blue, but in the next moment they were *blue de France* in a strange, shifting light. Glancing about at his neighbourhood then, all other colours appeared to be similarly heightened and unfixed while the veil of yellowish smog trapped in the hot air above had, somehow or other, drifted down to street level and swirled all about Greenthorne.

Saying nothing, simply gesturing for Oliver to follow her, she clutched his arm tightly as they clattered down the steps together and burst onto the courtyard's cobbles. Clasping his shoulders and looking at him imploringly, she took a deep breath. Her eyes were electric blue and rather wide then.

'Your m-mother said for me to f-find you... You must go... ehm... come... to her... at once, oui... yes?'

With a vision of Marion anxiously waiting for him in the shadows of Cranford Electric's lean-to, he asked –

'My mother?'

'Oui.'

'I didn't know you knew her.'

'I d-don't... not really.'

'Then why has she sent you? And what's wrong?'

'Je me sens... non... I-I f-feel... how you say... responsible,' she muttered with her eyes downcast. 'No time to... e-explain!'

With the queerest feeling that something was very wrong here, Oliver felt somewhat exasperated; his mother was dead, after all, and her spirit had just been haranguing him in the hallway.

'But my mother is...'

He could not quite bring himself to say it –

'... no... no longer alive!'

Simone was clearly not understanding him –

'S-sorry... Je ne comprends pas! I mean I d-don't–'

'Ma mère... is... morte!'

'Morte? Non! Vivante! Mais... ehm... b-but not for long. We... You can save her. But... m-must be quick!'

'Where is she, then? Cranford Electric?'

'Non, the Greenthorne Palace, bien sûr!'

'You coming?'

'I am there already... run, mon chéri... vite!'

Without further argument, Oliver then found himself running as fast as his legs could carry him because he sensed that Simone was hardly one to make mountains from molehills; something must be very wrong indeed! Having already passed the old smithy, Spring Gardens, and the Memorial Hall, he glanced behind and saw that she was merely a speck in the distance. How could she know Mother anyway, he wondered, and what on earth could she mean that she is there already?

With only the dissonance of his pulse thumping in his ears and his heels striking the ground, Greenthorne's quietude struck him as very strange. Middle Row was utterly deserted; the Oddfellows was boarded up – why? – and the town felt as if it had been evacuated, or perhaps the townsfolk had simply vanished into air? Despite this sense of desolation, however, everything was prettily cast in a rarely seen light, thanks to the coral and rosewood pinkness of the sunset; despite dusk's arrival, all colours still seemed unnaturally vivid. Cream was gold, brick was fiery orange, palest green was warm mint, and Miss Cranford Electric's gladioli stands were intensely purple-pink.

Having dashed all the way to, and then along the length of, Middle Row in surprisingly little time, Oliver neared the schoolhouse corner and was about to turn onto the old tramway. Its length filled him with apprehension for good reason: there was still so much ground to cover and, as he had sensed by Simone's anxiety, so little time.

Ducking into a side alley upon imagining that he could travel the length of the tramway along narrow passages that mostly ran perpendicular to it, he stormed past derelict factory backlots. Wooden spindles and their unspooled, serpentine cabling threatened to trip him. Offscourings of scrap wood, skewered with halfway hammered in nails, tore at his ankles. Although it was usually uncanny, he quickly lost his good sense of direction because the worry of what on earth lay ahead had seized his mind entirely; taking arbitrary lefts and rights then, he soon felt lost in a darkening and seemingly limitless maze.

'Where the devil am I?'

With dusk making way for night, and with the world's shadows rapidly thickening, his entrails wound tighter and tighter as the darkening alleys wended on and on unrelentingly; he could only hope that he was still heading perpendicular to the old tramway, but he had no idea which direction was east anymore, especially with such little visibility.

Then to Oliver's great relief, the walls of the alleyways fell away, and the echo of his footsteps flattened as he burst out onto the tramway at last. He was already under the viaduct and opposite those billowing drifts of steam in which the Queens Head and the Greenthorne Palace seemed to be perpetually shrouded.

Simone was indeed there already, with her eyes shimmering a very different shade of blue, which he could only describe as azure, or perhaps sapphire, as she greeted him with as much anxiety in her voice as she had had earlier.

'Ce n'est pas trop tôt!'

'She's here?' he asked while he tried to catch his breath.

'Oui... she is safe.'

'What's she doing here? Safe from what?'

'Le passé... ehm... The... p-past... and... ehm... safe from h-herself.'

'Why are you doing this?'

'Because her ch-choices were as few as ours.'

She could have chosen not to be such a rotten old harpy! he thought, then felt instantaneously guilty for doing so, especially since Simone was a mind reader –

'She... have to say s-something about this to you.'

Yelling from the Queens Head's windows, Ava and Kitty echoed Simone's urgency –

'Hurry up, chappy... Move it!'

'And quick!'

'Where is she, then?'

'I said it, the Greenthorne Palace. Allez, allez... No time to waste, mon chéri!' Simone also cried, anxiously ushering him into those swirls of steam that billowed about them – suddenly ablaze with a verdurous light that shone through the picture house's windows.

'Are you really there, Mother?' he whispered.

Although apprehensive, he felt intrigued enough, so, taking a deep breath, Oliver stepped forward and disappeared into those floodlit, swirling currents.

Feeling for a moment as if he were lost in a limitless void stirred only by smoky currents, he saw that already those dusty garlands that looped about him had begun to brighten, diffused with a hazy starlight; they became undulating garlands comprised of innumerable tiny golden flecks, which swirled and then settled, taking on material form. Looking up at the ornately wrought columns towering over him, supporting the sweeping arches overhead, it was an architecture of staggeringly monolithic proportion, and it was all exquisitely rendered with a marbled patina. Each viridian and emerald-hued surface of the palace's interior also glimmered with a twinkling, pearlescent sheen. Then more of those golden flecks condensed afresh and took the form of ornate fixtures: gold-shaded lamps upon the palace's walls.

When glancing up, he saw how a warm, golden light, flooding across the vastness of the hall's breadth, cast highlights of chartreuse and shadows of deepest jade; when glancing further up, he realised that this brilliance was, in fact, the strengthening sun's rays flooding through circular windows which were opening above. When craning his neck even more to stare up in wonder at those rows of arches far above him, they seemed an improbable sight – as if his mind could not calculate, let alone approximate, their massive number. That golden, shifting sunlight intensified then, refracting off those opalescent arches and rendering their sweeping curves and planes in shades of emerald, teal, moss, malachite, and forest green. Unlikely as it may have been, in light of all this, Oliver felt enraptured by the colour. Resembling the breath-taking movie sets of big budget films, and also the palatial cinemas that screened them, the dream palace's interior was an absolute marvel! One might expect to see circling rows of cheerful, spritely showgirls scissoring their legs on giant turntables while in the depths below, stagehands strong-armed them around and around, and while the cameras rolled.

The tinkling melody of a towering, oversized theatre organ at the palace hall's far end echoed around it endlessly while puffs of steam, wafting from its ranks of chrome pipes, drifted far overhead.

Then a slight tremor, momentarily alarming, along with an overhead clatter, but Oliver quickly gathered that it was only another locomotive cutting across the heavens above and causing the overarching frame of the viaduct to judder.

Appearing just ahead of him then, his siren from the south, Simone, had appeared, and she greeted him with an outstretched hand, having already slipped into a gown that looked as if she were tightly fitted into a giant carmine red rose. Its petals unfurled around her, with stamens of green forming a collar around her long neck, as if reaching for the sun; those petals fluttered then, as if another stagehand had placed a wind machine just beyond the periphery of his gaze. She was quite the sight as always, especially when glancing down at her feet and the ground on which she stood because that mirror-like floor reflected her gown as a corresponding carmine-coloured bloom beneath her. Clasping his hand then, she whispered softly –

'There she is, Oliver... ta mère.'

She gestured with her outstretched arm towards a bantam-sized figure standing far away across the vast expanse of the hall.

Quite suddenly, the air was scented with the sweet fragrance of fresh-cut hyacinths. Oliver stepped closer so that he might see his mother more clearly, treading the glassy floor, with its scattering of emerald sparkles, with some caution.

So far, he could discern that Marion's once grey hair appeared to be platinum again, and that she clutched the bouquet of flowers that he had already smelt from across the hall; when closer, her skin appeared dewy, and her arms were quite laden, in fact – filled with those sprays of pale lavender-coloured blooms. Once within yards of her, he faltered, feeling stunned by the vision before him; it felt overwhelming to see his mother in such a state of good health. She looked so young by consequence!

An auroral light shone from within her; while dressed in gauzy, gossamer silvery-white, with ruffled sleeves and with her arms bare, this luminosity suffused her dress, her hair, and even her skin – its paper-thinness and sallowness were entirely gone. In her ascension, aided by her 'sisters' from the Queen's Head, death and disease had only been her chrysalis state. Is this the afterlife, then? Am I alive or dead? he wondered, then swiftly decided that he could not care less if he would ever leave this realm.

Oliver knew that Marion would not speak; she did not need to because her gaze, filled with peace and accord, said it all. He remained quite still while absorbing its content and feeling everything that she wished him to feel; the deep sense of relief that he felt was beyond price! A smile of deep relief crept across his lips while he nodded in response to her wordless reassurances, and her eyes became as moist as his.

Upon feeling compelled to speak himself, his lips only quivered; with his soul feeling moved enough to reach out to his mother, his conscious mind struggled to find the utterances that a deeper part of him felt compelled to voice. Somewhere buried deep within his psyche, kept safely beneath the threshold of his consciousness until now, there was a certain something that needed to be aired finally: a grave misunderstanding, in fact, that should finally be remedied. Although Oliver felt deeply uncertain of how to broach this, she clearly did not, and although she still did not speak out loud, he heard her anyway –

'Oliver, dear... little Olly... as I've been trying to tell you–'

Cut short by an ear-splitting electrical crackle, Marion looked up as the dream palace's illumination seemed to intensify like a tungsten flame, until she appeared to be as overwhelmed as he was, and as the photographer, Albion Roper, had said, all warmth seemed to be washed from her face; Oliver followed her downcast gaze as he, too, noticed that the bouquet of hyacinths that she had clutched so dearly were dying, browning, and withering with a crumpling sound. They quickly became little more than dust, sifting through her fingers like time through life's hourglass.

He tottered towards her then, as she groaned, and her legs buckled beneath her. A trickle of blood ran from her nose, scarlet, like wayward tears of blood, and as she tumbled her eyes rolled up into their sockets. He knelt over her and shook her, then patted her face; isn't this what one is supposed to do, what people do in films? he anxiously asked himself because he had no idea how else to act. Her skin was terribly cold.

Sadly, his mother's resurrection had not lasted long; it had only afforded them the briefest window of reacquaintance between the realms of the living and the dead before fate swooped in to reinstate her fate. By then a scorching sun in its zenith bore down on them, and the mise en scène seemed also to brown, blister, and age like parchment through time. Already, it was as if she no longer saw Oliver, as if she stood alone, in fact, while glancing up and around herself in terrified bewilderment. Her skin, rapidly losing its vitality, dulled and coarsened while her body rapidly withered, her hair dulled to ashen grey again, and her overall appearance was all too familiar. Fast losing her corporeality, too, her body became more and more indistinct then, until finally she became only the vaguest outline of ash on the palace's floor. Her ashes and the few remaining husks of those dead hyacinths, that lay scattered around where she had paled into near-nothingness, rustled as they tumbled away on a sudden breeze.

Oliver faltered as another, far louder vibrational rumble shook the palace; it was not another locomotive clattering above, however, because it was the ground beneath him that had begun to tremor and quake. The building shook on its foundations while chunks of cracked emerald and onyx, ever growing in their mass, fell about him; they formed a random scattering of greenish shards, like a wrecked mosaic, about his feet. Alarmingly, the ground had also begun to pothole and crack open.

While feeling completely at a loss and unknowing which evasive manoeuvre to take, he forced his eyes shut as he shielded his head with his hands, listening to the terrible moans and groans of the destruction of the dream palace. Hoping for deliverance, he remembered Simone then, but while glancing speedily around, he realised that his usherette had vanished; he had, at least, noticed an archway leading to an ill-lit corridor to his left, however, and he made a dash for that in the hope that it would lead to an exit of some kind. Even bulkier chunks of masonry crashed perilously close as he ran for cover, and a giant, verdurous mushroom cloud of dust fountained up, flurried about, and then sifted back down in the crumbling hall behind him.

The hallway seemed to be secure, at least, although dark. Row upon row of porthole windows in wooden doors flanked this ill-lit corridor, bringing Cranford Electric to mind; the lighting was just as scant, and it seemingly leaked in drips from the lamps above – they flickered and flashed intermittently too.

Gigi! While looking at Oliver through a heavily varnished door's window, his nana's good eye twinkled, just as it always had, and the otherworldly-looking, clouded over one peered straight into his soul.

'I can see 'im and 'e ain't smilin',' she whispered to someone unseen out there with her, someone just out of sight.

'To whom do you speak, Gigi? It's Mother out there with you, isn't it?'

'She says she knows she were wrong, Olly... but she needs to 'ear you tell 'er... to get it off yer chest.'

There was indeed something he had wanted to say to Marion, needed to say even, but he had forgotten entirely –

'Tell her what?'

'That she were wrong.'

'About what?'

But then an even more pressing concern took hold –

'Am I dead, too, Gigi?'

She shook her head.

'No, poppet... yer alive, for what it's worth. But nowadays there really don't seem much difference, does there?'

He nodded in agreement; he quite understood what she meant.

***

While drifting aimlessly past the darkened exteriors of the Miltons, the Pattinsons, and the Shearers – folk whose lives Oliver knew intimately without knowing them in the slightest to greet on passing – he neared his favourite window through which to gaze wistfully at everything that he felt he had missed out on. But he was disheartened to find that his favourite theatre was closed; its stage curtains were drawn. Not even a sliver of light poked between them. Are they all upstairs, dead and rotting in their beds? he wondered of Hilda; Brian; their two daughters, Aida and Vera; and their son Archie. Oliver had not realised just how late it was: long past midnight already. The night was as soggy and stagnant as ever, yet the temperatures were the lowest that he had felt for quite some time, and that, at least, was something to feel thankful for. Greenthorne struck him as feeling singularly forsaken nonetheless, without a single upstairs house light anywhere to be seen; meanwhile, the streetlamps and house lights of the neighbouring villages of Chalk Hill, Bottoms Dale, and Middle Moor twinkled cheerily on the horizon. With only a wanting sliver of moon and the resulting scantiness of light, he had to narrow his eyes to make out his more immediate surroundings. The puzzling silence found him questioning whether he was still asleep – still lost in that baffling dream – but the aches in his back and haunches, owing to his lumpy mattress, felt very real, and they assured him that he was wide and painfully awake. It was deathly quiet, in fact, as if everyone had shuffled off this mortal coil, and the specific shade of night was, unquestionably, funereal black – no other shade came close.

Oliver had not been able to get back to sleep since he had woken trembling from the ordeal that his psyche had served up to him while snoozing at the living room table. He had found himself pacing Greenthorne's darkened tangle of dreary rows instead, wearing only his all-in-one, dressing gown, and the slippers that facilitated the night's stealthy exploration on his more planned night-time excursions; he had never wanted to draw attention to his nocturnal adventures with his footsteps echoing off of the cobbles, after all – a trick that he had learned long ago. But there was no one left to disturb anyway, at least that was how it felt even if the townsfolk were all merely asleep.

The darkened Oddfellows felt particularly bothersome, and the boarded-up store fronts suggested nailed shut coffins as he paced past them and along Middle Row. He realised that what had particularly perturbed him was that Doris usually left one or two of the saloon's lights on after dark, even after she had mopped, dusted, and done count-up; their gleaming ruby blooms had always felt reassuring – deeply so, in fact.

Tonight, however, an upstairs light at the Solbys' revealed itself to be the only beacon of hope, and it drew Oliver as close as Olive's front gate; he felt that he could not get any closer, though, let alone find the pluck to knock at her front door and beg for remembrance. But Miss Cranford Electric was alive, at least, and it heartened him that she had resisted this collective death, just as she had resisted the collective fate of her peers, and perhaps of her generation in general, most of whom had been worked into an early grave to get Britannia back on her feet after that terrible war.

He still wished that he could enter, however, simply to feel her home's warmth, to enjoy its familiarity, and to take shelter under her wing – to bathe in the blush of whatever it was that kept her impervious to life's abuses. She had always radiated a reassuring sense that life had order and meaning to it – even joy; in Olive's company, one felt that, despite all life's worries, its chaos, and its senselessness, there was actually nothing to fear. How he ached for her comforts and that special smile that she had reserved especially for him before she had forgotten him entirely.

After trudging back along Middle Row, Oliver leant against the creaking frame of a market stall; its awning cloth flapped in the warm breeze as he lit up again. He still had that God-awful feeling, but already the dream was barely memorised, at least; a vague awareness of his mother's involvement lingered, but he had no idea how. Gigi, on the other hand, he could clearly recall, speaking through an aperture of some kind while saying –

'She says she knows tha' she were wrong, Olly... but she needs to 'ear you tell 'er... to get it off yer chest.'

Hmmm... she'd always insisted that dreams have their own special significance, so what on earth had Gigi meant, that there's something I need to tell Mother? he wondered; isn't there something Mother should be telling me... 'Sorry', perhaps? Is she honestly expecting me to apologise? Am I still to be held accountable for all her troubles and her appalling behaviour? But then... Gigi knew everything, she had had the second sight, after all.

He had always sensed that Gigi had felt rather helpless watching him suffer at the hands of her difficult daughter. Whatever she had meant, then, it was surely in his best interests; as such, he then wondered if perhaps she had been trying to raise the alarm to a concern that he had not quite grasped yet.

'I miss you Gigi,' he whispered.

'Trust yer instincts, little Olly,' she had so often said. 'You're such a sensitive lad... Don't let 'er harden you too. Watch everythin', even yer dreams... They often tell t' truth.' But he had taught himself to forget his dreams so efficiently that it was a tactic which he could not unlearn in this instance.

'What are instincts, Gigi?'

'Joinin' life's dots, Olly... that's all... Intuition.'

Regrettably, then, despite Oliver's general reluctance to look inward, one thing about himself that he had no doubt about was that nowadays his intuition was in tatters. The relative peace of his early childhood had lulled him into a false sense of security, and it had made the coming avalanche of Marion's unravelling seem even more bewildering and brutal. The following teenhood of constant vigilance towards his mother's criticism had found him habitually second-guessing everything; every thought and action's virtue had to be debated down to the level of the microscopic and outguessed in advance, so that he should not put a foot wrong. Daily, it had felt much like fighting against a force ten gale. Metaphor aside, this he had done to the point that it had driven him near mad; he had sweated the small stuff as well as the big while being unable to sit easily in the middle of things – all much the same in the present day. How could one be in touch with one's intuition throughout all that?

Gigi, however, she would be the angel in his skies, if he dared believe that such a thing was possible; she would make such a magnificent one too! She had been beautiful inside and out; she had not been classically beautiful like her difficult daughter had been, yet his nana had been just as otherworldly, with that crown of mousy brown hair swept back from her face; her sharp, aquiline profile; her small smiling mouth; and with her good eye always twinkling! Even when the cataract set in, which only seemed to heighten her powers and sharpen her second sight, she still looked marvellous to him, even if others found it unnerving; she always peered past your shoulder with it, as if peering into the spirit world without the slightest fear of what she might see there. How his heart ached for her then, for her warmth, her wisdom, and her insight, but she... well... everyone was gone – everyone that mattered. Tears welled in his ducts. Although its details had mostly faded, the emotional distillate of whatever he had dreamt remained, and like life in general, felt profoundly devastating – shattering yet ineffectual, like one of Mr Turner's grenades missing its mark completely and incinerating nothing in a shrieking explosion. Everything felt the same, after all, even Greenthorne's deathly feeling, because his life was just as barren as this when the townsfolk were up and in circulation. Those tears dripped onto his cheeks then, as he sobbed gutturally, drowning in the utter emptiness and loneliness of that which he was always trying to fill with the noise of his obsessions and compulsions.

Oliver already missed his crackerjack, soft-hearted Simone, and he found himself wishing that he had just taken her for that drink after all. He mused on her magic, her empathy, the mystery, the woman. He wanted to tell her everything: his tumultuous past, his deadlocked present, and his fears for the future. He remembered her looking with curiosity at the other mantel photographs – the ones he had defaced – and felt that there was much that he could have explained to her while sensing that she would have understood completely if he had.

'J'ai une âme solitaire,' he informed her in a whisper, although he felt compelled to scream it as loudly as he could, had he the nerve; no answer came, however. Clearly, she had not heard.

Oliver wiped away his tears while feeling that he simply could not govern this grief a moment longer. Gripped by an irresistible urge to scour the back alleys, he wanted to feel the warmth of a body pressed against him and to lose himself in the heat of hot breath upon his neck. To only be admired would no longer suffice because an uninhibited desire had taken him over asudden while he so desperately craved that rush of physical sensation that drowned out all else. He wondered if he could bear the long journey to the heath, but at that time of night it would be creepy out there, and it would possibly be dangerous in the pitch-dark anyway. Instead, he thoroughly scouted every backstreet locale that he knew of, but the labyrinths of crumbling brick were also ominously empty. Only the darkened outlines of dustbins and pallets piled high with tea chests crowded around him. Storeroom extractor fans funnelled unpleasant-smelling winds around him, too, and with a ominous-sounding whirr while he peered wantonly into those otherwise empty shadows.

He continued to search for the cues that he had learned to look for: hot breath melting into cool air, appearing as smoke signals from behind passage walls and easily spied from the street's distance with a trained eye, and the tapping of a foot – a signal that desire awaited him with increasing impatience, yet nothing could be seen or heard. Also, the air was too warm for those smoke signals. But already, despite his hearty desire, Oliver was unnerving himself with such activity; the alleyways felt eerie, and despite their desertion, a vague sense of being observed had reared again. Suddenly, he could only imagine his nana's shocked appraisal of his behaviour; it had struck him rather coldly that since Gigi had developed the second sight, she was just as likely, if not more likely, to be watching him from the otherworld as Marion was. Perhaps, dare he say it, he was slowly becoming immune to Marion's judgments, but his nana's opinion mattered far more. That said, Gigi had never had a harsh word to say about anybody, and had never implied anything about his own sensitivities. But his father – he would obviously be appalled if he, too, was watching.

Someone's here! he thought upon discerning an advancing shadow, and he quickly forgot all that. His heart quickened, but as the fellow moved closer, it quickly sank; he became gripped by another familiar tense and fretful feeling once he had recognised the awkward, limping gait and the billowing rags that the creature wore. Draped loosely over his spindly, angular body, those rags lent the poor soul a wraithlike appearance, but it was only Quinn – a stalwart of the alleyways, yet he was an outcast, even there.

When considering an immediate, hasty withdrawal around the corner and cutting through to Overdale Lane, Oliver resisted the temptation because Quinn had seen him already and no doubt wanted to chat to him as usual; Oliver could not be so cruel as to shun him. As much as he felt uncomfortable in that man's company, he hardly wished to cause offence to someone who had suffered a lifetime's worth already. But the tension rose in him nonetheless, along with an intrusive soreness in his solar plexus. Quinn's ragged shadow was upon him then, and with the night's warmth, it was a wonder that he was not sweltering in that unravelling grey cardigan and that tattered cycling cape that was blowing all about him. His face was deeply wrinkled with clumsily applied splodges of rouge and eyeliner. Overall, it made one wonder if the ghost of an eighteenth-century vicomte had mated with a vampire and spawned poor old Quinn, or if the Widow Twanky's corpse had been reanimated somehow; Oliver kept these unfavourable musings to himself, of course. The tragedy of it was that Quinn was only trying to look pretty, but the paint's application only made his gaunt visage appear even more unnerving; it was all very unfortunate, and it inspired pity as much as unease, as did the broken, yellowed stubs of his teeth.

'How's tha doin', Oliver?' Quinn asked in a high-pitched yet creaking voice.

'Hello Quinn. I'm fine thanks... and yourself?'

'As well as might be expected, my dear.'

'Glad to hear that.'

'What's up with thee, dearie? Tha looks like tha saw a ghost.'

'It's pretty dreary out here tonight.'

Quinn sighed –

'Nobody promised us a rose garden, did they now?'

'I suppose not.'

'Dead tonight, is it?'

'It does seem so, yes.'

The usual awkward silence followed these stilted pleasantries, in which Oliver felt remorsefully assured that his unease was all too apparent. The faint odour of something strange and unpleasant seemed to always emanate from Quinn, which did not help him much either.

'Well, lad... shan't keep thee... cakes to bake.'

'Take care of yourself, Quinn.'

Quinn nodded and took leave of him.

The users of the heath's wilderness and this labyrinth of longing were sometimes as chatty as a sewing circle; Oliver had overheard all sorts of whisperings about Quinn. As hard as it was to imagine, the hearsay was that this roaring old pansy had been quite a looker in his younger years: a backstreet dandy whose fabled bloom had probably rivalled Oliver's own, considering his own popularity in all such places. He took a deep breath to steady himself as he watched Quinn stumble away. The sense of dread that the poor old fellow inspired had been difficult to explain at first; slowly it had dawned on Oliver, however, as he had bumped into Quinn more and more often, and he had elseways learned of his surprising backstory, why he disturbed him so much. It had become painfully obvious to him that with the march of time, Quinn's bloom had slowly withered, and he had been left with nothing but a lonely existence on life's margins. Again, he was nowadays shunned even in the back alleys – considered to be only a nuisance, a nutcase, a frump, an eyesore, and even a bogeyman.

It all boiled down to a singular worry: did Quinn hold up a mirror to his own wearied and forlorn future? Oliver had often wondered, and the probable answer was chilling. Oftentimes, a future life of being an outsider and a wretch, just as Quinn had become, felt guaranteed. The man reeked of ruin. Marion had insinuated many times that if Oliver did not forever cling to her modality for managing his own weaknesses and inferiorities, this was all he could expect of his own future: to only be sneered at, to be made a joke of, to be spitefully jostled in public, and to be manhandled in all the wrong ways, and with regularity.

He had seen Quinn knocked to the pavement more than once, when heartless townsfolk had circled about him and belly laughed. He was forever being butted by passing elbows, and when it rained, innumerable umbrellas 'accidentally' speared him as he simpered down Middle Row, trying to mind his own business; in light of such abuses, the mask of steely indifference that he had been forced to wear was betrayed by the unmistakable sadness of the hooded eyes that peered through it.

As much as all this stirred Oliver's sympathies, the unvarnished truth was that Quinn's situation frightened him; it felt too close for comfort, and it brought worry enough to feel too uncomfortable in his presence. He could not be as friendly as he felt he ought to be; he was pleasant but short. It was all he could ever muster.

With no woman ever likely to make an honest man out of Oliver, his future appeared to stretch gloomily ahead of him, with only other odd fellows to knock about with; that future appeared dim, dirty, and crooked. His mind raced with apprehension. He was not wealthy like Uncle Sheldon; that wealth seemed to shield his 'uncle' from a fate like Quinn's, somehow reframing the old nonce as a 'confirmed bachelor', which had its respectability. Furthermore, as much as Oliver liked to pretend that life's outskirts had their own shabby chic, that argument, in this moment, at least, felt like self-delusion in the strongest terms.

'But then again... with second thought, perhaps I'm just ahead of the times,' he murmured while remembering how Sheldon had so often intimated that they both were. From hearing his fake uncle's finespun subtleties and snooping through his diaries and letters, Oliver had gathered that Sheldon's older brother, Tristan, had contacts in London: philosophers, musicians, artists, and writers of some influence, most of whom were pure pillow biters, or had the nerve and greed to swing both ways, just as Oliver had.

The thought of them, and also of the heady lifestyle that he imagined they led, inspired a little jealousy, but more importantly, it brought reassurance. He could only hope that Sheldon was right: the harsh labels that Oliver had heedlessly embraced or feared dreadfully, depending upon his mood, were only a matter of perspective anyway, and perspectives may well shift across time, just as Sheldon and his older brother had predicted. Strictly speaking, this Bloomsbury set were not part of respectable society yet, but Tristan Bainbridge Senior had said that they were terribly modern and progressive, so the world would catch up with them soon enough; so, perhaps he need not worry about ending up like poor old Quinn after all... and, of course, this begged the question: what would Marion know about such things?

Oliver's worry began to dissipate a little while he drew on all the dissentience that he had felt forced to cultivate long ago; once again, he pledged to himself that until such time as society did catch up with this Bloomsbury set, he would remain cheerfully shameless for being such a debauchee himself. Hopefully, he would have his share of Sheldon's wealth before long anyway, if he played his cards well; that wealth would afford him similar immunity to such concerns as his fictive uncle had enjoyed. Oliver took in a steadying breath and then exhaled fully.

After skittering back onto Middle Row, he turned and looked northwards at the factories – at those darkened edifices silently awaiting the morning's scurries of worker ants. The rumble of the goods train over the viaduct signalled that the world was waking up. The stars were already obscured, and the heavens were a far lighter shade of azure, melding into heliotrope and lavender at the world's rim while briefly scattered with those curious clouds that manifest and then quickly vanish at summers' dawns. The sun was waiting in the wings while the day that stretched before him began to fill him with a little apprehension. He was utterly shattered; by consequence, he would be prone to feeling even lower than usual. Somehow, he also knew that, even if he put himself to bed again, sleep would elude him, despite such exhaustion and no matter how much he drank; he was overly tired. The only tactic, then, would be to lie in bed, close his eyes, try to relax, and try to empty his mind of everything for as long as he possibly could.

While traipsing back across the cobbled yard, it hit him harder than ever that Jonesy was not there to greet him; no butterscotch shimmer refracted from his eyes in the gloom, no tail twitched, nor could Oliver hear his purring as he chaperoned him up that darkened stairwell. Groping in the darkness to find his way, Oliver drudged upstairs alone.

Once he had tumbled into bed, as much as he tried to empty his mind, Quinn kept flitting through it; an eighteenth-century vicomte mating with a vampire indeed...

bahaha! Sometimes Oliver felt quite taken with his own wit. He rarely laughed, let alone this hard, except for the odd chuckle or giggle at Sheldon, of course, but this laughter was more of a hysterical outburst, which was propelled by another explosion of tears.

***

Having finally collapsed into leaden, unrefreshing slumber between lunchtime and four, Oliver awoke dry-mouthed and feeling quite bleary to that usual blur of yellowed skies, solitude, and sweat; oh, but the heat again! The days of summer's end seemed to hotten Greenthorne incrementally, becoming ever more unbearable.

A comatose darkness since noon... but last night... a peculiar dream... Mother again? he wondered; Gigi perhaps? He strained to remember... sketchy, indistinct outlines remained, but otherwise all detail was lost.

He wiped the rheum and sweat from his eyes while peering sleepily into his bedroom's emptiness. Regrettably, overnight that emptiness seemed to have been filled with a particularly bleak poignancy – palpably felt, as if it had also seeped into his every bodily cell while he had slept. While rising and dressing then, he felt bone-weary – utterly weighed down.

Once Oliver was slumped over his living room's table, it struck him harder than his mother's flat iron against his head that despite the sheer wonder of finding out that the sirens of the Queens Head were not merely myth after all, nothing of late had felt as dispiriting as his disastrous dalliance with Simone; a profound sense of impotence, as if emasculated by forces beyond his control, had gotten him by the scruff. It felt strangely like grief. He also felt furious, although he was not sure why, and not sure with whom, and these sentiments seemed to hold a mirror to the way life had conspired against him generally. It was a mirror that he hardly wished to gaze into, so, all as such, he felt that he could only embrace with greater gusto his usual, well-rehearsed routine; drinking excessively while smoking one coffin nail after another, he prepared to frenziedly apply himself to any vice that he had left available to him. Now that women had been entirely ruled out again, what was left was only his and his mother's haunts: the heath and the alleys. He decided that he would embrace the activities of the latter locale fully and stop being so half-hearted about them – instead, seducing all in every direction.

While cobbling together another sham of a breakfast with the incongruent and unpalatable scraps of mouldering food that he had left over, and then forcing the vile concoction down his gullet, Oliver noticed with some surprise that he had stopped glancing about nervously in the worry that Marion was lingering; with her bones rotting six feet under in the shadow of St Barnabas' steeple, she had, by his estimation, already overplayed her haunting. Her visitations were becoming so frequent, in fact, that he wondered if he was becoming somewhat impervious to them; that was how it felt presently, at least. Overkill was always her style, so to hell with her! he thought; even in ruddy death her behaviour borders on harassment! Despite this new cavalier attitude, however, and the fact that it seemed as if he had freed some mental space from her, thoughts of his mother, and all the anxiety that accompanied such thoughts, had simply become an uneasy disposition anchored in his innards while he buried her past and her present more deeply than ever – he told himself he simply had tummy ache.

Forget the crossway, he thought as he inwardly prepared to head outdoors; he could not risk bumping into Dennis Bannister so soon, but anyway, again, it was the heath's and alley's possibilities that were so urgently called for. But first he desperately needed a pint, of course, with which to insensibly squander his dwindling funds.

Heartsore Lady

While waiting for Doris to unlatch and swing open the Oddfellows doors with a benevolent smile, Oliver felt that he could not sit and stew in the horse hospital's stifling mugginess a second longer; a bottle of Murray's was glugged down, silt and all, and he made his escape into the midday's blinding light. Soon afterwards, he found himself loitering with hands pocketed and head glumly lowered on the periphery of Greenthorne's only serviceable football pitch; once, it had doubled up as a greyhound racing track, but like all halcyon days, those days were long gone. While standing adjacent to Greenthorne's penalty area, he felt comparatively inadequate while watching stampedes of similarly 'ill at ease' townsmen enjoying their frolic – a temporary release from their own thin-worn lives. Middle Moor was getting a pretty good thrashing today; while watching Greenthorne creep ever closer to victory, he cut a lonely figure, steeped in his own perspiration while swigging from his hipflask.

Both five-a-side teams were brought together by one of the 'occupational clubs' that the ministry had dreamt up to toughen those whom it feared had become as softened by long stretches of unemployment as he had become.

Once, while at the mercy of the labour exchange himself, Oliver had been forced to attend this very club, but the discrepancy between the instructor's agenda and the interests of the attendees had been all too apparent; the eggheads had known better, apparently, and this had made for an atmosphere that he had found too cringeworthy to tolerate, as well as tedious. He had quickly decided that there was little future enrichment to be had in learning to reupholster barstools, and he had not been able to see bookbinding becoming a new hobby by any stretch of the imagination. It had been a dingy, depressing place, too, run from the dimly lit chambers of the Greenthorne Workmen's Institute. On all such grounds, he had dropped out completely at the forfeiture of his dole, and consequently his sanity for a time.

These clubs for the unemployed insisted upon a wide range of sporting activities, too, such as tennis, football, track and field, and rounders; he had already been picked last for teams on St Mark's playing fields, however, and he was quite sure that he did not need to suffer the indignity of going through all that again. The ministry was more than keen, as everybody seemed to be asudden, that the great outdoors be used as an amenity for vigorous physical activity in order to improve the nation's health. But he felt that he had embraced that notion already, spending more than half of his life in the great outdoors, wandering many miles daily; furthermore, he had become quite game for certain other forms of vigorous physical activity, should he stumble upon a willing opponent. Therefore, he felt that they had little to worry about in his particular case.

Watching this sweaty bunch, who otherwise seemed impervious to the blistering heat, skirmish so exuberantly brought to mind how much he had envied the young boys that he had seen playing rough and tumble with their fathers when he had been a little one himself. He then found himself suspecting that this horseplay, at such an early age, might have been the necessary foundation for sporting ability; it felt like a good excuse for his failings, at least. Watching the ball being kicked about the pitch with such force and precision aroused a mixture of jealousy and melancholy, considering how two left-footed he had been on the sports pitch himself, and he found himself admiring the command that the players had over their own bodies; it inspired envy, actually, to the point of becoming a bit of a fixation. Thus, while scrutinising these sportsmen through a lens of infatuation, he felt somewhat akin to Uncle Sheldon. Perhaps the blood that he shared with his so-called uncle was more problematic than he liked to think, then? His mother had made many demeaning comparisons between them, after all –

'Stop being such a nelly like your bloody uncle, Oliver!' she had hissed. 'You should've outgrown poetry by now... it doesn't become a man at all... not a real man, at least!'

Since, with his face crumpling, Oliver had made no reply, she had gone on –

'What would your father, God rest him, have made of all this?' she had said while peering at the clutter of his beloved books: the works of Fisher, Harper, and Shenton; gothic romance novels; short story anthologies; and poetry collections, all spread out upon the living room table.

'Cringing little milksop,' she had added once he had been satisfactorily brought to tears. But this had hardly been her most bruising swipe at him, and once he had dried his eyes and realised that she had parroted this insult from a novel of hers that he had also read, she had abruptly lost credibility and authority in his eyes, as well as respect; Marion had spoken well but in a prosaic manner, with little linguistic flair, in all earnestness. Remembering her humble origins then, it was also as if he could suddenly see the vacuity that lay beneath all her pretentions – not that this in any way disproved her assertion of his limp-wristedness. He had nevertheless sworn that from that point on he would stop caring if he had inherited those dubious familial traits that had otherwise found their greatest expression in Sheldon's wing of the family tree. 'So be it, then!' he had said with a shrug; he had surrendered himself to it all, telling himself that he had no grounds to argue with her, and that, furthermore, he no longer cared.

But are these flippancies working anymore? Oliver had to ask of himself as he lit up another cigarette and continued to watch the match. Feeling somewhat exasperated with himself, he also had to ask why he was as much susceptible to the allurements of men as he was to those of women; it was rather bewildering at times, after all, as much as he tried to convince himself otherwise. Furthermore, it was hardly the done thing nowadays, even if that changed in the future, as per Tristan Bainbridge Senior, which seemed so unlikely by the harsh light of day. After trying to convince himself all would be fine only last night, here he was filled with anxiety about it all again, frustratingly. Meanwhile, his kinship with Tristan's younger brother felt undesirable, to say the very least, especially now that Sheldon was starting to repel him somewhat; whether fortunes changed or not, ending up like him or his less moneyed twin, poor old Quinn, was already beginning to feel like a pretty diabolical prospect once again. And with hindsight, it felt dreadful to have pandered to Sheldon's fancies when only a few months prior, while admiring Oliver's bare legs in his short trousers, the old lecher, flannel-mouthed as ever, had unmistakably drooled while saying –

'Oliver, if you must insist on smoking so much, then perhaps a smoking jacket would be fitting... or a veste de fumeur, as they say in frogland, patterned with motifs cachemire, I suppose. But, then, velvet, merino, or printed flannel might be more fetching, fastened with boutons brandebourg, I would imagine. Some matching short trousers, of course... We might pop you along to Manfred & Sons next week, my schedule permitting... Hmm... you could get a taste for this life, eh, champ?'

'I should say!' had been Oliver's swift reply, but then, thinking he should hedge his bets and sound more appreciative, he had added, 'If it's convenient enough, that is. I think that would be quite cheery indeed.'

'Indeed it would. Maxine, bring cake! I feel quite whimsical asudden. Don't you, Oliver?'

Oliver had been, quite simply, bowled over because Sheldon had always kept him dangling up until then. Unsurprisingly, it had not been convenient enough for his imitation uncle, however ; the garments never materialised. It had undoubtedly been throat clearing, though, before propositions would have finally been articulated.

Up until then, there had been no jollies into town in the Bentley, nor had there been any trips to the races; there had only been that weekly hour – Thursdays from eleven to midday – where Sheldon had filled the air with vague yet glimmering intimations of what rewards might be placed at Oliver's disposal if he remained compliant, pliable, and bucked his ideas up a little. Sheldon was usually too refined for the crassness of stooping to double entendres, but verbal wink-winks had been offered aplenty, along with many gesticular clues – cleverly passed off as the innocent gestures of a naturally lively and animated creature. Oliver knew that he had slowly been prepared by Sheldon, though; he had been groomed on and off by him for many years without knowing exactly what for, although lately he had begun to hazard a pretty good guess as to what that might be. On the back of these wink-winks and such, this throat clearing had found Oliver salivating with the taste of power, so sweet on his palate; presently, however, he felt ashamed of himself, sickened even, for having responded in such a way to Sheldon while realising that he must therefore be even more immoral than his best, most blithe guess.

While all this miserably wended through his mind, Oliver realised that the match players had begun to glower at him; feeling like a loiterer and a creep again, he realised that he had better pack it in and take his sorrow elsewhere while waiting for Doris to get her act together.

Once he had finally gained entry to his favourite bolthole, alone again in the corner seat with bitter as his bathwater, he tried to wash himself clean of it all and forget everything. He found that he could not help but study the townsfolk's utterances harder than ever, however, while desperately trying to figure out what it was that set them apart from him – why, despite their impoverishment, they remained cheerful overall. Comparably, he felt incredulous that life seemed to make sense for them when, for him, it felt like an utter chaos of opposing desires and moral sensibilities.

In view of all this, Oliver actually felt tearful again, with his tummy going into spasm, and Doris, who always had those few but very kind words for him, had even fewer today – she was rushed off her feet; Hard-Faced Auggy was off with shingles again. Roy played darts with Grahame, and he gave Oliver looks that once again felt as sharp as the arrows that he flung at the saloon's dartboard with terrible aim; Oliver felt that his sufferance of such an attitude was on the wane.

'Half-wit tuss needs a good old kick in the gnashbarbs,' Oliver muttered to himself, then worried that he had been overheard; when glancing nervously about, it struck him that the women in the snug had such a sense of solidarity between them while in the saloon there was no such geniality. The menfolk huddled together in groups, discussing the birds and bees and sport in the main, but groups that rivalled each other, much like sporting teams, and the spirit of their competitiveness no longer seemed so friendly. Turning around to look at Roy and dare to throw him a grimace that he could not quite muster, Oliver caught sight of Ava instead. The pretty gorse flower, the siren of the north, sat with her brunette tresses falling in flourishes around her bare shoulders while her pollen yellow parasol lay folded at her side, looking much like a fairy's wand. She had chosen a different yet equally elegant frock – canary yellow on this occasion. She was perched upon that barstool with such poise, too, sipping her tonic with immense elegance. Ava: so mature and composed, all yellow and gold, the epitome of womanliness! Thankfully, there was no fuss at all regarding her choice of seating. Morag and the snug's other drinkers simply had not noticed her upon entry; Ava, self-contained and quietly composed, was hardly as standout or loud as her equally magical 'sister', Kitty Kat, having discreetly tucked herself into the saloon's corner with Grahame.

The haze of cigarette and pipe smoke wafting in the saloon's air swirled gently about her; with the sun's rays slicing through the bar windows, it became just as golden as she was, as if to illustrate that she was just as spellbinding as the other two 'sisters', but was perhaps the most mysterious of the three. As well as quite taking his breath away, the picturesque sight of her warmed him unexpectedly, bringing the sirens and their magic to mind; that tummy ache lessened considerably then, and he felt brightened.

It seemed unforgivable upon reflection how scorned they were for their choice of profession, which was surely a noble and humane one; this had been evidenced by how delicately and tactfully Simone had handled his inadequacies – although Oliver did not want to labour that precise point too strongly with himself. Given the stock-still labour market of Greenthorne and the north in general, how could they be blamed? he had to ask himself. Most women looked old beyond their years, after all – ground down by their toil in the sweatshops where they spent far too much of their lives. So, who would not grab a chance to do something else, had they the right credentials? he found himself asking.

All three women wore outfits that spoke of the boldness of headier times; although they were often the teensiest bit worn and threadbare, they were far from sorry looking. And although it felt far too prickly to think of the disaster with Simone too much – his failings were his own, after all, and she could hardly be blamed – he felt that she – well, all three of them – were as faultless as they were stylish. As he continued to sup his bitter, he could not stop thinking of the sirens of the Queen's Head with broader brush strokes and with great reverence.

Perhaps they are comparable with entertainers, Oliver wondered; but, then... their craft is more physical... and judging by the way they had bartered for custom, despite their apparent camaraderie, market forces must drive them to be competitive. Are they not more like sportswomen, then? Do they not deserve similar prestige and recompense for the years of training that such skilfulness must have entailed? With a grin, he could picture them as jockeys then, nimbly riding the town's steeds towards the final furlong, down the home straight, and toward the finish line; if this were the case, he wondered what his own racehorse name would be. He liked to think that *Captain Crackerjack* or *Royal Lancer* suited him, but the sorry affair with Simone had suggested that something like *Milady's Endeavour* or *Tricky Business* would be more apt. He found himself tickled by the drollness of his own self-belittlement; it felt a queer thing indeed because it was somewhat uncharacteristic of him. He also found that he was quite enjoying this rather unanticipated and whimsical stream of consciousness while drinking so much, so he decided to remain seated, carry on with it, and put the heath and alleys off for a day or two.

The following evening in the Oddfellows saloon, Kitty Kat made her second grand entrance, this time draped upon the arm of Bert Greasley. They did not speak inside, but Kitty threw Oliver a look that communicated that her lips were sealed on sensitive matters; sometimes relief can be such a pleasant sensation that it is worth the worry, he thought. Regardless, he did not want more things whispered about him, despite the fact that had she not been so tactful, and had Bert and Grahame learned of his exploits, he would obviously have vastly shot up in their estimation. He hardly wished that Doris learn of his antics, however.

While nursing his bitter, Oliver watched her in his vision's periphery and listened keenly to all her froth and bluster. She was larger than life, as always, and it seemed unsurprising that he had previously wondered if she had merely been a happy dream; like the blue rose always pinned to her, nature rarely offers such surprises, after all, so once you have seen one, you wonder if it was of this earth or of another realm entirely.

With her body draped over Bert's, it was as if he wore her like a silk scarf while she wore him like a comfortable coat; while observant of them both, Oliver envied this physical ease that they had with each other. It was all too obvious, whatever the business side of things, that they had a genuine rapport. He decided, therefore, that Bert could only be the all-time racing great: *Warhorse*, and he was the odds-on favourite because he was clearly at the top of his game if he could please Kitty, professional girlfriend or not. Grahame Lowndes: *Seafarer*, cut a rather close second by Oliver's reckoning because he nearly always had a filly in tow. While watching them, Oliver glumly found himself burying his rekindled desire for women deeper and deeper among the wall-to-wall clutter of his psyche; watching their casual flirtatiousness with each other only sharpened his awareness of how hopeless he had been with Simone – and with Abigail, for that matter. No, he was not, and never could be, *Warhorse* or *Seafarer;* clearly, he was merely *Tricky Business.*

'I'll 'ave another Anne Boleyn, a pint of best for Bertie, and a top-up for Grah'... In fact... to 'ell with it... a round for everyone! Doris, 'ow much'll that be, darlin'?' Kitty asked while snatching an impressive wad of lolly from her purse. The saloon abruptly erupted with cheers and applause. However, it was surprising how little Doris seemed to mind her, or care that she upset the ladies next door, who no doubt sat stiffly with stern looks and trembling chins every time they heard her belly laugh. He could only imagine them becoming increasingly incensed that this intruder, mocking tradition or etiquette, however one might frame it, was lording it up in the saloon, and he knew that they would have guilted Doris for that, had they the nerve. They did not, though; she could be ferocious, could dear Doris.

Eventually, however, Kitty's rasping cackle did rankle the snug's drinkers, to the point that there actually was a complaint from Marina, Myrtle, and Morag, who tentatively entered the saloon; as they argued their case, the old prunes were shrill voiced while characterising Kitty as a wicked witch of some sort, but Oliver felt sure that she was actually a rather wonderful wizardess, and nothing short.

'Number one... women are not allowed in this bar... 'specially not that sort,' Morag hissed at Doris, and then she went on, ticking her points off on her fingers, 'an' number two–'

'My sorta wha'? Wha' you sayin'?' Kitty demanded of them as she rose from her bar stool and braced herself.

'Tha' knows exactly what tha' means!' squawked Marina.

'Not sure I do, darlin',' replied Kitty, scratching her noggin.

'We shall 'ave you kicked out!'

'I'm going nowhere, love,' Kitty barked back. She was clearly quite capable of holding her own, telling Grahame and Bert to 'pipe down and stay out of it,' when they went somewhat overboard in their defence of her. Thankfully, however, before things escalated, Doris, Kitty's unlikely comrade perhaps, put a stop to things –

'Now, now, ladies! It's not like it's wrote in stone, is it? This is t' modern world for 'eaven's sake! An' Bossman wants to 'ave that snug turned into a pool room... so, everyone'll 'ave to drink in 'ere soon enough. Think you need to back off an' leave this lass alone now, any road.'

'No 'ard feelin's, then, loves... I know I'm a right pain in the neck 'alf the time. Didn't wanna cause a fuss,' Kitty called after them with her voice softening considerably as the three 'M's returned to the snug, looking quite sheepish. She clearly got her hackles up easily, but there was a surprising humility and sincerity to her peace offering; for Oliver, this further illustrated that Kitty was as much misunderstood as she was maligned.

'What's up with you? You look right miserable,' Doris barked. Oliver did not turn around. He struggled with eye contact; he always did unless he was lying, of course, in which case he locked eyes mercilessly with the unwitting recipient of his rhubarb. It was a technique that he had learned thanks to Marion, and it was one that he had once depended upon for his survival. Doris was an exception, however, he often felt like she could see straight through him, after all.

'I'm fine Doris... Business as usual, really!'

She was spot on, of course; in stark contrast to the silly, joking mood of the previous afternoon and evening, today Oliver did not feel great by any means. He had no idea how to answer her truthfully or how to explain that even drinking had lost its charm asudden; now that its sole purpose was anaesthetic, it was beginning to taste like it. It was quite the pity, he had spent many a night lying in the gutter once Doris had shut up shop, and when he had first discovered booze, he had been having a terrific time of it in that gutter, looking up at the stars in wonder, three sheets to the wind.

With last orders called and served, in an attempt to re-enact that ritual, Oliver sat swaying on the curb. The stars were barely visible, however; they were obscured by Watkin's dreadful exhaust with the wind's direction as it was. He took this dreadfully hard until he became momentarily distracted by another curb dweller; Clive Turner, even after a long day's graft, for want of a better word, was still sat hunched upon the pavement while injecting something into his arm. Oliver felt compelled to ask what on earth it was –

'Mr Turner, what's that?

'An ooold fffriend of mine, Oliverr,' was Mr Turner's slurred reply. 'Would you llike to get aaacquainted?'

Unequivocally, the answer was a polite 'No thank you, Mr Turner,' for all too obvious reasons. He then watched Mr Turner slump into a quiet, dazed euphoria while unaware that Kitty had crept up behind him, until she gently clasped his shoulder

'You alright sweetie?' she inquired in a concerned tone.

Gripped by a sudden apprehension that she had gotten wind of his failures with Simone, Oliver found himself assured in the next moment that the French siren in question had far too much integrity to have blabbed about it all; yes, he trusted Simone. In fact, he trusted all three of them; their tact and kind-heartedness were all too apparent. Kitty's unexpectedly warm gesture and the tenderness of her voice coaxed tears again, though.

'I'm f-fine thanks... r-really I am,' he spluttered.

'Well... if you say so, lovely.'

She stepped around him and turned to meet his gaze; her eyes glimmered with concern. With a voice as soft as butter, she sang a song that belonged more to Rose Spence: *Heartsore Lady*.

'Come my sweet... Don't sit and weep... What have I done to make you feel so blue ...? I'm sorry too... What did I do...? Have I ever said an unkind word to you?' she crooned, but quite suddenly, despite those tears, Oliver's mind was on a far greater matter than his self-pity.

'My love is true... And just for you... I'd do anything at any time...'

Although it was night already, clear as day, Oliver could discern a bruised crescent upon Kitty's eye socket; it was not so well concealed, despite the makeup that she so liberally applied. It could not possibly have been Bert's handiwork – Oliver knew the chap was solid gold, even if he was a little coarse. While feeling utterly appalled, he hoped that the brute responsible was lying dead in a ditch somewhere! What a fool he had been about this game! He could not help picturing Simone having been similarly bruised by his own foolishness and depravity then; his mother would have been quite right – it had been utterly indecent of him to have sought out her services! It almost felt as if he may just as well have assaulted Kitty himself! Swiftly, in light of all this, he understood why women were better off without him; Marion had always been canny – he was in dire need of an exorcism of some kind, owing to his boundless depravity! He wondered if perhaps he should have words with Reverend Partridge, whom he had avoided like the plague since her funeral; at least then women would be safe, and as an added perk, his mother might finally leave him in peace! Moreover, it went without saying that he would not be scouring those alleyways again now.

But poor Kitty, he thought as she sang the last verse, feeling that it was she that needed his sympathy and not the other way around.

'Every cloud must have a silver lining... Just wait until the sun bursts through... And smile alike, my loveliest dear... While I wipe away each tear... Or else I shall be heartsore–'

'I'm sorry for whatever happened to you,' Oliver said, interrupting her. Glancing at her then, he found that the streetlight's illumination was not so flattering; she appeared to be far older than he had previously thought. Beneath her warpaint, her skin was, in fact, quite mature. Her hair was greying too; the blonde was clearly growing out. Perhaps her life had been tougher than he would have liked to have imagined, or perhaps it was merely that she refused to let middle age subdue her; either way, with all her bluster and bravado, she still made for a great raconteur and rabble rouser – and was no less beautiful.

'Else I'll be heartsore... Don't worry, love, I gave as good as I got,' she muttered while lighting up her cigar and offering him a puff. 'That Jock McAlloran, 'e got nothin' on me.'

'I'm sure... but I'm sorry all the same.'

'Bless you. Aren't you a diamond! I see it, even if this mob don't... So, leave all this behind, chappy... Polish yerself up a bit – I can see you'd scrub up well – and 'ead down to London. I got a friend... lives in Soho... Harold... The call 'im 'The Duchess'... 'E'd put you up... 'E won't want nothin' in return, mind... 'E's not that sorta poof... The big smoke'd be your oyster... I just know it... and you'd be its pearl.'

Oliver smoothed Kitty's arm a little awkwardly – the only comforting gesture that he could think of – and then he leant in and sniffed the blue rose pinned to her fedora. It had no scent; it was merely cloth after all. Feeling utterly embittered by this as much as by the square root of everything, he decided to retire from public life entirely; he decreed that he would not even champion the Oddfellows any longer because even it was starting to depress him. Preferring to wile his miserable evenings away at home instead, he lavished a large portion of his remaining allowance on a heavy haul of gut-rot, courtesy of Murray Pierce: *Yardbird's Pride* – an outsider, but still a favourite of his.

He tried valiantly to anaesthetise his troubled soul indoors instead then, emptying one bottle after another, but this technique seemed to be losing its effectiveness even more; it no longer tranquilized him satisfactorily, nor blot out those awful dreams of his. They remained half remembered yet wholly unsettling. Oh, if only he still had Jonesy to pet, to snuggle with, and to take his mind off it all.

Then slowly, while hours and then another day passed, something curious and unprecedented began to manifest within the storm clouds of Oliver's long-suffering brain; a vision of Marion, very much alive and in the Greenthorne Palace's refuge, began to resurface and regain some clarity. The dream had hardly been a night terror, at least not at first, and he was unable to get it out of his head – especially how serene and soft-hearted she had seemed. It felt like an unexpected counteractant to his memories of the shrewishness, grumbling espoused victimhood, and temper tantrums that had become the corpus of her character. It soon surprised him how often he found himself meditating upon the dreamt scene and trying to visualise it with greater clarity; there was an ease to it, a sense of accord even, that was as alien to him as it was compelling. It began to frustrate him, though, that however hard he tried, he could not contextualise the dreamt scene fully, or recall what his mother had said to him, or him to her, if that exchange meant anything at all. It made him wonder if his feelings towards her had softened somewhat; this felt pretty novel too. Perhaps, then, it was not fair to call her a sourpuss outright; she was far more complex than that. She was just... rather complicated, he thought as these phrases echoed about him –

'Boon for the dispossessed.'

'The poor made happy.'

Oliver remembered the headlines that he had proudly snipped from the *Greenthorne Gazette* when his mother had volunteered to manage the town council's latest initiative to feed the poor and homeless; the newspaper cuttings were still around somewhere, but there was scant chance of ferreting them out. It had likely been her way of coping with her tremendous loss, and whatever the weather's temper, she had gone to the soup kitchen daily, keeping herself as busy as possible. But once the last of the little savings that she had had left were spent and factory work had beckoned, machining overalls for Mr Crowther and tanning smelly animal hides for Mr Sharpe and Mr Beard, Marion's time and energy had become too depleted; she had not enough left of either, so she had reluctantly handed the reins to Mrs Crabtree, and that had been that.

But it was not as if she had been forced to do it, was it? he reminded himself; she could have stayed home and moped. It was not as if she had had a gun held to her head when organising her charity garden fêtes either; considering all this, he suddenly felt that he must acknowledge and even commend her surprisingly selfless actions, however capricious she was in the wider view. Somewhere, beneath all that haughtiness and affectation, there must have been some humanity left after all.

It lucidly came to mind then that many years prior, long before she had become so sour, things had sometimes been rather sweet. It was Oliver's fascination with hearing his mother self-teach French, and his desire to learn this new melodious-sounding language himself, that had brought them closer together – for a while, at least; along this joint endeavour, they had actually found each other quite companionable. He had picked up singular and plural pronouns in no time at all. First, second, and third person soon followed, and then nouns, adjectives, and such had crystallized in his mind. He had also found himself counting to a hundred *en français* in no time at all, just by observing Marion whispering this new magic; his own whisperings had clearly charmed her, too, because he had never seen her look at him with such adoration as when he had learned to say 'Très bien, chère maman,' in an impeccable accent. Soon, young Oliver had found himself ducking into her historical fiction novels and her D.S. Eades, Henry Pearson White, and Siegfried Coates poetry collections also, among many other poets that she had favoured; previously, he had been far too busy fighting battles with lead soldiers or piloting toy tinplate *avions* to know that their contents would soon capture his imagination far more – and as much as they had hers. Once they had, French had quickly been left behind; this was true magic! *L'âge d'or* followed between ages eight to ten or thereabouts. This was when he had had his dearest wish to be a mummy's boy granted, for as long as it had lasted, which had not been for long enough; nevertheless, for a time they had immersed themselves in poetry and prose on warm spring and summer afternoons, just he and she in Ashurst's lovely kitchen. She had read this alchemy aloud to him then, tracing the texts with the arrow of her fingernail. The sunlight had been temperate yet golden in those days; her shadow had been as soft and diffused as his. Only the gentlest of breezes had tugged at the sash curtains while Jeanette Le Blanc had been turned down to a whisper on the gramophone.

You that love England,
Who have an eye for her beauty,
Watch the light pouring
Gently over the uplands.

'Do you know what uplands are, Olly?'
'I think so. Are they hills, Mother?'
'Yes! You're a very bright little boy, Olly. I'm rather proud of you! I'm certain your father would've been too.'

In those days, there had even been a beauty and an elegance about Marion's smoking, just like Edith Granger, before it had become self-abuse with that fag perpetually dangling from her wrinkling mouth – smoking like Watkin & Rees' chimney. A pale, gauzy plume of cigarette smoke had swirled about her then, less like a widow's cap, more like a gossamer bridal veil because her love of literature had led her to remarry; she had become wedded to the catharsis of anti-war poetry primarily, while he, like her little page boy, had trailed at her skirts. It had clearly consoled her deeply after his father's passing. Occasionally, however, Oliver found some of those writings too chilling when he dipped into them –

Bethink one face that you loved before.
No one wears that face you knew.
Death has made it its nevermore.

And furthermore, while she was snoozing on a park bench, how she could have cheerfully been awoken by early spring rains and smiled down at snowdrops after reading these particularly grim lines seemed like an anomaly –

Time waits and then seeds
Crimson blooms in dry land.
Mingling muted sighs with thirst
Blowing dead leaves on parched winds.

Thus past and present, Oliver repurposed the portrait of Simone because in its defiance, it had been determined to portray his mother anyway; he entitled it 'Marion in the Greenthorne Palace'. He became so engrossed in rendering the background that he had to ride the Dales Express to Blandishford and back to replenish his Windsor, emerald, oxide of chromium, Prussian, and cadmium green oils. That Tuesday had undoubtedly been one of the better days of his week. For the accuracy and steadiness of hand required to render the long, willowy lines of Marion's figure, he felt grateful to Murray Pierce for steadying his hands again. He felt similarly indebted to Cranford Electric, of all places; he had learned by the example of Marion and the other dial painters in the way they had been taught to get a fine point to their brushes, and he had copied their technique when painting at home. He laughed then, remembering how Olive Solby had flown at him once for doing just that when painting with Abigail –

'Get that dirty thing out of your mouth! Germs, Olly!' she had snapped. He had never seen Olive so cross – or cross ever for that matter; she had then shown them both a way to point the brush without touching it. Sneakily, however, he had continued to point it with his lips; it was the best way to get the finest point possible, after all.

Thinking of portraiture in general led Oliver's thoughts back to Mr Roper again, and he felt an affinity with the photographer, owing to their shared interest in the subject. Also, now that Oliver had some distance, it became apparent that Mr Roper had a lovably sad air about him; one sensed that things were not at all easy, and the scamp had actually seemed a bit dejected overall while he also appeared to be as habituated to solitude as Oliver was. Oliver therefore decided that he would do him the kindness of sitting for him after all, partly because he felt that they could both do with the company.

'I would make quite an impressive subject and would likely furnish Mr Roper with the inspiration required to reignite his feeling for the lens,' he also mused while rendering his mother's bouquet; he then realised that, of course, the flowers that she had clutched in that dream had been hyacinths. They had been of the palest purple, but the green all about her was a hue that he had never felt comfortable working with, for all the connotations with which it had become irrationally weighted; for him, however, these unfavourable associations had always seemed utterly intrinsic, as if his mother's waspishness had been extracted, distilled, and added to the paints' formulas. Nevertheless, in this instance he felt like he was seeing the colour anew; shades of green that he achieved by blending his stock shades, such as Russian, pear, conifer, and Kelly green were particularly striking. He became so absorbed in this latest masterwork that he remained indoors for another day, or perhaps two, losing track of time entirely while finding intense engagement and even abstinence, despite his awakened libido – such was his absorption.

Meanwhile, he found the impetus to empty the living room of all Marion's things, even the disfigured photographs, while failing to understand or acknowledge the symbolism of this act.

'Tired of this gubbins,' he muttered as he tossed it all into her bedroom without looking in – once he had found the nerve to push her door ajar; he had begun to feel too encroached by her clutter. Furthermore, having lost the ability to gloss over it all, it reminded him too much of the barely recognisable creature shrieking its demands from the settee that it had never left – the cruel monster with the dead eyes. Somehow, this new painting of his felt like a soothing balm for all such eyesores, however, and it reminded him that once, despite her ill-fated marriage, before her dreadful 'career', for want of a better word, and before the 'illness' that eventually took her, his mother had been full of life and light and had quite simply been his queen.

Accordingly, it felt so pressing that Oliver illustrate this fact – that Marion had once been his matriarch and his monarch – some golden blush was needed to stipple an aura about her and the palace itself. He then decided to purchase some gold blush leaf from Templeton's Arts & Crafts Supply Store, which, when mixed with white and yellow, would form a tincture, the shade of which he could see quite clearly in his mind's eye: coronal gold. He also required some cadmium yellow deep to be able to achieve beeswax palest beige because the standard cadmium yellow was not cutting it at all.

The following afternoon, he managed to jump the Dales Express and ride the branch line to Blandishford without paying the fare; he curled himself tightly into a ball in the bottom of the luggage compartment as the ticket inspector swept by, so that he could afford the gold leaf and the yellow oil upon which his creative urges insisted. Templeton's had once made good profit from him before he had become such a shocking drunk that his allowance went muchly on beer; since then, he had stolen from poor half-blind Mr Templeton so many times that he no longer felt guilty for doing so.

While making his merry way back to Blandishford Station, and while feeling rather pleased with his thriftiness, Oliver slowed and then hesitated outside another old and once dear haunt of his: the Blandishford Picture House. He gazed up at it with unanticipated nostalgia while the traffic roared past. He had almost just ducked into the Lamp and Whistle to purchase a half pint of bitter with those coins that he had clung onto when pilfering the paint; the anonymity there – the novelty of not being so heavily scrutinised – was always such an attractive prospect, after all. But now he wondered if it was a good thing that he had passed it by.

Although it had similar form, the Blandishford Picture House was far more handsome and ornate than Greenthorne's dream palace had ever been. Red, blue, pink, and purple strips of neon-infused glass never failed to amaze – the modern world could sometimes seem like a pretty thrilling place! A terribly cheap ticket was all that was required to get lost in some adventure or fantasy unfolding upon its sizeable screen. All as such, he felt compelled to enter, even though he would have to spend those last coins jangling in his pocket.

Oliver could hardly forget that the sweeping curves and ornamented planes of its interior architecture were truly magnificent. Even the colour scheme of its décor, a medley of disconsonant greens, had not bothered him – such was his love of the place. The auditorium's admittedly rather noxious aroma of ingrained sweat, nicotine, and cheap, unfragrant perfume had not fazed him much either; those swirls of cigarette smoke, hazily lit by the projectionist, had only added to the sense of mystery and magic inside.

Back in the present moment and standing outside the place for the first time in many months, he gazed up in wonder at a poster of Edith Granger advertising her new picture: *Aurora*. On some level, he knew that he was peering through rose-tinted lenses while trying to forget how the flicks, despite more than pleasing him initially, had so mercilessly mocked him in the long run.

Two hours later, Oliver emerged from the auditorium's gloom, straining his eyes to retune them to the sunlight's ferocity. Charlie Ford he could take or leave, but Edith Granger, even though she had unexpectedly become as conniving as Patricia Lombard and Marion in this latest role, had still managed to set his heart aflame in *Aurora*. He had felt such sympathy for her, and he had forgiven her unconditionally for all of her character's bitchiness, owing to how unsuspecting she had been; she had pretty much been a fruit fly the entire time that she had sought refuge from her tumultuous past in Buenos Aires. He felt quite sorry for her, in fact, yet he was surprised by her character's naivety; it was a subnarrative that everyone else in the audience would likely have missed. It was not that he imagined himself as being any more sensitive to *Aurora's* undertones than them, however; it was merely that it was patently obvious, going by his own experience, what the two male leads had really been up to in that back alley! He had to admit, though, that he, too, would have curtailed his own susceptibility to men for the flame-haired goddess, and would have remained forever at her side as a kind of flower-girl-cum-walking-cigarette-lighter, given half the chance.

Regrettably, there had been no couples in the centre-back row's shadows to sit next to, however, nor had there been any sweets to suck because Oliver could not afford any. When the ice cream vendor had swept by during the interval, he had felt very dissatisfied indeed while casting the only other picturegoers in the auditorium – a courting couple who had broken their passionate embrace to purchase cornets lavished with generous dollops of vanilla ice cream – the filthiest, bitterest looks he could possibly have mustered. He still felt that this was deserved; if they had not possessed the decorum to confine their carnality to the centre-back row, then they should have had the graciousness to sit within easy sight, at least. It had been a very melancholy note to an otherwise reasonable viewing, and it had hardly reached the heady heights of his former excursions to the Blandishford Picture House.

While clattering back to Greenthorne, still ticketless but daring to risk taking a proper seat, and with the gold leaf and the yellow deep that he had stolen still stuffed in his underwear, he felt mesmerised by the locomotive's rhythmic rattle. He watched the setting sun illuminate Chalk Hill, Gorse Hill, Middle Moor, and Nether Moor in golden shades of amber and apricot; this all looked rather splendid, yet he remained fairly unmoved by it all while realising that the film had only dampened his spirits after all. Inasmuch as that, he should be so lucky than to meet a rich millionaire, get paid handsomely to shine his sword, manage his casino, and then elope with his knockout wife! Edith had been the only truly happy thing about it all.

With Miss Granger having set Oliver's heart so fiercely aflame, he began to re-entertain the notion, dare he even think it, that the female sex was not entirely lost on him after all – nor him on them, hopefully. Clearly, then, the problem with Simone had merely been that she was a smashing lass but was far too lanky; he had only himself to hold accountable for the disaster that had unfolded, then, because it was not as if he had not gotten wind of this in advance. So, gripped by new possibilities, he rushed down the hallway to his bedroom, to eyeball Big Sis and see if he found her any more appealing than when he had last clapped eyes on her.

Unfortunately, it was quite the reverse – he felt instantly unsettled by Big Sis' gaze and he was unable to understand his relationship to whoever it was that looked back at him, and he felt ashamed. Was she his sister, his muse, his mistress, his spirit guide, or his own personal god? He felt more unsure than ever because she suddenly seemed to be as duplicitous and as complex as Edith's role in *Aurora* had been; he had never quite been able to wrap his head around her. He had had Big Sis in his heart and his life ever since he had been a boy, when his childhood chum, Henry Finlay, had procured her from God only knows where and snuck her to him during their lunch hour at St Mark's. Oliver had not been in the least bit struck by her nakedness then; he had merely been spellbound by her beauty – particularly her sparkling eyes and her serene smile. He had realised in that moment that God could not possibly be a man after all.

But later that evening, Marion had caught Oliver in his bedroom admiring Big Sis similarly while knelt before her, as if in prayer; after the severe consequences that followed, involving slamming him against a wall, a fractured finger, and hearing that he was, for the umpteenth time, a 'little peep', this goddess had been snatched from his clutches, crumpled into a ball, and tossed into the wastepaper bin. He had known that he would never be able to part with his new patron saint the very moment he had clapped eyes on her, however; he had decided that he needed her in his life forever to watch over him like a guardian angel, so he had retrieved, uncrumpled, and then secreted her beneath his mattress, where she had remained for many years. He had only been able to safely retrieve Big Sis the day that his mother was buried. It was, in fact, the very first thing that he had done once he had returned home from her funeral; when bringing her out into the light, he had decided that she was not a surrogate matriarch, but more of a big sister that he loved deeply and depended upon because the horse hospital's emptiness had straightaway chilled him to the bone. Naturally, he had realised that he must safeguard his big sister's virtue and protect her modesty, as any protective little brother would have done, so he had painted Aphrodite's toga onto her in swathes of grey and silver. Unfortunately, however, as the months and then years had sped by and he had slowly spiralled into confusion, the paint of her gown had flaked away in tandem; she had become mercilessly defrocked by time's passing, giving Big Sis' bosoms a peephole effect firstly, by which time his hormones had been raging and had already gained a huge command over him. Her exposed areolas became a very guilty pleasure indeed. Soon enough, her appearance, that had once looked so virtuous, had appeared immodest and comely while she had simultaneously inspired the shame that his mother had prepossessed him with. He had still not given her gown a touch up, however, and he had allowed the toga to crumble while feeling worse and worse about himself. His relationship to Big Sis had become as complicated as it had to everyone, and it had ultimately come only to confirm what his mother had said all along: that he was utterly depraved and beyond redemption. This was exactly what he found himself feeling in that present moment while wantonly perusing her charms, searching for gratification, yet simultaneously despising himself for it. But in that moment, unsurprisingly, she struck him as godly again, just as she had in the first place; it felt as if he was caught up in her divine providence while being judged harshly.

Gripped by a sudden bright idea to remedy this problem, escape her unsettling gaze, and make her more palatable generally, Oliver remembered that he had stuffed the film's programme notes into his shorts pocket; they had quite a darling picture of Edith as Aurora on the front page. He decapitated his newly appointed diva-goddess then, cutting around her very carefully, especially her bouffant hairdo – the maintenance of which he imagined must have taken up most of the movie's production schedule. Then with tremendous care, which was difficult with his trembling fingers, he unthinkingly pasted her decapitated head onto Big Sis, without apology to Edith, or to the muse and sister that he had loved for so long. He immediately regretted doing so, unsurprisingly; straightaway, he knew that he had done them both quite a disservice. Not only did he then realise that he had defaced his poor sister, but he also felt that he had made rather a mockery of Edith too. Additionally, not only did her disembodied head look quite incongruous on his sister's body, but Edith's provocative, smouldering grin transposed on Big Sis' once angelic form seemed an absolute travesty. It was almost as if he had shamed Edith too; she had only been acting, after all, and she hardly deserved such a punishment. This also seemed only to add to the sense of hellishness about the collage that he had inadvertently created. The only way to set things right, therefore, was to fetch his oils and paint her over with a gorgeous black sheath dress, just like the one Edith had been wearing in *Aurora*, to tie the image together again, and to make her look more respectable, naturally.

It was a pity about the dress because it was only for a fraction of a second that he felt happy; it quickly dawned on him with horror that he had lost the only woman that he had ever truly loved. Big Sis was gone forever – trapped inside the visage of a flame-haired floozy that he barely knew, and that he had immediately lost all attraction and respect for. Women had driven him to distraction once again and he felt like screaming! Once more, confusion and shame were knocking on his front door; they had returned like old friends that had become so tiresome he had been trying to cut them from his life for quite some time. Since Marion never missed her chance to seize upon this, the coldly burning electric tingle emanating from her fingertips crept up between his shoulder blades, his vision's periphery became violated with flurries of luminescent sift, and his ears were once again filled with that voltaic hiss.

'Immaculate thoughts, Oliver,' was her stern instruction.

'Here we ruddy well go again!' Oliver cried. His mother, unannounced and uninvited, was making her not-so-grand entrance yet again, and his sufferance of her was on the wane too.

'Immaculate thoughts?' he hissed. 'Oh, come on now, Mother... I'm not playing this game, or cat and mouse with you a moment longer! It's actually become rather tiresome more than anything.'

She was clearly taken aback by his effrontery, and she retreated to the netherworld sharpish, and hopefully rather sheepishly, too, because clarity, silence, and his composure returned instantaneously. He easily swept aside her pestering, and he even managed to put aside his mistreatment of Big Sis for the meantime; his mind was far too fixed on wondering if he could dare to ride the Dales Express again without paying the fare, and on torching the ruddy Blandishford Picture House with his gas lighter. Such places, handily, were firetraps already.

Butler's Brouhaha

While stifling his grief over the heart-rending loss of Big Sis, as difficult as that felt, Oliver returned to his mother's portrait and he busied himself with her instead. Although he felt less enthused already, its completion felt non-negotiable; despite his feelings about its subject, which were already reverting to his former dislike, he knew that, technically at least, it must surely be his chef-d'œuvre.

Having emptied his pockets on alcohol and *Aurora*, days of eating leftovers while being consumed by this masterwork had taken its toll finally; this state of near starvation became insufferable. Knowing that life would soon feel even more unendurable, if such a thing were possible, he could not pretend that he had been anything more than pitiful at budgeting again, and he found himself entertaining thoughts of requesting yet another bridging loan. However, remembering that he had not paid back all the previous loans, and knowing how far the scales of power were tipped against him thereby, he decided that it would put him at too great a disadvantage with Uncle Sheldon to beg again, as tempting as it was. How on earth will I stick it out until Friday, then? he found himself fretting. Feeling sick to death with his perpetually whining belly, and with never having quite enough money for his weekly staples as well as foodstuffs, he oftentimes found himself hating Sheldon for his close-fistedness; he could be a bit more realistic in his calculations for me, Oliver thought peevishly, like so many times previous. As follows, he felt sick of poverty in general, sick of ending up on the bottom rung and as much with staying there, along with the hardship of it all. The discomfort of his cramped abode aggrieved him in particular – how everything about it made his body sore, such as that lumpy mattress with the springs poking through it. The horse hospital was too hot in summer while it was too damp and cold in winter – arctic, in fact. He had given up wooding around copses and hedgerows, however; he had similarly given up pinching nuggets of coal from the colliery slag heaps and ash pits once he had nearly been caught red-handed by the site caretakers. The likes of Bert and Grahame did it, but they feared the embarrassment of being caught less than he did, apparently.

The horse hospital was indeed far too small; he could almost feel his spine bending and his limbs shortening to adapt to such little space! For all his own misfortune, Clive Turner's digs were roomier, but Oliver felt that beggardom was beneath him. Oliver suddenly felt compelled to smash everything within his sight and emit a primal scream of outrage at the injustice of it all, and so he did, swiping the table's contents to the floor with the loudest yell that he could possibly muster while a tumble of blue bottles swarmed about him. But then he let out a whimper because he had given his elbow a nasty knock while doing so.

Later, while wandering listlessly through a dreary tangle of poky houses with washing lines strung between them, the south-easterly wind, still unusually warm, became even gustier; with the filth funnelling from Watkin & Rees' chimney down into that clutter of streets, he wheezed and coughed while the townsfolk's freshly laundered bedding and clothing became infused with the stench of its industry. On trudging through those rows, it sometimes hurt too much to sneakily glance through their windows and witness scenes of peaceful domesticity and familial ease; although life in Greenthorne had become a struggle for most, overall there remained a cheerfulness to the daily routine of these families. It was an ease which he had never known himself, with exception for that brief time at Ashurst, of course, but that was long, long ago and too much of a vagueness to hold onto. Soon, however, he neared another rather nondescript two-up two-down that he had always made exception for: the Bailey's residence, and on this Saturday lunchtime the stage curtains were thankfully open. The succulent smell of Hilda Bailey's cooking, stewed beef with carrots and onions, wafted out into the street and made that empty belly of his do somersaults. Mr Bailey, who was nearly always sunk comfortably into his armchair, hardly seemed to be 'ill at ease', nor did he appear in the least bit bothered to be out of work; forever splitting his children's sides, he folded paper darts with pages torn from the *Greenthorne Gazette* in this instance. It was the best use for it in Oliver's opinion because how young Aida and Vera giggled and larked about, throwing the darts back and forth between them! Hilda Bailey entered then, beaming while smoothing down her apron –

'Hark now children... Mind you don't go trippin'... you'll break things,' she warned and then belly laughed. But then little Archie Bailey, a lightly freckled but otherwise bantam-sized version of Oliver, with his hair just as blonde, returned his gaze with reciprocal curiosity and Oliver felt immediately caught out; he quickly moved on then, minding his own business just as Marion always said he should.

Motivated by the wonderful aroma of Hilda's cooking, he wondered if he should at least try to be constructive and pop into Greenthorne's library to see if there was a book on how to cook suet. He had not bothered with the place for seven or eight months – its main attraction for himself and the likes of Clive Turner was its warmth during the colder months; November through March, the reading room served as a refuge for him and all others that had as much time to kill – chaps who could only aimlessly walk the streets otherwise because their unheated homes had become intolerable to dwell in by day. Once inside, just like every other thumb twiddler, Oliver had pretended to scour the situations vacant in the *Blandishford Comet* and the *Greenthorne Gazette* while surreptitiously slipping off his shoes and warming his feet on the radiator. While doing so, it had always seemed rather incongruous to glance about and see shabby, tramp-ish-looking men reading books on philosophy, socialism, trade unionism, economics, and even psychology; following their example, he had given *Socialism Explained* and *The Challenged Mind* a try, but he had found that they left him utterly cold. He had then tried to revisit poetry, but he had quickly remembered why he had packed that in too – for similar reasons to the cinema. The newspapers served merely as props, with no real value whatsoever because Mrs Chivvers, the library's manageress, spitefully cut out the sports pages. Woe betide you if you dozed off or took a swig of Murray Pearce's finest from your hipflask either because she flaming well had eyes in the back of her head!

Once, having noticed the holes in his socks and his big toe reddening on the radiator, Mrs Chivvers had wrinkled up her snout and grabbed him by the scruff, just as she had with everyone else that 'abused the facilities'; he had quickly found himself out in the cold again then, watching his breath steam. How he despised the old prune! Her husband, of the same ilk as Cranford and Watkin, was no doubt busy working his own employees to death while she lorded over this place; anyone would think she was working in the effing British Library and not this sorry little collection of musty-smelling books, he grumbled to himself, just as so many times before. Mrs Chivvers had a face that she deserved, however, which was a small consolation; her snout was so large, pointed, and hooked that one had to duck when she advanced, for fear it would poke one's eye out. One had to be vigilant – one might have to sport an eye patch, like poor old Clive Turner, for the rest of one's life.

Why must folks like her and Mother be so overbearing? Oliver wondered; they had become just as waspish as each other. The two mothers had once joined forces to gang up on him when he had been bickering with her daughter, Avril, regarding who had been 'the greedy little thief'. It was a memory that still made the content of his bladder boil in this present moment; even though many years had passed since, he still felt like demanding of Mrs Chivvers why her silly, sodding daughter had not received the same punishment, at least. After all, they had said that Avril and he were as bad as each other, so it had hardly seemed fair; anyway, it was Avril alone that should have mucked out the French saddle ponies' stable that day in order to atone for the crime, and not him because it was she that had stolen and scoffed the Chelsea buns that Mrs Chivvers had been saving for their luncheon that day. Not only had it felt grossly unjust to be found guilty of a crime that he had not committed, the fact that he had never been allowed to ride those damn ponies had made the punishment seem even more objectionable.

Presently, however, while peeking over the top of the *Gazette's* pages and watching Avril's mother sweep the floor around her desk, she had clearly sensed that he was watching her and she threw him a withering, all too familiar look in return; how can she remember me and Olive Solby not? he wondered while wishing that he had a pail of water to hand with which to administer to Mrs Chivvers.

There were no books on cooking suet either.

'Quite a sorry little selection... Rather a lot of mouldy old books and nothing more,' Oliver grumbled as he took leave of the library's insufferable silence and equally insufferable manageress.

Speaking of mouldy, the leftover bread had become too much so – utterly grey-green – and could no longer be risked. While staggering up Middle Row and feeling rather faint with hunger, the tortuous smell of fresh bread wafting from Jennings was, unsurprisingly, the final provocation; he made a sharp about-face then, and he decided to turn up uninvited at Ferndale to request that bridging loan after all. As he hurried back through Middle Row and in Thorny Grove's direction, the townsfolk that he passed looked similarly sombre, as if they hardly believed in their own existence; by contrast, the alleyways flanking it were quite alive, however. Townsmen, playing pitch-and-toss, placed bets with each other and with unofficial bookies that loitered there by day while hoping that the coins that they gambled might amount to a down payment on a splurge at the pub later that evening. If their pockets were empty, then they would simply wager milk bottle tops for the heck of it; Oliver obviously did not have even a single penny to wager, however, he only bought condensed milk, if ever, and his luck was never good anyway.

By the time he reached Thorny Grove, hurrying past the old chapel and passing the charred remains of the church pews in the bonfire's ashes, he was dizzy with starvation and in quite a state of delirium. He had a vision of Uncle Sheldon warming his hands by that fire because the church had clearly been crushed by modernism, and it had faced rapidly dwindling congregations – a trend that his so-called uncle was increasingly thankful for. It brought an old discourse to mind: a design for life that Oliver had dreamily mapped out while sitting in the centre-back row of his own dream palace, the Blandishford Picture House, and while grasping boob. He considered knocking on the vicarage door and pointing out to the poor shepherd who had lost his flock that if they had kept their pews and simply reserved the back rows, which were always empty anyway, for similar activity then Christendom would have little more to worry about because churches would quickly rival cinemas in their popularity; as follows, religion would become as progressive as they were, and the cultural and religious zeitgeist would catch them up soon enough. He was resolute that he would embrace their message wholeheartedly and remain pious for the rest of his life if this possibility were ever offered. Who wouldn't? he had to ask himself; the answer seemed to be glaringly obvious.

He continued to mull this over as he waited impatiently on Ferndale's front step while failing to realise he had become so distracted by his musings that he had arrived completely disarmed; entirely unprepared, he had forgotten how unfortunate it was that he had never repaid a single bridging loan back, giving no thought as to how carefully therefore the request needed to be broached. It was Maxine's day off, so Sheldon: *Butler's Brouhaha*, terrible odds, answered the door himself finally, looking immediately displeased.

'I'll allow it one more time, but we'll have to look to some kind of arrangement,' was all that his pretend uncle had to say in a rather grave tone regarding Oliver's shameful insolvency. 'Quid pro quo and all that,' he added with his voice dropping another register, but Oliver did not know Latin. While Sheldon dug around for spare change, Oliver managed to peer past the wide diameter of the old nag – barely fit to run, to be put out to pasture, surely – and was sure that he could perceive the shadow of a young man sat in the dimly lit reception room at the hall's far end; Oliver immediately bristled with animosity. In silhouette, the lad's profile was fine indeed, reminding him of one of those rather becoming 'shades' that he had seen in Victoriana collections; he was tall too – much taller than Oliver who, regrettably, was only of average height.

'And what a strange sight you are, boy. You might think about a bath, Oliver... Anyone would think you were on the bloody tramp.'

Oliver took no offence to this; too busy feeling stung by pangs of jealousy and possessiveness to take any heed, he snatched the change from Sheldon's palm and stomped away. Who on earth was that lanky fellow? he wondered angrily; is Tristan Bainbridge Junior here already? What the dickens was Sheldon up to with him, then? And why on earth was that table tennis bat in Sheldon's hand?

***

After ravenously scoffing a Chelsea bun, a sausage roll, and an iced finger from Jennings, Oliver felt a little improved. He had already lost his resolve never to drink in the Oddfellows again; he simply could not resist upon passing because he had change in his pocket again and a tautness in his innards that he needed to soothe. Once inside, while peering through the stencilling on the saloon bar's frosted glass, it seemed a window into nothingness – Middle Row had become deathly quiet, especially now that the alleys had emptied. The townsmen's 'tea was on t' table' and all bets were therefore off. Doris, sadly, was nowhere to be seen again. It felt wonderful nonetheless to down a pint and he quickly became adrift on stormless seas again, as the sun shone even brighter and the ale reached and soothed his overwrought brain; he felt pleasingly distanced from the world and its woes already, safe from the spirits as usual, and he had pretty much forgotten the bewilderment of that Ferndale business already. He greedily glugged down the rest of his bitter.

This very late afternoon, Roy, Grahame, and Bert aside, there was only a handful of other fellas sitting in solitude, much like himself. Theirs were forgettable, grimy faces shadowed beneath felt caps and staring glumly into their ale; they appeared to be so wearied that they did not have the energy to take exception to Oliver – until he ordered again from the bar –

'Another pint of your very finest suds, dear Auggy!'

The saloon erupted into laughter, and even Auggy, hard-faced as she usually was, had the nerve to chuckle too.

'Don't worry lad, they laugh at you 'round 'ere,' an elderly gentleman explained. Oliver was not sure if the old chap was trying to be consolatory, or if he was merely adding insult to injury; thus, as he so often did, Oliver pretended not to hear. Staring at each other while sneering at this, Roy, Grahame, and Bert made that exception –

'Finest suds indeed? Bahahahaha!'

'Waffly as owt.'

''E 'as his amusing side, ah s'pose.'

''E'll not be amusing forever!'

'Look at 'im, sittin' there like a muffin.'

''E's that bandy legged, 'e couldn't stop a pig in a passage, that one.'

'Touché, gnashbarb,' Oliver replied in a muttered whisper.

The sound of broken glass sliced the air as Doris appeared from out the back.

'Oops, that's done it,' she said and giggled, then she promptly disappeared down the cellar steps before Oliver had a chance to catch her eye and wave hello; while looking over his shoulder, Oliver caught Roy in his sight's periphery instead. Goodness, isn't Roy overplaying today's performance, Oliver thought while feeling somewhat taken aback by the steeliness of his stare; he had always thought that Roy understood that he had little to fret about – Oliver was always utterly discreet on such sensitive matters as the alleyways' activities, not that he ever spoke to anyone anyway. Although he quite understood Roy's cold shoulder, he failed to understand his increasingly scathing look. Admittedly, Roy's delicately wrought hands were a charming contrast with his sportsman's build, and he had hazel eyes that were gold, green, and brown all at once; they were striking, admittedly, but Oliver still felt like reminding him that he was not the centre of anyone's universe, not even his fiancée's because when he saw them together, they already looked bored with each other. Perhaps, then, he should cool himself!

The townsmen – the inbetweeners – that used the alleys, heath, and other such places as a libidinous release were, for the most part, merely holidaying in a foreign land to which they had no intention of becoming permanent residents; Oliver believed Roy to be no exception. They were hardly in the same league as Oliver – they were not born degenerates, and neither were they flagrant fruitcakes like Quinn, nor were they stealthy ones like Sheldon. They were not stuck with it all for life either! They enjoyed an unspoken rule that served them well: as long as you weren't a painted, limp-necked, or simpering pansy like poor old Quinn, it was merely a convenient way to let off steam, and it was one which you easily outgrew once you married and started a family. Then you could forget it all with ease and had no repercussions to face. So, why are Roy's knickers in such a twist? Oliver wondered. Roy was not really an odd fellow at all upon reflection – he had many friends, some social standing, gainful employment, and a 'missus', Pearle, waiting in the wings, which meant conjugal duties to look forward to once their courtship had found its way. Yes, Roy had much to look forward to, and he reaped the benefit of these moral concessions while waiting for his future to unfold; the unfairness of it – Roy clearly had no inkling of how blessed he was! Furthermore, his scathing look reminded Oliver of his mother's gaze and he had already had quite enough of her scrutiny!

Roy's animosity was quickly forgotten, however, the moment Oliver felt crumpled paper tickling his leg. Bending down, he found what appeared to be nothing more than a discarded lunch bag dropped there under the bench. When he unfolded it and peered inside, though, its contents utterly astonished him. Inside, beside the breadcrumbs and smeared chutney, were a pair of 'views'. 'Views' were photographs in the format of cabinet cards which he had heard could only be purchased from under the counter in specialist newsagents in the bigger towns and cities with a nudge-nudge and a wink-wink. He had overheard *Seafarer* discussing his growing collection every time that he had found occasion to visit Blandishford. But these particular views were not the typical ones for which Grahame was so partial: 'shady ladies' baring all. No, these were, astonishingly, of young men – merry knaves of approximately Oliver's age leaving nothing to the imagination, nothing at all. Utterly unabashed while in their birthday suits, they posed in settings that looked to be straight out of motion pictures like *Hail Claudius* and *Aladdin*; there was a minimal smattering of props in each, which cleverly connoted the themes of hot, steamy Arabian nights and the decadence that became the fall of Rome. On the back of both cards was stamped the studio's logo: The Electric Light Company, Fort Lee, New Jersey. For Oliver, these were quite the discovery! He instantaneously ached for their beauty, their progressiveness, and their devil-may-care attitude while feeling utterly devastated that they had their life while he had his. Upon realising that he wanted nothing more in this world than to be one of these cocksure models, it struck him in the very next moment, in view of his own handsomeness, that he had all the credentials! No doubt, then, that once his own views were circulated on the underground-fantasy-portraiture market, he would be in tremendous demand! He would surely be invited to studios in far-flung, exotic corners of the world to pose before the photographer's lens, and perhaps even to frolic with these other princes of the radical age ahead. There seemed to be no doubt either that eventually he would wind up in New York City, where he had heard that the hedonistic spirit of the previous decade had not entirely been crushed; there, he would no doubt share a life of endless pleasure with these fine young gents, enjoying thrilling capers in opium dens and jazz clubs. Where the devil did these come from, then? he wondered.

'Sod that nincompoop and his new bloody nephew,' Oliver muttered to himself while realising that he no longer needed Uncle Sheldon, and a new destiny stretched glitteringly before him; luckily, Mr Roper had offered to photograph his portrait already, and once he had done a little sleuthing to ascertain the Electric Light Company's full address and mailed it to them, he had no doubt that he would be summoned for an 'audition', for want of a better word. Yes, the planets are clearly moving into alignment for my future to unfold, and finally the good life beckons, he thought as he forgave Marion instantly for all her snobbery, and he realised that he was his mother's son in more ways than he had previously imagined. But is it so wrong to want the good things in life anyway? he mused; shouldn't, as he had read somewhere, pleasure be the theme of life?

Utterly rapt, he sank deeper and deeper into these fanciful reveries while forgetting his setting entirely; while doing so, he had failed to notice that Dennis Bannister had hurried in. Dennis had spotted him immediately, strode over to the corner seat, and was already towering over him with a browned off look that illustrated that the crossway's outrage had not been forgotten. The fact that the 'queer little duck' quaking in fear before him was dribbling over a full-frontal photograph of some other uphill gardener only angered Dennis even more, who then threw Oliver a look that suggested sleeves might be rolled up; upon Dennis' firm request, Oliver did 'beat it and sharpish' after tremulously bagging the cards and stuffing that lunch bag into his shorts pocket.

'On yer bloody bike, slutchy-eyed weirdo!' Dennis then yelled after him.

'Leave 'im be, Dennis! No need to start throwin' yer weight around jus' cos yer strong in the arm an' weak in the 'ead!' Doris growled as she clattered back up the cellar steps with some urgency.

'Ah'm warnin' ya!' she added with another growl. She never missed a thing, Doris.

Watching only his feet, Oliver missed her consolatory look altogether as he slunk out of the establishment.

Feeling at a particularly low ebb that evening, Oliver, when necking a bottle of newly purchased extra dry gin and nearing unconsciousness, felt quite despairing that he was stuck in Greenthorne while his dreams of winding up in New York City seemed a little far-fetched by the murky light of his mother's rotting lamps. So did relocating to London, as Kitty Kat had suggested. Kitty had been quite right, Greenthorne was utterly pedestrian and lacklustre, but had he the confidence to head down to London? No, he would be entirely out of his depth, as much as he would like to imagine otherwise.

***

'Fancy a stab at table tennis, champ?' Uncle Sheldon asked.

'Really Uncle?' was Oliver's astonished reply. 'That'd be just terrific!'

'Better get suitably attired, then.'

'Time to change into your tighty-whites,' cooed Maxine from behind him; in the room adjacent, she tugged and yanked garments off and on his body, and then she goosed his rump.

'Don't touch that which you can't possibly afford, Maxine!' he snapped, but then he found himself chuckling with her.

'Always wanted to do that,' she purred, and then she tugged up his shorts and ushered him to the indoor sports room. How his heart quickened upon entry! He had to admire Sheldon's new-found taste because its ill-judged and rather odious decor had been reconsidered and remedied finally; the newly painted walls were that fabulous slightly dusky shade of red that they call 'metropolitan' while the philharmonic green wainscoting, Cavendish grey carpeting, and Cambridge blue drapes all tied together brilliantly. Moreover, the walls were adorned with another handsomely framed gallery of blue-ribbon champions and medallists. It was all most unexpected.

'But, Uncle, I didn't think you played.'

'I don't, you little twit. Your adversary has arrived... Oliver, let me introduce you to your opponent.'

Oliver immediately recognised the fellow who entered the indoor sports room stage right, already outfitted in his shorts and tee; it was that tall, gangly git that he had spied sneaking about in Ferndale's shadows.

'Oliver, meet Tristan Bainbridge Junior, my other nephew... down from London for some country pursuits. Tristan, meet Oliver.'

Tristan made his feelings plain by exhibiting a rather supercilious-seeming smirk. Oliver insisted that that newly lain Cavendish grey carpeting tear open and swallow him whole then; it refused to furnish him with such a kindness, however. What had he been thinking? As much as he would enjoy thrashing Sheldon's new toy, of course, the hard truth was that in every aspect of sporting ability he was incurably inept. While feeling incensed by this ill-conceived invitation, it then dawned horribly on Oliver that it was not that it was ill-conceived, but far more likely that it was ill-intentioned.

'The match winner shall be awarded a handsomely paid scholarship, paid fortnightly, to finance and facilitate their table tennis training. Naturally, I shall be delighted to lend my undivided attention and support to such a noble cause... for what is sport, if not the necessary cultural force that civilises man's primitive physical urges,' Sheldon cried.

Upon stepping up to the table and confronting his opponent, acrimony and indignation scalded Oliver's innards enough to forget the hard truths learned on St Mark's playing fields, however; he was going to wipe the conceited smile off that overgrown tallywag's face – nothing else was on the menu!

'Serve!'

With his fancy footwork and good aim, Tristan returned the ball with such devastating velocity that Oliver could not even see the wretched article as it sailed past him, and Sheldon, rapidly losing breath, ran off behind him to retrieve it each and every time. It was upon Tristan's tenth or eleventh consecutive kill shot that Oliver realised that his desired outcome was indeed an impossibility, and that Sheldon had cleverly unearthed the well-hidden secret of his utter uselessness in the sports arena. Oliver's opponent's agility, and his masterly handling of the table tennis bat, earned nothing but astonishment and admiration from Sheldon. Only heckles and boos for Oliver, however, and not from Sheldon, who was too absorbed in his admiration of his opponent; they came from that gallery of the world's finest title holders.

Oliver blinked, and the room slowly came back into focus while the drool dripped off his chin. Well, thank heavens it had only been a rather wretched dream! But he could not shake the worry that this weasel, Tristan bloody Bainbridge Junior, was hard on Sheldon's arse, upstaging him in reality. Oliver had been going off the idea of pandering to Sheldon's fancies until that silhouette of a shit had shown up in

GREENTHORNE

Ferndale. Country pursuits indeed? He had no doubt that his cousin, so to speak, had arrived already and would be moving in with Sheldon; if he was as much the shameless Lothario as his father was, then he had probably got some debutante pregnant and was relocating to Greenthorne to avoid the scandal among London's polite society, was all Oliver's racing mind could imagine. If Oliver lost the real game to this hijacker, then he would never get out of his poverty-stricken life. He could not work, after all; the factories were absolutely shocking, and everyone had shunned him at Watkin & Rees. He had no qualifications either, except in art, which had no vocational application. The word was that only Sharpe & Beard were hiring currently anyway; since Marion had been a former captive of that tannery, it seemed unthinkable to apply, along with the fact that he had too sensitive a nose. It is said that a tanner can only marry another tanner, after all, owing to the unfortunate fact that no other soul could tolerate their stench; it was a stench that he well remembered in all its repugnance.

Worry over his future, with infrequent exception for his darkest moments – moments such as this – was not something that he allowed to have much command over him generally, but when that worry did hit him, its force felt flattening.

Another worry: Sheldon's father still owned the horse hospital, as he did half of Greenthorne, but if Oliver fell out of favour with Sheldon, would his father allow him to remain? The family connection was fairly tenuous, after all. Oliver could then only picture that large photograph hung above the mantel of Ferndale's largest reception room; it was a snap of Sheldon and his chums – the kings and queens of Greenthorne – gathered together at some classy function or other. Quite suddenly, he realised that his admiration for the Grove's businessmen had actually been underscored by much resentment. Once again, he was abrasively reminded that Sheldon, in his days as a company lawyer, had specialised in malfeasance, which had essentially meant book cooking and getting the bigshots off the hook for their misdeeds towards their employees. In the photograph, with a cigar clenched between his teeth, Sheldon had the guests of honour, Minty and Bunny Baxter, on each arm. The three of them stood centre frame in that picture, utterly cock-a-hoop and swelled with self-importance while rubbing shoulders with profiteers such as the van Hildas, the Grosvenors, the Drydens, the Summerskills, the Chivvers, the Spooners, the Cavendish dynasty, 'Sparky' Cranford, and 'Big Bucks' Bradshaw. So, at that time Sheldon had defended and protected these sweatshop owners, who had worked the likes of his mother to their bitter ends while making a mint in the process. He then also thought of how, when at the end of her tether finally, Marion's co-worker, Rose Houghton, had complained to her union, who were not particularly thrilled with the fact that women had recently infiltrated their ranks either; she had brought attention to the inhumanely long shifts at Cranford Electric, the infrequent breaks, poor pay, and such, stating that it was all affecting her and her colleagues' health, and that it all urgently needed to be negotiated. 'Sparky's' counteraction, since he was being sued for stealing trade secrets anyway, was that he was in no position to negotiate; he had also claimed that with the economy as it was, too, he simply could not afford to, and then he had retired to northern France and lived off a hefty stash, or he had moved the outfit abroad perhaps – the gossip had not been conclusive.

Either way, the place had quickly shut its doors – fallen deathly silent suddenly – and the workers had lost their jobs, which, although arduous, were much depended upon; with no other companies hiring at that time, the dial painters, particularly the widows, had faced great difficulty and scarcity thereafter. Marion had hit the settee then, as well as hitting the bottle even harder; her gay feeling of being 'let go' had not lasted more than a day or two either. Quite suddenly, Oliver had found himself at a complete loss with her heightened mania and despair – a resentment towards life that had seemingly doubled overnight.

The injustice of it all! Oliver presently griped to himself after remembering how it had all unfolded; by association with the dial painters, he felt that he, at least, deserved some compensation from Sheldon and his cronies. Yes, he definitely deserved a share of their wealth; this was exactly what he and his mother's cousin had been working toward anyway. Relatively recently, an invisible wireless had been crackling away, attuned to the electric charge of that infinite field of possibility that lay between Sheldon and he; quite recently, however, the airwaves had fallen silent. His chief priority, then, especially now that he had a rival, would be to recharge those airwaves and potentiate their connection – to restore their rapport.

'Marion in the Greenthorne Palace' was signed and dated, and although he had felt very pleased with himself along the way, in its post-mortem things felt anticlimactic and it inspired familiar sensibilities of inadequacy; after his initial self-congratulation with his artistic prowess had simmered down, he noticed its numerous faults. No, it was not at all the runaway success that he had expected of this potential masterpiece while he had been so immersed in it; he glumly concluded that when one takes a step back to facilitate a wider appreciation, one realises that the success of the overall piece is not always the sum of the parts so exquisitely rendered. Overall, the portrait seemed to be visually incohesive somehow. Also, the portrait had already begun to unnerve him because he had not been able to capture her unusually sincere and clement-seeming gaze at all. In fact, she looked far more like she had become in life: haughty and critical. Her prying eyes, the ones that he had unwittingly reanimated, followed his every move then, looking either weed, fly trap, or cactus green, depending upon the light.

'Why has Mother changed?' Oliver had once asked his nana.

'She 'asn't changed... not really,' Gigi had whispered while Marion had slept off her hangover on her settee.

'Always 'ad a good old sulk when she didn't get what she wanted, an' were always t' first to blame everyone but 'erself.'

'Why doesn't Mother speak like you and everybody else, Gigi?' he had also asked regarding those patrician tones that he had picked up from his mother.

'She learned all that fancy lingo off t' radio... What were 'er name now... Lady Westville Sack, ah think it were... Always some fish story 'bout her fancy trips to Persia an' all that guff!' Gigi had replied sharply while plonking her teacup down so forcefully that she had cracked it in two.

'She wanted to be one of them society girls in t' big cities when she were older. It were 'ard to explain to 'er it would never be so. But then she sorta got 'er way in the end, ah s'pose... by marryin' 'im! Your father thought 'e were cock of the flamin' walk an' all!' she then said with a chuckle.

''E did 'is bit for king and country, though, an' 'e were alright, really... your dad... old Terry... God rest 'im. But your mother... blimey... it were queer... as if she were born into the wrong life... if such a thing were possible,' she had then muttered while mopping up the spilt tea.

'Ah do love my Mari... of course ah do, but she don't exactly make it easy, does she now? She's just like your great aunt Florry. She thought she were to the manor born an' all... An', just as stubborn as your mother, she found 'er way there eventually... Married into a title! That were unlikely an' all. Our lot were treated like dirt at the weddin'. Properly looked down upon. Nasty fella she wed... Just ghastly... Small wonder Sheldon an' 'is brothers are such a bloody handful. An' all that money, Olly... good grief... What good did it do for 'em? And you know your mother hated Sheldon... hated him... even when she were cosyin' up to him with her eye on his chequebook.'

It had been a good answer; Marion had been a born snob all right. She had nevertheless been quite bearable until things had begun to go wrong for her. In view of this, it was sometimes hard to hold on to the fact that there once was a time when her disposition had been much more agreeable. But many other women of her time had lost just as much as she had and wound up in the realm of the downtrodden; somehow, however, their humanity had remained intact, owing to the fact that they had been humble enough to accept their misfortune and get on with life as best possible. Could it be, then, that some of the faults of character that she had projected on to him were also her own? he dared to wonder.

Although they had had that special rapport during their *âge d'or*, things had quickly fallen apart once it had passed. Back in the present prickly moment, Oliver found himself revisiting all that had followed with painful clarity. He could not help but browse through their history yet again: past her stay in the infirmary where the doctors were little help, past Crowther Overall Manufacturing, past Sharpe & Beard, past Gigi's passing, and finally through Cranford Electric and beyond. It felt like a rehash of how dramatically their camaraderie had paled away until eventually the only ally that he had left once Gigi had passed had vanished and then reappeared centre stage as his nemesis. He had become a teenager by then – just; his pubescent, raw-boned body had become alien to him as new hair had sprouted in the most peculiar of places. He had suddenly become all hard angles, he had formed pimples, and there had been a roughening of his skin. All this had seemed to disturb her as much as it had him – the way she had so often looked at him with what could so easily be read as aversion, after all, while he had scurried from the harshly lit bathroom to the comforting dimness of his bedroom. In tandem, she had become increasingly judgemental of his interests and habits while becoming even more quarrelsome. By then his poetry recitals, which had previously won him such praise and adoration, were beginning to grate on her instead –

They bathe in beauty,
Like spirits in the palest shroud,
Of love's great mystery,
While dandles and kisses abound.

It was written by John Fisher. It had been one of his absolute favourite poems, and it was written about love, so what on earth could be wrong with it? Oliver had wondered. It had once been the kind of text that she had loved to have read aloud to her. But by those days she could only cock her eyebrow and grimace or even cringe – yes, she had actually cringed sometimes.

'Cloth ears! I've told you enough times to have lost count, this really isn't suitable for your sex or your age, Oliver. You're a man now… Well, you're supposed to be.'

He had indeed become a young man by then, albeit an inferior one by her yardstick. Since he had finally been furnished with a sigh-ridden explanation of why poetry should have been outgrown – particularly the kind he favoured – he had turned to silently sketching and painting instead whenever she was indoors – an activity which, unsurprisingly, she took no interest in whatsoever. He had continued to read poetry by torchlight, however, under the covers, as if it were pornography. It was perhaps as if, buried in her psyche all along, she had actually thought that such sensitivity was passable in a young boy, or even cute, but could only be deemed a weakness when nearing adulthood; perhaps, owing to the war's brutalities, she had felt deep down that men needed to be thick-skinned and hardy – things that he clearly could never be – in order to protect their loved ones and their communities.

'But Mother... it was written by a man.'

He had thrown her for a moment; she had gone quiet while searching for her retort, and when she had answered finally, it had merely been a stumbling deflection –

'That's quite beyond the point, Oliver!' she had replied tartly. 'To write, and to write badly is one thing. To only read, and to read badly is quite another.'

How on earth does one read badly? Oliver had thought. Nevertheless, seemingly, she had resented him for not stepping into his father's shoes, despite them both being size tens. She had no doubt wanted a copy of her Terence, not this stripling, this 'stringy little beanpole' that she had peered at so dimly, straining her eyes with incredulity at what her womb had served up to her amid the carnage of childbirth: a 'nelly', a 'never-do-well', and a 'skinny little sprat'. She had mocked the slenderness of his young body; when measuring the thinness of his wrists by wrapping her own spindly fingers around them, she had expressed astonishment at their slender girth with shrill, grating laughter. From then on, he had hated to be touched – not that he often was. Quickly, then, the world's shadows, once so soft and diffuse, had sharpened and darkened as the years passed after puberty's onset; newly, the world had appeared to be picked out in painfully sharp relief, revealing everything that was wrong with Oliver, and with awfully harsh clarity. Feeling horribly overlit and overexposed, he had grown to dread summers particularly, when the daylight's intensity had become utterly unbearable; every chin pimple had felt stage-lit. The roughening of his skin had also bothered him greatly, particularly the roughening of his hands – the hands that Mrs Dennis-Hunt had so fallen in love with.

When advancing down the hall with a towel draped over his slender hips, the summer sun's rays, slicing through the high stained-glass window with the reddish flourishes pained upon it, had cast his shadow in sharp relief amid a maroon pool of light upon the living room floorboards. His shadow's darkness and elongation amid that pool of blood red light had been another talking point –

'Odd, Oliver, to say the least. Your shadow looks much like your father's... but there you are with such little meat on your bones that anyone would think I've been starving you. I've seen the way other mothers look at me. Do you do it on purpose somehow? You do, don't you...? You mock me!'

'Sorry again, Mother.'

'On purpose? How?' Oliver had later grumbled to himself. 'She's no dummy, but she sure acts like one sometimes!' Gigi had been told numerous times that his mother had academic potential, after all, but her Mari had been hell-bent on that charm school rather than furthering her formal education. Regardless, perhaps Gigi had been correct in her consolations when he had occasionally turned up red-eyed: it was likely that he was beginning to remind her too much of her lost husband while falling short in terms of his manfulness.

'But you're still only a boy, Olly,' Gigi had said. 'Don't take it to heart.' Although the fact that introspection always led to trouble had been more of a feeling that Oliver could not quite articulate to himself, he had still had a vague sense that it had been a problem for both of them – he and his mother; Gigi had probably been right once again.

Soon after the Big Sis incident, Marion had said sneeringly, 'One always sensed that there's something a little uncanny about you, Oliver. I've noticed the way you look at young ladies... I think I shall have to have difficult words with Mrs Solby regarding young Abby, now that we know what a little peep you are. It isn't easy for a mother to admit that her son has become so... well... such a dirty little grub. Dear oh dear, Oliver, whatever shall we do about you?'

'Bent little bugger,' she had also muttered when noticing the way that he gazed at the men's underwear illustrations that featured in her magazines. Thereafter, she had not been able to make up her mind whether she feared that he was a danger to women or to himself; secretly, he had also become confused about such matters. He had slowly grown so desperate for attention of any kind – let alone affection – that he had become inclined to leave his options wide open; Oliver was beginning to tread a path that led towards becoming somewhat of a romantic omnivore, secretly charmed by young men as much as young women. It quickly became apparent that, for Marion, he had thus become a bit of a social embarrassment; since he had perhaps become a little too light on his feet for her tastes, she had decided that it would be for the best if he stopped spending so much time with Henry, Silas, Trevor, and his other boy pals when he was out of school. The words that she had used to lay out these remedial measures had been typically choice. Her provocations and reprimands had not fazed him half as much as she had hoped, however; he was becoming increasingly blasé because Marion had unwittingly been fostering a devil-may-care attitude within her only son. She had pointed out his dubious character traits so unrelentingly that he was feeling increasingly numb and, as such, impervious to it all.

As follows, that maverick take on life that he had felt forced to cultivate became his armour as her malignancy invaded their relationship like a cancer and more years passed; inside his mind, at least, he had become Little Miss Mary Quite Contrary. Although having those traits pointed out would be a pill too bitter for most to swallow, he had decided that he preferred to suck that pill gently, savouring it like the sweetest of *bonbons*; sometimes he regretted that he had never dared to retort and point this out to her. She had hated his sauce on the rare occasion that he had found the nerve to dispense it, however, so he knew that he would have only wound up with another wonky, fractured finger if he had.

While revisiting all this, Oliver became struck suddenly by the realisation that he had been thinking of his mother, and of his history with her, more and more often over the last few days – shocking, it was not his way at all! It felt as if those mental closets, where things had been stockpiled and left for the moths to decimate, had become overstuffed before the moths had even had a chance; having had one too many once-unbearable memories flung into them, they clearly could no longer contain their contents and their doors fell open while it all spilled out rapidly, yet he felt relatively unscathed by this avalanche, surprisingly.

While staring down at the finished portrait, with which he was already quite sick, and which was perhaps another reason all these memories were resurfacing, those eyes still fixed upon him were less chilling asudden – simply bothersome. Had they been goblin, crocodile, or grass snake green? He just could not recall.

'Wish to God I'd never begun this piddling painting... What the devil was I thinking?' Oliver muttered, flipping it face downwards while feeling partly relieved, partly disappointed, and entirely dispirited once again. How will I fill my evenings now? he wondered.

With his gaze once again drifting to the mantel, he felt no fear of witnessing Marion reprise last Friday's pitiful performance. Having seen her so corporeally rendered on that visitation had refreshed his visual memory of her physicality; ever since, her slender bone structure had struck him as rather insubstantial. She had, in fact, resembled a twig that one could easily snap, and she had looked quite brittle, especially towards her end. It was her spirit that had once been so forceful – a spirit which, as much as she liked to pretend otherwise, was trapped in another realm entirely nowadays; had there ever really been anything to fear, then?

While glancing at the mantel still, Oliver found his gaze fixing on his father's portrait instead. What had that fellow really been like? he wondered because his mother's more than favourable endorsements of his father's character were possibly losing their sway; she had naturally been biased, and she was prone to exaggeration generally – she would say anything to impress. He had been full of mettle, grit, and all that good stuff by her account, but plenty others had died in that war, and in far ghastlier ways; they had died slow, agonising deaths upon the battlefield's wastelands, or they had simply rotted to death in those terrible trenches while the fighter aces had skirmished in the skies above. When pilots like his father were shot down, they, more often than not, perished in a mercifully immediate manner; was the old man any more of a hero than those fighting it out tooth and nail below, then? The way his mother had praised his father's war effort, she had certainly seemed to think so. But could anyone be such a faultless specimen of manhood? And could Oliver really be such a poor imitation of him? How could he ever know? Terence Alan Gidley was unknowable. Death had made him its nevermore too.

Nether Moor

While chewing on another uninspiring, zestless breakfast, Oliver found himself mulling over these grim lines –

Tired, trembling, and heartsick,
While the skies give no shelter,
No warmth where the rain pelts,
Beaten, sodden, and spiritless.

He then snatched up his mother's D.S. Eades poetry collection and tossed that into her room too. Within a sweep of the mantel clock's minute hand, he was long gone.

Kicking off his brogues, he then tossed them into his satchel to facilitate his stealthy exploration of the old, disused station's crossway, now that a passing Dales Express had doused it in thick steam; his socks were in desperate need of darning, but the warm concrete underfoot made no argument with his exposed toes. But, having crept entirely along the overpass' length, he felt heavy-hearted because it was entirely deserted.

With equal disappointment, he found that 'Granny' Rogers had shut up shop, which seemed surprising, but then he wondered if perhaps she went to church or choir on Sundays. Sadly, then, there were no confections to be bought and stuffed in his pockets, although they were filled with cigarettes already; he supposed that he would simply have to make do with those.

Oliver came to no harm, much to his relief, as he once again followed that march of steel from the heath's border across its uncultivated lands – a wilderness that, for him, would serve wilder callings than it had ever done previously.

While straining his eyes to survey the place again, the heath suddenly reminded him of one of the tableaux of the 'Dark Continent' that adorned Ferndale House's 'ethnic room', along with all the other exotic swag that Sheldon had come to favour – including all that Egyptian revival nonsense. The ebony wall masks, busts of African ladies with baskets of fruit upon their heads, and other such carvings had always felt misappropriated somehow; the faded photographs of the previous century's explorers, shooting elephants or 'civilising' impressively muscled natives that obviously had no need of this, had always felt just as unseemly.

'One might expect to see zebras or monkeys here, though... elephants even... not these weary rabbits and this scorched gorse,' Oliver muttered while feeling sorry that there was no sign of the particular prey that he was searching for. His newly found carnal urges had marched him the many miles that stretched between the horse hospital and this wilderness rather speedily; they clearly had quite a command over him, but although he had not long arrived, the sunlight's intensity and the long hike there had him feeling overheated and tired already. He could not enjoy the notion that he was some hunter in the wild, as he would have liked to have imagined; bored already and hot and thirsty to boot, his zeal was once again fading fast. Registering no movement whatsoever, Lady Luck was being quite mean-spirited, or so it seemed so far.

He had not bothered stuffing his sketchbook into his satchel to use as a prop because he had barefacedly declared to himself, when he set out on today's excursion, that he would make no bones about its true purpose: to furnish himself with a thrillingly impassioned liaison! This newfound honesty with himself had felt refreshing upon its declaration – exhilarating even.

Perhaps a dickybird finally… but after hearing the snapping sound of dried grass underfoot, Oliver saw that it was only a hare that had hopped rather feebly into view as it gasped at the stale air and then padded sluggishly away. In concert, Oliver felt increasingly mopish while his shoulders were starting to ache with the rubbernecking required to check each nook and cranny of the heathlands thoroughly.

'Cock of the walk!' he told himself while trying to raise his spirits. Remembering how Gigi had affectionately called his father this for his ceaseless bravado, Oliver felt that it rather became him too; he decided in that moment that he would embrace it as his own post-nominal title: Oliver Gidley, Cock of the Walk.

While he continued to wait for Lady Luck to make her grand entrance, he lit up yet another coffin nail and it wrapped him in pale ribbons of smoke before they were thermally sucked skyward. While he savoured his cigarette and drank from his hipflask, he glanced in the aerodrome's direction where birds of war taxied along its airfield. The specks in the far distance were a different kind of aeroplane entirely to the ones his late father piloted; they were streamlined, modern, and ferocious looking up-close. While they glided across the aerodrome's expanse of withered grass, they were still the only movement that he could spot, sadly.

After savouring the last of his smoke's taste upon his leathery lips, Oliver carefully stubbed it out underfoot, minding the tinder-dryness of the underbrush; he felt quite sure that he did not want to start a fire that could easily consume the heath's entirety, and perhaps even Greenthorne itself, within minutes!

'Nothing for my trouble,' he muttered glumly to himself, then he pressed his sweaty palms over his face, shielding himself from the sun's brilliance. That sunlight reddened his eyelids while the heath sounded uncannily quiet again; quiet, except for the chirrups of crickets and the rustling sound of stale air shifting about the lifeless remains of hawthorn and bracken. But then, upon removing his hands and peering about again, he saw that the shimmering outline of a man had appeared amid the haze on the shrubby grounds ahead. Almost a silhouette and verged with an orange blaze – the sun's fiery outline upon him – the man paused, loitered, and then glanced

Oliver's way fixedly. Oliver's breath quickened because he had the queerest feeling that something extremely curious was about to transpire – the significance of which he just could not grasp.

It would have been natural, and all too obvious, to presume that this gentleman was looking at him wantonly, as they so often did in places such as this; if that were the case then Lady Luck would have finally paid her dues. Once, stirred by such aphrodisia, Oliver would have spontaneously gone into kiss chase mode: batted his pretty eyelashes at his admirer, allowed the fellow to pursue him for a while, and then he would have deftly performed a vanishing act. Presently, his response would have been quite different, of course – informed by equally bawdy intentions if he had not felt a peculiarly unaccountable instinct that this was not the case. This was something else. He had an inexplicably haunted feeling as he tentatively glanced in the fellow's direction.

The man just stood and stared. What could this chap want? Oliver had to ask himself. While exceedingly tall – quite intimidating, actually – the stranger had hair the colour of red brick, and even at this distance, he could see that the man's face, although attractive, wore the most baffling of expressions that Oliver could not decode at all. Oliver's heart beat so fast; no one had ever looked at him this way – with such intensity – not even Mr Roper, nor anyone in the darkened alleys. Despite the steely stare, which could so easily have been misread as hostility or desire – he had long ago learned that, with men, they were expressions which could closely approximate each other – Oliver's curiosity was piqued because it was a peculiar stare, as if the man were somehow gazing upon him from another realm entirely.

Breaking from that gaze momentarily, since the intensity and perplexity of it all had become immense, when Oliver did glance back the man had vanished. Just the summer's stillness remained, along with the murmur of stale air as it funnelled about the heath's deadened flora and fauna; beyond that only the faintest scurrying sound of weasels and stoats could be discerned. The cabbage whites, impervious to the heat, still performed their bawdy love rite as they tumbled around the sun-scorched spinneys.

Trying to shrug off that encounter's puzzlement, he plucked another coffin nail from the carton in his pocket, lit up, and took another swig from his flask – watered down extra dry today because he had decided to be far more sensible with his rationing going forward; the last thing he needed was to end up in the sorry situation of having to beg Uncle Sheldon for more money. He had cautioned himself about this during breakfast that morning while also making a mental note to dig around for coinage beneath the cushions of his bogus uncle's armchair at the very next opportunity; Sheldon's pockets could be heard perpetually jangling like Father Christmas' sleigh bells, after all. But thinking about Sheldon and then his new rival, Tristan Bainbridge bloody Junior, if that was who he had seen at Ferndale House, was already making Oliver's stomach feel taut and queasy, as was the cigarette that he gave up on and carefully stubbed out underfoot.

Undoubtedly, the unnaturally landscaped area beyond the tennis pavilion, buried beneath a tangle of brambles and briars, was the start of the old golf course. Oliver had a vague inkling that he may have swung a club himself on one of its teeing areas; as such, he supposed that it was possible that he had been brought there by Sheldon once, but it would have been too long ago to be sure if this was memory or merely fancy.

Only a short while later, just after Watkin & Rees announced a break with another shrill whistle, and without knowing why, he found his gaze drawn to the old tennis pavilion; he wondered if perhaps he was imagining the dim figure that he could just about discern lurking in its gloomy interior. Wishful thinking? he wondered because the eyes played many tricks upon the heath. He paid that ruined empty shell little mind usually; it was too hot to take shelter in by day, so he had clearly missed this other fellow who had awaited his audience all along. Yes, as hard as it was to adjust to the sunlight's brightness, he became certain that he could just about make out a darkened figure waiting as impatiently as he had been in its gloomy confines. A spasm of readiness moved through Oliver, and he found himself propelled in that direction. Within only a few strides, the man ventured out a little, leaning against the pavilion's creaking doorway where he paused, allowing the reddening sunlight to sweep across him. Before Oliver had time to study his face, he noticed with some interest that the fellow was wearing an air force uniform, and must therefore be stationed at Camp Nether Moor. Noticing the redness of his hair then, Oliver realised that he was the very same gentleman who had vanished from sight ten minutes prior. Within a beat of a racing heart, a more far-reaching realisation dawned on Oliver, and how his heart leapt in his chest!

Father! Terence Alan Gidley! His hair was rust red, just as Oliver had been told – the same colour as Jonesy's had been after all – while his cheekbones were high – Oliver's inheritance, as were his small, protruding ears! He had that milky pallor, those biscuit crumb freckles, and those haunting silvery-blue eyes too! That face was his father's, no doubt; Oliver had studied the landscape of that face daily using the picture on the mantel as his guide, and he had come to know its form as intimately as his own. Although he had only the barest of memories and that one photograph to know him by, Oliver was convinced that this was the soul that had sired him and then left this mortal coil before they had ever had a chance to be properly acquainted; Oliver had no doubt that Terence Alan Gidley had returned to make that acquaintance!

Incredulous and amazed thoughts crowded Oliver's mind, and since he could no longer process anything, the scene before him blurred as his head began to pound. His father had moved closer and was already towering over him with an expression of complaisance and purposefulness. He had begun speaking, but Oliver could not process his father's introduction because the noise and chatter in his head, sounding much like all the Morse code that had ever travelled the airwaves, drowned him out completely; the words that Terence spoke – likely to be outpourings on the subjects of regret and of reunification between the realms of the living and deceased – were just incoherent sounds to him, so Oliver simply smiled, nodded, and tried to appear calm and composed even though his innards had seemingly turned to aspic.

Among his racing thoughts, he considered for a moment whether there had been some dastardly contrivance – some plot of his mother's making – to conceal from him that his father had returned from war very much alive; perhaps it had simply not worked out between them? But no, he realised that this could not be – that would have meant that his nana would have been in on the ruse too; she had never minded a white lie if it took the edge off a harsh truth, but Gigi would never have stood for the outright deception of an innocent child. Undoubtedly, then, Terence was yet another revenant; it was unsurprising really because they crept around Oliver always.

Oliver was quickly so awestruck that his whole body trembled. He wanted to fling his arms around the old chap while half expecting his father to do the same as he edged even closer, his eyes still fixed firmly upon his own. He was so tall and manly looking, yet graceful in his gait, cutting exactly the figure that Oliver had always imagined.

But, then, surely this tennis pavilion where men secretly met by night was not a fitting place for their reunion? It had dawned on Oliver rather horribly that the juxtaposition of his father's angelic form with the site of his own deplorable lustfulness felt like an absolute travesty; he was not, therefore, the son Terence would have wished for, nor deserved. It seemed abundantly clear, in fact, that Oliver was entirely unfit. Feeling sick to his stomach then, he dodged his father's embrace, swerved, and hurried back through the heath's scrub, which was suddenly cast in a vexing reddish light. As if propelled by a gust of the deepest melancholy that one could possibly suffer, Oliver increased his stumbling pace. Tears streamed down his cheeks while the shame revisiting his churning innards felt indescribably dense.

He had blown his chance of reconciliation by reason of his tawdry past, and this felt like the final blow. Perhaps, he wondered, when he reached home, he should take that kitchen knife to his throat rather than merely slashing his forearms half-heartedly; it had always felt like a pointless performance anyway, with no one present to witness him becoming so wooed by his self-destructive urges. In any case, since his father had, to all imagining, returned to reprimand him for all his sins, it felt like yet another diabolical visitation by supernatural custodial forces. But, then, life had become a prison already, with Marion's thoughts as his cage, had it not?

Time seemed to have become curiously cockeyed, which only added to the awful sense of the uncanny and unnatural. The sky was darkening rapidly, and the sun had crept surprisingly close to the dales' uplands; he had not realised that he had slept through half of the day before he had risen and arrived so late. He would soon be in darkness. Above, a murder of crows encircled him while a hot gust of air abruptly crashed over him, and the dried-out grass all about him seemed to hiss ominously as it swayed and bent to its will.

Everything was lost – such anguish, such tenderness and tension in his solar plexus as dusk quickly made way for night. The setting sun, already scarlet against the horizon, backlit Camp Nether Moor and its aircraft hangars, which had become the blackest of silhouettes. Glancing nervously around to be sure that the angel had given up on him, Oliver saw that he had, thankfully, because the dimming figure of his father was trudging in the opposite direction, back toward Nether Moor, and then he faded entirely into the darkening undergrowth.

***

Supper, as it so often had been in the past, was simply bread and butter, but without the butter in this instance; with no cold store, nor one of those newfangled fridges that had suddenly become all the rage in Thorny Grove, it liquefied with the summer's heat, becoming utterly vile.

The traffic squeezing through Water Street and the ticking of the mantel clock underscored the quietude of that long, baking summer, as always. Only Terence Alan Gidley's portrait, confined to its tortoiseshell frame, lay on the living room table's stained tablecloth because its clutter had been swiped to the floor. Bathed in his own sweat, Oliver had stiffly sat gazing down at it for quite some time while the moths crept out from the horse hospital's nooks and crannies and fluttered about him before feasting on the drapes and his mother's lamps. He ran his outstretched palm over that face again, trying to feel its morphology, like a blind person upon making a first acquaintance. His cigarette, burning down between his fingers, wafted ringlets and wreathes of grey-blue smoke that quickly paled into nothingness; its ashes, irritating his nostrils, caused him to sneeze, however, and a scrim of mucus splattered his poor father's visage; he felt even greater self-hatred as he hurriedly wiped it off with his sleeve.

Father had looked so imposing in the 'flesh', he thought after having calmed himself a little. The portrait had not really done him justice, as it turned out. Terence was just as tall as his mother, if not taller. So why on earth am I of average height, then? he had to wonder. At school, he had always been the tallest in his class, and he had been the tallest in his year with exception for Johno Webster, who had always had an inch or two on him. But at aged fifteen, or thereabouts, his own body had seemed to have given up and had not bothered to grow even an inch taller; this was around the time he had sneakily begun to pocket and puff on his mother's cigarettes, so maybe it was that that had stunted his growth. Regardless, he could quite understand how enamoured Marion had been with Terence; they had clearly gone together like carrots and peas, and he began to understand her disappointment that he was not particularly modelled upon his father. Oliver knew that he had bloomed, of course, long after her heart attack had dispatched her to the otherworld, so she had not had a chance to witness how much his appearance would change for the better. But to a great depth, despite the good looks that he had become so self-congratulatory about, it hit him that he was hardly the strapping lionheart that one would have expected from the fruit of Terence Alan Gidley's loins – as well as lacking his integrity, bravery, and moral fibre, of course.

'I'm sorry, Father, truly I am,' he whispered while brooding upon his terrible conduct, 'for everything.'

There was a metal trunk, upon which many yellowing copies of the *Greenthorne Gazette* and *Daily Herald* were piled, that he abruptly felt compelled to throw open – to lift its heavy lid and peer inside for what would be the first time in ten years or so. After scattering that pile to the floor, he found that he had forgotten that the wretched article was padlocked. With no key to be found, it was a painful exercise to break that lock – kicking it firstly, then trying to smash it with his mother's old flat iron which still lay under the sideboard along with her sewing basket. He felt like such a weakling again, such a sorry excuse for a man while trying to shatter its lock that he could almost scream with frustration and self-loathing. Finally, a large mallet from the kitchen cabinet's bottom drawer did the job rather nicely, and with only one blow.

The contents were mainly clothes: a suit, some carefully folded slacks and sweaters, a winter coat, some presentation boxes containing cufflinks and a wristwatch. Beneath were letters from ghastly old Grandma Gidley, who Oliver had never bonded with at all; books on aviation; military documents; a birth and death certificate; and condolence letters from the ministry – all quite faded. While feeling surprised to find that these keepsakes stirred no emotion and meant little, despite how much he had idolised this man his entire life, Oliver quickly tossed it all back in; feeling utterly underwhelmed by its contents, he despondently allowed the heavy lid to slam shut and a cloud of dust rose as it did, scented with a curious cocktail of stale cologne, pomade, and other unnameable odours. It assailed his nostrils to the point that he almost sneezed again; it all commingled as a weird-smelling, musty aroma that was most unappealing. But he supposed that it was the smell of a man – a good man – and that such an aroma should be so utterly alien to him was hardly surprising. This realisation, at the very least, furnished him with a truth that, although harsh, he felt that he could take squarely on the chin: there could be no more pretending – ever – that Oliver could be anything other than that which he had always been told. But, then, it was hardly his fault that something had gone awry and he had been born this way: chinless, such an inferior specimen, and such a disappointment to both his parents. It instantaneously became apparent that he simply had to make the best of what paltry qualities he had been born with, which meant stooping to the lowest mode of conduct in most matters while remaining in life's shadows. Small wonder, then, owing to his inherent weakness of character, that he had become self-schooled in such depravity, with extra tutoring from Uncle Sheldon of course; it was absolutely in his blood to be a delinquent, a sinner, and a bent little bugger after all. Clearly, he had a knack for knavery that could not, at this late stage, be unlearned. After making these observations and confessions, he felt lighter somehow.

'So be it!' he exclaimed in utter resignation while raising yet another jam jar of extra dry. Like all those times previous, it at least felt as if he meant it as he glugged the gin down, fast approaching his favourite destination: blotto. The shame that his father's visitation had rekindled paled even more and he felt far less uneasy.

Soon afterward, however, Oliver found himself fixating upon his reflection in the harshly lit bathroom mirror – and with little of the self-satisfaction that he usually felt in what had become such a pleasurable pastime of late; the fondness that he had felt for that looking glass had suddenly become nothing but acrimony. His body, having become quite skinny again, had begun to bother him just as much as it had in former times; he wanted to be broader and manlier – more like his father. Feeling disgusted suddenly by the fullness of his lips and their resulting sensuousness, he felt equally displeased with the rosiness of his cheeks, and he also came to resent the way that his eyebrows and his olive green eyes slanted towards the ridge of his nose. He was, in fact, far too pretty, and being pretty was, needless to say, a female virtue; no wonder, then, that he had failed to inspire Simone, and that Abigail had not appreciated his advances either! The fact that he resembled Marion far more than Terence made him wonder if he should have been born a girl, and whether something had gone terribly awry in utero; he then found himself wondering if this was actually the reason that his mother had grown increasingly critical of his changing body throughout his teenhood.

Either way, all these comparisons, from which he just could not desist, were making him feel utterly wretched, and in a fit of agitation he tore down that shrine to his father's domain: the pictures of military aeroplanes and such pinned opposite his bed. He disposed of the aviation books that he had once been so keen on, too, tossing them into Marion's room also; doing so had felt just the tonic to abate his self-loathing, along with another generously sized measure of extra dry of course.

Finally, after what had felt like several anxiety-ridden eternities in succession, Thursday came around, and his appointment with Mr Roper loomed. As the day had approached, Oliver had found that he was barely able to think of anything else – not about his awakened libido, the heath, the alleys, the crossway, his father, or even his mother. After a reappraisal of the 'views', he submissively came to accept that his brand of beauty, however pixieish or fey, still had tremendous capital in the right circles, which brought motivation enough to become significantly reinvested in it – an allure that Mr Roper had obviously recognised as such. He could only think of Mr Roper's penetrating stare then. *Bachelor's Button* was the photographer's racehorse name, surely, owing in part to those dark but lustrous eyes of his – shiny as buttons; he had become Oliver's odds-on favourite suddenly. Unsurprisingly, however, as the hours passed that Thursday and their appointment loomed even closer, he found himself fretting over his appearance even more. Oliver tore through every item of clothing in his wardrobe, spent considerable time deliberating which were the most flattering garments of his, and then he laundered those that he had picked.

That evening, after giving himself a brisk wipe down, dressing hurriedly, and then briskly making his way to the Old Stores, cutting straight across Middle Row without even glancing in the Oddfellows' direction, the night's stuffiness was upon him. He passed behind and then cut through a factory's forecourt, scrambling through a tear in its wire fence until he finally reached Mill Lane. On nearing the Old Stores at last, his breath quickened. Anxiety rose within him while he slowed his pace and furnished himself with another smoke, making the most of each of those final nerve-wracking seconds before the session began; there could be no turning back, after all – not that he really wanted to, despite some apprehension.

For the first time ever, Oliver was entirely sure that the clickety-clack of those footsteps behind him was only the echo of his own; he found himself wondering then, also for the first time ever, whether he had simply imagined Marion had returned from the dead –

'I do have rather an imagination, apparently. Gigi had so often said so… and I'm also a bit of a pisshead,' he chortled to himself. Following on from this confession, he found himself wondering whether his father's appearance on the heath had been yet another trick of the mind, but that particular visitation had been so uncanny while convincing, he could not hazard a guess either way; whatever the truth of it, in this moment he felt that he had more pressing matters to set his mind on anyway.

Foxes, foraging for leftover scraps of food from tipped over rubbish pails, reminded Oliver of Jonesy by the manner in which their eyes glimmered in the darkness. For the first time ever, however, this provoked only fond memories; no tears followed. The foxes felt like kindred spirits of sorts because he had often found himself foraging in those bins too; with the Old Stores looming, he could only hope that he would never have to stoop to such desperation again.

***

The way that Mr Roper had greeted him, with his kindly looking face awash with anticipation, along with the way he had shaken, or perhaps caressed, Oliver's hand had spoken volumes about his own excitement about the artistic project upon which they were about to embark. Oliver could not help foretasting the photographer drinking in his allure then. *Bachelor's Button* had been just as amiable as he had been during their last acquaintance, and Oliver felt assured that the contents of his penetrating stare were not processed through the workings of a devious mind like Uncle Sheldon's. Oliver still hoped that this sitting might serve as a flirtation ritual of sorts, however. Mr Roper was rather attractive, after all – pleasantly frayed at the edges again. He had not buttoned his shirt up properly, and the top rungs of his chest were quite a savoury sight.

While waiting for his host to get himself organised, Oliver listened to *Bachelor's Button* mutter to himself as he crashed and clonked about in his storeroom; it was quite endearing to hear, however, and it had given him time to adjust to the glare of the photographic lamps, at least, although their sizzling heat remained a test. They still lit every square inch of that place without leniency, and it surprised him, since he would soon be photographed while lit without leniency, too, how little that prospect kept him on tenterhooks now that he had arrived; again, the way Mr Roper had looked at him with such admiration, just as last time, had bolstered his confidence tremendously.

'Now, where is that bugger? S'pose ah musta left it 'ere somewhere... Ah'm a daft apeth sometimes,' Oliver heard his host mutter to himself back there. That man is clearly a rather delightful scatterbrain, he mused.

He felt somewhat comforted because he had expected the same clutter that he had witnessed on his first – well, actually, his second, come to think of it – visit to this studio; the three-quarter bottle's worth of extra dry gin that he had necked on his way there would have helped smooth away the harsh edges of that shambles anyway, but he still appreciated that the place had been tidied in preparation for their sitting. After all, lately, when his mind became cluttered with as much anticipation as this – or anxiety otherwise – any physical clutter around him had become rather hard to bear; he felt similarly pleased that the studio's high windows had been unlatched and remained ajar, not that there was much airflow, but the industrial odour had dissipated a little, at least.

While glancing around then, Mr Roper's portraits struck Oliver as quite remarkable! How had I missed their charms when I came here last week? he had to demand of himself as he studied them in turn. But then, when noticing the photographs of the war's martyrs among them, he found himself thinking of his father again, and he had to look away. Glancing nervously at the display album instead, still lit by the emerald flare of the lily lamp close by, he heeded the empty spot where the crinoline lady had once stood and was instantly revisited, and unfavourably, by the deeply affecting image of her smashed on the floor; its symbolism became painfully apparent as he relived his mother's collapse, and he felt that sickening thud as she hit the floorboards again before paling away to nothingness. Accordingly, anxiety immediately besieged him with an array of stressors and his soggy body, sweating even heavier, quickly saturated those cleanest and nicest of clothes that he had so thoughtfully selected and thoroughly laundered. He then noticed that he could smell himself, too, regrettably.

'S'pose ah'll 'ave to tidy this lot up an' all... What a flamin' bombsite...' Oliver's host muttered while he continued to forage.

Glancing up again, Oliver inadvertently caught the servicemen's collectively stern glare once more, which unnerved him even more acutely; what right had he to be photographed, after all? What great achievement or noble act deserved his own immortalisation? Unlike those heroes, he had no doubt that he would be quite hopeless if he were drafted into the armed forces himself; being so spineless and timorous, he would have no utility whatsoever because he generally shrank from even the slightest of disagreements, let alone confrontations. Reminded again of how much he was the antithesis of his father, and his mother for that matter, who had never shied away from conflict either, Oliver found that his self-loathing had reared and taken hold; unsurprisingly, then, in the next moment he found himself brooding anxiously over his appearance again, and he felt repugnant. Then, remembering how he had hoped that one of Mr Roper's photographs would serve as a calling card to a company that would provide him with a similarly ill-gotten income to the one that he had sought from Uncle Sheldon, Oliver felt even greater self-disgust. Feeling flushed and overheated, too, the sweat continued to drip from him, and he had no doubt that he had become a frightful sight by then.

'Please, stay back there.'

By the time his host had finally located his light meter and re-entered the studio, Oliver had lost every shred of his confidence, and he knew that he was visibly trembling while feeling quite tearful.

The look on Mr Roper's face was hard to interpret when he came rushing back in; Oliver found himself looking sharply away from the dark depths of his host's eyes, nevertheless. The silence in the room was overwhelming until Mr Roper said –

'Er... what does? Er... just 'old on a minute... Ah'll e-er... ah'll be back in just a tick.'

The photographer rushed back out of the room, and Oliver frantically searched for a way to salvage his composure while Mr Roper searched for and fetched whatever else he had forgotten. It was only a few minutes later that he, with some surprise, felt a blanket being thrown over him, swaddling him up.

'T-that's quite all right Mr Roper... I-I-I'm not cold at all.'

The photographer's voice was sincere-sounding but grave in tone –

'Then why's tha shaking, lad?'

'I-I'm not sure... S-sorry.'

Despite himself, Oliver found himself trembling even more, then even more forcefully as tears quickly followed; all he could think was how ugly and absurd his reddening face must have looked.

'I'm sorry Oliver... if this makes thee uncomfortable, we should just stop,' *Batchelor's Button* said gently.

Unable to absorb what Mr Roper had just whispered, Oliver found that it was not the eerie electrical whine of those awful lamps, which illuminated his unsightliness with such cruel clarity, that bothered him as much as the portraits of the war heroes; they had nobly martyred themselves in that terrible war, and seemingly stared down at him in utter disbelief at the disgraceful spectacle that he had made of himself, and at the life of immorality that he had also made for himself among the freedom that their sacrifice had afforded him. Furthermore, his host's well-meaning gesture – swaddling him up with that blanket – had left him reeling; it had provoked a myriad of emotions that Oliver could not possibly untangle in the present, wretched moment. It had been peculiarly comforting for the briefest of times, but even when covered by it, he still felt like an eyesore. Surely, then, his bloom was more like one of those rotten-smelling flowers of flesh, carrion flowers – revolting plants that Sheldon had mentioned during his insufferable, sleep-inducing prattling on about the exoticisms of the 'Dark Continent'.

Sobbing ever more gutturally, Oliver felt that he needed to flee from Vale Studios as soon as possible. Mr Roper had sat himself down and was poised anxiously with his hands covering his face while Oliver, feeling ever more blinded and overheated, searched for his satchel, sobbing all the while.

'L-l-look,' Mr Roper stuttered, 'p-praps we can just wind things back a bit... S-start over.'

Oliver, having found it finally, tottered unsteadily towards the door. Hush up, he thought, and then he turned to his host and snapped –

'Fat chance, Mr Roper. I seem to have made quite the fool of myself!'

'You 'ave not! It's me that's made a mockery of thee, lad...' Mr Roper muttered, 'an' ah couldn't be sorrier for what ah've done.'

'Actually, it would be a great kindness if you could forget me altogether,' Oliver barked as his shadow melted into the hot night.

Indoor Sports

Oliver had not had a wink of sleep, and he was in no mood at all for Uncle Sheldon; his patience had worn rather thin with their charade – the tiresome parlour game that they had been playing all year.

Despite his extreme fatigue, as predicted, sleep had been an impossibility, owing to his overstrung mood. It had been far too dark to lie awake the whole night, however, without switching on that frightful machine-like lamp, with its light flashing and flickering, and with its faulty wiring emitting that obnoxious singeing aroma; popping, arcing, and crackling still suggested that some connection had gone terribly wrong, but since electricity increasingly repulsed him, he felt disinclined to try and fix it more than ever. After tossing and turning for what had felt like hours, he had relented finally and switched it on; while lying there in complete surrender to it, he had felt on the verge of a seizure owing to the light's frenzied pulsation. To pass the time, he had attempted to read the book that Uncle Sheldon had given him for homework. Poetry was a thing of the past, after all, bringing his mother's disapproval too much to mind, he had read all his adventure and spy sagas a thousand times already, and he could hardly revisit *Geronimo Bill* so soon. So, although he had already assumed that Dickie Shoosmith's offering, *Psychoanalysis for the Feeble-Minded*, deserved nothing but contempt, he had decided that he would humour it, and Sheldon, for a brief time, perhaps in the hope it might free his mind of the horrendous fiasco that had transpired at Vale Studios. 'Bugger all that, then,' he had muttered while trying to convince himself that his increasing anger and frustration at Sheldon had somehow trumped the shame of it all; Oliver was still cock of the goddamn walk, after all! But it had still felt as if he had been hiding from his mother all night while hoping that she remained in her bedroom and kept all thoughts on the unfortunate matter to herself. Thus, he had felt that he dare not leave the safety of his own bedroom for the constancy of the living room's lamps. Poor, overwrought Oliver had to suffer all this until dawn broke finally, and it furnished him with some natural illumination, much to his relief. Then he had switched the horrendous item off finally.

While flicking through the book's strobing pages with jittery fingers, lines such as 'A permanent malaise lays claim to the mind of the feeble-minded, giving rise to many problems of which they are entirely unaware...' had marked that it, unsurprisingly, was going to be rather aggravating reading. Then lines such as 'Every human feels directionless from time to time, but the feeble-minded would not know a map, even if they had been forced to draw one...' had aroused acute exasperation.

'Heavens to sodding Betsy,' he had huffed miserably as he had continued to flick through its densely worded pages; all the while, the lamp's strobing effect had left visual afterimages – as if those lines had been stamped onto his retinas permanently. Finally, the line 'Work is a common phobia for the feeble-minded, but has tremendous therapeutic benefit, given the right conditions ...' had touched an already raw nerve, and it had irked him enough to risk the hallway, quickly dash downstairs, throw the book onto the outhouse lavatory floor, and then urinate upon it until its pages were a pleasing shade of Naples yellow. While doing so, he had wanted to shake his buggersome fake uncle violently for all his nonsense, and for this book especially; it had clearly been another jibe, and was another diversion from the road to riches and privilege – possibilities that Sheldon had dangled before him like carrots for too long.

Yes, Oliver wanted the comfort of Ferndale House permanently; yes, he wanted money, fine clothes, and trips to the races in the Bentley parked out front of Ferndale;

and yes, he was quite willing to offer himself up without reservation to Sheldon's every freakish fancy. Well, he would make it appear that way, at least; it was time for the real game to begin!

'So, what's the delay?' he muttered to himself incredulously as he passed the Jolly Gamesman by. 'Surely Bainbridge should feel blessed to have my attention! It really takes the cake... Pearls before swine...'

Oliver saw Ferndale House on the horizon, at last, and his indignation deepened; his anger had become so great that it did indeed trump all of last night's shame – Mr Roper and Vale Studios were completely off his mind.

'And why was he so aloof last time?' he carped in his next breath. Is it something to do with that weasel, Tristan? he could only wonder when thinking of the good-looking beanpole that he had spied seated in Ferndale's shadows, wantonly awaiting some suspicious caper with his unfaithful sham of an uncle. He remembered that, mind-bogglingly, Sheldon had clutched a table tennis bat when answering the door, and Oliver then remembered the dream that that sight had inspired; as hard as it was to swallow, the loathsome table tennis champ of his dreams must have been playing indoor sports with Sheldon. Oliver immediately found himself worrying that the silly old buffoon might drop dead of a heart attack, due to physical exertion that he would be woefully unconditioned for – dropped dead before he had won his favour enough to have been written into his will!

'What on earth is the old twerp playing at, allowing that cuckoo... well... anyone, for that matter... into the indoor sports room anyway...' he muttered, '... especially when I've been denied that right for so long?'

This stinking dung worm was undoubtedly stealing his birth rights from right under his very nose, threatening to pilfer everything that he had worked so very hard to get his own hands on, and before the dirty deal with Sheldon had finally been struck. By the time he reached Ferndale's front gate, Oliver decided that this simply would not do!

Without bothering to knock, he simply let himself in through the servants' side entrance, and after helping himself to a slug of ginger wine from the decanter, he plonked himself down on the chaise, facing that poor facsimile of the 'uncle' that he had once so admired. Sheldon already appeared pleasingly agog at his impertinence.

Upon entry and while making his way to their usual spot, he had scrutinised Ferndale's ground floor thoroughly and was satisfied that the lanky lad was not present. He told himself that he would grill Maxine about it all the second he got a moment alone with her. Sheldon could never be direct about anything, after all; he enjoyed his games, but at least he had had the courtesy of being punctual on this occasion!

Making himself quite comfortable, Oliver flippantly threw off his shoes and socks, and then, since he was in short trousers again, he stretched out his sun-kissed legs while feeling pleased with how their fine golden hairs shimmered in the morning sunlight. While dangling one leg over the chaise's headrest in a pose of pure provocation and ruthless determination, he felt that he had already dealt Sheldon a formidable blow; he noted that Sheldon appeared quite flustered while picking at his tightly buttoned collar, as if he were struggling for breath. Oliver had, in fact, arranged his limbs very carefully to mimic the pose of one of those lewd luminaries that featured in the 'views' that he had been studying with such admiration all week. But then, somewhat regrettably, pungent odours wafted about them both and he realised that his feet were hardly the freshest; after a brief flicker of embarrassment, he salvaged his devil-may-care attitude. Plucking a cigarette from his shirt pocket, he then tapped it three times upon his hand, just like Wade Noble or Randolph Stewart. He lit and proceeded to smoke it with elegance, in a tribute to those matinee idols that he had once so idolised; it was a well-rehearsed act, and one which was paying handsome dividends already. Yes, it was clear by Sheldon's muteness and wide eyes that Oliver's charms had been reinvigorated and were considerable; he had all the power again. Sheldon's eyes were as wide as dinner plates, in fact, ogling the main course finally after far too many tastebud tickling appetisers. The Cranford Aurora two-valve K63 – a shameless Plakativ Apparat rip-off – was switched off and the silence was quite delicious.

'Are you quite comfortable?' Sheldon asked in an unusually weak tone. He was clearly aflame; Oliver had no doubt then that he had successfully reignited his taste for the diabolical – just in the nick of time too! Of course, Oliver realised that he could never actually let the old fruit anywhere near him – that would be unthinkable! Sheldon was an utter eyesore! Once again, Oliver told himself that he would simply have to give Sheldon the impression that he might one day have a place in his bed, and meanwhile play hard to get; Oliver would be the one dangling the carrots in future! The tension once again crackled in the air between them like an invisible wireless. Prudent not to answer just yet, though, Oliver savvied as Sheldon shifted uneasily in his chair.

'Yes... well... ehm... tell me, Oliver, how have you been?'

Oliver glanced about the room, and while keeping his mouth firmly shut to suggest indifference, he noticed the latest additions to the room's increasingly absurd-seeming display, and he could not suppress a giggle. More ridiculous props had appeared – for starters, a gold-lacquered badminton racquet, of all things! I mean gold, I ask you? he thought as he surveyed Sheldon's other newly acquired *objets d'sport*. In the far corner, a tailor's mannequin sported a rather well-worn cricket jersey while an admittedly rather sweet bronze of an aerialist sat atop the grand piano that had never once had its ivories tinkled, and yet more pewter shot putters had appeared, poised and ready to wield their discuses about the place.

'Eating well? How have you been managing your bridging loan? Carefully, I hope.'

Oliver still gave no reply. Sheldon was clearly transfixed by his smouldering stare now that he had returned his gaze.

'And your homework... how much have you read?' Sheldon asked just as weakly. Oliver took another puff, refusing to furnish him with a reply until he had drained his cigarette of its nicotine yield and felt quite satisfied. Garlands of smoke looped and whorled around them in shades of tear drop blue and scotch mist grey. That'll do beautifully, he thought as he stubbed it out.

'I found it rather tiresome Uncle... In the end, I preferred to watch television,' he answered finally.

'Television?' Sheldon looked very surprised indeed. 'How could you afford such an appliance? Bit of a luxury – what!'

'Oh, Mother bought one... or perhaps she borrowed it from Cranford. She said it was an invention that would improve our lives immeasurably.'

'I see.'

'Yes, Mother said information is fired at little phosphors on the screen and pictures form... That it's like the eye in reverse.'

'Fascinating.'

'It is, actually. Look, I'm rather thirsty, Uncle Bainbridge. Can you please have Maxine bring some refreshment?'

'Well... yes... but first... I really think–'

'Now please, Uncle! I'm utterly parched!'

Although he was feeling quite pleased with his showmanship, Oliver quickly became aware that his lips and palette had been wicked dry by the cigarette, and they tasted quite unpleasant. While wiping his mouth with the back of his hand, he realised how chapped his lips felt, then he quickly felt just as brittle overall, and quite depleted; as his bravado quickly dwindled, his underlying achiness and exhaustion became all too apparent. Glancing down at his legs and arms, he realised how grubby his skin actually appeared. Additionally, those hands of his, having always looked old beyond their years, appeared shocking to him in the harsh sunlight streaming through the bay windows; their lines had seemingly deepened. Glancing down at his bare feet also, he could not ignore their reek any longer; shame seeped through him while another electrical-sounding hum became audible. Mr Roper must have been truly aghast at my appearance last night, he thought; what a polite fellow. Clearly, I have just misread Sheldon's reaction too.

A murky haze seemed to swirl about Oliver again, infused with that peculiar luminescence that had marked his life ever since Cranford Electric had appointed Marion their dial painter number eight; those shimmers in his vision's periphery seemed to morph once again into apparitional, figural form.

He then understood that he must calm down since he had gotten rather carried away. Marion, all-knowing and ever watchful, was presiding over this appointment, of course, but perhaps with a little less disapproval than he had previously imagined; she had, more than likely, come to coax him into less shameful behaviours, then. He guessed that in all her pestering, she must have had his best interests at heart all along, which might well turn out to be a saving grace. After all, he had made an utter fool of himself in a very similar manner only last night, and if he carried on acting this way, the ruin he could bring upon himself! Feeling ashamed for all this as much as for his feet, he curled himself tightly into a ball on the chaise, feeling utterly contrite. He could see quite clearly, just before he closed his lids tightly, that Sheldon's changed expression signalled that he was consoled with having the upper hand again.

'You really don't look great Oliver, or smell great either,' Sheldon said, then he called for his servant girl –

'Maxine, can you find and fetch my snuff, this really is too much to bear. And can you open the window. Christ... you reek like a butcher's apron, boy!'

Yes, Oliver knew it and did not need it pointed out – the shame of it all was already enormous! Maxine trotted into the room with the snuff and a tray of refreshment while Oliver, with eyes still tightly closed, did not dare to look at her legs to see if they were covered or bare; instead, he tried to focus on having immaculate thoughts. From this low angle, however, once he had opened his eyes again, he noticed that odd fellow out once more: a portrait of a rather doe-eyed Dales Express engine driver that was always turned facing the wall. Although it seemed unthinkable, the portrait's placement may have hinted that buried somewhere beneath all that blubber and avarice, Sheldon must have had a heart to be broken once, and could not entirely be such a monster therefore. While wondering if his dummy uncle's intentions – at least some of them – might be more noble than he had ever given him credit for, Oliver still felt reluctant to give him too much latitude, if he were really being honest.

'I know Uncle... I'm quite a state. I've just not been sleeping at all well... and you know that when I do, I suffer from nightmares... the most awful kind.'

Sheldon, while idly doodling upon a notebook in his lap, scratched his head while his eyes rolled back in their sunken sockets again; he wearily replied –

'And what are these nightmares?'

'Often to do with Cranford Electric... damn that place.'

'Ah.'

'You worked for them, too, though, didn't you Uncle? In a manner of speaking.'

Sheldon dodged that inquiry, and while probing his revoltingly hairy nostrils, he only replied –

'What sort of things do you dream about?'

'Oh, I don't know how to explain... just awful things.'

'Cranford, eh?'

'Yes... yes.'

'You dream of your mother also?'

Oliver did not reply; he did not need to. Sheldon laughed then and said –

'Well, no wonder you call them nightmares!'

Oh dear, Oliver thought, I've walked right into this.

'Well, she was rather mean to you, wasn't she...? Cruikshank told me all about it,' Sheldon said with a smile, unsurprisingly.

'Mother was perfectly all right really. She just expected a lot. She was a stickler for discipline, that's all!' Oliver yapped back at him. But is this what I really think? he found himself wondering; he had tried to avoid the subject for so long that he was no longer sure. Regardless, it still felt far safer to leap to her defence, with her eavesdropping as always.

'No, Oliver, you forget... I knew her since childhood. She was always a difficult woman, your mother, believe me.'

'No, not always,' Oliver countered, defaulting to that curious mode of defending her; surely only he had the right to think badly of her, if allowed at all.

'Oliver, as I've tried to tell you many times already, your mother was born petulant. She had an axe to grind and a bone to pick with everybody. Moreover, nothing that happened to her didn't also happen to many women of her generation, thanks to that regrettable yet unavoidable war. You haven't seen them becoming so bitterly unhinged, though, have you? She acted as though she were singularly picked out and stalked by misfortune because it suited her. I begrudgingly applaud her performance, however – a pity she never tried her hand at acting. She'd have been quite the success if she had. Again, though, you haven't seen others behaving as she did, have you?'

While Oliver was consumed with thoughts about Sheldon's awful accusations, the spark and din grew fiercer in his eyes and ears, and the smell of overheated fuse wire suggested that Marion's ears were also burning. However, despite all this, he still could not stop fretting over whether it was in any way fair to call his mother 'bitterly unhinged'. It was undeniable that she had become quite insufferable toward the end of her life, but Sheldon was being too cruel again, surely. She had been incredibly unfortunate thrice over, after all. Widowhood. Sickness. Cranford. But then Oliver had to acknowledge that, along the lines of what Sheldon had just pointed out, other women had actually felt empowered by their entry to the labour market, and they had not felt in the least bit exploited or diminished by it; he had heard this on the wireless once and he had also overheard Olive Solby say as much, but Olive's and many of those other women's husbands had survived all that – most had come home from war and were earning a wage again. Once more, his mother had not been so lucky.

Bone picking? Oliver then wondered; Bitter? Acting? Hmm... acting? It's far too simple to align her with any of that, surely. A bit of a snob, obviously. She had never really wanted to work while demanding the good life, of course... but when she was forced into work, she had not looked down on her co-workers at all, who were of a different class; theirs was the class that she had been relieved to leave behind, admittedly, but it still seemed too simplistic to call her an outright snob even, or bitter. She had admired them for doing their bit too. She had said so many times; it was not that she looked down upon them for being happy with their lot... merely that she demanded far more from life. Well... that is what she had so often said.

Following straight on from this, however, he found himself wondering if this was merely what Marion felt that she ought to feel... or perhaps she felt that this was what others needed to hear, so that they would not think badly of her. Perhaps, then, dare he even think it, Sheldon was right... at least in part on this particular point of contention; as post-war realities became apparent, and it had dawned on her that her wages could not possibly maintain the lifestyle to which she had grown so accustomed, she was not best pleased, after all. He supposed that when facing widowhood and a future of hard work, she had become embittered without fair cause because many others had been in the same boat... but rowing it with greater determination... and, more pertinently, with far greater humility.

'Well, have you?' Sheldon said, quizzing him again.

Oliver had no doubt that his mother felt just as uncomfortable with this dissection of her life and character as he was, yet he still could not desist from this internal argument; he could not let Sheldon berate his mother any more than was fair – if it was fair to speak ill of the dead at all.

'No, perhaps not,' Oliver said reluctantly while wondering whether even a fraction of her embitterment was understandable; but, then, her work as a dial painter at Cranford Electric was a soulless kind of drudgery that they had all found difficult to endure, and she had often found herself working even longer shifts than Rose, Olive, and all the others... That certainly had not helped matters... The jobs that she had had prior, all of which had been fairly demanding, must have slowly robbed her of her resolve and energy, with Cranford – the worst of them all – being the final straw... And, again, one should not forget that she had been a single mother... a sole earner... quite a different scenario to those women whose husbands had been fortunate enough to return home in one piece!

Sometimes Oliver tried to hold Cranford Electric entirely responsible for Marion's ruin while knowing deep down that it was far too easy and simplistic to lay all the blame at its front steps; years of suffering had done damage to her already. Sheldon had assured him that 'Sparky' Cranford was a perfectly decent fellow anyway while reminding him that a demanding work culture was merely what was required of Britain's workforce to get Britannia fighting fit again. But then again, he thought, what with all that industrial espionage, and the scandal of the stolen radio technology trade secrets that he had uncovered when stumbling across Sheldon's erotica, how could Cranford ever be trusted, or Sheldon, for that matter? That month in hospital and all those tests had revealed nothing much... but was it really so mysterious, the malady that had gripped her? Was she not simply being worked into the ground until her heart simply could not take any more? Still no clearer on the matter, all Oliver could retort to Sheldon's accusation was –

'But she had a terrible illness.'

'Or so she said. She always had an imagination, your mother. You forget that all the doctors that she ever consulted, Doctor Dryden included when I sent her for a private consultation, could find little wrong with her. A malady so serious yet repeatedly overlooked seems infinitely unlikely. No, she brought it all on herself, with all that hatefulness festering inside her, along with her drinking. No wonder her heart, if she actually had one, couldn't take it!'

Even the wireless coughed and spluttered in objection to that!

'Yes, okay, don't shout...' Oliver replied sharply. 'Think what you like... but, if I may, I'm sure your memory fails you, Uncle. That's not at all what the hospital doctors said.'

'And what was their diagnosis exactly?'

'They said p-perhaps founder's fever... or the... ehm... brass chills,' Oliver said in an improvised, faltering reply. In truth, all he could remember was how much those quacks had apparently scratched their heads while looming over Marion's gurney in the infirmary; the truth was that they were at rather a loss with her, deciding finally that she was likely suffering from extreme exhaustion and moderate malnourishment.

'Well, neither of those are fatal, are they? Doctor Dryden found her to be as fit as a fiddle, but he warned her about her drinking,' Sheldon said while topping up his sherry glass.

'Her illness was real! I was there, Uncle. I saw what it did to her. She had a heart attack, for heaven's sake!'

'Hmm... you'd be surprised, Oliver, at the illnesses people dream up and manifest. I cannot think of any purer expression of the spite that burned within her. And for someone that heartless, to have their heart fail them comes as no surprise.'

Really? Is it actually possible that one can make themselves so ill by thought or feeling alone? Oliver wondered. He supposed that all her rancour, whether justifiable or not, alongside her years of backbreaking labour could have manifested an illness of sorts. But 'heartless'? What arrogance! He briefly browsed through Marion's career history after her husband had been lost: Crowther Overall Manufacturing, Sharpe & Beard, of course, and some odd jobs here and there that he could not quite remember. Throughout most of that she had seemed as if she was managing reasonably and accepting her fate with the teensiest of grace, at least, however she truly felt, disclosing only the odd complaint here and there. But by the time Cranford Electric had gotten its grubby hands on her, it had become an umbrage that could no longer be suppressed. Perhaps, then, that umbrage was the cause of the malady after all, and not merely the expression of it, as Sheldon seemed to be suggesting, but this rather muddled inquiry only seemed to go around in circles, revealing nothing.

'Oliver?!'

Oliver's head brimmed with so much clangour and chatter around these thoughts that he barely registered that Sheldon was trying to bring him back into the room and the present moment.

Whether the illness was real or self-imposed, it makes no difference ultimately, he thought decidedly; it was clearly beyond her control – how she changed and became, at the very least, brainsick. By sense of that, what happened to her was deeply unfair; no one deserves that, not even your worst enemy!

'Oliver, are you actually still with us?'

Finally, Oliver reached a familiar conclusion: he could only remind himself that he had found great mental relief in ceasing to deliberate whether his mother's awful behaviour was excusable or inexcusable in light of the illness that she had possibly suffered from, and the unfortunate hand that life had dealt her. Overworked, embittered, or diseased, it made no difference, at the end of the day. This still felt like the best approach; it also felt far simpler not to brood on it all and keep it closeted in the recesses of his psyche, just as before. It made him, and no doubt her, increasingly uncomfortable to have Sheldon prod him this way!

'Yes, yes, Uncle. But perhaps we might change the subject. I'm not sure I like you talking about Mother this way,' Oliver finally said as he reopened his eyes. He saw that Marion had already paled away, mercifully, so it was just Sheldon and he again. His gaze became lost in the luminosity of the jade Saturn lamp parked next to the chaise.

'It's incredible the lengths you'll go to in order to defend her... you still feel that these problems justify the harm she caused you?' Sheldon cried.

'Harm? I never said it was harm!' Oliver cried out as his vision became clouded and that maddening hiss sounded even louder. Harm? He had never imagined, not even for one second, that such a term had any bearing upon him. Harm? The word rang out in his mind like an alarm bell. Was it at all relevant? Dare he even consider it? His temples throbbed while he felt their veins becoming distended; he knew immediately that he would be in the grip of another migraine if he could not find a way out of this. The discordance of the electrostatic noise that coursed along his ear canals grew fiercer. This still did not deter him from pressing on, however; his psyche was on its own trajectory, cross referencing and investigating this accusation of harm thoroughly.

Oliver found himself blown hither-and-thither through his past then; already, he was back in his bedroom at age thirteen, tentatively unfolding that torn out picture of Big Sis that his schoolboy chum, Henry Finlay, had snuck to him in St Mark's lavatories during their lunch hour that day. Again, she was not at all naked in his eyes – merely undraped. Utterly entranced, he stared down at her while Marion barged in without bothering to knock, as usual; she snatched Big Sis from him then, crumpled her into a ball in her fist, branded him a 'little peep', and walloped him hard enough that she managed to fracture his finger when he and the wall collided.

'From now on, think only immaculate thoughts, Oliver!' she barked, and from that point on, with eyebrow cocked, she grilled him with regularity on this matter –

'Immaculate thoughts Oliver! Don't forget, I can see straight into your soul... and believe me, there's nothing good to see,' she hissed from behind her permanent veil of cigarette smoke.

'Oliver, are you listening?' Sheldon whinnied, but Oliver, oblivious to Sheldon's rising agitation, and with his hagridden past distressing him even more, could not even hear, let alone answer. Sheldon felt so stymied, in fact, that he plucked three oranges from the fruit bowl and began to juggle them in the hope it might draw Oliver's attention back to the present moment; Oliver's mind's eye was so focused on the past, however, that they merely appeared as a faint blur in his vision's periphery while he was being blown all about the horse hospital and across days, weeks, and years, fleeing from and tussling with his mother and her increasingly frightful countenance.

Yes, she had acted like a total monster by his teenage years, and it seemed quite symbolic how her physical appearance had taken on a terrifying aspect over time: skeletal, ghoulish even, as if she had one foot in the grave already. Additionally, as she exhaled that plume of smoke from her cigarette, its gauzy wafts semi-obscured her, making her look even more colourless and phantasmal. The grey smock in which Cranford had outfitted her and the other dial painters, with its little barbed metallic hooks instead of buttons, had become her *robe de chambre* once they had all been laid off, and it had become increasingly ragged and threadbare. In uniform, her bare arms had become thin and sinuous with the sharpest of nubs for elbows. Her face, so hollowed by then, had sunken cheeks so deeply carved that they had resided in permanent shadow while her eyes had become eldritch glisters of blackest black and greenest green.

Once, sometime earlier, in a rare moment of thoughtfulness that was rather misguided, she had brought some of the dial painter's luminescent paint home for him to paint with, but Oliver was not particularly taken with it; the stuff was too eerie, after all.

'Stupid brat... So ungrateful... Don't know why I ever bother!' had been her reaction, which had not helped at all, nor had the fact that she had put him over her knee for a thorough hiding, which had felt utterly horrendous because he had been too old to be spanked by then; he had become a teenager, after all, and it had felt bizarre and rather inappropriate, whereas it had merely felt unfair before. A clip around the ear would have sufficed, surely? It did not get any better either, not in any respect – he spent his teenhood perpetually soaked in her disapproval, of course. While remembering all this, he could only wonder if Sheldon was right; perhaps he should hate her for all that, and wear that hate upon his sleeve!

'Please, Oliver, snap out of it,' Sheldon brayed.

Oliver could not, however; his brain certainly was not ready to, despite the distress of having all this dredged up. He felt hot and bothered, to say the very least; the ambient and cellular heat had him feeling like he might internally combust while sweat poured off him profusely.

With fresh hindsight, there seemed little excuse for what he found himself reliving with such unbearable clarity; he could hear her caterwauling, the door splintering, and the lock snapping yet again as she forced her way into the bathroom that she was so very proud of. She straight off informed him that he would have to pay for the lock's repair while pointing to the grime that he had not cleaned up yet, despite him having every intention of doing so; severe consequences followed if you did not leave it sparkling, and he had learned this long before. It became apparent to him suddenly that she had broken in once again to find an excuse to rebuke him because he had become so adept at damage control that she was running out of opportunities to do so, and she had to manufacture her own.

'But Mummy, I always do I... simply haven't dried yet.'

'My name is Marion!' she screamed. Yes, that was around the time she began to insist that he address her as 'Marion' – 'Mummy' or 'Mother' absolutely infuriated her.

While clutching a towel close to protect his modesty, her ambush made him feel vulnerable and queer again; he hated to be seen so unattired – so very scrawny, as she had so often pointed out.

'Quite a sorry little article, as per usual,' Marion muttered while flouncing out again. After some time gripping the tiling's grout with an all-too-familiar ache in his innards, he turned and caught sight of his reflection in the mirror again, finding himself despairing of it more than ever for its lack of lovability.

After wearily dressing and then dutifully cooking both their suppers, she frowned at the dish that Oliver served her, as always, saying that he had 'made a right muck of it'. But then, finding himself back with Sheldon and remembering what she had followed that up with, he felt an immediate stab to the heart. Ever since, what she had said had been forced safely below the threshold of his consciousness; he suddenly realised that he had not been aware of how his psyche had served to protect him thereafter. But how could I have forgotten that… what she had said and thought, he still had to wonder, in view of its gravity. His throat clamped shut and tears pricked his eyes; it was just too awful to recall, after all.

'Per-perhaps I did mind…' he blurted out in a timely and calculated deflection while all din and spark was quickly damped down.

Sheldon, relieved to have him back in the room again, checked his timepiece, yawned out yet another unfragrant, billowing cloud of pipe smoke, and said –

'Right, now that you're back with us–'

'… but I wouldn't say it was harm… It's not my place to, not with everything that happ–'

'Yes, yes, Oliver, but time is of the essence. You've been wittering on for almost our entire hour together, and there's still a final item on our agenda.'

'No, I haven't, have I? But what about my mother?'

'Yes, yes, I suspect there's much there that you need to confront,' Sheldon said snappily, 'but another day. So, pressing on...' he added while checking his timepiece and extinguishing his pipe.

'Maxine, could you fetch the indoor sports bag from the games room? It's the rather large burgundy one with all the bats and balls and such.'

'Right you are, Mr Bainbridge.'

'And finally... as to our arrangement,' Sheldon murmured as he stood up, stretched out his arms, shook out his legs, and then cracked his thick knuckles. Crossing the room with surprising grace then, he briskly drew the sash curtains, and the room became dim.

So, here was the showdown finally, but it was arriving far too early for Oliver, who felt too tired, too overheated, and too unsure of Sheldon's motivations; addedly, the disturbing droning in his ears had yet to simmer down. He instantly regretted that he had sought that extra bridging loan because he knew how much the scales of power were tipped against him in that moment; the moment had arrived nonetheless and felt unpostponable. The plentitude of possibilities that had existed between them had collapsed into singular form; Sheldon's will had shaped that form entirely while Oliver's mind had been elsewhere. Disaster clearly loomed.

'Come closer, then, boy.'

Once Maxine had retreated into the gloom of the house, Oliver, with all confidence a distant memory, crossed the dimmed room, shuffling on bended knee toward Sheldon's darkened shadow. While doing so, he swallowed hard and hoped that it would not be too awful; somehow, however, he knew that whatever was about to take place, it could not be anything but awful.

'And perhaps a little forced contrition for your flagrant abuse of my generosity and charitable nature,' Sheldon said in a cruel-sounding whisper.

All around, the showcase of admirable athletes, gymnasts, and other such blue-ribbon champions watched silently, their gaze filled with contempt and disgust for the disgraceful spectacle unfolding before them.

***

Although it had felt like an eternity, little more than fifteen minutes had passed before Sheldon had slunk upstairs and Oliver had set off in the dourest of moods. An utter fury had propelled him through the maze of chambers and halls that led to the front porch, and along the way he had conspired with himself to smash every vainglorious trinket therein, but he only managed one such act of wreckage: Sheldon's 1:100 scale model of the *Grande Rue de Paris* had gotten a pretty good kicking, at least. When reaching the front entranceway, he turned and glanced into the large Rococo mirror placed there and was astonished by the barely recognisable creature that returned his gaze. His nicotine-stained fingers; his long, straggly chin whiskers; his blemished, bruised, and dirty skin; and his greasy, matted hair were all quite an eye-opener. The dismay of having his true countenance revealed to him was quickly turned into furious rebellion, however; swiftly, he gloried in his dishevelment!

'What about your socks and shoes, Master Gidley?' Maxine called after him, but he felt that he could not turn back. He wondered if, after fetching the bag of torture instruments masquerading as sports paraphernalia, she had stood silently in the hallway, eavesdropping whilst smirking to herself – loathsome harpy if she had!

While tearing across Ferndale's front lawns, Oliver grabbed fistfuls of soil from the flowerbeds and smeared them across his cheeks.

'I'm a madman! Look! A madman for ever bothering with you, Bainbridge!'

Accordingly, the housewives of Thorny Grove stared at Oliver with horrified amazement as he passed them by; they may have looked like roses, but he quite understood why the old garden village was called Thorny Grove nowadays. As well as disarming those smug, prickly gnashbarbs, this bizarre act also paid off rather well in Middle Row because he enjoyed looks of incredulity and astonishment from passers-by, although the hot and sticky tar underfoot had become unbearable by then – scorching his tender soles too much. On passing Olive Solby, who was dutifully weeding her flower beds with all the speed and dexterity of her ancient tortoise, he found it quite tempting to throw her a look of fury that she no longer acknowledged him at all. But he was still a person of civility even if his appearance no longer reflected it, and, more importantly, he loved her. His allowance, which had been made up in advance and then tossed onto the chaise after the atrocity, amounted to nothing more than damages in his opinion, and this inadequate compensation would cover a barrel's worth of beer, at least.

A sign outside Allsop Florist read 'Horse manure, well-rotted'. He decided that he would purchase a sack, haul it back, and empty it over Ferndale's front steps, had he the strength.

Showering his bare feet and Jennings' entranceway with crumbs and jelly, Oliver stood and scoffed a pork pie with all the table manners of the rats that foraged for scraps of meat and shortcrust in the bakery out back. Soon after, however, Doris foiled his plan to shock and dismay her customers too – he had gone too far, apparently, and he would not be served until after he had gone home for a bath. She spoke to him as if he was a petulant child in need of a firm hand, which he did not appreciate one bit, not until she laughed while squeezing his dirty cheeks, and then squealed 'Filthy beggar!' while gaping at the muck that came off in her hand.

'You've been got!' she called after him.

The warm, soapy water was surprisingly edifying, however, and he felt grateful for the first time ever that Marion had been such a stickler for cleanliness. She had spent the last of her savings on that bathroom, with its bath, wash basin, and mint green tiling all around; there were conveniences that she had refused to relinquish, despite their downward mobility and the resulting change of living standards. He watched sadly as all his defiance and rage gurgled down the plughole in brown swirls of mud, and he made sure to leave the tub filthy.

Why not go the whole hog, Oliver then thought as he dragged a rusty, blunt razor over his chin whiskers and attacked his mop with a pair of scissors, leaving himself with only the barest crown of straw-coloured tufts. A quick glance in his bathroom mirror was reassuring; he looked much, much better after his bath and trim, and he dared to believe that he was not quite as ravaged by sin as he had feared. When wondering, in all seriousness, if he should return to Ferndale to slit Sheldon's throat, he decided that a pint was more pressing.

'And why is that damn thing still on,' he cried upon noticing the machine-like lamp was still flickering and flashing upon his nightstand; he was sure that he had switched it off that morning.

'Blighted damned contraption!' he screamed as he sent it sailing through his bedroom window and across the horse hospital's rooftops.

'That better, Doris? I'm chuffin' parched, as they say. A tall glass of ale then, if you will.'

Doris was still unimpressed with Oliver's barefooting; he had barely passed muster, but he had passed nonetheless, and his greeting had charmed her enough. The Oddfellows had emptied out somewhat and was extremely quiet, with the saloon bar empty except for Roy Wilks and some other dimwit who Oliver did not know from Adam; he made sure to appear as if he had not noticed either of them upon entry. Does that gnashbarb ever work? was Oliver's indignant gripe. But even in his dear old sanctum, he did not feel any better – not yet. His backside still smarted from the sound thrashing that Sheldon had given him; it brought back lucid reminders of his mother doing exactly the same thing countless times past. All hope that it would not be as miserable as he had sensed it would be was quashed the moment the table tennis bat had bounced off his derrière; the pain had seared through him with an unexpectedly vivid charge, and all he could imagine was Marion's phantasm watching the scene; she had probably gotten up from the chair in the corner where she always sat, and then crossed the room towards them, dripping luminescent ectoplasm in her wake. Then, with her ghostly hands clasped around her villainous cousin's, she had no doubt gleefully assisted in the heave-ho of the bat as it bounced off his tender cheeks.

'I'll admit that you've had a brush with misfortune since both your parents passed away... and you've been left comparatively down at heel... but you're too old to act like an orphan, for goodness sake! And you stink, boy. You stink!' Sheldon had cried while they had played indoor sports finally.

'Bastard effing tuss!' Oliver muttered to himself while his fists bunched in his pockets – a rebuke that came a little late.

'What were that love?' Doris queried as she wiped down the tabletop behind him.

'Oh, nothing Doris... Don't mind me. Just having a word with myself, as you've so often said I should,' he replied.

A joke always served as a good deflection, especially with Doris because she enjoyed a bit of banter; she laughed and moved away, allowing him to sink back into his revulsion.

In retrospect, it had been a profoundly disturbing experience, as well as physically painful – not at all the heady power play that Oliver had hoped for, wherein riches and privilege would be traded. While making his getaway, he had looked grievously about at all the treasures of Ferndale House, understanding finally that they would never be his; perhaps they had never been available to be bartered for in the first place, as he had presumed – again, that preposterous pillock, Sheldon, and his insane bloody games! The thwack of the table tennis bat had dislodged intense yet fathomless emotions; every cell in his body still screamed with their charge. Now that he was seated, they could not be suppressed, and tears pricked in his eyes, ran over his cheeks, and topped up his beer.

'I'm such an idiot!'

As usual, when emotions became too intense to be borne or grasped, he thought only of Jonesy's bright butterscotch eyes and reddish and orangey-striped tail; at least then he felt that he understood the precise composition of his tears. He yearned suddenly for the simplicity of their bond when no other relationship, except with Gigi, had ever made any real sense. Most folks behaved unthinkably, after all! But he realised that he had better stopper up his tear ducts and stop acting like such a heartsore laddie before Roy or Doris noticed, and especially now that another chap had just entered the saloon, had seated himself in the alcove opposite, and was browsing through a copy of the *Greenthorne Gazette*; Oliver hardly wished this stranger to look up from that rag and witness his weepiness and wallowing in self-pity either.

That said, perhaps a more pertinent reason to stop whimpering was that this was exactly the horsewhipping's intended purpose – to reduce him to a blubbering wreck, as well as giving bastard Bainbridge his jollies, of course. Again, the abuse that Marion and her dastardly cousin had just administered horribly echoed all her own good hidings, times past when she had been alive. No, I shan't give either the satisfaction, he assured himself as he wiped his nose and blotted his tears with his sleeve. He still had a good mind to break into Ferndale, however, accost Maxine so that she could not alert the police, creep into his vile quasi-uncle's boudoir, and cleave open his skull while he snored like a horse. A pity, he thought upon remembering that he had left Marion's bone-headed walking stick – the intended murder weapon – at home. I should have at least kicked humpty dratted dumpty squarely in the gusset before he crashed back upstairs, he also thought while feeling driven asudden to smash his pint glass upon the saloon bar's floorboards.

Admittedly, Oliver had initially felt disgruntled that the stranger seated opposite had chosen to sit so close and might notice the tears that he was still struggling to wipe away; Oliver soon came to notice, however, how the fellow was dressed, and he realised that he must be another airman, likely stationed at Camp Nether Moor. From the corner of his eye, he began to study this gentleman more closely, but without the greatest of clarity because his vision had already begun to shimmer, owing to his tipsiness. In the ruby-coloured cast of the electric lights that Doris had just switched on, due to the sun's disappearance over Greenthorne's horizon, the stranger's handsomely carved features had become dapples of cerise and deepest maroon. He was tall, and he was yet another ginger, with biscuit crumb freckles amid a milky pallor. Sinuously carved mounds of muscle, bulging beneath his air force blue pullover with overstitched elbow patches, impressed Oliver once he had removed his long overcoat. He had remarkable silvery-blue eyes too.

'Crikey!' Oliver muttered as he recognised the fellow and took a reflexive intake of breath. While returning Oliver's unassured glances with the same thousand-yard-stare as he had during the previous dusk's uncanniness, the chap felt far less unnerving in this setting; on this occasion, despite his drunkenness, Oliver understood how mistaken he had been upon the heath. The stranger did indeed share his father's red hair and freckled fairness, and he had similar height and breadth to what Oliver had always envisaged, but the fellow was hardly his father's double; with such close proximity, Oliver could discern that the stranger's brow was far heavier than his father's, and his lips were much fuller while his eyes, although the same silvery-blue, had a startling honey-coloured halo around the pupil. His father's eyes had actually been far colder looking, in his portrait, at least.

Appearing to have become gripped by a sudden urgency, the serviceman gulped down the three-quarter pint of ale that he had remaining without pausing for breath, threw his overcoat back on, rolled up his newspaper, stuffed it into his coat pocket, and then rose to his feet with his eyes locked upon Oliver all the while; his alluring expression undoubtedly beckoned Oliver to follow him as he left. Although Oliver did his level best to appear as if them both leaving at the same time was happenstance, that piece of elastic strung from the stranger's coattails to Oliver's toecaps was all too apparent to Roy, who enviously watched Oliver trot out of the saloon bar, hot on the heels of this striking stranger. As Roy heard a motorbike being kick-started and then its engine growl as it sped away into the night, he found himself resenting Pearle more than he had ever done.

***

Although he had let this gentleman in already, Oliver soon found the stranger forcing open another door, but he forgave the intrusion the moment the stranger had made his way in because he immediately felt an incredible fire kindling in his loins, which then crept up along his spine, and then on through every nerve fibre in his body; this was something altogether different to the showy swordsmanship that he had witnessed in the alleyways! The mere sight of this sinuous, stocky thoroughbred beneath him set his mind equally ablaze while the glorious sensation of flesh against flesh upstaged the sharp stinging that Bainbridge's spanking had left upon his rump and haunches. The room shimmered and blurred at the edges. Pushing against him was, with each thrust, a revelation! This was *Captain Crackerjack*, surely! *Captain Crackerjack* wore a necklace with a propeller-shaped pendant, which reminded Oliver that he was an airman of some sort; Oliver's body felt like an airborne vessel entirely at the aerialist's command.

It felt like the perfect antidote to the abuse that he had suffered at the hands of Sheldon and his mother's spirit only hours before; what had he been thinking, bothering with that berk and entertaining soft thoughts of that harpy? He steadied himself again, swearing that he would not stop until this exquisitely fashioned dynamo had pummelled every trace of their reproach and his shame out of him; he even found himself hoping that his mother was watching him because it would be the brickbat to all her disdain and criticism. Now, he had some sense of what he should have done with Simone, yet he felt that he would likely never want to even try again.

After the explosion, which felt incendiary, their shared petite mort was peaceful. Oliver's only thought then was how relieved he was that he had tidied away his toys.

Finally, *Captain Crackerjack* lit two cigarettes and handed one over. They both smoked quietly then, wafting ribbons and circlets of smoke that captured the moon's brightness; thus, the clouds inside his room became just as silvery bright as those drifting in the night sky. Finally, after this surprisingly comfortable silence, the captain whispered in a Scots accent –

'Damn, laddie... yae sure are a pretty one. Ah want tae dress yae up like a proper lady an' take you oot on the town...'

'Oh, really?'

'Aye... jus' like yae lady friend up there,' his bedfellow added while pointing up at Big Sis supplanted by Edith Granger. For a moment, since he felt oddly liberated, this sounded like quite a gas to Oliver, and he almost pointed out the lipstick that Simone had left on the bedstand, but then thought better of it.

'Ma name's Gordy, by the ways... wha's yours?'

'Olly,' Oliver replied quietly.

'Ahm pleased tae meet yae, Olly... She's the doughboy's sweetheart, ye ken?' Gordy said of Edith, who was probably being painted on the side of fighter planes at that very moment on the Atlantic's opposing shore. For a moment, Oliver missed Big Sis terribly, but he then realised that he still had his big sister in his heart, and he no longer needed her picture to remember her by.

'Charmed,' Gordy whispered as he shook his hand. That huge shovel of a hand engulfing Oliver's slender one felt a little overwhelming, and he felt a twinge of self-consciousness, but this pang of anxiety quickly passed.

'Likewise, I'm sure.'

'Yae lost yae shoes?'

'Something like that,' Oliver replied, then smirked when remembering where he had left them.

'Ah seen yae before... yae dinnae ken?'

'I do... I know... I'm sorry... I thought you were somebody else.'

'Whit?'

'Oh, it doesn't matter... I was just mistaken... Very mistaken.'

'Aboot whit?'

'Nothing... It really doesn't matter anymore.'

'Well... tha's okay then, laddie.'

It truly no longer mattered. Blimey, what a dashed-handsome devil, was all Oliver could think of the surly Celt lying alongside him; he trumped *Warhorse* and *Seafarer* without a doubt. Gordy, or *Captain Crackerjack*, as Oliver still preferred to think of him, had become the odds-on favourite – no contest.

Oliver felt glad that he had left his bedroom window open since Simone had graced him with her presence because the breeze – unusually cool – seem to cleanse the room, as well as cleansing his mind of all possible remorse or any other ill-thought on what had just transpired; he freely allowed himself to be kissed again.

The captain's eyes were most arresting to gaze upon until they finally flickered shut and he drifted off to sleep. It felt like a curious sensation to lie in the arms of another and drift off oneself – wonderful, actually.

Tungsten Flame

Blown southerly by a chill wind, the exhausts from Watkin's, Spooner's, and Sharpe's smokestacks hazed the air around Oliver. With Greenthorne sprawling far below, the clouds drifting alongside him were a stippling of raw sienna, fringed by the setting sun with fine strokes of cadmium yellow deep.

His outstretched arm was, oddly enough, that of a boy's while his chubby little hand was being clasped tightly by a far larger one with a thickly knuckled wrench for fingers and thumb; it belonged to his father, of course, who was also flying wingless alongside him, and wearing the tightly collared buttonless tunic and side cap that Oliver had always pictured him attired in.

Terence Alan Gidley turned and looked at his son then, with those grey-blue eyes of his; his gaze contained no discernible affection and was steely.

'Time to be a hero, Oliver... to do your bit for king and country,' was his father's instruction.

Eagerness and compliancy immediately took Oliver over as he signalled his readiness and willingness with a nod; despite the firmness of the directive, he would unhesitatingly do whatever his commandeering father wanted of him – such was his devotion.

'We tied the knot there, your mother and I... You were but a glint in my eye then,' Terence said while pointing in Thorny Grove's direction. Oliver followed his gaze as they drifted high over Ferndale, Ashurst, and the Jolly Gamesman, looking toward the deserted chapel and at the smudge of cinders nearby – the pews that had lost their utility. After passing over where the brook that ran between the grove and factories met the river – which itself looped its way through the heathland and dales towards the horizon – they then passed over Mill Lane, Middle Row, and the Oddfellows. A little further along, he spied Olive Solby – a speck far, far below, dutifully pruning her privet hedgerows.

'A fine family, the Solbys... upstanding. They broke the mould once they made Alec.'

Oliver nodded in agreement. His father was spot on, of course. He would unhesitatingly agree with anything that he said anyway; how could he do otherwise?

With Abby's old primary school already drifting directly below, and with the factories only a little further ahead to the north, Oliver felt drawn to look west, down toward St Barnabas' cemetery; there, unsurprisingly, was Marion standing upon her plot, leaning against her own headstone while the shadow of the church's crossed steeple fell upon her. While waving them both off with her handkerchief, the look on her face was indescribable; conceivably, then, it was 'a broken heart' and not 'heart attack' that should have been written on her death certificate.

'Love? I'll admit it wasn't a question I often asked myself,' he heard her murmur, 'but then... when they told me he wasn't coming back... I knew I'd loved your father more than anything.'

This sentiment appeared to be entirely lost on his father, who showed no acknowledgment; Oliver hoped for her sake that it was not indifference, but rather that he simply had not heard her.

'Where exactly are we going, Father?'

'As I've said already, boy, to the glories of war.'

Oliver immediately felt panic-stricken; war was a place you could quite easily never return from. Quite suddenly, he had no desire whatsoever to follow his progenitor – a stranger who had, in truth, never been anything more than a fanciful idea to him –

and an impossible yardstick to measure himself by, as much as he had been taught to use him as such. Theirs was certainly not a bond strong enough to see him rushing headlong after his father on some kamikaze mission into dangerous territories.

'But what about Mother?' Oliver asked furtively.

Again, Terence had no reply.

Feeling increasingly troubled by Marion's abandonment, Oliver desperately wanted to touch ground and remain with her. He wanted to take hold of her and assure her that he, at least, would not forsake her, and that he would always be there for her no matter how much her loss might embitter her; he would offer himself willingly as her pincushion – who could blame her in her pending bereavement for needing somewhere to stick all her grievance, someone to sound off on, and someone to vent her despair to.

Sensing his changed mood, Terence merely gave him a formal salute and looked back at the horizon; he appeared to be disturbingly eager for the atrocities that lay ahead as his velocity increased, and he vanished over it without once looking back. If he had thought his son cowardly, there was little Oliver could do about it then; both their priorities were elsewhere anyway.

***

Oliver awoke to a woefully empty bed; his Romeo had crept out while he had slept. The horse hospital felt more devoid of substance than it had ever done. It had taken him over an hour of peevishly stomping about the place, slamming doors, and kicking his *arrangements* irritably about, before he found a note left on the living room table that read 'Hope we meet again, laddie – Gordy'. He felt far less aggrieved then, mostly wistful.

Despite this wistfulness, an unfamiliar sensibility, an emboldened one, resonated strongly within him, however; having dispensed with enough of his indignation, it had become apparent that, down to a cellular level, he felt quite transformed by their brief acquaintance. The aroma of his own body commingling with that of *Captain Crackerjack* spoke vividly of the glorious dance that they had performed together that night. Furthermore, Gordy's was the agreeable smell of a good man, and one who had actually liked him, at that! But then, as it dawned on Oliver that there was no certainty that he would see the captain again, that sweaty, earthy aroma began to taunt him; he found himself bathing again.

While in the suds, Oliver cast his mind over the racy details of the whole shebang, but then he remembered the curious chain of events that had ultimately wound up with Gordy as his bedfellow; it had begun with him mistaking him for his father upon the heath, after all. He could not help but wonder then, when he had seen Terence's face like a mask upon Gordy's own, whether he had been searching for that face in every man that he had ever locked eyes with; he still had some vague sense that he had dreamt of Terence that night also. This questioning made him doubt whether his heinousness could ever be pardoned, and whether his soul could ever be deserving of absolution; although he had long ago accepted that his indecency must be intrinsic, there were limits, surely? Could I really have stooped to such depths as to have wished my own father into bed with me? he wondered with horror; he quickly found himself scrubbing his flesh raw then.

While his skin reddened and stung, another matter began to overshadow this particular worry because last night's dream was coming back to him – not so clearly remembered in its detail, but strongly felt in its emotional resonance; it, in feeling, at least, clarified his sentiments on at least one of two extremely pressing matters. Somebody was going to be taken to task rather soon. All ambiguities around the matter of Gordy and his father were put aside because Oliver finally felt done with self-reproach; wasn't it rather terrific, after all! he thought. A tentative glance in the bathroom mirror was surprising: he looked shinier and had roses in his cheeks again. A similarly tentative glance at his father's portrait confirmed that he had nothing to fret over. Furthermore, with Gordy it had not been the pantomime of romance, nor had it been the vulgarity of the alleys or heath. It had been, quite simply, a revelation, so he felt that there should be no apology for it either; it had felt, despite its impermanence, so right! By result, his body's soreness stemmed not only from Sheldon's whacking, but also from the captain's manhandling, which ached in a surprisingly satisfying way. It emboldened him somehow for the task ahead – the one regarding his dastardly former uncle. The things that the 'proper shit sack' – his newly named archfiend – had muttered while Oliver had been so vulnerable, bent over his knee, had been utterly reprehensible –

'... you're too old to act like an orphan, for goodness sake! And as for your mother – as if the mere act of dying somehow makes a monster a saint!' This vilification still echoed around him as if emanating from Cranford's tannoy.

'Yes, Mother may have lacked the modesty and humility of the likes of Olive, for instance, and she was undeniably beastly at times... but for Sheldon to dare characterise her as such, when he is no more beyond the pale than she, is beyond belief!' he grumbled. 'And furthermore, how dare he make such damning commentary on someone who is in no position to defend themselves! She would have in life... she never shied from any altercation; she practically sought them out, after all!'

At last, Oliver understood there had, in fact, been two villains in his life; one could just about be forgiven, however, while the other one never could be. Unable to remember ever feeling more livid, he glugged down at least half a bottle of gin, and for the first time ever, he found himself spoiling for a fight.

***

For the first time in a long, long while, Oliver found himself running; for the first half-mile he found his pace quickening the more Sheldon's unforgivable utterances rattled around his head, the more his disgust took hold of him, and the more he imagined the odious old gnashbarb getting his comeuppance finally. His fists pummelled the warm air as he hurtled down Middle Row; somehow, he had found such intestinal fortitude that he could easily pay the stinging cuts and abrasions on his bare soles little heed. His entrails seemed to bubble and boil with a molten fury that fed a turbine in his chest, pumping it into every fibre of his being. Upon careering into Middle Row, the rag-and-bone man, his cart on a collision course, had to swerve out of his way and steered headlong into a market stall; its produce tumbled across the road and made for quite the spectacle.

Roy Wilks watched all this bedlam from beneath the Oddfellows awning, open-mouthed and with an ale moustache. Oliver, whatever he was up to, had appeared utterly incandescent as he had galloped past; even the scrim of sputum that Oliver had spat at Roy's feet did not diminish a desire that was instantly rekindled.

'Tearing off down t' high street 'e was... an' spat at me an' all, the queer little gnat,' Roy griped to Doris while secretly wishing that he had torn after Oliver and torn all his clothes off too.

'Give over... My Oliver's far too restrained for all that... 'E got manners! 'Ad a little too much to drink, Roy? Imagining things?' was her terse reply while hiding her intrigue well.

Being poorly conditioned for such exertion, especially in such heat, by the time Ferndale's trim lawns came into view, Oliver had lost considerable momentum, his lungs felt fit to burst, and the grazes and scrapes on his feet could no longer be ignored; as he hobbled up the driveway, its gravel felt like a bed of nails underfoot. Much of his fury had been consumed as fuel for the considerable effort of getting there so quickly, it seemed; by the time he had rung for Maxine's attendance, he was armed with only smouldering ashes of the fire that he had set off with.

'Christ almighty, what a scorcher. Surely the hottest day of the year,' he muttered while waiting and staring up at the sky's rufous complexion. He was awash with sweat.

'Come for your shoes an' socks, 'ave you, Master Gidley?' Maxine chirped after flinging open the front door and dropping them at his feet.

'No I've come to see Unc... Sheldon, if you please, Maxine.'

'Now, you know your uncle doesn't like to be disturbed so early.'

'He's not my uncle, Maxine, and I must see him now!'

Maxine stiffened, surprised by his firmness, tongue-tied.

Christ, she's a pain, Oliver thought; rather than argue, shouldn't she lower herself in genuflection, and then summon his nibs immediately?

'Now, if you please, Maxine! It's a matter of extreme urgency!'

'Ooh, what's gotten into you, mister?' was all she could say while flicking her rag at him in annoyance; he pressed past her with ease, however, marched through the house, and was grateful to find his way to his usual seating in the room where he and Sheldon always met. Christ, bloody Maxine, he had thought as she had flapped and clucked while in pursuit of him; he would dare say that with her big trap, those buck teeth of hers, and that boxer's jaw, she could give Jock McAlloran a fright.

'Ah'll allow it this once,' Maxine had called after him, her voice weak with unsure authority. 'An' mind the place now, we don't want another accident, do we?' she had added, reminding him of the Parisian landmark that he had destroyed while leaving the day before. Once he had switched off Sheldon's frightful counterfeited radiogram, she had sighed, shrugged, and withdrawn, and as he parked himself on the chaise, he realised that Ferndale's usually cool interior felt more like an oven; by consequence, he felt even more diminished. Feeling akin to a Victorian lady swooning on her fainting couch, he tried to consolidate what little energy he had remaining while hoping that Sheldon would not descend too soon. He had to clear his throat and set his teeth the moment that elephantine-sounding footsteps were finally heard on the stairs. The old clod looked considerably put out as he entered, and he was satisfactorily dishevelled, too, almost tripping in his slippers while tugging on his waistcoat inside out. Oliver thought all this was a pretty good start until Sheldon opened his mouth –

'Well, Oliver, I'd like to say that you calling in like this is a surprise… but, of course, you've come asking for another loan again – what!' Sheldon said snippily while staring at Oliver's bare, bloody, and dirty feet with incredulity.

Oliver shook his head stiffly, somehow managing to keep his composure, despite his unease.

'You do r-realise, I'll have to s-seek similar r-recompense, I hope?' Sheldon then spluttered amid unshared laughter. Oliver was immediately incensed –

'Look, Bainbridge... no more rhubarb, thank you very much... nor funny business either, that's for bloody sure.'

Sheldon merely cocked an eyebrow wryly.

'You know that's not why I'm here... don't you...? Well, don't you?'

'Hmm, well... yes, I gathered. What's all this in aid of, then, eh?'

While catching his breath and wondering how to phrase himself, Oliver looked censoriously about the room's absurd array. He noticed that the singular table tennis bat, still divorced from its spouse, had been put on display next to the gilded badminton racquet: another provocation that Oliver had a good mind to smash his chops with!

'I gather you've not slept well, then?'

'No, I slept soundly, like a dead dog, in fact. But... I'm just so... angry!'

And how Sheldon's head shot up at that! He appeared to study Oliver quizzically, yet more keenly than he had ever done – keener even than before things had begun to fizzle out between them; it was as if he was really seeing him at last.

'Oliver, as I've been trying to tell you, anger is a good place to start. In fact, I'd say it quite becomes you–'

'Oh, piddling down my back at last, eh? But you do realise that it's you I'm furious with, not Mother! I cannot b-believe the th-things you've said,' Oliver muttered, visibly shaking while his fists clenched tightly, seemingly of their own accord. 'You didn't know my mother, Bainbridge... not really.'

Sheldon appeared quite stunned and replied weakly –

'B-but, dear boy, you must understand–'

'No, I've nothing to understand! Even if I were angry with her, so what!'

Beads of perspiration dripped off them both. Oliver stayed stiffly braced, his heart thudding inconveniently, and his breath far too short for his liking while watching Sheldon's expression shift to one of incredulity.

'So what? Well, that's rather easy! If 'so what' is such an effective strategy for you, then why am I always picking up the pieces of your pitiful existence? She's clearly ruined you, Oliver!' Sheldon cried while his eyes narrowed.

That's fudged it, Oliver thought as his face crumpled instantly with embarrassment and indignation. He knew precisely what was being alluded to: last year's breakdown and the way his mock uncle had swooped in to restore order and decorum. Is Sheldon right, though? he had to ask. Was all that Mother's fault after all? Should she really be blamed entirely for all the messes and scrapes I've gotten myself into? Perhaps she should? But then... surely not? These quibbling thoughts filled his head with muddled interior monologue again, and his focus became entirely blurred. He could already hear the electrostatic crackling along his ear canals, and knew that he might expect another migraine.

'No, the thing is... or rather was...' Oliver's voice fractured. 'The... the r-real p-p-problem is...'

'Yes? Out with it then!' Sheldon gasped in exasperation.

Finding this unanswerable in the wake of Sheldon's snappiness, 'Please don't shout,' was all Oliver could whisper imploringly. He then realised that he had not turned the radiogram off properly as he had marched in, and it spluttered noisy interference while off-channel, which did not help either. All in all, he had never felt so flustered, nor off-kilter.

'Well, she... she... she... g-gosh, I can hardly breathe... Too bloody hot in here.'

Unsurprisingly, Ferndale's rear gardens were no refuge; if anything, the heat was more stifling there, even in the shadow of the aspidistra. Oliver wilted into a trellis chair while Maxine rushed glasses of iced lemon water out to them both, then withdrew. Sheldon then removed his waistcoat, rolled up his sleeves, and mopped his wattles and the fleshy rolls of his neck with a hanky as he called after her –

'And bring tea, Maxine – piping hot. The boy needs a good sweat to cool off.'

Hushfulness pervaded Ferndale's grounds while they waited for her to prepare the beverage, underscored by an orchestra of crickets. Oliver still felt saddle sore, but the warm grass tickling his bare soles was an agreeable sensation that grounded him a little; his feet felt less painful, at least. His hands, tautened by his perpetual dislike of them, as well as his desire to clasp them around Sheldon's neck until his fat face turned blue, gripped the chair tightly, however.

During this awkward-feeling interval, Oliver looked across Ferndale's flourishing gardens and saw that the white lilies, red roses, and pink-flowering thorns remained in their seats, anxiously awaiting the final act. In childhood's innocence, these gardens had been full of wonder – a place where he had once searched for the fairies that he had had no doubt flitted around their shrubs; presently, however, they bore witness to the impurity and brutality of adulthood, and as such had sadly become the stage for it. The way Sheldon had greeted him, and had casually remarked of the 'arrangement', without having the faintest inkling of how infinitely horrendous yesterday's vile queening had felt, confirmed that the bastard deserved garrotting. But with little strength of hand, Oliver knew that he was hardly capable of such a gallant act; he no longer felt capable of administering a stern oral reprimand either because Sheldon had bloody well shut him up already! Touché dear uncle, he said to himself begrudgingly. But, then, the atmosphere, at least, felt so twisted and awful that this must surely mark the end in itself, Oliver thought amid the silence. The malignancy of their relationship seemed to have been spectacularly unmasked before them finally; Oliver could not bear its unsightliness, and he presumed, judging by Sheldon's downcast gaze, muteness, and apparent unease, that he could not either – he really did look out of his depth for once – his tongue unusually still.

Yes, this is it, Oliver thought; nothing could reanimate the corpse of their acquaintance now, surely. He plucked another coffin nail from his pocket, but then he thought better of it, knowing that it would only make him feel worse. While Sheldon sat motionless with his eyes pressed into his palms, Oliver peered about at Ferndale's grounds again; the sunlight was so bedazzling that they appeared curiously dark – his eyes simply could not adjust to its brilliance, as if the sun had blindsided him as much as Sheldon just had. But again, by contrast, how bright, colourful, and alive these gardens had once seemed – as had the universe in general during childhood; that had been when the young dreamer and would-be entomologist had, with wonder, realised that the green velveteen of grasshopper lamina, the spotted crimson oilskin of ladybird pinions, and the pearlescent nets of dragonfly wings were the apparel of the fairies that he had sought for so long.

While meditating further upon his childhood days there, the way his mother's vile cousin had begun, as far back as then, to prepare him for all this seemed infinitely distasteful... and, actually, utterly reprehensible in the present moment! But, then, perhaps that is not fair to think, Oliver found himself wondering because he had to admit that he had eventually come to offer himself willingly at times to the game they had been playing; his spurious uncle had always been a figure of fluctuating importance, depending upon his own level of financial desperation, and that desperation had become too great in recent years. But had he not really been desperate for guidance more than anything? True guidance: help with finding a way forward, rather than wrongful intentions masquerading as a concern for his welfare.

Just as he should, in light of all this, Sheldon continued to appear quite tense as he slowly prepared and lit his pipe without looking up once.

Should I just get up and walk, then? Oliver wondered of himself; why am I still sitting here, waiting in this strained atmosphere while my head feels like it's going to explode? Should I say, 'Au revoir... farewell... toodle-oo, Uncle,' and take my final leave? Or am I waiting for Sheldon to wrap things up?

With his own eyes closed then, the sun still pressed through his eyelids and left sunspots in his visual field when he reopened them; as difficult as it was to see clearly, he wondered if he had caught that familiar wispy haze in the corner of his eye – something, or somebody, appeared to linger in front of the mass of ivy that throttled the gardening shed. It could not be Mr Doubleday, the gardener, because Sheldon only employed him on weekdays nowadays.

Tea was served with a clatter, and Sheldon, much to Oliver's disbelief, gestured for him to continue while saying –

'Alright, then, champ, out with it.'

But now that he had noticed Marion and Sheldon had derailed him, Oliver had lost all train of thought completely; he was on shaky ground. The situation had become entirely stripped of context; now there was only her and the worry of her while the smoke from Sheldon's pipe smelt simply awful – its billowing fumes clouded his mind even more. What had I been saying, then? he wondered; ah, yes... he had been asked what the more pressing issues were regarding his mother –

'Well, she... she...'

'Yes?'

No, Oliver felt that he actually dare not mention it, not only for the pain that it would cause himself, but also for the pain that it would cause her; he hardly wished to aggrieve her spirit again by raking up the past once more, even if he could have explained it all without breaking into tears.

'Do... do you think it's possible she's still here?' he answered helplessly with a wondering frown.

'Who? I'm not sure what you mean, dear boy.'

'Here, right here,' Oliver whispered in embarrassment, then he nervously glanced across the gardens in her suspected direction again.

'Oliver, it's very common for the bereaved to imagine–'

'Because if she were here, she'd know!'

Sheldon was clearly anxious to hurry this up –

'Know what?'

'That she was wrong!' Oliver cried while looking back at Sheldon in confusion. 'I'm not crazy, am I?'

Sheldon, looking immediately reinvigorated, lurched forward to clasp Oliver's knee.

'Yes, she was wrong, dear nephew. I'm glad that you're–'

Recoiling in horror that was utterly abject, Oliver imagined a table tennis bat might smash down on his knee at any moment.

'But I'm not your nephew... and don't touch me... You've no... you've no right!'

Sheldon, clutching only empty air, looked crestfallen for only the briefest moment, then his face simply froze over as Oliver fled.

In his getaway, Oliver sidestepped Maxine, who had locked the back doors in an effort to contain him – likely to put a stop to any other acts of vandalism – by trampling through the densely tangled vines that clung to Ferndale's east side. Once he had emerged out front, he found his shoes on the front steps, hopped into them, and fled as fast as he could; by the time Maxine had reached the front door, Oliver was beyond sight. Meanwhile, out back, Sheldon simply shrugged and, while tapping his watch, ordered more tea –

'But quick, for I've an appointment at Manfred & Sons in just short of an hour.'

His newly appointed valet and butler required chaperoning to the outfitters. He marvelled at how picture-perfect that lad would look in a white jacket and dickie bow while floundering over his knee, but then he found himself quibbling over whether the bowtie should be plain or spotted.

***

Having already marched himself through that thorniest of groves, Oliver stopped to rest at a stile which crowned a footpath that he had not trod for over a decade. While trying to catch his breath, he promptly recalled how on one of their walks, Sheldon had lectured him on the rules of cricket while Oliver had felt far more interested in the fungi and conkers hiding in the tall grass; with exception for when Sheldon had taken him to the fairground's boxing booths, which had admittedly been quite exciting, the truth was that his sport schooling had been deathly dull. He would have bored the spots off toadstools!

Admittedly, he had not brought his former uncle to task in quite the fashion that he had hoped, but his point had hardly been lost, and for that he felt rather pleased with himself; what remained was a queer feeling, like a great weight had been lifted off of him, leaving only the worry of his lost income and how his future might look without it. But that worry was for another day.

This path, which was scattered with countless wisps of dandelions, led from the grove's border all the way to the grassy meadow behind Watkin & Rees, circumnavigating Greenthorne entirely. The babbling of the brook that accompanied this track soothed him as the breath returned to his body and he found his mind curiously calm; cutting Sheldon out had proved to be an instant spring cleaning for his psyche!

Watkin & Rees marked the afternoon shift with yet another shrill whistle, and with his attention drawn in that direction, he noticed beyond the sycamore trees, which were already dropping their spinning winged seeds, Cranford Electric.

'Meet me there, Mother. Please.'

Upon getting even closer to Cranford, trepidation flooded the mental space that the encumbrances of being tangled up with Sheldon had previously cluttered. Oliver remained resolute, however, that he would not shy away from confronting it either; he had a new determination to put the past behind him – one inspired by the great dividends that his bravery with Sheldon had just paid out. While crossing through Thornebridge and still gazing at his mother's last place of work, Oliver knew that he had more to face up to, and despite his reticence when confronted with Sheldon only minutes prior, he swiftly felt better equipped for it than he had ever imagined possible.

***

Oliver looked tentatively about at Cranford Electric's forecourt; it felt strangely emotive to be there because he had always kept that safe distance from it since it had closed its doors. What was unexpected with close proximity was its modest size; it was hardly the imposing spook house of his nightmares. It looked extremely forlorn, actually, with its windows cracked and its brick crumbling while entirely hemmed in by droves of weeds.

ALEC S. IRESON

The day's climate seemed to have increased even more in Fahrenheit and humidity, so Oliver felt thankful to take shelter beneath the lean-to that reached over the side steps to Cranford's first floor, or the 'clockworks', as they had informally called the department where the dial painters had laboured. It never ceased to surprise him that it was still standing, although some of its wooden slats had rotted and splintered, allowing shafts of sunlight to dapple him; with it diffusing the harsh sunlight, he had never expected to feel shelter there. As he took pause, all around seemed extremely quiet except for a warm, whispering breeze and the faint rumble of Spooner and Watkin's workings across the way.

Allowing himself this brief hiatus from his campaign to lay the past to rest, Oliver lit a cigarette, and while savouring its vapours, he found himself wishing that Alec Solby was sat with him; Alec had also enjoyed a fag, that momentary escape from the world, and he had smoked one with such dexterity, balancing it nimbly upon those large, squared-off fingers of his – fingers belonging to wonderful hands that Edwin Cranford had not deserved to put to work. While smoking, marvellous old Alec would entertain him with card tricks or war stories while the women packed up for the night. His boss may have been a tyrant, but Alec, one of his middlemen, had been a lamb; with promotion he had become charged with second tier quality control while he sat in a raised booth above the dial painter's own booths in the 'clockworks'. Somehow, however, he had managed to keep his higher-ups happy while also endearing himself to the women in his charge; that had been no easy task and was a testament to his diplomacy. He had always found ways to boost morale, and with a great sense of fun, he had occasionally given the painters a bit of a lark during the days when management were out of office.

'Thirty-one, get up and run. If only we all could, eh, ladies!'

'Thirty-five, tea-time jive. Turn up the wireless, Olive dear, time for some fancy footwork.'

'How do you get the fairer sex to say the 'f' word, then, ladies? Someone shout 'Bingo!"

Unquestionably, then, he had had more of the air of an entertainer, or even that of a priest in a pulpit who had managed to endear himself to his flock, than that of a taskmaster. But to have his good company again was an impossibility, of course, because Alec, or rather his remains, resided in a mossy plot in St Barnabas' churchyard – only a few plots away from Marion's. It was sadder still that so many of their generation resided there – the workhorses of Greenthorne, worked into an early grave while putting the country back on its feet.

Upon stubbing out his smoke when waking from this melancholy, Oliver noticed that from this vantage point Middle Row looked more like a miniature scale model while the townsfolk upon it were merely specks. The sky above those specks had grown unexpectedly dense and heavy looking, however; the dense veil of water vapour that had hovered in the air for too long was quickly distilling into clouds of a brilliant hue. It seemed as if all the summer's building ferocity had finally been distilled into vast swathes of burnt orange and cochineal, garnet, and cardinal red.

Is that just the rumblings of the tannery opposite or the distant echo of thunder? he wondered; as hard as it was to imagine after months of baking sun, rain seemed to be imminent. Already, the sky's intense chromaticism was dulling and greying; one could feel the weight of the air – the intense pressure of a sky ready to crack open and release its heavy burden finally. Knowing that the lean-to could not shelter him from this, Oliver took a deep breath and then pressed against the doorway, readying himself to enter into Cranford Electric's darkness, as had been his intention all along.

Trapped inside, the heat and humidity had built all summer long. Sweat promptly dripped from his brow once he had forced that door ajar; he was utterly awash from the moment he had stepped in. The smell was overpowering too: that abrasive smell of industry that had marked his life one way or another, combined with the pungent smell of rot. Decomposition had certainly added colour and texture to the place. Nature – ever ready to take the reins again when man disembarks – had been transforming the place too: moss green made for a striking contrast with the brown and orange of rusting metalwork.

ALEC S. IRESON

It was so gloomy inside. The large circular window above Hattie Blake's old desk was so grimy that he could barely make out Spooner & Sons' chimney; it also afforded Oliver little light because the sky had dulled and greyed even more. While trampling over the fallen masonry and flakes of rusted metal heaped on the floor, he made his way down the central hall, past the washroom where he had once fled from Marion's raised hand, to booths five, six, seven, and eight at its far end.

Opposite was a stairwell, which he well remembered led down into the darkness of the 'teleworks'; thankfully, it was cordoned off with densely laced spider webs. He had found those stairs just as foreboding as a child, knowing that the ominous sounds that bounced up their steps annunciated the manufacture of those creepy contraptions that he had come to loathe; he had never wanted to venture down there and had politely declined that part of Alec's guided tour. He had gladly taken a peep upstairs, however; wirelesses were cheerful devices, after all, that merely filled the air with music, stories about the world, and the sporting triumphs of the day without pretending to be anything more than they were.

Once he had pushed through the sweatshop's groaning doors instead, 'G-goodness,' was all Oliver could stutter; it was every bit the atrocity exhibition of the dial painter's exploitation. It felt suitably sequestered, and as such was so depressing to revisit. The iron roof and its supports had certainly seen better days, but the rusted holes in that ceiling allowed scant shards of light to provide a little illumination, at least. Here, too, plucky weeds crept up through the ruptured cement floor, vermin squeaked, and a crow nesting in the rafters squawked as if sounding an alarm. More thick tangles of gossamer spider webs coated arrangements of bottles and canisters of chemicals which were crawled over by beetles and woodlice. The wireless that Marion had bought for herself and her comrades, the moss had wormed its way into that too; it was a testament to Edwin Cranford's miserliness that she had had to source one herself because they were manufactured in such large quantity upstairs.

Looking about, Oliver could only acknowledge again how soul-destroying it must have been for Marion to have worked there: a job that was utterly thankless, servile, and numbingly repetitive. He could suddenly recall with such clarity how, with Alec as his chaperone, he had watched the women peering wearily through their magnifiers with reddening, strained eyes, pointing their brushes every ten seconds to maintain the precision that their livelihoods had depended on. Elsie Smith and Rose Houghton would, despite Alec's defence of them, often be cautioned for their inaccuracy via the booming tannoy, and they were even threatened with the sack occasionally if they did not raise their game. In such cases, Alec would wince and offer prompt consolations, insisting that their understandable overtiredness accounted for their failings; he had tactfully and strategically argued their case to his higher-ups, too, and although nothing had really changed – that tannoy still issued its reprimands – in doing so he had saved them from the sack, at least. In Reenie O'Brian's case, however, developing severe short-sightedness had been a misdemeanour that he had not been able to acquit her of, and she had been sent packing.

With all this in mind, and while struggling for breath in the heat, Oliver had to remove his cap while crossing to his mother's old locker; inside was her alternate smock and hair net – now a rotting rag and something that more resembled another spider web. But then, amazingly, pinned to the inside of its rusted door were the sacred, long-lost photographs for which he had mistaken Mr Roper's! They were faint, yellowed, and brittle-looking, but he could somehow see the coral glow of Gigi's gown, despite the images' monochromaticity, and how beaming and alive she had been that day; Sheldon must have sneakily snapped her with that Coronet camera of his. Another photo of his mother and he, both smiling and looking quite luminous while picnicking in the common land beyond Ashurst's back garden, also crumbled to ash with his touch. He promptly snatched his hand away.

He turned then, and he noticed that the magnifier, which had unsparingly demanded such painstaking accuracy of Marion, was still standing upon her booth among the flakes of rusted iron that had fallen from the roof; with his surroundings speaking so loudly of her, he expected that he would feel his mother's presence more strongly there than anywhere, especially since he had asked that she show herself there.

But no, quite the reverse, in fact – no crackles of static electricity, nor electrical waves washing over his skin, nor any shimmering whorls in the corner of his eye.

'Mother?'

The day before, Sheldon had inadvertently unearthed the sharpest point of contention between his mother and he – one that Oliver had buried safely in his subconscious and come to forget – a grave misunderstanding that had become the final brick in the wall between them not long before she had died. Although it had hovered very uncomfortably in his mind before and after the distraction of Gordy, it had, at least, dawned on him what she had been about to utter in the Greenthorne Palace while he had been dreaming; in that sequence's possibilities, she had quite clearly tried to reach out and make amends before she had collapsed. It was a misunderstanding accompanied by such awful emotion that, with his own readiness to address it finally, it felt like an unbearable tension building in his chest. To break an opening between their worlds, Oliver closed his eyes, and in that darkness, he finally allowed the past, in all its fullness, to rise from the sinkhole in his psyche.

***

It had been another long, blistering summer, much like the current one, which facilitated Oliver's recall; back then, summers no longer felt like a holiday – they had felt more like a reform school, wherein he had attended to his ailing mother's needs as best as he could, and then he had recovered from her angry outbursts in the confines of his bedroom.

Attending primary with all the other spoilt little rascals of Thorny Grove had been a blast, but secondary school at St Mark's had been a bit of a shock, socially as well as scholastically. Apart from Mrs Dennis-Hunt's classes, it had been a fairly unpleasant experience and, as such, was not much brooded upon henceforward. That said, he had had a few much-cherished friends there. The other pupils whose company he had enjoyed – the twins, Paula and Liza Slack; Lorna Stubbs; Silas Baxter; and Henry Finlay

– had disappeared from his life once school's routine no longer brought them together and Marion had shackled him to her. Yes, as he and his mother had increasingly come to blows, it, surprisingly, had no longer been a case of her pointing at the front door and clicking her fingers, or him being forever told to scat, shoo, or get out from under her feet – quite the reverse: he had become her house servant, more or less. He had already lost his dear Abby by then, too, and Marion had been so relieved to hear that they had parted ways, despite the fact that Olive had expressed sorrow at the split. Cranford Electric had shut its doors already, and Marion and he had been forced together in the stuffy horse hospital while she had grown angrier and sicker, and he had felt increasingly hemmed in by her and her clutter; it had become a life battened down to near nothing.

Amid all that, it had been another unbearably hot day, and another when she had forced her way into her bathroom, and had scolded Oliver for the mess that he had not yet cleaned up. Then, as was customary, she had made damaging commentary on his character as well as his appearance. After dutifully cleaning the tub, he had prepared both their suppers, as had become his daily duty, while wiping the tears from his eyes and the sweat from his brow. Leaving his to cool, he had carried hers through to her, finding that she had reclaimed her throne already – sprawled on the tattered settee with its ragged mouths of torn leather grimacing at him also. Unsparing as ever, Marion had straightaway found fault with the 'slops' that he had served her –

'Oh, I don't know,' she had said while staring disapprovingly at the plateful that he had handed her. 'Look at this... potatoes dry as ashhhes, meat burnt to a crissssp, peash like mushhh... Do you d-do it on purpose? You must, sh-surely.'

Shot down once again, Oliver could only stare at the floor, but she had become too sore a sight to look at anyway: such a state, and she had been so tragically drunk. But then she had said in a slurring voice loaded with self-pity and spite –

'Goodnessh... can't even look your own mother in the eye, eh? You don't love me... A mother knowssh... But don't you worry, little one... I sh-shan't be here forever... not at thisss rate, anyway... Then you'll be a happy little orphan, I sh-suppose?'

With his heart's seams immediately splitting open, Oliver, amid an onslaught of bewildering and saddening thoughts and emotions that he could not possibly have been able to untangle at such a tender age, had not been able to find the words to tell her that she was wrong. And until he had finally forced himself to forget the matter, his heart had felt torn to pieces.

***

Oliver opened his eyes and took in Cranford's gloom again. An energetic charge seemed to resonate about the room. He could hear a low, electrical-sounding hum; smell burning fuse wire; feel a galvanic current wash over his skin, causing the fine hairs on his neck and arms to bristle with its charge; and see wispy, luminescent whorls in his vision's periphery. He had summoned her. Taking a deep breath, he then said aloud –

'Mother… you were wrong.'

And to be exacting on the matter –

'You were entirely wrong, Mother… I d-did… Well, I still do… l-love you… I love you, you cantankerous old crow!'

That luminescence intensified in its glow, like a tungsten flame, while a cacophony of jumbled, rasping noise raged against his ear drums, but then the din and spark died out just as quickly, followed by a flicker of lightning as another vast roar of thunder shook the skies, and then… finally… rain. The crow above and the rodents below cried out before the workshop fell utterly silent except for the sound of rain drumming on the roof. He then lifted his head with his eyes closed, allowing the freshening drips of rainwater that had found their way in to splash his face.

Finally, he had no doubt whatsoever that an analysis of their relationship's peculiarities was pointless, even if it were possible; moreover, it seemed entirely inconsequential. Whether her conduct towards Oliver could have been described as harmful, or not, and whether it was an excusable consequence of her inadequacies allied with the unfair hand that life had dealt her, or not, it no longer mattered – she was gone, after all;

all that did matter was that he had loved that complicated, crotchety woman, despite her severe shortcomings. And with that declared, it no longer mattered what she had thought or felt about him. Amid such enormous relief, he could not tell what was rainwater and which were tears trickling off his chin while he spluttered and sobbed with a long overdue release of acute emotion.

As he emerged from Cranford's darkness, and from under the lean-to's shadow into the cast of silvery-blue light that newly illuminated Greenthorne, he gladly allowed himself to become utterly sodden by the downpour's cooling waters; with the change of light the world looked so very different. While looking to the distance, at rainswept Middle Row and its occupants, he found that the impact which their judgments had once exerted upon him had greatly diminished too; his whole being abounded with the sense of freedom that this afforded him as he gazed upon Greenthorne with a refreshed sense of its possibilities.

Busman's Picnic

On rainswept Middle Row, Olive Solby rushed outdoors and praised the skies while tying her headscarf; she could at last stop fussing over her wilting gladioli and snapdragons, although her crocuses and pansies were long gone. No need to commiserate with Archie either, who was immediately set free – allowed to let the moisture seep into his dry hide.

'Well, we really needed it, didn't we?' she enthused to practically every passer-by. Upon turning to admire her garden then, it seemed as if her sight had sharpened somehow, just as the dramatic change in weather had seemingly restored clarity to her mind, which had also become foggier and foggier in recent times.

A few hundred meters down puddled Middle Row, Roy Wilks, while enduring his wet shoes, soaked socks, and sodden trousers, emptied the Oddfellow's awning of rainfall with an upturned broom; while being splashed with rainwater, he glumly contemplated his imminent marriage to Pearle Gill. With the Indian summer at an end, the townsmen's activities in the open-air places would peter out until early spring; thus, wintering with Pearle, holed up in their tiny two-up two-down, seemed a claustrophobic prospect, to say the least.

Inside the saloon, Doris Pert felt thankful that trade was brisk because she liked to be kept busy. With rainwater drumming on the empty ale barrels in the yard out back, it sounded a percussive, mesmeric rhythm that set her mind wandering; she found herself hoping that her prince charming was dry, warm, and had some shoes on his feet, at least.

Upon noticing that a new patron had entered the saloon, one that had caught everyone's eye, Doris supposed, judging by her bohemian appearance, that Bossman's new tenant for his other establishment had arrived. Carrying several suitcases, the young lady had also travelled with her cat, which was mewing in a wicker basket. She was a striking-looking woman – Mediterranean, South American, or Romani perhaps – who introduced herself as Vida. When she asked where the Queen's Head was, Doris hissed at her to keep her voice down unless she wanted things to begin on a bad footing with Greenthorne's womenfolk.

While Vida Collins, lowering her voice, made small talk about her train journey from Darfanwhy, Doris scribbled a map on the back of a bar mat, marking the route around a few corners and along the length of the old tramway to Iron Bridge and the Queens Head. Doris took her envelope of cash then – Vida's first month's rent for Bossman – and stuffed it into her brassiere, gave her a wink, wished her well, and told her that she would come around in a day or two to see how she was settling in.

Meanwhile, some waterlogged miles away and at the wrong end of town, Simone Cranford, née Aubert, having left her laundry in a wet heap out the back, crossed the darkened saloon bar of the Queens Head, and wiped the misted windowpane. Peering through sheets of rain, she kept a lookout for the tenants that were replacing Kitty Kat: her half-sibling, an exotic dancer and photographer who would apparently be accompanied by her cat. Kitty's half-sister's name was Vera, apparently, but her stage name was Vanessa, or Vida, or some such. She was travelling in from Wales because their father had – without a word to anybody, even his wife – run off with Vera's gitana mother there some time ago.

Staring out at this sodden and forsaken part of town, Simone found herself wondering once again where her husband may have absconded to – not that she overly cared. She had to smile again at the irony of it, however; it was the fact that her husband had continued to frequent the Queens Head, even after he had nested her in Greenthorne, that had drawn her attention to the trade being plied there. After she had grown suspicious and begun her investigations, she had found Ava and Kitty to be extremely friendly and sympathetic, and had quickly been taken in by them. She had fled from Edwin's raised hand without even taking her clothes. The rest was history.

Feeling that she had been left with no other choice than to become an agitator because her eyes had been widely opened by that abusive and unscrupulous man, Simone found that it emboldened her knowing that she could not possibly be accused of being a mild-mannered crusader, now that women's rights and worker's rights were her main priority; after all, she had first-hand experience of ending up on the bottom rung, the abuses that you become prone to there, and the desperate measures that are often necessary to survive. She realised that she should return to Paris, not Borseau, however, because she would be more likely to find kindred political spirits there; for her, 'comrade' and 'sister' had become more tender terms than 'lover'.

While continuing to wait, and while hoping Kitty's sister would soon arrive so that she would not miss her own train, Simone found herself musing upon how, with her affluent background, she had felt ashamed to have come from money; she had felt somewhat relieved to have lost it, however, until she had learned how hard life could be without it. Her businessman father had insisted that she marry Edwin, and she had done so rather thoughtlessly because up until then, she had actually had her sights set on running a little épicerie or boulangerie, in Orphine maybe, and leading a more modest, uncomplicated life.

While Simone contemplated her politicisation, upstairs Kathleen Rooney – Kitty Kat was only her professional name, after all – sat on an enormous, overstuffed suitcase, trying to lever it shut with her gymnastic thighs. While feeling that she had half a mind to say 'auf Wiedersehen' to everyone and scurry east, since east of anywhere always seemed to be where she most felt at home, Kathleen imagined slipping across borders to give Berlin a 'butcher's'. But to her great disappointment, she had heard how the political and cultural climate had been changing there, so London would obviously be far more sensible; she then wondered whether she could get her old day job back at the bookstore on Shipton Cross Road and read D.V. Adderman all day. Either way, it seemed best to slip away before Bert Greasley's imminent proposal, to which she had been tipped off by Grahame Lowndes. Or should she simply insist that he go with her? she wondered; it would be the only way the big lug would have a chance with her because she had had more than enough of Iron Bridge, and of Greenthorne in general, for that matter.

While Kathleen considered her future, in the room next door, Ava Glewe, the yellow gorse flower of the north, welcomed the downpour, which pooled in and then sploshed from the clogged gutters; it provided an assistive tempo to which she would later write down the poetry that it inspired, and to which she could skilfully ride Grahame Lowndes, or *Seafarer*, as Oliver had so enviously called him. She had trained *Seafarer* to be a pace stalker, but on sensing his readiness to claim his prize, she jockeyed him into position and galloped him down the home straight and towards the finish line.

Meanwhile, the graves in St Barnabas' cemetery lay silent and waterlogged. The rain licked their headstones and watered the floral sprays and wreathes garnishing those that were still tended to; the forgotten inhabitants of those that were neglected could voice no complaint.

***

Oliver asked Avril if he could ride the ponies of fortune.

'Please,' he once again implored her, but she was still having none of it –

'No, you can't... You're far too heavy for French saddle ponies. I've told you already!' Avril snapped.

With a matchbox handily pocketed, young Oliver thought it prudent to appeal to Mrs Chivvers before setting fire to her silly daughter.

'Mrs Chivvers, can you please have Avril behave nicely?'

'If Avril doesn't want you to ride her ponies, then I can't very well force the matter, can I, Oliver dear,' Avril's mother replied, then she turned and whispered something to Marion and Sheldon, but they just groaned in unison – a chorus of misery that did not bode well for Oliver.

'Avril dear, can't you just this once–'

'No, I shan't! They're my ponies!' shrieked Avril.

'Gnashbarbs!' Oliver complained bitterly.

'Oliver, I should wash your mouth out!' Marion gasped.

Oliver discarded the matches, for fear he would grow wilful. Sheldon snickered to himself, nearly choking on his cigar as the two mothers quietly conferenced on how to resolve the dispute. They were all extremely glad that Mrs Shanks had taken little Wally home for a bath already; he had not been too happy with Avril either. Finally, they informed little Olly and Avril of the best course of action, but little Olly begged to differ –

'Mother dear, with the greatest of respect to you and Mrs Chivvers, perhaps we should knock your bloody heads together instead.'

'Ha ha! Jolly good show – what! Hear, hear!' Sheldon spluttered while convulsing on the patio.

'Shut up, bastard tuss!'

Yes, Oliver had had quite enough of him too. Marion almost choked as she spat her martini over Mrs Chivvers' chiffon blouse. Avril shrieked with shrill laughter – quite delighted with all of it. Oliver had vastly shot up in her estimation, and she then decided that he should ride the ponies of fortune after all. And so they both did – riding off into the sunset, leaving their carnage behind them.

***

It was mid-afternoon already when Oliver woke. The sleep that he had so desperately needed, and had finally caught up on, had mostly been a dreamless, undisturbed darkness; he chuckled at the vaguely lingering image of Avril Chivvers and her ponies. It was so refreshing to wake without lingering dread or hangover; his sleep had, in fact, been the most restorative that he could remember! Hopping nimbly out of bed then, he glanced outside and learned that the storm had not simply cleared the air of humidity while the Indian summer continued on its trajectory throughout the autumn, as everyone had wearily anticipated; the rain continued.

How light-footed he felt as he padded down the once feared hallway without giving it a second thought! Upon entry, the living room struck him as surprisingly spacious, and he finally appreciated the elbow room that he had afforded himself by having emptied it of so much clutter; it felt akin to an empty canvas now that he had cleared it up, waiting for him to make his first carefully considered mark. He turned on the Radiophonic then, hoping for sport or suitably upbeat music; delightfully, it sounded as clear as a bell –

'There goes Manwall's forwards again... Oh, it's a close shave for the Helsham goal... Helsham keep on pressing, however... Yes... here it is... It's a goal...! The first goal has a tonic effect in a game like this, and Fred Adair went all out to get that goal...'

While peering through the living room curtains at the scatter of wet roofs and chimney pots, Oliver saw that Greenthorne appeared to have dressed itself in cool and comfortable apparel; the world appeared to be far more hospitable than it had seemed for quite some time. He could not wait to get outside.

'There goes Brian McKinney, Helsham's number ten... Missed a lovely chance to launch... Still, one of the best in the Helsham forward line...'

While wrinkling up his nose at the mouldering scraps of food scattered upon the living room table, he decided that he would purchase a far tastier breakfast from Mrs Spence, and he dressed hurriedly because hunger stirred already.

Upon leaving, and on passing his mother's bedroom door again, Oliver remembered how, upon returning home the night before, he had felt compelled and surprisingly unafraid to open her bedroom door and even to enter because he had finally freed himself of her. He had not once set foot inside since she had passed and lain in state there, without any mourners coming to pay their respects, and for only the briefest of times before Nurse Cruikshank had called Doctor Fairbrother, and he had in turn telephoned the mortuary.

Inside, her bedroom had smelt quite fusty; her old perfume – a stale-smelling melange of lavender, rose, orange blossom, rosemary, and geranium – had commingled discordantly with the odour of cigarette smoke and wet rot. It had assailed his senses enough that he had felt forced to heave her window open. A whistling gust of wind had entered and bestirred the thick dust that had long since settled there. It had formed an ashen shroud which had hung ominously in the air; it had quickly thinned into a pale, gauzy veil, however, before that air had totally cleared, leaving the room feeling quite empty.

Stepping back over the floor's clutter, Oliver had sat on her chenille bedspread while the springs beneath him had groaned, much like his own bed. The nostalgia of seeing all her other curios for the first time in years had been unexpectedly emotive – yet more unreturned library books, her jars of face cream smashed on the floor, empty packets of her slimline smokes, vases containing the ashes of posies, more photographs of the old man, yellowing copies of *The Lady About Town*, and showy ornaments salvaged from Ashurst, all along with the other items he had thrown in a few days prior.

He had then noticed, propped upon her dresser, a much unappreciated leaving present: a withered potted plant of some variety, from Mrs Crabtree, and he had laughed. He had almost forgotten that other golden yet short-lived period at the start of his mother's decline, when her increasing disgruntlement with life had begun to fray her airs and graces. Apparently, Mrs Crabtree had made quite a muck of running the soup kitchen once Marion had taken double shift at Crowther and could no longer supervise it herself; oh, the way his mother had called Mrs Crabtree 'a quite useless, tasteless old bag who does sod all but piss and moan!' upon receipt of that leaving gift! Bahaha! Revealing her true heritage, she had occasionally begun to resort to low-class vulgarity, which had her son tittering hysterically because it seemed so out of character. So, he had laughed again as well as wept a little, feeling much the same as he had in the downpour when leaving Cranford. Then, after glancing about one last time, he had reasoned that the shade which she had chosen for her own bedroom could only be named royal green, even if she had come to rule with an iron fist in her queenliness.

Forgetting all that while clattering down the outside steps, Oliver took a deep breath and the horse hospital's yard smelt wonderfully germinal. He breathed in these moist, earthy aromas while feeling bowled over to see sprouts of green poking between its cobbles already; with all this and the way the birds were in song, the afternoon felt fresh and harmonic, as if gifted by some deity of tranquillity after having overthrown a warmongering god, who must have been picking new fights elsewhere. Those swathes of silver up above would soon be cotton white again, drifting in bluebird skies while all below would be orange and gold. A favourably fresh breeze caressed him with a satin touch while he anticipated all of this.

Upon ducking into the outside lavatory to relieve himself, he found Shoosmith's book had dried out upon the floor. Although it smelt ghastly, he picked it up, and although most of its pages had stuck together, he found a note tucked inside the book's back cover, just about legible, from Sheldon to Shoosmith that he had missed all along.

Rah, rah, rah... He runs me around the block with all his demands, and I am doing my level best to assist him. I cannot help myself in that regard. I have a thing for the weak – a meritorious need to assist, often to my detriment. Yet, alas, there is a softness of character there that his father would surely have loathed. His mother certainly did, and she tried her upmost to knock some sense into him before his contrariness ground her down. And, more gravely, my nephew has a real talent for exploitation. He has actually been trying to hustle his way into my private affairs. Rah, rah, rah...

'Ha! The old lecher is utterly unbelievable!'

Oliver could only chuckle at Sheldon taking the moral high ground because he knew that they had almost been as bad as each other; they had both become transactional creatures that charged by the hour. With the note stuck fast to the back cover, he could not peel it off to read the rest, yet deemed it unnecessary as he tossed the book into the dustbin.

Although his taste for colour had hitherto been as high-key as Sheldon's, while walking Oliver found even greater appeal in the more muted tones about him. Greenthorne appeared to be rendered in pigeon, school yard, tin roof, pewter, and blue point shades of grey, along with saddle, otter's dam, and horse wrangler shades of brown. Ale foam and tea caddy shades of yellow seemed to befit the Oddfellows' signage as he glimpsed it upon reaching Middle Row.

Cheerfully, a kazoo band played up ahead. The townsmen and women also appeared cheerier, despite the rain, as if a great weight had been lifted from their shoulders now that the murderous heat of the lingering summer had passed; the tension between them had lessened greatly, and they even had smiles for one another.

Upon sighting Alfred Goldfinch, the grocer's son, who was still as generously proportioned as a delightfully plump cherub, Oliver found himself grinning while staring deeply into the blue irises of his oh-so pretty eyes again; unperturbed by Oliver eyeballing him from across the street, and just as amiable as ever, Alfred simply smiled back and uttered a cheerful 'Alright mate!' just as he did with everybody. Noticing what cute, tiny little ears Albert had – in need of being nuzzled and tenderly bitten – Oliver then decided to restrain himself from acting on such fancy; whether Alfred was particularly taken with it or not, it would hardly go down well with his father, nor with the good people of Middle Row. Oliver bought liquorice to chew on instead while feeling surprised to find that his sudden yearning for Albert, and his liking of his ears, had felt like nothing more than a harmless sway of heart towards the fellow; this reassured Oliver that nothing about him had ever been warped, despite his mother's insistence otherwise. He was, needless to say, simply poetic, romantic, and passionate by nature.

It began to drizzle again, and it actually felt pleasant to wear a coat, or rather a cycling cape that he had sneakily lifted from the Oddfellows saloon's coatrack on one stormy night a while back. While cheerfully wiping the rainwater from his eyes, Oliver turned and took in a wider view of the high street and the townsfolk that busied themselves upon it, feeling great affection for Greenthorne's residents, even from an outsider's viewpoint. Sourpuss Sybill Woolgather looked beguilingly glum as she stooped to pick up her umbrella. Enterprising 'Granny' Rogers had just exited the General Stores with her basket piled high with sweets and cigarettes that she would resell to the heath's ramblers and ravishers with a big markup; she stood discussing entrepreneurship with that other shrewd profiteer, Murray Pierce. Just a little further up, Quinn, with his effeminately nursed hair protected by a headscarf, nodded wearily to Albion Roper, who then turned and trudged away just as wearily. Pity about all that at Vale Studios, Oliver thought; when wondering if he should run, catch Mr Roper, and apologise, he then thought it best to deal with it once he had had a chance to think how to best approach it. Just across the street, Roy Wilks, with his fiancée, Pearle Gill, transparently pretended that he had not noticed Oliver and turned to his future wife to discuss the price of potatoes; Oliver found himself wishing Roy only peace.

Despite his late afternoon stroll on Middle Row feeling pleasantly temperate, avoiding the emotional highs that were always too high and the lows that were always too low for a change, he suddenly found himself stripped of this restraint when a striking-looking diva swept past him, carrying several suitcases and with her cat mewing in a wicker basket; he then did an abrupt about-turn to gape at her, slack-jawed. She had chosen a rather witchy-looking wide-brimmed black fedora, pinned with a poppy. Although she was wearing her mother's clothes, or perhaps those of her grandmother – black lace-frilled and sequinned gowns – she looked utterly bohemian. This was particularly the case because she had accessorised them with all manner of metallic charms and trinkets; even her Victorian boots had been given an enterprising twist with gold appliqué that he found utterly ingenious as well as eye-catching. It made him wonder if he should tear through his own wardrobe armed with scissors, a darning needle, thread, some decorative gold buttons, and as much creative ingenuity.

Oliver already felt besotted enough to tear after her and introduce himself as her new favourite minion while showering her with compliments and liquorice twists;

or perhaps I should darken my own visage with soot from the grocer's windows and present myself as her newly appointed *mucamo* while operating castanets, he wondered because she also looked every bit the Spanish *señorita*. At the very least, it only seemed gentlemanly to snatch up her bags and insist that he carry them for her to wherever she was heading. She looked so beautiful, and he was almost overcome with such foolishness, but he managed to calm himself, take a deep breath, and simply let her go.

Up ahead in the very next moment, with the rainwater blurring his vision, he saw a flare of yellow, fuchsia, and vermillion which quickened his breath; it was Simone, of course, heading in the station's direction with a suitcase. He found himself imagining, perhaps even hoping, that she was making her escape to Paris, Marseille, Toulouse, or wherever she hailed from – it had slipped his mind to ask. He did not rush to catch her, however; as much as he felt compelled to do so, snatch up her hand, and invite her to dance the quickstep, he did not. He did not want to be disappointed to learn that she was only off to Blandishford for the day, or something like that, and would remain stuck in Greenthorne for the rest of her life; she was clearly destined for far greater things than the town could ever offer. Tellingly, her case was rather large indeed, though, so he felt assured that she was not coming back, and he accordingly felt a swell of gladness that rivalled his sadness. Although their acquaintance had been brief, and awkward, to say the least, somehow it had a special significance for him. Looking back, his main regret was actually that along their journey that day, he had not sung 'Dance little lady... leave it all behind...' instead of Wally Shanks' song.

Upon seeing the outline of Simone up ahead, and without being distracted by the dreaminess of her face, it then became apparent to Oliver that the spell that she had cast on him – and the reason that he had felt so unnerved once she had crossed his threshold – was that she had a similarly otherworldly and rarefied countenance to that of his mother. Simone's looks were softer, but otherwise, with her height, blonde hair, and physical grace, she did, in fact, echo Marion somehow. He then found himself wondering if all that damning commentary characterising Marion as bourgeois and pretentious – of which he had been as guilty as anyone at times – was completely off the mark after all; Marion's aristocratic bearing was something that she had clearly been born with, even if she had had to carve and shape herself further in terms of dress, comportment, deportment, and diction. Perhaps, then, just as Gigi had once said, her daughter had been born into the wrong life, just as he sensed that Simone may have been – not peas above sticks after all.

This hunch was companioned by frustration as he struggled to comprehend why, although different, Simone and his mother's faces did indeed seem interchangeable somehow. The dreams that he had spent half his life trying to forget, he suddenly wanted to remember and revisit very carefully; how else could he have come to suspect that their interrelatedness stemmed from some kind of real-life entanglement, as if all their fates were somehow intertwined? Perhaps, he found himself wondering, his dreams had all along been dramatising an explanation of why everybody's lives had become so adverse. Gigi had once suggested that they could, after all; perhaps they had whispered a reveal to him of some kind – coded *en français*? But then again, he thought, the truth surely is this: as much as people want reasons for their difficulties and somebody or something to blame, life is complicated and random for the most part. With a multitude of forces that one can only be partially aware of, all of which play their part, there must be an equal measure of forces that one could not possibly grasp.

'Let her go. Let it all go,' Oliver murmured while feeling thankful nonetheless that he had found cause to revisit what had become his favourite dream palace again; the Greenthorne Palace once again seemed just as magical as it had when Marion had taken him there all those years prior. Thanks to that place, and to Simone, Kitty Kat, and Ava, too, he had rediscovered the magic that he so desperately needed in his life; by reason of this, the sirens that dwelled in the pub opposite the dream palace seemed to be just as enthralling as those that had once graced its silver screen.

As Simone vanished from Middle Row, he considered entering Mrs Spence's tea-room before heading to the Oddfellows because he still craved those ice cream sundaes and the liquid gold that poured from Doris' taps; the journey began as a meander, though, not a rush, which felt something of a novelty. It was too wet for the heath or the crossway anyway; the former would surely be soddened, and the latter would be just as empty. But then he realised that he did not feel the need; if nothing else, his frolic with *Captain Crackerjack* had taught him that these anonymous outdoor encounters were nothing to write home about, even if one had a depraved relative with a thirst for scandal to anxiously await such letters. Although undeniably thrilling, it was not the intensity of his encounter with Gordy that had been the revelation; it was the lying in his arms afterwards that had been. No, not the heath, he decided; the thought of it just depressed him. At that juncture, even the teensiest and most restrained nibble on Alfred's pretty little ears would be far more rewarding.

Once he had turned back and just as he was about to pass the Solbys' residence, he saw that Olive was labouring in her garden, as usual, and looking vaguely in his direction; once closer, however, it appeared as if she was looking at, rather than through, him this day, and he dared to think that there was even a glimmer of recognition in her eyes. He slowed in his stride while wondering if he might dare to say hello, but he did not need to –

'Olly? Oliver Gidley... is that you?'

'Yes... Hello, Olive,' Oliver replied, beaming.

'Is it really?'

He nodded.

'Oh, Olly, ah were only jus' thinkin' about ya t' other day. I was sayin' to our Abigail on t' telephone when she called, "Whatever happened to our Oliver?" We were, in fact, gettin' rather worried.'

Oliver did not bother to mention that he had passed her almost daily for the longest time, realising that there must be some explanation; had his former dishevelment and discomposure made him that unrecognisable to her? he had to wonder.

'Oh, Abigail'll be chuffed. She were so fond of you Oliver... Always asks when she calls.'

'Really?' Oliver blurted out as his smile broadened.

'Always! Any road, she's learnin' art at a fancy school in London nowadays... Won 'erself a bursary, thank 'eavens. Money bein' 'ow it is, ah never could 'ave sent 'er there... Oh, ah remember 'ow you used to play out 'ere, you two... while Margaret and ah put t' world t' rights.'

Her voice dropped a little –

'Oh, 'ow ah miss 'er, Os-Olly... ya must do too. It were sad 'ow we lost touch. But then ah heard about h-her illness an' what followed... an' ah understood. Can't say it surprised me, though. Our generation 'ave been droppin' like flies... although ah don't n-need to tell ya that, do ah? Sorry, love.'

Margaret? Clearly, something was a little off with Olive's memory, which perhaps explained a little more of why she had not recognised him. The look on her face, however, showed that she had not forgotten their bond, even if she struggled with the particulars.

'No, I'm sorry... well, sorry to hear about Alec, rather.'

'Thanks, pet. But the dead n-never leave us... not really. Ah'm... see... ah'm sure 'e's still 'ere. We feel 'im around. You know... it's queer s-sometimes... as if... well... out of the corner of my eye... well, never mind that! Ya should come out t' rain, love. Though ah must say, we needed it, didn't we? Ah've a brew on... and... l-look... fruit scones in t' oven that only need a few more minutes,' she said as he pushed open her gate.

'If you're sure it's convenient enough?'

'Ah see ya've lost none of your politeness. Of course it is, ya daft apeth. Follow me.'

Oliver felt exalted as he ventured up her path; Olive's garden was a miniature paradise upon closer inspection – one that he would exuberantly render in shades of catnip, leapfrog, grocer, and cruciferous green.

Inside, Olive's kitchen was warm, clean, and, most pleasingly of all, just as he remembered it. There, propped on the kitchen cabinet next to her prized Tempograph alarm clock, was dear old Alec's portrait. Abigail, pictured next to her father, was still recognisable as a young woman; her photograph was coloured, but it did not appear to be hand-tinted, curiously. Abigail herself wore bright, primary colours, had a sharp haircut, and wore bold red and yellow jewellery; she looked like the same bright little sparrow who was brimming with life while she also appeared so cutting-edge and modern – looking every bit the vanguard of a new and exciting age to come.

So, Abby's at art school in London, having been awarded a bursary... Hardly surprising, Oliver thought; she was exceptionally talented. Her technique had been the freest out of the two of us, and more painterly.

Their masterpieces had always been a joint endeavour; he had begun them with impressive backgrounds, but because he had no knack for figures, she had drawn them in afterwards. Oh, how he missed Abigail all of a sudden, and their 'busman's picnics'. Olive would bring ploughman's sandwiches out into the garden while they would draw and paint on paper – and even on Archie's shell, much to their mothers' amusement. He remembered Marion laughing then, and he could picture her so clearly – the lineaments of her face and the exact shade of her hair's blondeness as she had leant over that very table while chatting to Olive. Despite her general snootiness, Marion had made exceptions; she had not looked down on Olive at all, and had regarded the Solbys as good friends before she became so sick and gave up on everything. Again, she clearly had had her virtues. As of now, mother and son's war seemed nothing more than a high drama pantomime when thinking back, even if he knew, deep down, that he was veneering the past with a rose-tinted varnish.

'Ah'll just be a moment, O-Ol-Os-Oscar. Ah've got to pop upstairs. Wish I'd sorted that leak long ago. Still, a bucket'll do for now... Then ah'll be back d-down... an'... w-well... ya... ehm... l-look... ya must tell me what you've been doin' with yaself all these years. H-help yourself to a brew in the meantime.'

Well, that's a bit worrisome, Oliver thought while wondering how on earth he might explain himself; he supposed that he would just have to say that he had been doing odd jobs for Sheldon. Olive got halfway upstairs then stopped and called back –

'Oh... l-look... ehm... Abigail'll be home shortly, by t' way. She got a fortnight off 'tween terms at C-C-Cumberley... or is it Canderwell?'

He heard her chuckle heartily then, before she added, 'Search me Os-Oliver, ah... gosh... ah can never quite remember. My Abigail does get cross sometimes.'

Oh dear! As much as he was wishful to be reacquainted with Abby – rekindle their friendship even, if that were possible – Oliver suddenly felt rather anxious. He had to wonder how on earth he would explain himself to her too – that he did not have a job currently, and that he had never managed to hold one down, for that matter; would he have to lie again? But then a far more pressing matter occurred to him: he had no income whatsoever as of the day before. Momentarily, he felt a twinge of anxiety, but then, saved by the sight of one of his and Abby's childhood paintings, still tacked to the wall, he was reminded that art classes featured in his local occupational club's syllabus; these, he remembered from the attendant's grumbling complaints, were classes where hands that were once bone idle rendered countless still life studies of tattered hobnail boots that were being reheeled in other classes. More pertinently, however, he also remembered that these masterworks had been declared of importance by the condescending twits of the art world; they had even gone as far as being exhibited in the fashionable galleries of Middle Moor, Snobbshill, and Blandishford, under the title 'They Paint Their Own Lives'. Although he had sensed upon hearing this that these students were being ruthlessly exploited, this quickly struck him as rather opportune because it would give his own talents a chance to shine; it surely would not be long before he would have critics and buyers beating a path to his door! Moreover, on a more practical note, he realised that if he played the labour exchange's game, as he should have done in the first place, he would be able to claim dole again, which would tide him over until he had achieved such success! All foolish fancy, maybe... but then again... who knows? He supposed all he could do was give things his best shot and leave the rest to Lady Luck; he relaxed and poured the tea.

Glancing idly out of the window, Oliver caught sight of Clive Turner, standing further down the street beneath a tattered umbrella and clutching today's merchandise:

bunches of crocuses – torn from Spring Gardens, no doubt. While thinking that he would offer Mr Turner the opportunity to double his money and resell *The Picture-goer's Who's Who and Encyclopaedia*, Oliver chuckled; Mr Turner was a survivor, and Oliver vowed that he would follow his tenacious example.

The rainfall became heavier. Feeling himself sinking into the comfy kitchen chair, he felt solidly grounded while being somewhat entranced by the pitter-patter of rain drops upon the misting-up windowpane. The master of his mind finally and in a place beyond harm, Oliver realised that his life's story was one that had been ghostwritten for too long, and that was all about to change! Overall, Oliver felt much better than he had for a good while – better than he could ever remember, in fact; somehow, looking forward, he just knew that everything would be quite alright.

Sincerest Condolences

T he letter read:

My dearest Abigail,

My sincerest condolences for your loss. Although we have never been properly acquainted, I can only think of you as family, considering the strength of the bond that I shared with your late husband. I dare to hope that over time you might come to think the same of me. I quite understand why, owing to our Oliver's industriousness, he became far too busy with his work and the management of his happy home life to arrange our introduction, despite my hopes to the contrary – hopes that sadly became dashed by another unexpected and most terrible war.

As proud as I felt of his readiness to defend his country, I became inconsolably afflicted when I learned that we had lost our dearest one upon the battlefields. In his great self-sacrifice, I am sure you will agree that he vastly uplifted the esteem in which we already held him so highly.

That said, despite my own unshakable grief, I dare not insult you by claiming to possess any inkling of how much you must have suffered yourself – especially now that you are widowed and are faced with the unenviable task of childrearing alone. My own heartbreak is my own encumbrance, of course, and I hardly wish to deepen your wounds by articulating it any more starkly than I have already.

This censure does not stop me from deploring the situation that you are left in, in any case. Should you ever want for anything, please do not hesitate to call upon me. With regard to our beloved one's loss, there would be no greater consolation for me than to contribute financially to the future wellbeing of his wife and darling daughter. I can only hope that, with your agreement and in time's fullness, young Amelia will feel less alone in the knowledge that she will always have a great uncle standing by to unhesitatingly support her future endeavours. Such assistance would only be proper, and is the least I could do under the circumstances.

Yours with great sympathy, yet equal optimism for your future,

Great Uncle Sheldon.

Abigail, feeling quite on edge suddenly, promptly crumpled the letter into a ball and flung it into the wastepaper bin. Her recollection of its sender was of a swollen, deathly-looking creature lording over Oliver's wake; in her pictorially oriented imagination, its inflamed, bloodshot appearance had brought a vampire to mind – engorged with the blood of his last victim. He had also appeared utterly unmoved while she, her mother, Rose Spence, Doris Pert, Bert Greasley, Ava Glewe, Vera Collins, the Baileys, Albion Roper, June Lovesey, and countless others had wiped tears away. Moreover, Oliver had once revealed a little of this man's lack of scruples, so she knew to steer well clear of him – he was capable of much unpleasantness.

She found herself reasoning that she was fiercely independent anyway; as challenging as being a widowed mother might be, her paintings were selling reasonably, and she alone would shape her and her daughter's future, thank you very much! And why was Sheldon fixating on her? she had to ask, but the answer seemed instantly obvious: Oliver had disclosed that Sheldon had a predilection for the vulnerable – or those whom he might assume to be thus. Also, she could only imagine that Sheldon might be trying to salvage his reputation with her because she was well-known and liked in Greenthorne. He was probably sweating over what Oliver might have revealed about his frightful game plan with him, and over what she might reveal in turn. She then supposed that she should just be thankful that he wasn't trying to sandbag her with what he might reveal, not that it would have worked! She knew all about Oliver's past; theirs had been a union based on sincerity, frankness, and friendship – somehow it had just worked.

Turning then and glancing at the mantel where Oliver's photo took centre stage, Abigail found that he still looked just as gallant and saintly as a martyr should. The photograph had not been hand-tinted, but she could still see the greenness of his peepers and the sandiness of his hair – it had dulled a little over time; Albion Roper had perfectly captured the essence of the man that he had become – from sweetheart to lionheart without losing any of the tenderness of the former.

'Oh, Oliver, why am I still without you?' she moaned under her breath. Then, blotting her tears with her sleeve, as had become her routine, she looked back to her easel.

'Oh, I don't know,' she muttered, then flung her brush down while feeling even more angered by the letter's patronising waffle. It had stymied her creative flow as much as it had disturbed her. She found her sight drifting away from her easel then, and settling on a patch of green that they had missed when she and Oliver had repainted the horse hospital's living room autumn sky blue. If she could not continue with her latest commission in that moment, she thought perhaps she might just about manage to raise a brush to that instead.

'Ooh don't, it's too awful... Our poor young lives cut so short... Oh, don't! Don't! You can't have your funeral and watch it, young lady!'

The young lady then let out the most spine-tinglingly shrill cackle imaginable. What on earth's this ghastly radio play about? Abigail had to wonder; it was not helping at all. She quickly turned the wireless' dial and found music –

ALEC S. IRESON

Cuddle up and don't feel blue
All your fears will diminish greatly
When you see, dear, that I'm all smiles for you

'W-what were in that l-letter love?' Olive asked.

Turning to her mother, who coddled sleeping little Amelia in her arms upon the settee, Abigail felt brightened by the sight of her daughter; her untamed red hair tumbled so sweetly about her lightly freckled face as she slept.

'Oh, nothing worth wasting any breath on, Mother,' Abigail replied. 'Anyway, I'd like to keep my cheeks as dry as possible today.'

Every cloud must have a silver lining
Wait until the sun bursts through

Abruptly then, out of the corner of Abigail's eye, she registered movement and imagined that a breeze must have moved something. However, all the windows were closed, and the air was quite inert.

'Well, that's strange.'

Yes, despite this stillness, a gentle waft of air, emanating from no discernible source, tugged at one of her and Oliver's drawings that had been tacked to the wall. It had become her favourite of theirs: a scribbling of them holding hands, drawn at age nine, or thereabouts, with the words 'friends forever' also scribbled upon it.

And smile alike, my loveliest dear
While I wipe away each tear
Or else I shall be heartsore too.

'Oliver?'

Behind her, Olive gasped, and Abigail turned again to find her mother's gaze fixed on the fluttering painting too.

'Is it wishful thinking, Mother?'

Olive's eyes quickly became moist while she said –

'L-look, love... I did say... they never do leave us, not really.'

Acknowledgements

A thank you to all those who gave help, support, and inspiration:

Agnes Kruger, Willow Garms, Mrs Wagstaff, Vera Rodriguez, Anton Johnson, Sophie Besgrove, Helen Hagon, Russell Clarke, Sheena Elliot, Kenneth Runcimun Annand, W. James Chan, and Alana Bates

About the author

Alec S. Ireson is a new writer who hails from Penzance, Cornwall in the United Kingdom. He studied film, media, and communications at Goldsmiths in London in the late nineties. He has made a number of shorts in the years since. His current project, a short film entitled Drum Heart, is currently on the international film festival circuit. Meanwhile, his next novel is underway – a meditation on love, life, art, and poetry. Alec loves living in lively east London with his much-cherished cat, Valentina. He loves hearing from readers, so don't hesitate to contact him!

alecsireson@gmail.com

Maker Books is an east London-based collective of writers who publish independently under their own stamp. If you enjoy this novel, Alec would be very grateful if you could leave a review on Goodreads and/or Amazon. If you don't like it, you can still leave a review, however, and/or burn this book during wintertime to briefly warm your hands. Thank you!

Also by Alec S. Ireson

Bright Spark:

While trapped in the stuffy confines of bourgeoise Thorny Grove, Simone's life is filled with strangers; she really does not know anyone, not her new husband, not her only 'friend', and least of all herself.

It will not be long, however, before her husband's exploits lead her to the Queen's Head Public House and Hostelry and a discovery of the controversial trade being plied there. While wearing her detective's cap and investigating his shady conduct, she will find two comrades there who will transform her life beyond all imagining, seemingly for the better.

But there could so easily be fallout, scandal, an outcry that Simone Cranford should be classed as a fallen woman henceforward. Indeed, many will predict she will wind up in the gutter, but God willing she can prove them wrong as she continues her journey of self-discovery.

With another unconventional take on the interwar period, Bright Spark delivers eccentric characters and risqué scenarios as it advances towards a surprisingly upbeat conclusion.

www.ingramcontent.com/pod-product-compliance
Ingram Content Group UK Ltd.
Pitfield, Milton Keynes, MK11 3LW, UK
UKHW021029110925
462789UK00004B/48